THE GIRL ON POINTE
THE BALLERINA

BOOK ONE

Patricia Bowman-Stein

This book is a work of adult fiction containing light sexual content. Not intended for readers under the age of eighteen.

Any similarity to names, persons living or dead, ballet companies, actual ballets or costume apparel are strictly coincidental. Characters and events are figments of the author's imagination. However, historical places in 1965 New York City are real.

DEDICATION

For my son, Paul Nicolai Stein, a visionary and successful playwright, producer and director who sees the bigger picture then creates his own.

Cover created by Michael David

Author's Website & Video Design within the Website also by
Michael David

www.patriciabowman-steinwriter.com

ACKNOWLEDGEMENTS & THANK YOU'S

Sandy Robinson – the editor, critique partner & beta reader.

Kathy O'Rourke – publishing organizer, critique partner, beta reader & edits.

Laurel Haberman – copy editor & beta reader.

Karen Ehrenberg – critique partner.

Marie Miller – critique partner.

Lynn Stein – daughter-in-law, cheerleader & adviser.

Monica Gyulai – stepdaughter who caught such words as "Coke is the drink & capitalized, not the drug."

Paul Stein – advice.

Martin Henry Mosher – first cousin, cheerleader.

Miklos Gyulai – husband, "Write what you know. Is it done yet?"

Patience Arminta – ballet teacher for our newest generation of baby ballerinas & a good luck charm during the writing of this book. A true balletomane.

Hedda Brinley – cheerleader. "Finish the book so I can make Martini's at the party. Have a copy ready for me."

Judy Reisner – cheerleader. "When is the book signing party? I'll bring my daughter Debbie."

Zoya & Andy Yamamoto – cheerleaders & tech persons.

My beautiful Irish support friends – Noreen, Kathleen, Majella, Shawneen, Pauline, Patty D and Madeliene. "Ladies, the book contains some sex. Maybe you should skip those parts ... or not. Sincerely, the author."

IN MEMORIAM

I wish to thank the people who trained me to dance and act and left a lasting respect for theatre, ballet, music and film.

Lew Christensen, San Francisco.

Anna and Igor Yoskevitch, Vladimir Konstantinov, Madame Alexandra Danilova, Madame Valentina Pereyslavic, Matt Mattox, Broadway Joe Piro, New York.

Sandy Meisner and Martha Graham at New York's Neighborhood Playhouse. Stella Adler at her class on Broadway.

Eugene Loring, Louie DaPron and Nico Charisse, Los Angeles.

And to my mother, Annamay Mosher Bowman who taught me how to tap dance at age four, "I'm a Little Teapot" and at age five, "The Darktown Strutter's Ball," I love you.

And my devotion and heart to Madame Alexandra Danilova for sharing her stories, discipline and love of ballet. I've saved her cards, letters, ballet class memories and ballet role variation's class mishaps and triumphs. A band of angels sing her soul.

During the reading … if you're unfamiliar with a word meaning or phrase, kindly refer to the glossaries at the back of the book.

Yiddish/Jewish Glossary
French Glossary
Ballet Terminology

CHAPTER 1

"We never know how high we are
Till we are called to rise;
And then, if we are true to plan,
Our statures touch the skies—
The Heroism we recite
Would be a daily thing,
Did not ourselves the Cubits warp
For fear to be a King—"
Emily Dickinson (1830–1886)

New York City, September 1, 1965.

BEADS OF PERSPIRATION trickled down my spine inside my already damp, lavender leotard as I stood in the center of Studio A.

Biting my nails and hoping for a place in a real ballet company, I watched five judges grimace, throw their hands in the air and argue. Their final decision would guarantee a contract for one, lucky girl.

I heard from ballet friends, some dancers spent years applying to professional companies but never got the chance to audition. And here I'm wringing my hands until my knuckles turned white because I just tried out.

"Please, judges," I muttered under my breath. "Pick me, see me," and stared at the five men and women seated behind the long table.

Shifting from side to side, antsy as a flea on Aunt Lucy's Yorkshire terrier, I couldn't stand still. *How could I?* Paying attention to five decision makers intimidated us applicants and the crowd now entering the room. *Why?*

The judges included a legendary prima ballerina, a Sadler Wells ballerina and three male soloists and choreographers as austere and stand-offish as Odette and Siegfried. Occasionally, to fend off an impasse, a judge would break his or her Swan Lake pose and point to our resumes or their notes.

Wow, stunning blue-grey eyes and blonde hair as bright as straw when sunshine streamed through the windows in the roof. The vision was Yuri Konstantinov, a premiere dancer, formerly of the Leningrad-Kirov Ballet. Seated in the center of the judge's table, he defected from the U.S.S.R. six months earlier while dancing in Paris. *Holy cow!* The guy was so handsome I thought I'd stop breathing when he glanced up and stared at my face. My pulse rate spiked at this mighty pang of anxiety. Good thing he looked back down at his notes, I could breathe again and not turn blue. *Whew! I'm telling Aunt Lucy and Bubbe I saw this gorgeous man. Like a movie star, he looked better in person than his picture in the Sunday Times.*

Judges, please hurry. This waiting is awful. The clock over the studio door told me eleven minutes passed since we ended with thirty-two fouettes. *Dollars to donuts*, if I could scream or jump up and down to help these deciders make up their minds, I'd do it. Patience is not a virtue to my way of thinking even when my dad yelled at least a hundred times, "Wait your turn, Sarah! Enough!" *Huh?* I never thought it necessary.

Should I make a run for it? Sprint out the door and quit this torture? No way. I'd danced too many hours in front of these people to quit now.

We seven finalists, with a number pinned to our chests eyed one another like a Halloween spook show checking out costumes. No "Miss Congeniality" would be awarded here. Every time the red-haired girl next to me looked my way, she crossed her eyes. *What's with her?*

I turned my head and focused on more fresh faces marching in single file through the opened doors of Studio A. Parents, teachers and friends waiting in the lobby could now enter the room and hear the judges announce the winner. They took seats on benches, along the floor to ceiling mirrors and stared at us finalists.

Some families whispered among themselves. They looked nervous wiggling in place, swinging their feet or as the two women seated in front of me, filed their nails. Six stage mothers belonging to six finalists stood gawking at the judges. Inch by inch, they moved a little closer to the judge's table trying to listen.

Oh gosh, I could use a hot shower, a gigantic hamburger with everything on it except the sweet pickle and a chocolate egg cream.

Good night! Without any fanfare, Mrs. Pace, the company director, stepped up to the microphone and my heart skipped a beat.

An eerie silence hit the room. Mrs. Pace, dressed like a Vogue Magazine model in an elegant pale grey suit with fancy gold and grey braided trim, stood and smiled. She hesitated and fingered a string of pearls around her neck.

"Thank you, all," she gestured to the group seated at the long table, "to my panel of esteemed judges and artists. You took time out of your busy schedules, to help decide which finalist should dance with our City Center Ballet Theatre."

The audience applauded.

Mrs. Pace turned to us seven finalists standing in one, long line.

"And to our talented young ladies, we thank you for your hard work by taking part in this grueling, audition process. We wish we could pick more dancers but we can only choose one. But, before I announce the winner ..."

A groan echoed throughout the room.

"Wait, please." Mrs. Pace held up her hands. "The happy news is ... our winner will perform as a soloist in a new ballet, choreographed by Mr. Yuri Konstantinov."

The room thundered with applause.

"Mr. Konstantinov will dance the lead in his new ballet, *Colors of The Rainbow*. His first, full-length production and we are thrilled to introduce his genius to New York City."

Applause.

"The world premiere is set for mid-October at the City Center Theatre." She paused ... "Ladies and gentlemen, I present, Mr. Yuri Konstantinov."

The Russian dancer shoved his chair back, stood up and waved. The crowd rose to their feet and clapped like crazy loons.

As the applause continued, Mr. Konstantinov walked over to Mrs. Pace. He kissed her hand and gave her the envelope.

Two girls in the audience shrieked and the crowd laughed and applauded.

Mrs. Pace put on her glasses and opened the judge's decision. The crowd stopped applauding and grew silent.

"Ladies and gentlemen. The winner is ... Sarah Rothman. A seventeen-year-old from Brooklyn Heights, New York."

Holy cow! My heart beat like a jackhammer.

"Miss Sarah Rothman, a student from the Brooklyn School of Ballet, welcome to the City Center Ballet Theatre. Please, step forward. Congratulations!"

My hands flew to my mouth stifling the word "yes" and I walked up to Mrs. Pace and accepted a bouquet of long-stemmed, red roses. She touched my shoulder and smiled. "These flowers represent the first of many. Congratulations, Sarah Rothman."

I choked back tears of joy. The moment so special I'd never forget. A few tears did escape down my cheeks and someone in the audience offered me a tissue.

"Thanks," I muttered looking at the woman whose eyes glistened as much as mine.

Mrs. Pace kissed my cheeks and put her arm around my shoulders. The crowd applauded her affection.

Me, the kid from public schools, the streets of Brooklyn and Miss Candy's ballet class at the St. Felix Playhouse, the Academy of Music. I mumbled, "Thank you," several times and meant it.

Yuri Konstantinov kissed my hand and in a foreign accent, I thought he said "Congratulations" but wasn't sure. He leaned in and said something else but all I understood was, "Sa-rah Rotting-man or ham."

Good golly, he smelled so good like the subtle scent of suede and leather. Not the odor of my brothers and dad who used Old Spice, that stinky stuff in the television commercials I hated.

REPORTERS FROM THE New York Times and New York Post interviewed Mrs. Pace, Yuri Konstantinov and me. Their newspaper photographers asked us to pose for pictures and we did. The Russian dancer put his arm around my waist and gently yanked me to his side. Startled by his warm body, I flinched.

He laughed, "Da, okay, fo-toe."

"Really a photo?" The hair on my arms stood up.

"Da, fo-toe," he nodded and Mrs. Pace chuckled, "It's al-right, Sarah. We're posing for the press."

I blushed feeling his hand slide around my waist for the second time. He pulled my hips against his hard body. *Wow! Some introduction.*

We three smiled for dozens of popping flashbulbs and became blinded by the flashes but only for a minute or two and then it was over. Everybody thanked everybody.

Mike Kravitz, a reporter wearing a New York Times Press Pass with a photo I.D. asked, "Miss Rothman, how do you feel at this very moment? What are your thoughts?"

"Oh, um, ah, I, I guess I have to say, I'm dreaming. I mean ... yes, I love ballet ... I loved 'The Red Shoes,' I saw it twice."

"You mean the movie? The Red Shoes?"

"Yes, Aunt Lucy took me. It was the best birthday ever. I was eight years old. Did you see it?"

"No. I was more into hockey and baseball."

My chest started to heave and the tears welled up.

"Miss Rothman, I'm sorry. I didn't mean to hurt your feeling."

"No, no, no," I sniffled.

"What is it?"

"I'm alone," I blurted out. "Nobody in my family came to see me audition. Aunt Lucy tried to get Uncle Al to close the deli but he wouldn't do it. My family worked."

"But, when they hear you won, they'll be happy."

"Why?" I sobbed. "I took the subway alone. I danced two hours alone. That's not happy, nobody cares."

A tall, young man shouted, "I care. The audience cares."

"But, I didn't share it with my family."

"You shared it with us. Hey, I'm Gary. I'm a friend of one of the judges. I got to stay and watch you dance."

I smiled at the tall, young man, "Thank you."

Several teenage girls circled around me. "Congratulations. You're really lucky to win. We're going to buy tickets to see you dance."

"You are? You're coming to see me? Ah, wow."

"See, Miss Rothman," interrupted Gary moving closer. "You're not alone. We're cheering for you."

"Yes, I guess," I sniffled. "Do you have a hankie? I have to blow my nose."

Gary shook his head but the reporter offered me his.

I blew my nose long and loud. "Honk, honk ... there, I blow my nose like everybody else. Are you gonna print that?"

"Sure, can I quote you?"

"No." I stopped blubbering and frowned. "I'll wash the hankie for you."

"No, keep it." He glanced over his shoulder, "I have to go. Good luck."

Mrs. Pace walked up and whispered in my ear. "Sarah, let's put on a happy face and smile for our guests. That's what we do."

"Yes, Mrs. Pace."

"Good girl."

EARLIER IN THE day, when I rode the BMT alone into Manhattan, I looked forward to this final audition. Knowing my family couldn't make it wasn't a problem until Mrs. Pace announced my name.

Three hundred and twenty-two girls competed for the prize and I won. The New York Times reporters considered my winning an achievement; a real accomplishment. As Mike

Kravitz wrote the following day, "Inspiring and awesome for one so young."

And being a soloist without dancing in the corps de ballet first? "It's you," said my Aunt Lucy. "You grabbed the brass ring on the Coney Island, Merry-go-round. An honor, dancers struggle to achieve. A few make it, most don't. Consider yourself ahead of the game."

"And to be young and talented and win the lead role in a new ballet by a Russian premiere dancer?" quoted the New York Post and the local television news, "surprised everybody."

But it didn't surprise me. At seventeen, I knew what I wanted. What could go wrong?

CHAPTER 2

Everything backfired in Brooklyn Heights.

MAMA SHRIEKED, "NO fancy dancin'. That's not a real job. Find a nice boy and get married."

"I don't like it," said my dad. "Go to college like your brothers and sister. Be a responsible adult, not a silly girl with pipe dreams."

With such negativity, let me back up, three days to Sunday when there was a heat wave on the East Coast. Adults and children sizzled and suffered. Dogs walked the streets with their tongues hanging out. Kids opened fire hydrants and played in the gushing waters while firemen drove around the boroughs turning them off. And during this sweat inducing misery, one cool thing happened.

A search was on for "a rising star" to emerge from the student ranks of any ballet school. The prize? A chance to perform with a professional dance company.

When my Aunt Lucy heard this news from a pianist friend, she kept it a secret and hurried to tell me. Usually this type of gossip traveled fastest by yelling out a window. Why spend a dime on a phone call? We're talking Brooklyn where families know the art of communication; a good shout out gets the message across and clears the lungs.

But this time Aunt Lucy thought the news, too precious to include the neighbors. Instead, she took the elevator from the fifth floor where she lived to my family's third floor apartment.

When I opened the front door, Aunt Lucy blurted out the details like ticker tape at the stock exchange. Her excitement so infectious, I jumped and banged my head on the doorjamb.

"Ouch!" I leaped into her arms. "Wow! An audition."

"Yes, but let go of me. I can't breathe."

"Oh, right," I giggled and bounced backwards.

Her eyes twinkled. "Can I come in? Will you move your clodhoppers from the doorway?"

I grabbed Auntie's hand and pulled her inside the living room and kicked off my pink bunny mukluks.

"Now," her finger tapped my nose. "You go tomorrow morning."

"Tomorrow? Egads!" I plopped down on the plastic-covered couch. "That's fast."

"Yes, it is. Take the early morning subway, the six-ten into Manhattan. The auditions start at eight."

"But, I, I ..."

"Schuss." She put her fingers to my lips. "Don't say a word, pay attention."

From her purse, she handed me a ten-dollar bill, subway tokens and a piece of paper. "Here's the address. It's a ballet school in midtown. You'll be changing trains so watch out."

As I listened, I rocked back and forth, getting antsy on the slippery plastic couch. For all the bagels and cream cheese in Brooklyn, I couldn't sit still. Up I jumped, like a rocket to Mars and paced back and forth. This irritated my aunt but I had to move.

Annoyed, she grabbed my arm. "When you pack your dance bag, take sandwiches. And pack the purple leotard I bought you at Gimbel's and the tiny polka dot lavender and white skirt."

"No way, not that dumb skirt. I hate it."

"Yes. That dumb skirt will make you stand out."

"Yeah, like Dumbo the elephant cause nobody else would wear it."

"It's a cattle call. There'll be hundreds of girls trying out. You need to show off. Wear the diamond stud earrings grandma gave you. By the way ..." She stopped talking and looked around. "Where's Bubbe?"

"She's sleeping in her room." I nodded towards the hallway.

"And something else ... wear make-up ... only a little. You're not dancing Carmen and it's not Halloween. Don't outline your eyes in black pencil like a frightened possum."

Suddenly, a key opened the front door and in walked two men. Aunt Lucy reared back in surprise and I plunked down on the couch.

My older brother Jeff and a tall, sun-tanned stranger stood in the center of the living room.

"Yo, sorry, Aunt Lucy," said Jeff. "Didn't know you and little sister were here. Dad needs his car keys and I couldn't find them in my apartment." He walked past Lucy and into the dining room. "I'm going to try his bedroom."

"And, try the key rack in the kitchen," said my aunt raising her voice.

Jeff disappeared down the hall, leaving his friend standing next to dad's overstuffed, plastic-covered chair. The stranger scrutinized everything in the room until his ocean blue eyes rested on my face. His gaze deepened. My hormones perked up and I pushed out my small breasts.

My aunt harrumphed and glared at the stranger. He broke his stare but not his interest. The man's eyes traveled my body like an elevator at the Empire State building. *Oh, dear!* I swallowed hard and my heartbeat kicked up a notch.

He never spoke and Aunt Lucy didn't attempt small talk. Just as well because Jeff rushed back into the living room wearing a smug smile. His right hand dangled the car keys above his head.

"Found them! Sorry we barged in on you girls. Didn't mean to scare you Aunt Lucy."

"It's okay. I'll live."

"No harm. No foul. Yo, ladies," smirked my brother. "Take care."

The stranger nodded.

Jeff opened the front door and walked into the hall. His friend followed but stopped in the doorway and glanced over his shoulder. His eyes rested again, on my eyes. Aunt Lucy moved from her chair to the door and pushed it shut with her butt causing a thump.

I bounced up and down on the couch, "Wow-weeeeee." My hands covered my mouth unable to stifle my delight. *He was the most beautiful man, I'd ever seen ... tanned, tall and strong.*

Aunt Lucy's lips parted like a grumpy Pitbull showing teeth. Any man inspecting her niece like prime rib at the butchers? Was no gentleman. In a quick turn-around, my aunt shoved her back against the door and glared daggers.

"What?" I asked.

"Close your legs, young lady and stop drooling. Don't think I didn't notice what you were doing, Miss Scarlett O'Hara flirting with Ashley Wilkes."

"Auntie?"

"Don't Auntie me with innocent eyes. We both know that man was too gorgeous and sexy as sin. And if I was twenty-five years younger?" She straightened her shoulders. "Or even fifteen years younger? I mean ..." She pushed the hair out of her eyes. "Anyway, don't get any silly ideas, missy. He's too old for you."

"Okay, okay." I jumped up from the couch. "What else? The dancing thing."

Aunt Lucy switched gears. "Alright, the auditions will last three days. The finalists will be called back in the afternoon, of the third day and they'll compete against each other."

"Until somebody wins. Which is me. Ta-da!" I bowed and flapped my Odette arms in Swan Lake.

Auntie gave me a disapproving look. "This isn't a joke."

"Sorry." I yanked her sleeve, "I wanna win."

"Then do it!" Her eyes widened. "Put that energy to work."

"Right." I stared at my bare feet remembering warm water soaks in Epsom salts to toughen the skin.

Lucy leaned into my face. "Tomorrow at the audition. Think of gladiators fighting in the coliseum, fighting to the death."

I shut my eyes and scrunched up my face. "Yes, I see it ... I'll fight to the death but don't you mean dance good not kill anybody?"

"Sarah!" she barked. "Just do it. You know what I mean, damn it!"

"Okay, sorry."

She exhaled, "Whew. So, where's your father?"

"He's playing in the dance band tonight. Mama's working in the deli."

"I'll tell your dad, but your mother? I'd rather shuck oysters for a week in Narragansett and break my eight-dollar acrylic nails.

"Mama will be furious. All she talks about is college."

"And finding you a husband. But we girls know better. Your career is dancing."

"Like the girl in *The Red Shoes*?"

Auntie shook her head. "No, not that girl, she killed herself. Why did Hans Christian Anderson write that stupid fairy tale for kids?"

"*Swan Lake's* a fairy tale."

"That's different. The girls run around in white skirts."

"Huh?"

"How do I tell your mother?"

"She likes to shop and buy cooking pots."

Auntie laughed, "That's it. I'll take her shopping to Macy's Herald Square and treat her to Rumplemeyers on West 59th."

"I love Rumplemeyers."

"Everybody loves Rumplemeyers," said Lucy patting my cheek. "Three scoops of hand-churned ice cream can make anybody happy even a troll."

"What?"

"Never mind."

"But you said?"

"I'll tell your mother when her mouth is full of whipped cream and maraschino cherries."

I hugged my aunt, "I love you, forever and ever."

"Love you too, baby. Get a good night's sleep."

She pulled away from me with tears in her eyes.

"Listen to me. Nothing matters but the audition. Don't think of anything else."

I watched her push the button to the elevator.

EARLY THE NEXT morning, I took the BMT into Manhattan standing most of the way and held on to the overhead strap. The screeching of metal, scraping against steel tracks irritated my teeth. I faced open windows breathing stale, humid air. And when the brakes slowed at every stop, they'd grind and squeal like raucous parrots gone berserk.

And if that wasn't bad enough? A man brushed up against me and smelled worse than three day old garbage. *Yikes!* When he grabbed my mini-skirted rear, I turned and screamed in his face, "Don't touch me, you pervert." *That's tellin' him.*

At the next stop when the doors opened, he ran out. But

then, a shiny cockroach the size of a half dollar scurried across the train floor. The bug made my skin crawl.

"Nothing matters but the audition," I muttered over and over.

Just before noon that same morning, my focus must have worked because I was asked to return to the call-back on Wednesday afternoon.

MY HEAD FLEW back to reality. It's again September 1st, Wednesday and I just won the contest. I had my picture taken for the New York Times and the Post. It's six p.m. and I'm dressed in street clothes ready to leave the ballet school. But, Mrs. Pace waved at me through her office window.

"Come here," she shouts. "Shut the door."

"Yes?" I ran in carrying my dance bag and the bouquet of red roses.

"Sarah, dear girl. Because of your age, I'll need your parent's consent so you can join the company as a full-time employee."

"An employee? Getting paid?"

"Yes, for money. Can you meet me here in my office? Tomorrow morning at ten with one or both of your parents?"

"Yes, uh-huh." I bobbed my head up and down.

"We'll set you up with a schedule, discuss some details and sign the paperwork."

"Paperwork, wow, that's great." My chin trembled and my eyelashes fluttered. "Thank you, Mrs. Pace."

"We're done. I'll see you tomorrow."

"Okay, goodbye." My heart pounded a joyful noise. I'd be dancing *Swan Lake* and *Sleeping Beauty* and *The Nutcracker*. *Gee whiz!* I couldn't wait to tell my parents.

CHAPTER 3

Later on September 1ˢᵗ. I should have waited.

*T*HAT NIGHT, *HOLY cow,* the news shocked my parents. Their enthusiasm fell flatter than leftover A&W Root Beer. The celebration I expected at Mama Leone's Italian Ristorante, went poof into thin air.

"Nessie!" snapped my dad. "Call the relatives. Tell them to get over here. Now!"

Mama ran to the kitchen, pushed up the window and hollered for my relatives to come to our apartment. I got nervous watching her hang over the ledge. She held the clothesline and screamed, "Emergency at Ben and Nessie's. Hurry!"

The first to arrive was Jeff. He bolted through the opened front door and plopped in a chair. "What emergency?"

"Your sister got a job."

"I ran up two flights for that?" he panted. "Tell me Dad, you're kidding."

"No, I'm not," he growled while standing at the living room door ushering everybody inside. When they all showed up, he shut the door and announced, "Sarah's gone meshugeneh. She got a job in a ballet company as a dancer. She'll wear short costumes and make-up. Maybe you can talk some sense into her. She won't listen to her mother or me."

Uncle Al, the designated CEO of our family because he owned the deli and gave everybody a job spoke first. "Sarah, darling, you're a good girl. You applied to Brooklyn College already. So go and find a husband. Have a mortgage, have babies, be happy."

"Yeah, such happiness, I should die from happiness," said his wife, my Aunt Ida Mae seated on the plastic-covered couch smoking a Lucky Strike. "Cook and scrub floors, shop, bake, wash, iron. Raise five screaming brats. Have a headache every Friday night. Take your time getting married, Sarah. Thirty is soon enough."

"Ida Mae!" yelled Uncle Al who looked like he could strangle her. "Didn't I buy you a mink coat?"

"Yeah, sure you did Al, but you won't take me any place to show it off. So, what? I should sit at my Singer sewing machine and mend your clothes in a mink?"

My other relatives had similar comments. "Be smart, go to college and look for a husband." But as the advice continued, a few relatives had second thoughts. They mentioned how impressed they were with the two dozen, long-stemmed, red roses "because they were perfectly matched. Maybe," said Uncle Louie. "This ballet job isn't so bad if the boss gave her beautiful flowers."

Aunt Lucy spoke, "Sarah should take the job. It's her dream." She clucked, "I'm so proud of you, baby, you're a working girl and not at the family business. Give me a hug."

Then Aunt Sophie chimed in, "Benny, let her dance a few months, a year, then send her to college. No crime in that. You both get your way."

Bubbe reached for my hand. "I go with Sarah to her ballet and I sit and knit. She dances beautiful. She can get married anytime. There's plenty of men. I beat 'em off with a stick on Atlantic Avenue walking her to the subway."

"Oh, Bubbe," I gushed. "You're funny."

"I know."

Aunt Lucy heard enough and left our apartment. I followed her up two flights of stairs and listened to her rant.

"The feminist movement ... free love, equal pay. Listen to me, Sarah, women should be allowed to pick and choose what makes them happy. We have minds that matter. We have bodies that count and produce the next generation."

"What are you saying?"

"Everybody tells you what to do. No one asks you what you want to do."

"I didn't expect them to."

"But you should, Sarah. Women's rights are changing and your generation will make the difference. You are not your mother ... not anymore."

Lucy unlocked her front door and I started to cry, "What should I do?"

"Come inside. Don't blubber in the hall. Mrs. Goldberg is always looking out her peephole."

"I don't want college or marriage. I wanna a professional career on the stage."

"Leave it to me."

Of course from my lips to Auntie's ears, she just heard me state a fact. "One of my parents had to co-sign my contract with the City Center Ballet Theatre."

"I can't convince your mother of anything never mind signing her name but I can twist my brother's arm."

"How come, Auntie?"

"Your dad is a different kettle of fish" and she dialed the phone.

Ten minutes later, Daddy sat in Lucy's kitchen drinking coffee.

"Benny, for goodness sakes, go with Sarah tomorrow and sign the contract so your daughter can dance her little heart out."

"No, Goosey Lucy, I won't do it. Sarah should go to college like my other three kids. She's not a flower child, dancing with hippies smoking pot."

Lucy flipped her wig and flung her coffee cup across the sink with the force of a Yankee pitcher. "Bullshit, Ben. She's dancing with a famous ballet company not hippies in Central Park. Wake up, you moron."

The porcelain cup hit the wall and shattered into tiny pieces on the linoleum floor. "Benny, read my lips. You will go with your daughter tomorrow and sign those papers."

Benny slid his chair back and stood up, "Make me."

My aunt sprung to her feet and glared at her brother. "Should I drop a bombshell right here in front of your daughter or do you want her to leave?"

Dad took a moment then gritted his teeth. "Sarah, get out of here and go home. I'll be down later."

DAYS LATER, AUNT Lucy told me, her brother had secrets. It seemed my dad as a teenager hung out with the wrong crowd. He got into trouble hot-wiring and stealing cars. No one knew, not even Mama. Aunt Lucy threatened to tell everybody in the family if, Dad didn't sign the ballet contract.

CHAPTER 4

Thursday, September 2ⁿᵈ. Met a milestone.

DAD AND I ate a quick breakfast, walked three blocks to the subway station and rode the express into Manhattan. After a quick bus ride, we arrived at the school at precisely ten o'clock.

With outstretched arms, Mrs. Pace greeted me and shook Dad's hand. Her attorney (a gray-haired thin man wearing a three piece dark blue suit) briefed us and Daddy and I signed two contracts. The first, for the CCBT and the second, the AGMA union contract for professional ballet dancers. But, taking money out of my bi-weekly salary to cover initiation fees and dues?

"Not kosher," mumbled Dad in disgust.

"Yeah, why so much?" I screwed up my face at the short and pudgy union representative.

"It's a sliding scale. If you're corps de ballet it's one set of fees or if you're hired in as a soloist as you are, we take more."

"Why every paycheck? Can't you wait?"

"No."

"I'll end up with bupkis."

"Not really. But, if you want to get rich. Choose another profession. Most dancers I know are starving."

Mrs. Pace gave him a dirty look.

"Well, face it Mrs. Pace," he defended. "You know, they live on nothing."

"No, I don't." She dismissed him with her hand, "We're

done" and glared at her attorney. Both men rose, shook hands with everyone and left Mrs. Pace's office.

She turned to me, "Sarah, you'll need to go to Capezio's. Go tomorrow morning. Order ten pairs of toe shoes and anything else you need. It's a commercial account. All your purchases are paid for by the CCBT."

"You mean if I like something, I take it and you pay for it?"

"Yes, dear, anything you need. In return, you dance as beautifully as you did at your final audition and we'll call it even." Mrs. Pace smirked and winked at Daddy.

"Tit for tat ... I like that." I flung my arms around her in a hug. "Wow," I giggled.

A startled Mrs. Pace smiled for a brief moment then pushed me away and stepped back. She straightened her red suit jacket and blue and red scarf. "Okay, Sarah? I'll see you Monday morning at ten-fifteen to show you around. The professional class is an hour and a half and begins at eleven."

She turned to my dad, "Any questions, Mr. Rothman?"

"No, but keep an eye on her. I'd appreciate it."

"Of course."

"She's a scraper but she works hard."

"I kind of suspected, Mr. Rothman" and they shook hands.

I moved to her office door and turned and grinned. "Thanks for everything, Mrs. Pace. I can't wait for Monday."

"Break a leg!"

"Oh, noooo."

"Not literally. Means the opposite, good luck in the theatre."

"Really?"

"And the French say merde for good luck."

"Shit," I giggled.

"You know French?"

"Yes, I kind of half to, I dance ballet."

"Touche ... and one more thing. Do you have a current passport?

Dad and I looked at each other, "No."

"Mr. Rothman? Take her to the passport office at Rockefeller Center and fill out an application."

"Why? Where are you taking her?"

"Nowhere for now. But sometimes, our dancers are invited to perform elsewhere like London or Paris."

"Will you give me some advance notice? So I know what to expect."

"Of course, Mr. Rothman. Right now your daughter is dancing in New York City. But to be prepared, leave right now and take a cab to the passport office and apply."

I choked back tears. London or Paris?

SEVERAL HOURS LATER, when Dad and I finally got home, Mama was furious and wouldn't speak to me when she learned I signed two contracts. My decision to join CCBT was "a slap in the face" (her words not mine). Mama babbled and kvetched driving us all nuts. And the guilt?

"How could Sarah do this to me? A fancy dancer parading like a circus animal? Why not stick a knife in my heart?"

Dad tried the velvet glove approach. "Honey ... Sarah's not like our other children. She loves the ballet. Let her try it for one year. Get it out of her system. Is that so bad?"

"Just because my Sarah graduated high school in June doesn't mean she finished her education."

"I know that."

"Benny, our generation had to work. We never got education. But, our three older kids graduated college. They're teachers. Sarah should go to college, find a husband, be a nurse, a librarian ..."

"A dance career can be honorable. Later, she can teach ballet to children."

"What Jewish girl does that? Miss Candy? A meshugeneh shikse? I don't think so." Mama followed Daddy from room to room talking non-stop. "Sarah should be like her big sister, Michelle. Go to college, get married and teach school at P.S.89 on the upper Westside. That's what a nice girl does."

"Because she doesn't want to," said my frustrated father.

"The girl gives me grief, Benny." She screamed, "No ballet dancing. Tell her, Ben!" The neighbors heard her screams and telephoned Aunt Lucy who ran downstairs to join us for dinner.

But, when we sat down to eat in the dining room, Mama threw my place setting and hers at Daddy's head. Fortunately, he ducked and none of the Melmac dishes I hated so much broke. Silly, ugly, turquoise and orange plastic crap made in Taiwan. They didn't chip or crack.

With the urging of Aunt Lucy, Mama calmed down and the four of us finished the meal. However, when Auntie and I washed the dishes, Mama threatened again.

"Talk to her Ben. Make your daughter stop this nonsense."

"No!" replied Dad. "I won't."

Mama tossed the metal, chicken soup pot and grazed the top of Daddy's skull. The pot caused enough damage to require eleven stitches at Dr. Adelman's office.

Lucky for us, Dr. Adelman had his office across the street on the ground floor of the rowhouse. My brothers walked him over.

When Dad returned home, he mumbled, "I'm never going in Mama's kitchen again. No more cooking pots. My banged-up noggin hurts too much."

"I'm sorry, Daddy," I whined unable to look him in the eye.

He waved his hand, "Go to your room, Sarah. Leave me alone."

I tip-toed into the kitchen and tried talking to Mama. She ignored me and stared out the window. Her indifference escalated the guilt. My worst fear; she'd turn my picture to the wall and sit Shiva. Hives broke out on my neck and chest in red, ugly blotches.

AT ABOUT NINE o'clock, Daddy went upstairs to Apartment 4A to talk to Mama's brother. Upset and worried, Dad needed advice and Aunt Lucy suggested, "Al. Talk to your brother-in-law. Maybe he can help."

Uncle Al, angry over his sister's behavior took charge. He contacted the entire family to meet at his apartment, tomorrow night for dinner. He and Aunt Ida Mae would discuss "what to do with Mama" following the Friday Shabbos dinner. Since everyone lived in my building except my sister and her husband, it was "a must show, no excuses, see you at sundown kind of invite."

Aunt Lucy thought Al's dinner meeting was a super idea. She hated seeing her brother tortured by her sister-in-law and lamented, "I felt guilty making him sign the two contracts but it had to be done. Aside from that," she grinned. "Isn't it a good thing I bought this building two years ago? Our family stays together and can help each other out."

Geez Louise, since Auntie mentioned her building I'd been dying to ask her for the longest time, "Aunt Lucy, why did you name this apartment house, 'The Valiant Arms?'"

She laughed, "Valiant sounds to me like a knight in shining armor."

"No, it doesn't."

"Think about it. Valiant reminds me of Sir Lancelot and King Arthur's Court."

"No, Auntie, we're not valiant in Brooklyn. The plumbing leaks, the steam radiators knock and hiss and the wood floors squeak."

"Never mind. The building is my Knights of the Round Table and the name stays."

And two years ago, when Aunt Lucy purchased the two brownstone rowhouses across the street and the Valiant Arms, she brokered the deals with Uncle Al's attorney. She insisted in writing, that all her buildings if rented out to her relatives, "should have low monthly rents and rent control as long as her relatives lived in her apartments and signed leases."

"Badda bing, badda boom," said Uncle Al at the time, dancing a soft shoe which he called, "The off to Buffalo" shuffle.

When Mama heard Lucy bought the buildings, she told Aunt Ida Mae and Aunt Sophie, "Lucy is too rich for her own good. It's not fair. She got money from two dead husbands and a Chock full o' Nuts bribe in a divorce settlement."

"And," said Aunt Ida Mae, "she spoils her nieces and nephews with cash and presents. She bought one of my kids a car, damn her ... how could she? And behind my back!"

"A regular Queen of Sheba," said my mother rolling her eyes.

"A prima donna," snickered Aunt Ida Mae.

"A diva," squeaked Aunt Sophie.

But, Uncle Al scolded all three women. "Spending money is not one of the deadly sins."

"Spending too much money on you Al, is!" said his wife. "Just because Lucy paid to remodel your deli inside and out, doesn't make it so. Hoop di do."

When I'm called a real grown-up, I don't want to be like any of them.

So, what were the rules of my upbringing?

No person or subject was off limits and no one knew from quiet. Everyone and everything was fair game and we should leave no stone unturned. And we all talked at the same time, louder than the next person and we had opinions. But, not me. I was too young for opinions and was never asked. *But here's hoping that changes when I turn eighteen.*

And because of my upbringing? I dreaded tonight's dinner at Uncle Al and Aunt Ida Mae's. Yes, I'm to blame for Mama's madness. My relatives will remind me, a hundred times. Gosh darn!

But what if my relatives insisted I quit the ballet job and ask Mrs. Pace to tear up the contracts? What if that was the only solution to make Mama happy and healthy? *No way, that can't happen.*

Should I ask Aunt Lucy for help again? She pulled one rabbit out of a hat. Can she pull another rabbit out and save my job and contracts?

I have a lot of praying to do tonight before I sleep. I'd better eat a snack first.

CHAPTER 5

Friday, September 3rd. My Manhattan adventure begins at the store for dancers.

"*I* NEED TEN pairs of toe shoes. Size 3, Capezio Pavlowa." I stared at the shop girl trying to act nonchalant but the butterflies in my stomach told a different story. *Imagine asking for ten pairs of shoes in one visit I could scream.*

"Yes, Miss Rothman," responded a smiling, thin shop girl just a few years older than me with her hair slicked back in a tight bun.

"You know who I am?" I gasped.

The shop girl stared at me in awe. "Yes, we all know who you are. You photos are in the New York Times and the Post. Congratulations!"

"Thank you," I murmured.

She giggled, "We're thrilled you came in to see us in person." Why do you say that?"

"Because some of the principal dancers send in someone else to order and pick out their things."

"Really?"

"Did you find us okay, Miss Rothman?"

"Yes, I got off the subway at Times Square and walked over on Broadway."

"Some people complain about climbing the stairs."

"To the second floor?"

The shop girl reached for her order pad. "Let's measure your feet, shall we?"

"Pavlowa pointe shoes, size 3."

"Shall we double-check, Miss Rothman? Please, take off your shoes."

I stood barefoot as the girl traced both my feet on white paper and then verified my shoe size. "And so it is, size 3, Pavlowa, ten pairs… what else?

"Pink satin ribbons and elastics enough for ten pairs and five boxes of lamb's wool. How much are the toe shoes? I'm curious."

"Eight dollars a pair. Anything else, Miss Rothman?"

"Yes," I pointed to mannequins in the window. "One pair of rosy pink woolen leg warmers. One black short sleeve leotard and two long sleeve backless leotards, light blue and lavender, size small."

"Would you like to see our Capezio catalogue?"

"Why not?" I turned away feeling a blush.

As I thumbed through the pages, I had to stop myself from wanting everything, so I ordered, "Two dance belts, size small and four pairs of pink tights and another pair of leg warmers in light blue, size, medium. And, ah … the short sleeve, sweetheart neck leotard number 330 in purple."

"Is that it?"

I exhaled a deep sigh, "Yes … that's it."

The shop girl frowned. "Sorry, I can't get your order filled from the catalogue. Won't have a delivery until later today. Can you come back after three o'clock?"

"I guess …"

"Miss Rothman, sign here please."

"Do I have to take everything with me?"

"No, take what you want. A messenger can deliver the rest

on Monday to the ballet school."

"I see ... then for today ... I'll take two pairs of toe shoes, the light blue leotard, a dance belt and one pair pink tights."

"Anything else?"

"Yes, the rosy pink woolen leg warmers."

The shop girl pointed to the window display. "Do you mean the ones in the window you already ordered?"

"Yes, include those leg warmers."

"Of course, I'll pack them in your take today order."

I looked at the clock near the cash register. *How do I kill four hours? Oh, dear.*

"Miss Rothman, we'll see you back here after three."

"Yes, thanks."

OUTSIDE IN THE sweltering, 102 degree heat, I walked Broadway feeling my skin itch and my hair frizz. Nasty, smelling black plastic bags lined both sides of the street. Another garbage strike, *lovely!*

I changed direction and walked over to Eighth Avenue and took the uptown bus to Central Park.

At Columbus Circle, I hopped off and walked inside the park, bordering Central Park South. Passing one-hundred-year old swans gliding on the pond, a conversation I had with Aunt Lucy previously came to mind.

She told me, "Swans mate for life and so do wolves." She didn't know why "women called a man 'a wolf' if he chased women." I answered, "Maybe because they whistle, Auntie?" She laughed at my response. "Don't be silly."

On the path bordering Fifth Avenue, I stopped at the Delacorte Clock at 64th Street and waited because it would go off in less than five minutes. A brass band of eight whimsical animals revolved in a circle, playing music every half hour. The penguin on drums and the hippo on violin were my favorites.

And just beyond the clock was the children's zoo, the Carousel and the bronze statue of Alice in Wonderland on a mushroom. The Mad Hatter, Cheshire cat and White Rabbit posing alongside Alice in Wonderland were photos taken by my dad when I was five or six. I smiled thinking of those happy afternoons.

At the zoo, I passed up the monkey house to sit alone, outside on a bench. I recognized my old pal, "Edgar the Gorilla" thrashing about in his cage. I waved at the primate and he hollered and waved back.

Edgar drank gobs of water, puffed out his cheeks and spit at innocent passerby's. No one could stop this rude behavior. How do you discipline a naughty four hundred pound gorilla anyway?

The zoo staff tried and warned visitors to stay away from the cage and not to encourage his awful behavior. But some children refused to listen and did as they pleased. No wonder "Edgar behaved badly. He'd spit and scream at visitors." Why? Because the kids teased him. They'd puff out their cheeks and laugh at him.

Suddenly, I felt movement on the bench.

"Remember me?" said a man's voice.

Startled, I jumped up and walked to another bench.

The stranger spoke louder. "I went to Erasmus Hall High School and NYU with your brother Jeff Rothman. He's a friend of mine."

"What?" I turned and looked. *Holy smokes!* I swallowed hard and stared.

The man said, "Didn't you and your family used to live in Flatbush?"

The lump in my throat got stuck. I swallowed again, "Yes, but we moved."

"I know. I saw you at your new apartment last Sunday. Jeff said your Aunt Lucy bought the Valiant Arms and two others."

"*Really?*" *Jeff shouldn't tell family secrets. I'm gonna tell Dad on him.*

The man stood up and walked over. My heart pounded watching this arrogant, self-assured move. *If I'd been a flame in a fireplace, I'd crackle and pop.* But instead, I looked down at my folded hands and tried to stifle a giggle.

Edgar hooted and beat his chest. *I wanted to do the same but on second thought, maybe it wouldn't be ladylike.*

The man extended his hand. "Hello, I'm David Katz. And you are ... Sarah Rothman."

I'm not sure if he smiled because when I glanced up, the sun blocked my view. I saw grey slacks, a starched white shirt and loafers. When shielding my eyes, I saw from the knees down. No pennies in the loafers.

"Your brother began teaching high school geometry after I finished law school and went to work in the D.A.'s office."

I bit my lip.

"Last Sunday, Jeff and I met up. That's when I found out, your family moved to Brooklyn Heights. What? Almost two years ago?"

I put on my sunglasses and looked up at the tall stranger. An athletic body, well-chiseled face and flawless skin. *Oh, my stars!* Aunt Lucy nailed him. *Hello, gorgeous.* My heart did a cart-wheel. *He could be a matinee idol on a TV soap opera if Bubbe was asked to describe him.*

Aunt Sophie and Bubbe were fans of "The Guiding Light" and "As the World Turns." They worked split shifts at the deli so they could rush home and watch their afternoon soaps. They also swooned over the Marlboro Man cigarette commercials.

Mr. Hello-Gorgeous grinned. "May I sit down? Next to you?"

Oh, that clef in his chin definitely belonged in the movies.

He waited.

I nodded. "I guess, I mean ... I know you? Were you at my sister's wedding two years ago?"

"Yes," he smiled. "You danced with me."

"Nooooooo," I formed a heart-shaped mouth.

"You did." His eyes caught my mouth.

"I did?"

"Twice. I remember. You talked about your sister."

"I still do."

"I've seen you a couple times since."

"Oh?" I tilted my head. "When?"

"At your uncle's deli and with your grandmother at the Academy of Music."

"And last Sunday?"

"Yes, Sunday." He hesitated and shifted on the bench so he faced me full on.

I moved away, "Wha, what?"

"I wanted to ask you out."

"Really?" I averted my eyes feeling a flush.

"But your brother said no."

"Huh?" I looked up.

"He was emphatic. Promised to punch my lights out or kill me if I messed with you."

"That's him." I giggled fighting a quiet panic.

"How old are you?"

"Seventeen."

"Ah, no wonder he threatened. Nice meeting you. Goodbye, Sarah." He stood up and walked away.

"Oh, crap," I said.

He stopped and spun around. "What did you say?"

"Nothing!" I snapped.

He chuckled then turned and walked towards the zoo exit. He waved over his shoulder.

"Oh, noooooo," I cried out watching him pass the end of the animal cages. My heart sank.

"Waaaaait! Mister!" I yelled springing to my feet. "I'll be eighteen on November 5th." I yanked off my sunglasses.

David whistled and turned, "November 5th?"

"Yes, don't listen to Jeff," I stamped my foot. "He doesn't know anything."

As if a symphony conductor signaled the downbeat, Edgar screeched a primal scream. Zoo visitors stopped moving. David ran his hands through his hair.

Edgar screamed again even louder.

And with that signal, David took giant strides and walked back to me.

"Thanks, Edgar," I giggled watching David pick up his pace until he stopped, right in front of me.

Hands on hips and blocking the sun, the man declared, "For the record Sarah, I had no intention of listening to your brother." He cleared his throat. "I'd already decided to ask you out when it felt right ... out of respect to your parents."

I sat up straighter and smiled.

"Are we on the same page?"

I nodded.

"Good" and he sat down next to me but a little too close for comfort.

I shifted in place and looked away. Having read only one Jane Austen novel, I wasn't sure what to do next. *Emma might faint but I couldn't do that. Not in 1965, the modern age.*

He searched my face looking for a response.

So, I gave him one. "My Aunt Lucy said, 'You're too old for me.'"

"I'm twenty-eight, the same age as your brother. Why did she say that?"

"She saw how you looked at me last Sunday."

"Like how I'm looking at you now?"

The heat rose to my cheeks. "Don't do that."

He smiled. "You make me want to look. You're beautiful."

"What? No, no, I mean ... a, stop it," I stammered. "But ten years?"

"Why not? If there's an attraction?"

"I don't know. My grandpa was eighteen years older than Bubbe."

"There you are. You just said it."

"That was different. It was an arranged marriage to a man with money in Odessa, Russia. She never met him until her wedding day."

David shrugged. "Families married for business and religion. Tradition."

I smoothed my hair. "She was fifteen on her wedding night. Imagine, taking off your clothes getting naked with a man you don't know to have sex?"

"No," he chuckled. "I don't imagine but you do."

"Oh, dear." I hung my head and covered my face. "I, I didn't mean to say that. Sorry."

David laughed. "Say anything you want. I'll never tell."

Humiliated, my cheeks burned.

David touched my hand. "Sorry, Sarah. I shouldn't have laughed at you, finish the story. Were they happy?"

I turned back and heaved a sigh, "I think so. Bubbe said she loved him after the birth of their first child. Her husband kept his vows as a devoted husband and they had six more children."

"That's a lot of happy wedding nights," he smirked. "If you count all the rehearsals."

I punched David's arm. "You're bad. Don't talk about my Bubbe that way."

"It's a mitzvah, Sarah. A woman should love her husband and in return, he'll adore her. C'mon."

I looked down at my clenched knuckles turning white. "Yes, she should."

"That's the assumption," he said. "But why is it? Half of all marriages end in divorce? And, we know this because?"

"I don't wanna know."

"Happily ever after? You're a romantic?"

"Yes, I believe in happy ever after."

"Even with hard statistics proving otherwise?"

I smiled.

He smacked his lips, "And so it goes."

David turned to Edgar sound asleep in his cage. "Gorillas are odd creatures. Almost human sometimes when they look deep into your eyes."

"I can't imagine Edgar being one of the guys."

"You know, I visit the zoo to make decisions."

"Why?"

"In a couple weeks, my work ends at the D.A.'s office and I start a new job in a private law firm." He shifted his focus to the other animals in cages. "Not sure if I made the right decision."

"How will you know?"

"I guess after I've worked there."

"I have a new job," I grinned. "I start rehearsing this Monday with the CCBT."

"Doing what?"

"I'm a soloist in a new ballet. I auditioned with three hundred and twenty-two other girls and they picked me."

His eyes held my gaze. "Very impressive. A soloist with the CCBT? They're world famous."

"I have six weeks to rehearse before the premiere. At first I was a little nervous but now, I'm petrified. If I think about it ..."

"Don't think about it. Jump in heart and soul, one hundred percent and eyes wide shut."

"Eyes wide shut?" My jaw dropped, "How?"

"You'll figure it out." He reached for a loose strand of my hair and tucked it behind my ear. "You're a smart girl and someday I'll say, I knew her when." He sat up straighter. "Are you hungry?"

"Ah ... not really."

"I'm starving. Let's celebrate our new jobs."

"Huh?"

He stood up from the bench, "Carnegie Deli or the Russian Tea Room?"

"I don't think I should."

"Why not?"

"Aunt Lucy wouldn't like it and neither would Jeff."

"Where's the chutzpah girl who beat three hundred and twenty-two girls to the finish. That person needs to eat."

"But, we just met?"

"C'mon Brooklyn. That's your argument? Your conjecture? Won't hold up in court."

"But, I don't know you."

"Unless we talk over lunch and you ask me questions how will you know me? Call it due diligence."

"Due what? What does that mean?"

"It means you'll have to do better, Miss Rothman."

"But, I've never visited the Russian Tea Room is that an argument?"

He reached for my hand. "That's grounds for investigation. The tea room it is."

"Yes," I squealed and jumped to my feet.

"Good."

We put on our sunglasses and left the zoo and Central Park.

STROLLING DOWN FIFTH Avenue, we passed the fountain statue in front of the Plaza Hotel and the 58th Street Theatre. David read the film title on the marquee. "The Sleeping Car Murders, have you seen it, Sarah?"

"What?" I mumbled admiring his black curly hair caressing the nape of his neck.

"I caught you." He reached for my shoulders and stopped me.

"What?" I gasped and snapped back after visualizing a girl kissing a handsome sailor in a TV commercial.

"I know what you were thinking, Sarah."

"Noooooooo."

He looked me in the eye. "You were asking yourself, am I six foot, one or six foot, two?"

"Wow, David. You're a mind reader," I lied.

"Nah."

"Okay, I guessed six foot, one."

"You're right, Sarah. And you're, five foot, four?"

"Exactly," I exhaled a slow sigh.

We walked briskly down Fifth Avenue and passed Bonwit Teller's and Bergdorf Goodman's. When rounding the corner on West 57th Street, we walked west. Across the street and beyond the exclusive Henri Bendel's, David pointed to the grey concrete building at 157 West 57th Street.

"The entire eighth floor is my new office. The firm of Loeb, Lieberman, Loeb and Strauss."

"Say that fast three times."

"Whoa."

"I meant it's a long name."

"Solid and prestigious," he shot back.

I screwed up my face.

At the corner of Sixth Avenue also known as Avenue of the America's, David took my hand to cross the street. His hand so large it totally enveloped mine. I looked up at him, "Do you play the piano or basketball?"

"Yes ... No!" he yelled and I shrieked feeling him yank my body back to the curb to avoid getting hit.

"Sorry," he muttered keeping his eyes vigilant on the traffic. "That truck turned too close. He could have hit you."

I pulled my hand away. *He should have looked before crossing. Not my fault.*

Continuing on West 57th and nearing Seventh Avenue, David stopped before the building on the corner. "You recognize Carnegie Hall, right?"

"Yes," I smirked *thinking duh?*

"Have you been to a concert?"

"Nope."

He pointed across the street to a tall building on the far corner. "That's the Osborne."

"Never heard of it."

"Built by James Edward Ware in 1883. Tiffany glass, gold gilt and a two story attic for the servants. The walls at the base are four and a half feet thick and eighteen inches near the top."

"Sounds spooky but it's missing a moat."

"Could be ... I heard it has secret staircases connecting the luxury apartments like in the Dakota."

"Really."

AT THE RUSSIAN Tea Room, under a maroon-colored canopy, David took my elbow and guided me through the front door. Inside, chatter and laughter filled the mostly red-colored restaurant with leftover Christmas balls.

"Madam, sir, right this way," said a soft-spoken Russian-accented waiter. He led us to the last red leather booth in the corner.

Audrey Hepburn and several other famous people sat in the booth next to ours. I tried not to stare at the celebrity but I couldn't help myself. She was delicate and beautiful and had a soft laugh.

While David ordered for us, I kept peeking over my shoulder at the movie star. David gave our menus back to the waiter and smiled, "Do you want to ask her for her autograph?"

"No, I'd be embarrassed."

"And, maybe she'd be annoyed if you disturbed her lunch."

"Ya think?"

"I would guess."

The waiter served the Borscht and we ate the warm beet soup topped with sour cream. Pirozhkis filled with potato, meat and cheese accompanied the soup on tiny plates. The Pirozhki pastries, too yummy for their own good were a delightful addition to the sweet and savory Borscht.

A second waiter brought the plated Chicken Kiev. A breast covered in a pastry shell with boiled parsley potatoes on the side. When I used my knife to cut into the shell, melted butter splattered everywhere including my chin.

David dabbed my chin and lips with his napkin. "Can't take you anywhere." *Gadzooks, I'm totally embarrassed until ...* David sliced his Chicken Kiev with a sharp knife and hot melted butter sprayed. We both laughed.

Time for desserts and David asked, "Charlotte Russe or Peach Melba?"

I shrugged and stared at the ceiling in thought.

"Waiter, bring both for the lady, thank you."

I giggled, "I've never eaten fourteen thousand calories at one sitting."

"We're celebrating and you'll insult the pastry chef if you don't at least taste the convection."

"Okay, one bite."

"You're on, one bite," he chuckled. "Ah, right."

I tasted the Charlotte Russe and fell in love. I slurped the Peach Melba and dove in for more. Within minutes, I consumed half of each dessert.

"Slow down, Sarah. You have cream on your upper lip."

He leaned in and kissed it off.

Shocked at the kiss, I came up for air and stared him down. Then giggled and giggled like a looney tune. The sugar high hit fast and I turned giddy as a fourth grader playing Spin the Bottle.

"Son-of-a-bitch, you can't handle sweets, can you?"

"Bubbe told me I have an addictive personality."

"No, shit, who knew?"

I took another spoonful of the Peach Melba dripping with raspberry jam. "Such deliciousness, I love the Russian Tea Room." I laughed, "Thanks for bringing me here."

"Yes, I can see we'll be returning."

Wound up like a cuckoo clock, I talked faster and faster telling stories. "You know, when I was a little girl and my grandpa was alive, he drank hot tea from a glass with a sugar cube between his teeth. Bubbe yelled at him because he'd leave the spoon in the glass and she was afraid he'd poke his eye out."

David touched my arm, "Hey, slow down."

I kept going. "No, he didn't poke his eye out and to please Bubbe and make her happy, grandpa took the spoon out. But, when Bubbe left the kitchen, he put the spoon back in the glass."

"To cool the tea down?"

"No, to make her really mad when she returned again to the kitchen."

"Grounds for divorce."

"Grandpa said, "Divorce never, murder maybe.'"

David laughed.

"His uncle was murdered by a robber on horseback. Shot him six times in the head. And Bubbe's sister married her fifth husband when she was sixty-three. A scandal because he was twenty years younger. The women liked younger men after arranged marriages with old guys."

David leaned in and whispered, "Please, stop talking."

"Oh gosh, you smell delicious," I licked my lips.

"We need to calm you down, Sarah." He motioned to the waiter, "Two glasses of warm milk for the lady."

The waiter nodded and I pouted, "I'm not a baby."

"No?" He slipped his arms around me and hugged me like one. Inhaling the odor of his neck, I stayed in the hug sniffing orange blossoms and a lemony men's cologne. *The scent could knock my socks off if I'd been wearing socks with my sandals.*

"Ahem," I cleared my throat and pulled away.

"Right, I shouldn't have done that."

"You smell so good," I giggled. "Like another dessert."

WE LEFT OUR table and started to leave when an older, gray-haired man dressed in a dark blue suit stopped us. "David?"

"Mr. Lieberman?" David sounded surprised.

"My client and I..." The man nodded towards the bar at the entrance. "Had a liquid lunch and saw you two enjoying yourselves."

"Yes, we had some laughs, Mr. Lieberman."

"David ... call me, Bernie. And this young lady is?"

"Sarah Rothman."

"Nice to meet you, Miss Rothman." He nodded.

"David, I can't schmooze. Got to get back to the office. Not this Sunday but in a couple Sundays, the senior partner Loeb turns fifty. His birthday party. You are coming, right?"

"Yes, of course."

"A chance to meet everybody on friendly terms, huh?" He slapped David on the back.

"And, bring Miss Rothman. She'll fit in just fine. A lovely young woman always does. See you both at the birthday party."

"Yes, sir."

"Bernie, I insist. Call me, Bernie." Mr. Lieberman turned a quarter degree and scooted past the bar and out the front door.

AS WE LEFT the tea room, David immediately hailed a taxi and opened the door.

"Get in, Brooklyn. You mentioned picking up something after three?"

"Oh, I did? Right. What time is it?"

"Four o'clock. What's the address?"

"Damn it, er, dang ... oh, yes ... 1650 Broadway, Capezio's."

David yelled to the driver, "Broadway and 51st."

I jumped in the backseat and David slid beside me. He touched my arm. "Sorry, I made you late. You can sue me. It's a litigious society."

"What?"

"I know a good lawyer." He reached for my hand and squeezed.

I gasped in surprise and yanked my hand away seeing Aunt Lucy's pit bull face.

FOLLOWING CAPEZIO'S, DAVID insisted on carrying two of my three plastic bags and walking me to the BMT. *Which was sweet of him as long as he didn't touch my hand.*

We trudged down the subway stairs into the crowded station bumping elbows with strangers. In the congested area at the entrance to the token boxes, we pushed forward where riders dropped tokens. Out of nowhere, a tall, lanky teenager leaped up and over the turnstiles without paying. His body could have smashed me if it weren't for David's quick thinking.

David glimpsed him coming and yanked me into his chest. Our bodies slammed together hard. My voice hitched in surprise.

"Fucking idiot!" muttered David, holding me in his arms in a protected grip. "He just missed your face." The beat of his heart pounded against mine.

Startled, I clung to his upper arms and inhaled the sweetness of his skin through his open shirt. Again, the pleasant scent of orange blossoms and light sweat radiated a desire to bury my face inside his shirt. He certainly smelled a heck of a lot better than my brothers. Especially when they returned from playing baseball.

Incoming trains, slammed on metal brakes. They screeched and clanked in the high octaves. The going-home-from-work crowd moved at a clip and hurried to squeeze through the last few inches of open train doors. Whoosh, the doors shut tight and we watched the subway take off.

"I hate train stations," I mumbled into David's chest.

He moved his head against my neck and sang, "Here we go

round the mulberry bush, the mulberry bush, the mulberry bush. Here we go round the mulberry bush. On a cold and fro-sty morn-ing."

I dropped my arms and stepped back. "It's not frosty. It's hotter than the beach."

"I know it's hot, I'm playing with you."

"Don't. It's, it's not, not, very nice," I stammered taking the Capezio bags off his wrist. "You treat me like a baby."

"You're no baby, sweetheart and playing can be nice, Sarah. You haven't had the right partner."

"Huh? Oh! Not today, Mister." I adjusted the bags and rolled my eyes. I took a token from my coin purse and dropped it in the slot.

"Sarah, wait." His hand caressed my cheek.

I pushed through the turnstile and ran along the inside plat-form gripping my purse and bags.

"Sarah?" he yelled. "I'll call you, okay? I'll call you!"

My heart leaped over the moon. Yes, I heard him but I didn't dare look back. *When he held me in his arms, I wanted to stay forever.*

CHAPTER 6

Same Friday, September 3ʳᵈ. David's burden of proof.

SARAH ROTHMAN INVADED my thoughts when I needed to focus on other things, namely work. Bumping into her at the zoo seemed a strange place to meet anyone other than animals. But the accidental meeting, lasting into the late afternoon proved a pleasant surprise.

Sarah was beautiful; no argument there, counselor. She had fistfuls of blonde hair, a great ass and amazing tits when most dancers were flat chested. Nipples that exploded through a nylon blouse when the idiot leaping over the turnstile sent her flying and I caught her. Matter of fact, she had an alert body chiseled in hard muscle and softness in warm curves. But the girl was young. Not young enough to label me a "pedophile" if I dated her, but still young. Probably sweet and naïve, qualities I never admired in women but in her?

My usual choices were working women my age, give or take a couple years, college educated, fledging feminists and skilled in the positions of the Kuma Sutra. Birth control pills, gin and tonics, trips to Puerto Rico and bikini waxes added to their allure.

So, why did Sarah Rothman linger in my head? Not my type of female and grounds for reasonable doubt. Could be, a frivolous lawsuit in the making. Yes, flimsy thinking and wholly without merit.

However, in the subway station? I defended my case for holding her too long when I should have let go immediately. I reasoned to make her safe. But when her silky skin touched my skin and she smelled so good, her femininity startled my senses. No wonder my thoughts flew south and I'm not talking Jersey.

My one-week engagement to Shoshana Baumgarten left me suspicious of women. Shoshana exemplified the term "bitch" in big bold letters. She used me to ramp up her social standing among her girlfriends.

On the night of our ten year Erasmus High School reunion last May, she sealed the deal. That night ended our betrothal, cut me off from old friends and delivered the coup de grace.

Classmates, on learning or our engagement, demanded to know why her. "Why are you marrying Shoshana?"

"Why not? She's a great girl."

Simon, the former editor of the high school newspaper, put his arm around my shoulders, "I hate to break the bad news but you deserve to know, Shoshana was the class slut. She gave head to almost every football player during our senior year."

I shoved him away from me. "What? Fuck you! You're lying."

"No. Ask the football players. They're here tonight."

"You know," said Annabelle, Simon's wife. "Several years ago when Shoshana lived with Nathan Silverman, she was two-timing him with Rocco Amatoro, the United Vintner's liquor distributor for her dad's restaurant. And do you want to hear about her uncle's partner?"

"Not really," I huffed and went looking for another drink.

Minutes later, I ran into Jeff Rothman, a buddy back in high school and college. Even though I hadn't seen him in months, I asked about my fiancée's reputation.

"Yeah, David," said Jeff. "Sorry, it's all true. Shoshana

boasted she'd stay a virgin until her wedding night. She gave blowjobs, never went all the way. My own girlfriend, that's all she wants to do, not that I mind."

The answers made me sick to my stomach. I felt humiliated in front of people I respected and hadn't seen in years. I wanted to slam my fist in Shoshana's face but by some miracle, I didn't break her three-thousand-dollar nose job daddy gave her for her sixteenth birthday. Rage twisted my heart.

Of course, Shoshana denied the stories at first and shed fake tears. Later, she shrugged and handed me back the sapphire and diamond engagement ring.

Her parting words hurt. "I never really loved you, David. I wanted to be married to a hotshot lawyer. Have a nice house and pretty clothes. Is that so wrong?"

"Yes, wrong on so many levels!" I sprinted to the school's parking lot and gunned the engine. When I drove away, I nearly hit an on-coming car.

My late grandfather used to quote Solomon, "And this too shall pass." But, I doubt it.

Since that night, I've spent some time with Laura, an attorney friend. Sex is all she wants. No commitments and no hearts and flowers. "Just fuck-my-brains out David and go home."

I'm not sure Solomon would agree but it works for me or, it has up until now.

CHAPTER 7

Sarah, same day, September 3rd. Minutes later.

I PLOPPED ON the bench-seat on the 4:48 p.m. express BMT to Brooklyn. My heart pounded David's parting words, "I'll call you, I'll call you."

WHEN I GOT off the train at my usual stop, Court Street/Borough Hall, the station clock read 5:46 p.m. I still reimagined David and me at the zoo and lunching at the tea room. I giggled out loud recalling how the Capezio shop girls swooned over "Hello-Gorgeous" as they watched him carry my packages and open the front door.

Oh, Gosh, I'd better stop thinking about David. No one can know I met him as I walked myself home, three long giddy blocks from the station.

Inside the lobby of the Valiant Arms, the neighbors from the back apartments sat on couches, noshing on soft pretzels.

"Sarah? Why so late?" said the beady-eyed Irma Green checking her watch.

"Huh?" *Oh, please Irma Green, don't talk to me. Don't spoil my perfect day.*

"Yoo-hoo, darling," said Mrs. Goldberg.

Son-of-a-gun, now she's talking. Do I have to be nice to the neighbors?

I answered, "Yoo-hoo, yourself, Mrs. Goldberg," and watched her drip spicy mustard from a half-eaten pretzel down the front of her blouse.

"Sarah?" said Irma Green. "How's by your Uncle Louie? Is he renting out his three spare bedrooms in his Taj Mahal apartment? I mean renting to any, eligible, unmarried bachelors?"

"Don't know," I shrugged and turned my back.

"You know at our ages us girls need a little fun," she snorted. "Get my drift?"

"No, I don't" and I stepped inside the elevator and pushed the button. The elevator moved, jiggled and groaned until it shook to a stop, on the third floor.

I unlocked Apartment 3A, turned on the lights and stashed the three Capezio bags in my bedroom closet. Being Friday, Mama and Bubbe were upstairs at Aunt Ida Mae's cooking. I quickly took the hall stairs to Apartment 4A.

INSIDE IDA MAE'S kitchen, Mama hollered, "Sarah, you're late. So, where were you?" *Holy cow! Mama was speaking to me after the Arctic deep freeze.*

"Sorry," I smiled watching her glare at me with a wooden spoon in one hand and a potholder in the other.

"Is your arm broken?" she frowned. "Can't dial a phone?"

I almost giggled seeing the splattered egg yolks and matzo meal on the Zabar apron I bought her last Hanukkah.

"Really sorry, Mama."

Bubbe kissed my cheeks. "We were worried. You should call. Nu? Next time?"

I inhaled and blabbered, "I shopped for ten pairs of toe shoes, can you imagine?" My eyelashes fluttered. "I asked for ten pairs of toe shoes today and I could pick out anything I wanted and I did!"

Bubbe gave Mama a funny look, "Why?"

Mama shook her head. "Sounds fishy to me."

"Oh, Mama it was wonderful choosing pretty things and telling them to deliver my things to the school." I kissed her cheek and she pulled away.

"What? They can't deliver to Brooklyn? Too hoity-toity?"

I moved closer. "And Mama, I went to Central Park and visited the zoo. I ate lunch and it was very hot."

"So, what else is new? It's hot everywhere. Tell me something I don't know."

"Sorry, Mama, I thought I just did."

"Your Uncle Al's a rich man. Seven air conditioners in seven rooms. You can sit here all day and be cool. Why sit in the park and be hot?"

"I know."

"Sarah," said Mama. "Can a fancy dancer set the dining room table? Can the swan queen of the lake help?"

I bit my tongue and wondered if David's mother spoke to him like that? *But, I can't think of David* and hurried to the dining room. I took out clean white tablecloths from the buffet drawers.

"Sarah," yelled Mama from the kitchen. "Set the table for twelve. Use Ida Mae's Rosenthal Dishes her mother left her may she rest in peace on top of her husband, her favorite place in the cemetery wall."

"We know," chuckled Bubbe. "She liked to be on top of him every Friday night when he was alive. She told everybody their sex life."

"Bubbe," barked Mama. "Don't talk dirty. I'm washing your mouth out with soap. And Sarah, don't listen to Bubbe. Cover your ears and put out crystal wine glasses."

"How can I cover my ears and put out wine glasses?"

"Smart talk. You want soap in your mouth, too?"

I set out the glasses, plates and soup bowls from the mahogany and glass cabinet.

"What?" yelled Mama. "Cat got your tongue?"

"Yes, Mama. I'm doing it. Everything's on the table."

Bubbe yelled, "My silver candlesticks?"

"Yes, your wedding present you carried on the ship and through Ellis Island."

I returned to the kitchen. "All done."

"Challahs and wine?"

"Already there."

Bubbe grabbed my cheeks and pinched hard, "Shaineh maidel."

"Ouch, Bubbe. Stop!" I whined. "I'm not a child anymore."

"You're not a child anymore? Nu?" said Bubbe. "Since when?"

Mama stopped stirring the soup. "So, now my daughter is too big for her britches. Why so grown-up all of a sudden? What got into you?"

I hesitated before answering. "Nothing, Mama."

I'd die before mentioning David Katz or write about him in my diary.

Bubbe threw her chubby arms around me, "Bath-sheeeba," she cooed.

"Sorry, Bubbe."

"No need for sorry." She wiped my tears with the embroidered hankie from her apron pocket. "I give you a hundred kisses" and she started counting and kissing.

AUNT IDA MAE and Uncle Al arrived home to Apartment 4A and yelled to us women in the kitchen, "We're here." They had just locked up the deli like all the neighborhood businesses. Sunday after eleven, they'd reopen for brunch, lunch and dinner. Aunt Ida Mae started checking on the cooks, "Shabbat Shalom."

My older brothers, Jeff and Max walked in carrying wine. They lived on the second floor, Apartment 2A.

Uncle Louie from the first floor, Apartment 1A, tripped coming in the front door and landed on his tush. "Too much blubber. I'm okay, I won't die."

My sister Michelle and her husband, Leon the jeweler arrived, "Shabbat Shalom." They rode the subway from Manhattan where they lived and worked. Aunt Lucy and Aunt Sophie followed carrying flowers from the corner store.

Aunt Sophie? She lived with us and shared my bedroom which was not okay. She belched and farted in her sleep. *Eeeeeeewww!*

Why did Aunt Sophie share my room?

Her fiancé jilted her on their wedding day and the shock nearly killed her. Out of the goodness of my parent's heart, they invited Aunt Sophie to stay with us for two weeks to recover. That was seven years ago.

Last year, I asked Bubbe, "How can grief last so long?"

"Beats me, child. Men are like taxi cabs. Miss one, grab another."

"You mean Aunt Sophie should go out and grab a cab?"

"Why not? Plenty of men driving cabs in America."

FOLLOWING SUNDOWN, MY relatives gathered around the large, oval, dining room table. Mama and I, lit the candles in the silver candlesticks and Mama waved her hands over the flames three times, welcoming the Sabbath. Covering her eyes, she recited the blessing, the "Bracha."

When she uncovered her eyes, everyone greeted, "Shabbat Shalom," hugged, kissed and sat down. With a glass of wine in everyone's hands, Uncle Al sang the "Kiddush," a blessing for our day of rest. "Amen" and we drank.

The two challah loaves were uncovered, blessed, broken apart, sprinkled with salt and passed around.

"Let's eat," bellowed Uncle Al.

Fluffy matzo balls in chicken soup, overcooked pot roast to kill the germs, yummy sweet potato tzimmes, carrots, sticky egg noodles and various wines and sodas.

Among the several wines was Uncle Al's favorite Manischewitz Blackberry which daddy hated. "Too sweet. Don't try it, Sarah. There's no afterlife for a Jew." Daddy lived to annoy his brother-in-law, Al. Why? Who knew?

But Uncle Al could care less. He believed himself a class act and to impress us, he had a messenger deliver two large, strawberry cheesecakes to die for. They came from Lindy's Restaurant, located in the theatre district of Manhattan.

"So, Al?" asked my dad ready for a fight. "Why couldn't you order cheesecake from Junior's, on DeKalb and Flatbush Avenues, right here in Brooklyn?"

"I wanted the best."

But Junior's bakes a sponge cake bottom so delicious. No sticky graham crackers."

"Enough!" scolded Mama. "Cakes, smakes! Eat already!"

Bubbe reached for another slice. "Once on the lips, forever on the hips, more of me to love, oye vey," she chuckled. "But, I don't like so much the strawberry kind from Lindy's. I like pineapple cheesecake better."

"Yo, pineapple cheesecake at Junior's?" said my brother Jeff. "And the blueberry cheesecake? Now ... we're talkin' the real taste of New York, right Dad?"

My daddy with a mouthful of the strawberry topping, bobbed his head up and down like the Cupie Doll in the rear window of his second-hand 1956 Chevy.

"Keep talkin', Jeff," said Uncle Al. "It don't make no difference. You and your Dad don't know nothin'. You're not rocket scientists or food gourmands."

Uncle Louie opened his eyes. "Put that in your pipe and smoke it, boys."

"Go back to sleep, Louie," grumbled Mama.

Uncle Al checked his watch. "We're done eating," he boomed across the table. "Sarah! Take Mama and Aunt Sophie downstairs. The Dick Van Dyke Show is about to start on the television."

Dad whispered, "Sarah, we're gonna discuss Mama. So, go."

AN HOUR LATER, Dad telephoned. "Sarah? I want you should pack a toothbrush, your clothes, shoes and all your dancing things."

"What?"

"Do as I say."

"Why?"

"We decided… Michelle and Leon the jeweler are taking you home with them, tonight on the subway. You'll live with them in the city."

"No! I don't want to." I started to cry, "No, Daddy."

"Sarah. You'll be rehearsing long hours and we can't let you ride the subway at night. You heard Mrs. Pace. The choreographer wants you to rehearse whenever he's free. That means nights."

"Maybe, I guess."

"Baby, I'll miss you but it's only five weeks."

"No, Daddy. It's more. I perform for the next two months after the rehearsals."

"Did I know that? Okay. Take a cab to Michelle's when it gets dark so I don't worry. I'll pay the two bucks."

"Daddy?" Crocodile tears rolled down my cheeks. "I'm gonna miss you and Mama and Bubbe."

"Don't cry, Sarah."

"I can't help it."

"Stop it, Sarah. There's no time. Hurry up and pack your things. Michelle wants to leave in an hour."

"What happens to Mama?"

"She'll be fine. Uncle Al and Aunt Ida Mae are taking her to their friend Maury, the psychiatrist."

"What will he do?"

"Al says Maury can talk to Mama and give her some pills. Maybe, Libriums and Seconals. The doctor eats lunch every Wednesday and Friday at Al's deli. He orders the George Burns Hot Pastrami on Rye with spicy mustard and creamy horseradish. He's a big tipper according to Al."

"I love Mama."

"I know Sarah. We all love Mama. So, hurry up. Take the suitcases out of Grandma's closet. They're on the top shelf."

"I don't want to..."

"Go... do as I say."

"No!"

"Do it now!" Dad hung up and the dial tone buzzed.

BACK HOME IN 3A, Mama refused to look at me while making sandwiches from the sliced challah and leftover brisket. She slapped mayonnaise on bread like a butcher chopping beef.

"Just in case," she told my dad, "what's her name," she pointed her thumb in my direction like a hitchhiker, "gets hungry on the train." To further emphasize her anger, she bounced her head up and down like Mrs. Levy, her psychic friend reading the Tarot Cards. That was Mama's way of cutting my heart out with an imaginary knife.

However, her next move proved bizarre. Mama took cash, her "pushke" money from the Snowman Cookie Jar on the kitchen counter. She tied the money inside a cotton embroidered hankie. *Holy mackerel,* she used the hankie I made her for Mother's Day when I was eleven. *Now I'm gonna cry seeing her take my gift from her apron pocket.*

Mama pushed the hankie in my hand, closed my fingers and gave me a sad smile.

At the elevator, Aunt Lucy and Bubbe hugged me goodbye and cried. Mama stood a couple feet away, imitating the iceberg that sunk the Titanic when I kissed her. Stiff as a two by four, she said nothing and didn't kiss me back.

Uncle Al used to warn us kids, "A Jewish mother who says nothing? That's the kiss of death. Watch out."

On the subway, I sat between Michelle and Leon the jeweler and sniveled the entire ride.

11:38 P.M. MANHATTAN.

Michelle, Leon and me … arrived by cab at their Second Avenue apartment in the Murray Hill district. We climbed the dimly-lit fourth floor walk-up to their three room apartment. When Leon unlocked the front door, their apartment sweltered with hot, humid air.

"Leon," hissed Michelle. "Turn on the air conditioners! I'm

dying. Do it fast in all three rooms."

Leon's dad, Charlie Spinell, the furrier, bought this small, apartment building three weeks before Leon married Michelle.

Charlie immediately said to the couple, "Why not live in one of my apartments? It's a bargain. Rent-controlled and all new appliances. One hundred and forty-five dollars a month. Great location between 33rd and 34th Streets."

"Sounds perfect," said Michelle. "We both work in Manhattan."

So tonight, because Dad insisted, I slept in my sister's living room, on a Castro Convertible Couch. The black and white zebra upholstery I recognized from the TV commercials shot in Times Square.

Michelle tried soothing my tears, "Don't mind Mama. She's going through a rough time. You're her baby."

"She treats me like I don't exist."

"Give her some time. She'll come around. Besides Al and Ida Mae will get her to their friend Maury, the psychiatrist and he'll give her pills to calm her down. So, Sarah, don't cry anymore. It'll all blow over like the wind. Here today, gone tomorrow. Now you must be so excited thinking about your new career ... all the people you'll meet!"

Like David? Discussing David Katz with my sister wasn't safe. The yenta would holler anything I told her out the windows. So I didn't dare tell her David bothered me like hives needing to be scratched. Or, he was out of my league and too-well educated. Or, I was the girl who needed hand-holding when crossing Sixth Avenue. The man "made nice" as Bubbe would say.

Geez Louise, as I analyzed the David situation, the obvious became clear. Why would he call? I cried at the truth and sewed pink elastics and pink satin ribbons on my new toe shoes. I sniveled and packed my dance bag and made tomorrow's lunch. At eight o'clock, I watched Ed Sullivan on TV, took a shower and stretched out on the convertible couch. I prayed, "God bless Bubbe, Mama, Daddy and oh, yeah, David Katz. Please keep them safe and healthy. Thanks."

CHAPTER 8

Friday evening, September 3rd. David addresses a sidebar.

I DIALED THE phone in the study of my Manhattan Eastside townhouse. I counted the number of rings when suddenly, she answered.

"Hello, Laura? It's David. Just so you know, I have the speaker phone on. Is it okay?"

"Why?"

"There's too many papers on my desk and it's easier to handle the phone without strangling myself with the cord."

"I get the disclaimer. Is anyone with you?"

"No, I'm alone."

"In that case," her tone changed to a sultry whisper. "Hello, lover. What can I do you for Mr. Katz?"

Her voice, reminiscent of warm brandy sliding down my throat made me mindful of our carnal trysts. Her wanton and thirsty demands appealed to my psyche using every ounce of my strength. When she finished the sexual Olympics triumphant and satisfied, I was discarded like yesterday's news.

I took a deep breath.

"Who's got your tongue, David?" said the silky, come hither voice. "It's not in my mouth."

I cleared my throat. "I'm driving to Southampton for the weekend. Would you be interested? Pick you up in an hour?"

"I can't. Not possible. Although sex on the beach sounds my

kind of fun but you know me, I get bored."

I shifted positions in my chair.

"Besides," she purred. "I have a backlog of research on a case going to trial in ten days. I should stay in the city and spend Saturday and Sunday in the office. But on your return, if you're got an hour or two?"

"Right, goodbye, Laura."

I hung up thinking just as well. Dating wasn't part of our arrangement. I dialed another number.

"Hello, Aunt Eleanor? Yes, it's me, David. Do me a favor. Cancel my two night reservations at the club. Yes, I'll stay with you and Harry, thanks. Is the spare key under the hydrangea pot? I'll be late. See you at breakfast. Bye."

DRIVING THAT NIGHT in heavy traffic, on the Long Island Expressway seemed a slow boat to China. My mind drifted to lunch with Sarah Rothman. She, innocent and silly on a sugar high and me, the horny tomcat on the prowl. I fantasized all sorts of delicious things I could do to her and with her but probably shouldn't.

Unacceptable illusions, counselor. Get real.

My little black book had phone numbers of attractive, single and grown-up women. And where was I driving tonight?

To the beach community in the Hampton's where South Shore women outnumbered the men, two to one, or three to one if the men were straight. Singles, divorcees and widows rented summer places to party or they owned beach houses, attained from divorce settlements. Women eager to drink, get high and get laid. And now at the summer's end, they were desperate for a last hurrah.

Especially, the South Shore playground of the rich and some famous, sex trumped lying in the afternoon sun. "One partner, two partners or "three potato, four."

Husbands and wives with open marriages threw their room keys in a swap wives bowl at the tennis club. If I had a wife, no way in hell would I share her. The concept made my blood boil.

Quickies in bathrooms and locker rooms also held sway. Doors had to be opened with caution. Other than massage therapy and sex in cabanas, spare the flashlight when strolling in the moonlight on the south or west shores at night.

And yes, there were drugs. Discreet Hampton party hosts willing to make guests high for a price, masqueraded in Brooks Brother's suits and designer name dresses from Henri Bendel's and Saks Fifth Avenue. They tooled around in Jaguars and Lamborghini's serving LSD, cocaine, hash, black gold, pot, uppers and downers for free flowing cash. "You could party hardy like there was no tomorrow" was code for dealers.

Altering my mind didn't interest me. Sure, I smoked pot in college, who didn't? But since college? I wouldn't touch the stuff. Ambition outdid bending my mind.

Near midnight, I arrived in the village of Southampton and stopped at a friend's house. I joined a poker game, had a couple beers and talked politics. When I went to leave, I noticed two women on a den couch, spacing out on acid they'd just dropped. I wondered how they'd feel come Monday morning at work. But hey, not my problem. I wouldn't be banging them anytime soon. I left and drove the Sunrise Highway.

At my aunt's house, I found the key under the clay pot filled with lavender-blue hydrangeas. I unlocked the front door and tip-toed in. Moonlight shining through the uncovered windows furnished light to climb the stairs. I entered the house like a cat burglar so, I wouldn't wake my aunt and uncle.

Moving along the hallway on the second floor, past three guest bedrooms, I opened the last door on the right. When I flipped on the light switch, I couldn't help but laugh. Eleanor had redecorated the room again and went overboard. There were deep pink roses on a white chintz bedspread, throw pillows the shapes of flowering pink tulips, pale pink tea roses on the wallpaper, fuchsia-pink lamp shades and a metal flower chandelier, painted in every pink hue on a painter's palette. The cotton candy wonderland decorated by my sweet Aunt, made me think of Sarah. If she was to visit? She'd probably adore this room. I unpacked my suitcase and put that never going to happen thought out of my head.

Wide awake, I flung open the French doors to the balcony and stood outside. The Atlantic Ocean, mysterious and dark, held heavy fog over the horizon at 2 a.m. Deciding to run, I changed into sweats and running shoes.

Descending the outside stairs two at a time, I kicked into a patio flower pot, "Shit!"

On the beach, I ran several miles and tasted the salty air and wind chill. Exhausted, I showered and called it a night.

Lying in bed, I thought of Sarah, energetic and unspoiled full of excitement beginning a new career. So different from the jaded women I'd dated in the city and here on the island. My next two weeks at the D.A.'s office would be hectic. I'd be transitioning the new person into my position. Sarah would be learning a new ballet.

My head sank lower into the pillow and I closed my eyes. *Forget it counselor. Don't open Pandora's box; don't call.*

CHAPTER 9

September 6ᵗʰ, Monday morning. My first day at the City Center Ballet.

I TOOK SEVERAL deep breaths to calm myself before walking through the front door and into the high-ceiled lobby of the ballet school. Still a bit rattled, I noticed an announcement on the bulletin board and walked over for a closer look.

> *The professional class meets daily 11 a.m.-12:30 p.m. except Sundays.*
> *Attendance is mandatory. No exceptions. No excuses. Keep in mind, if*
> *you miss one class, you feel it. If you miss two classes your partner feels*
> *it and if you miss three classes, the audience knows it.*

I muttered, "They take no prisoners."

Mrs. Pace waved at me through her office window. I hurried across the lobby and walked in.

"Sarah, my dear girl, good morning."

She shooed the two dancers out of her private office and gave me the welcoming speech and a few rules regarding my new CCBT home.

After these announcements, I left her office and found the girl's dressing room upstairs. Moving quickly, I changed into a light blue leotard, pink tights and leg warmers and old toe shoes no longer used for *en pointe*. I picked up my dance bag loaded with street clothes and entered Studio A. Tiny droplets of perspiration dampened my forehead.

The enormous room felt brighter than the lobby. Glass windows covered the ceiling, casting illuminating sunbeams everywhere. It hit me ... I'd be under a microscope. Every nuance in the brightness would be noticed.

I glanced around the room, seeing professional dancers huddled in groups. They spoke in whispers. My heart skipped joyful beats seeing visions of my favorite film ... on the day of my eighth birthday.

Aunt Lucy took me to see *The Red Shoes* on a snowy afternoon. The film played at the run-down Thalia Theatre on Manhattan's upper Westside. When the movie ended, I wanted to be a dancer and begged Auntie for lessons. Today, I'm standing in a scene from the 1948 classic.

But reality can be tricky.

When I moved among the company dancers, there wasn't snow on the ground only ice in the air. No one smiled or said Hi or welcome. They ignored me like an intruder in their sacred world. *How mean and scary.*

Spotting an empty spot at the barre, I walked over and set my dance bag down next to the mirror. But, a tiny girl raised her hand to stop me.

"This place is taken," she said in a snooty, high-pitched voice. She dismissed me with a flick of her wrist and turned her back.

"Well, hello to you, too," I muttered and found another empty space about ten feet away. I started to get comfortable and stretch my legs when a tall girl wearing knitted white leg warmers approached.

"No way! These spaces are taken. There's no room here." Her male companion dressed in blue tights smirked. He folded his arms across his chest and flared his nostrils.

How disgusting.

I continued to meander from place to place being pushed away until I finally ended up, at the last opening at the barre. Which meant, I faced the back of the studio with hardly any room to extend my legs in a grande battement. Seeing how sad I must have looked, one of the dancers took pity on me.

"Hey, I'm Anna," she called out waving her hand to come join her.

I rushed over, "Hi."

"Hello, I'm Anna Zvyagintsev."

"Yes, hello, golly," I smiled grateful for the greeting. "You're the only nice person in the room."

"Never mind. These girls are cows and bitches. They treated me the same way when I arrived here three years ago from Seattle. They want you to fail."

"Is that professional?"

"Dorothy, you're not in Kansas anymore. There's plenty of witches, Sarah Rothman."

"You know my name?"

"Oh, yes. Everybody knows your name."

"What? They don't act like it."

"You'd better develop an elephant's tough hide."

"Why?" I blinked.

Anna poked my shoulder. "Sarah. You're the youngest soloist in a national company. These girls are jealous chimpanzees vying for attention having never danced a solo in their lives."

"What are you talking about?" I sniveled a half laugh. "You talk like this is a zoo."

"It is a zoo. Know why you're here?"

"I won an audition."

"No! You're here for Yuri Konstantinov's new ballet. Every girl in this room … would kill or fuck that man, six ways to Sunday to dance your principal role."

"What?" I choked up.

Anna stepped into me and cupped her hand to my ear. "Mrs. Pace is always scheming. You're here because of a bet."

"A bet?"

"Psssst. Quiet. I'll tell you after class. Did you bring your lunch?"

I nodded.

"Me, too. We'll eat together. Have you met Yuri Konstantinov?"

"Ah, sort of," I shrugged.

"He's so handsome and dreamy." Anna drew her hand across her face in a mock swoon.

"Don't know. Never really looked."

"What?"

"Today, I meet him at three o'clock to rehearse."

"You know, he doesn't speak English. Hope you guys get along."

I stared at Anna and gulped.

Gosh darn, just then, the man we talked about entered the room. He carried a large, tan leather bag and dropped it in a corner. Without a word, he began warming up. Tension filled the air feeling his presence. Males and females shut-up and split-apart. They moved to their places at the barre in front of mirrors, and focused on themselves stretching long and lean bodies.

Anna whispered, "Sarah, my advice? Watch your back and dance with the passion of going to war. Don't let anybody stop you. This is the battle royal."

My clammy hands rubbed the back of my neck. "Right, this is my first attack. Jeepers, Anna."

"Good girl. Stay focused."

I placed my hands on the barre and stretched the backs of my legs. My hamstrings and Achilles needed very gentle and slow, easy lengthening. *Please God, help me be strong and alert.*

At precisely eleven on the studio wall clock, the door banged open and in paraded a short, stocky woman dressed in black. She wore leather shoes with Cuban heels, slacks and rested a silver-handled cane over her shoulder. She greeted the man seated at the baby grand piano in Russian and walked over to Yuri.

They kissed three times on rosy cheeks and babbled in their native tongue.

Anna whispered, "She's the ballet mistress. Svetlana Madyaslavic. Call her Madame."

"Shouldn't I call her Mister?"

"Hah," replied Anna. "You mean she's the only female relative on the male side?"

Madame Madyaslavic clapped her hands and looked grim. "Bon jour, Madame's et Monsieurs. Tout le monde est pret? Alors, commencons, allons-y!" She nodded to the pianist.

Talk about a drill sergeant, Madame's cane banged out the tempo on the wooden floor. "Une, deux, trois, quatre." As she counted again only this time in Russian, "ah-DEEN, dvah, tree, che-TYH-ree," the dancers morphed into a parade of the wooden soldiers. Their right hands on the barre, feet in fifth position and stomachs sucked in, pulled up and under rib cages.

The music began and Madame's voice pierced the air, "eeeeeeeeeeee ..." The knot in my stomach flip-flopped. My mouth went dry. Hiccup ... hiccup again. Deep breaths didn't stop my bouncing chest. Hiccup.

"Grande pli ... é," sang out Madame. "Advan-cer doucement, slowly ... eeeeeeeeee, port de bras ... rel-e-ve... tendue a la seconde, eeeeeeeeee, grande pli ... é... doucement." Madame emphasized ballet terms in such a rhythm, stressing the importance of movement married to music. Hiccup.

I wasn't at the Brooklyn School of Ballet anymore. No more St. Felix Playhouse and Mama and Bubbe's encouraging smiles. No more, "Very nice, sweetie," from my ballet teacher Miss Candy whom I adored. Hiccup. She being a former Miss New York Beauty Pageant contestant holding my hand with fiery red nails. Hiccup. Her beehive hairdo smelled of Aqua Net Hair Spray.

And unlike Madame, *Miss Candy never articulated ballet terms while singing Madame Butterfly to nine girls and one skinny thirteen year old boy.*

Hiccup. I surveyed the room and counted forty dancers packed in like anchovies in a can. Each artist outshining the other. Hiccup. I chuckled and sucked in a slow deep breath. The comparisons between Miss Candy and Madame were comical and I laughed. *Gee whiz* ... no more hiccups.

Then, an ominous, dark shadow moved behind me in Cuban heels. She tapped her cane on the floor observing my right foot, frappe and tendue plie to tempo. She stepped around and faced me. Battement sur le cou-de-pied. Standing at equal heights, her hand pushed my chin. "Head up. Nyet, look down. Rond de jambe en l'air, eight count, tourne, other side."

She stroked my face and murmured, "Pret-ty child, tres jolie ... so young ... breathe, ma petite chou. C'est ca." She poked my belly. "Tight." She poked my thigh. "Frappe, sharp. Tendue soft plie ... Staccato battement sur le cou-de-pied." She poked my mid-section. "Strong ... ici, votre core, danse ici."

Suddenly, Madame heard giggles. She turned and moved quickly to the cackling sounds and stood before two females. She hit the taller girl's arm with her silver-handled cane. The girl winced feeling the sting.

"Something funny? Nyet funny."

The pianist stopped playing. The girls trilled, "Sorry, Madame. Sooorrry."

"Get out," yelled Madame. "Get oooouuuut." She pointed her silver-handled cane at the door. "Crocodile nyet laugh. Eat people." Madame changed her limited English to her Russian language and screamed a tirade. The embarrassed girls ran out of the room in tears.

I trembled watching the faces of frightened dancers endure Madame's temper. But the ballet mistress recovered and signaled the pianist to play what else? A Chopin Polonaise. Class resumed as if nothing happened.

Madame next directed thirty-two grande battements using the right leg. She counted the first few in French, the next few in Russian. Then the class turned to the other side. Madame started the count aloud for the left leg, thirty-two more repetitions. To say my thighs and calves had spasms. Yes, the muscles burned.

At the end of sixty-four grande battements a la seconde otherwise known as high leg lifts up to my ears, *I wondered if my legs would shrivel up and fall off at the hip bones like Bubbe's boiled chicken.*

Minutes later, the class moved to the center of the room. The dancers formed lines to dance adagio starting with a grande plie in fifth position. Each time, I attempted to step forward to get a better view of Madame demonstrating a combination, someone pulled me back.

When Madame noticed what was going on, she insisted on rotating the lines. Hence, I finally made the front row during a waltz ending in a double pirouette. If Anna said this class was a zoo *well, by golly,* I found my tiger. Let the elephants and wildebeests beware. I caught the jungle fever and danced fearless.

But to be fair, some of the older girls were incredibly talented. They were swans and flamingos and graceful leaping gazelles.

Some of the men, highly trained and athletic jocks, moved as majestic as lions on the Serengeti.

And it was a fight for power. During a floor leap across the room on a diagonal, two aggressive swans crowded me out. They spiraled sideways making me look foolish. No matter. I forged ahead and retried the leap alone and succeeded. Anna grinned and gave me a thumbs-up.

At the end of class, the dancers applauded Madame and she exited the room stomping her two inch heels.

When the door slammed shut, Yuri walked over and greeted Anna and me with kisses. The spurt of energy from his penetrating attention, could light sparklers on the fourth of July if I had sparklers in my hands and it wasn't September.

He attempted to speak in English making no sense. We tried not to laugh but couldn't help ourselves. But, who cared? And "Yes, Anna he was handsome, gloriously handsome and dreamy" and a magnificent dancer. "Without equal," alleged the dance critic at the New York Times, "the greatest male dancer in the Western World today" and I agreed seeing him dance for the first time.

From his dance bag, Yuri grabbed a small towel and dried his face and neck. Strands of light blonde, straight hair – fell over his blue-grey eyes upsetting his view and made him upset. After redoing his short ponytail, he relaxed his anger and smiled.

Anna's eyes shone bright and opened-wide when Yuri moved closer and kissed her mouth. She turned cuddly as a mushy, ripe strawberry. *Wow! Can love do that? And no, I didn't have to ask Anna if she had feelings for the man. It was obvious.*

Yuri and Anna kept speaking in Russian and had eyes only for each other until ... he switched his focus to me. *Holy cow!* His hands waved around my upper body expressing something to Anna in staccato phrases. He pointed to my legs and then at my face, adding a confounded stare. Not used to being scrutinized like a prize steer up for auction, I tensed up and chewed my lip.

Yuri ignored my unease and rested his fist against his chin. He resembled Rodin's statue, "The Thinker" in the gardens of the Museum of Modern Art. And, as he continued to examine me at arm's length, he contemplated every inch of my one hundred and three pounds.

Would he bid on me like a coveted bull? Or, raise my lips to examine my racehorse teeth?

Creepier still, his eyes narrowed and fixated on my face. He broke into a sheepish smile and tapped my nose in a playful move. His shoulder bag fell down his arm and bumped my hip. I flinched and gasped, "Oh, dear."

He blew it off in a laugh and kissed the back of my hand. Then he kissed Anna's lips. "Do svidaniya," he said in Russian which sounded like "duh svee-dah-nee-ye" and walked away.

I watched the curvature of his back in a damp sleeveless white tee-shirt and beige tights. His muscles rippled down the length of his body. I'd never danced in a class with a man before. The closest I'd gotten to a male was thirteen-year-old Joseph who played a skinny prince in our dance recital.

So today was a bit daunting. Several men, all wearing tights showed their anatomy in front. I tried not to look but I looked. And right now, I tingled standing before Yuri with visions of David Katz. *Good grief!*

My mind's eye saw David's strong, sexy, athletic build ... wide shoulders and narrow hips walk towards me in self-assured strides. My blood ran hot and I began to sweat.

Anna shook my shoulder.

"Huh?" my breath caught.

"Come back to earth girl, you're in outer space. Are you

okay?"

"What? Yeah, I'm fine."

"Well then … Yuri was all compliments about you holding your own in class, strong and sensuous. He especially grinned mentioning the sensuous."

"How do you know that?" My cheeks flushed.

She laughed and elbowed me in the ribs. "Your face is red. Are you blushing?"

"No."

"Don't tell me you're embarrassed by the word sensuous? Oh Jesus, you can't be that naïve."

"You're making it up."

"Sarah? My parents are Russian immigrants. I spoke Russian at home and learned English in school."

"In Seattle?"

"Yes. There's Russians in Seattle, duh." She laughed.

"You don't have an accent."

"Why should I? I was born in America."

"So Yuri said I danced sensuous?"

"Yes, and don't ask me again." She locked her arm in mine and we left Studio A.

AT THE HORN & Hardart Automat on West 57ᵗʰ Street, Anna and I found a table. We ate our homemade lunches and purchased drinks. The Lemon Meringue Pie looked tempting in the tiny, glass, coin-operated windows but too many calories.

"Anna, tell me about Yuri."

"Okay, but it's only what I've heard."

"Better than nothing."

"Five months ago, Mrs. Pace signed him to the CCBT when

he defected from the Soviet Union."

"That's when he was seeking asylum in Paris when performing with the Leningrad-Kirov Ballet."

"Right. Mrs. Pace flew him to New York to dance the lead in two ballets. The audiences went wild. His electrifying leaps and jumps made the people want more and more of him and his performances were sold out."

"My aunt tried to buy us tickets but she refused to pay the scalpers fifty dollars a ticket price."

"Fifty dollars? Jesus! Anyway, everybody was thrilled. The critics loved Yuri and there was SRO at the theatre. Because of his success, he asked to choreograph something new."

"Is that my ballet?" I asked in innocence.

Anna grinned and gave me a playful slap on the arm. "Yes, you lucky little shit. It's called *Colors of The Rainbow*."

"Mrs. Pace announced that ballet at the final audition."

"Right, but what I'm about to tell you, Sarah. You must swear not to tell anybody. Swear?"

"Yes, I swear."

"Well ... Yuri told me in confidence, Mrs. Pace decided her choreographer Karl Kreisler had to go."

"Why?"

"She hated the son-of-a-bitch. He created a few worthwhile ballets but he refused to wine-and-dine her wealthy patrons. He demanded free tickets and house seats to Broadway shows and concerts like a pompous ass. The man was so rude, he didn't ask in a quiet way. He yelled what he wanted. So, Mrs. Pace asked her attorney to get rid of him and make it legal."

"You mean fire him."

"No. That's a breach of contract and a fight with the union."

"What did she do?" I sat up straighter biting my nail.

"She proposed a wager. She knew Karl loved to gamble on

the horses and poker games. If two fleas crossed the street, Karl would bet on which flea got to the other side first."

"No kidding," I chuckled.

"Yep … Mrs. Pace bet she could determine a student's potential for greatness. Karl scoffed at the idea saying it was impossible. He laughed in her face."

"What was the bet?"

"That she could turn a female student from any ballet school into an overnight sensation. A soloist that audiences would adore and do it, in six weeks. The student would debut in Yuri's new ballet."

"What happened?"

"Karl freaked when he heard Mrs. Pace hired Yuri to choreograph a new ballet for the fall/winter season. Normally, Karl produced the big gala opening night ballet every year for five years straight. Also, Mrs. Pace refused to use either of Karl's favorite ballerinas, Irina and Sonia."

"So, who's the ballerina?"

"That's the bet. You!"

"Oh, nooooo. No!"

"Karl screamed at Mrs. Pace in front of the professional class. 'You will fail, Mrs. Pace. Not without a magic wand and you're no magician. You're a crazy woman.'"

"Oh, God forbid." I held my spinning head in disbelief. "This is awful."

"You wanna know the prize, Sarah?"

"Do I have to?"

"If she wins, Karl forfeits his three-year contract and leaves the company immediately. No farewell parties and no lawsuits."

"That's what could happen?"

"Those were the terms and she asked him in front of her professional class as witnesses, if he understood?"

"He did and wanted to know if he won, then what?"

"She would increase his salary twenty percent and pay for a two week vacation in Puerto Rico for him and a friend."

"Can she afford it?"

Anna nodded. "Her family's rich. She's born with a silver spoon up her ass."

I shook my head.

Anna held my upper arms. "Sarah. Work hard. Devote yourself to Yuri. He can make you great."

"You think so?" I frowned.

"Yes, I know so. I watched you in class. You're fearless. Your technique is strong. This is your chance, your passion."

"You believe in me?"

"Yes, you idiot. The audiences will love you."

"Don't say that," I snapped. "My grandma would spit three times if she heard you say that."

Anna looked stunned. "Are you superstitious?"

"Yes! I'm spitting, "Toi, toi, toi, against the evil eye."

Anna laughed and spit, "Toi, toi, toi."

"Good. How did you find out about the bet, Anna?"

"Yuri told me."

"Really?" I glanced up at the red neon clock on the wall. "Anna, I have to go."

"Yes, we both have to go," she wiped her mouth and bounced out of the chair. She handed me my dance bag and picked up hers.

"Anna? What's Yuri's favorite color? I have to change into clean leotards when I get back."

"You'll need more than his favorite color to please him. But you're right. His nature is sensitive to color. He hates pink."

"I'm gonna throw up."

"If you have to? Do it fast. I have to catch the 104 bus."

I shook my head. "Just nauseous. See you tomorrow, bye."

Anna ran to the automat's front door and yelled over her shoulder. "It's red! Yuri loves red!"

I hurried back to the school in a tizzy. In my dance bag, I had one clean leotard. It was pink. *Gosh, darn.*

CHAPTER 10

Monday afternoon, September 6th. Brooklyn meets Leningrad.

DRESSED IN LOLLIPOP candy pink from head to toe I met Yuri, a few minutes before three. We smiled at each other in the smaller room, Studio B. Joining us was an unfamiliar face, the rehearsal pianist hired for Yuri's new ballet.

Mrs. Tupper, a thirty-something woman was an American wearing a tan suit and tan pillbox hat. She introduced herself and walked over to the piano. The original musical score to *Colors of The Rainbow* laid on top of the baby grand waiting and ready.

While Mrs. Tupper looked over the score, Yuri and I warmed-up and stretched our legs. Minutes later, he smiled, "Red-dy?"

I nodded, "Yes."

He started designing an entrance step then stopped. He scratched his head, "Sa-rah danse Red Rain-bow? Da? ... da, da, cabriole, assemble, da, da, grande jete?"

"Yes, Red Rainbow," I nodded. "Cabriole, ah ..." *I'm dancing his favorite color but his steps are weird. Do girls cabriole?*

Yuri walked over to the piano and showed Mrs. Tupper where he wanted her to begin playing. It would be the theme music for my solo variation in Act I.

At the time, I didn't know I'd appear at the opening of the ballet, with six other rainbow girls in a tableaux behind a scrim.

But, several rehearsals later would come the news. And a week after that, I would learn that during Act II, the character of "The Sun" danced by Yuri, falls madly in love with the Red Rainbow. No one told me this was a romantic fairy tale and I caught the prince.

Yuri started teaching the first variation. I followed along marking the steps. Although I stumbled when dancing full-out, I did okay or so I thought.

"Stop!" he bellowed. "Sa-rah, danse vid mu-sak?"

"Didn't I?" Tears filled my eyes. *He hates me. I'm gonna get fired.*

Yuri walked over to the piano and picked up the score and hummed the notes on the page. He pointed to where Mrs. Tupper should play.

She grimaced.

I danced the variation to the Red Rainbow melody theme. But, as Mrs. Tupper played the ballet score, I recognized several wrong sounds. *It wasn't me dancing badly. It was her awful sight reading.*

Yuri held his head and stormed to the piano. "Nyet!" *If he were a dragon he would have breathed fire.*

I hiccupped in fear.

While glaring at Mrs. Tupper in anger, Yuri reached across the keyboard as if to smack her hands but he didn't. Her mouth dropped open watching him close the lid to the baby grand Steinway.

Yuri explained something in Russian. The pianist's eyes bugged out and she sat motionless. She didn't understand. Frustrated, he grabbed the musical score and pointed to the notes singing the melody in the treble clef. "Da, da, daaaaaa, da, da…" Then he sang the bass clef chords in a deeper voice, "dum, dummmm, dum, dum, dummmmmmmm." Each time he indicated through pantomime that Mrs. Tupper should follow and sing.

She sang after several attempts to goad her into trying and she succeeded. So when Yuri stopped singing, she sang alone. He smiled and with the lightest touch, he opened the lid to the keyboard.

THAT NIGHT AT Sutton Place, Yuri dined with Mrs. Pace. Anna told me this at lunch the following day. And, to make the dinner conversation run smoother, Mrs. Pace invited Madame Madyaslavic to act as the evening's translator. Yuri learned from Madame, Mrs. Tupper wasn't at fault. Mrs. Pace hired her at the last minute and for a fact, never showed her the musical score.

During the meal, Yuri complained about me and Mrs. Tupper. They could get a leading soloist to understudy my part but Mrs. Tupper?

Yuri threatened to have Mrs. Tupper executed by a firing squad if, they rehearsed in Russia. "Pianist should know … sight read." Mrs. Pace didn't learn about this until a week later when Madame told the truth. The exact translation: "Tupper should be shot dead; burn in hell; crucified Yuri ball-let mu-sak."

MEANWHILE, OUR REHEARSAL continued and Mrs. Tupper's mousey brown ringlets, dripped sweat. Thankfully, her sight-reading improved and Yuri yelled less. I couldn't tell if she played the right notes or the wrong notes. It could have been Mama's washing machine chugging along in the wash cycle. I hated every note.

During the second hour of our rehearsal, I noticed a bottle of cough syrup sitting atop the piano that hadn't been there before. Mrs. Tupper took repeated swigs but she never coughed. Soon, the bottle looked empty.

She confided in me several days later, the bottle was to calm her nerves. I kept her secret, knowing if anyone with half a brain could guess she had a problem.

Yuri's enthusiasm for his new ballet showed in his physical strength and mental agility. I thought my energy was endless but I was no match for his "he-man strength." I quickly realized I'd better get eight hours sleep and stick to a high protein diet if I wanted to keep up with him. That being said, the next setback was me.

I'd never danced with a man before and hadn't taken partnering classes in adagio work. So when Yuri switched my solo variation to our opening duet, he began demonstrating the first lift.

Yuri stood across the room and yelled, "Sa-rah ... run!"

I ran to him, his hands reached for my hip bones, raising me high in the air over his head. Arching my back, I soared like an eagle. *Okay, I got that part right give me a gold star.*

The next part he demonstrated with his hands ... I would slide down his back and in snake-like moves, wrap myself around his body, chest and slide the length of his leg to the floor. *Oh, my stars you've gotta be kidding.*

Yes, he showered and smelled of pine soap but I didn't expect such intimate body contact. My female parts rubbing against his muscular physique. I'd never been kissed by a boy never mind, sliding up close and personal with a man's torso and thighs. *What would my family think? Oh, crap, Mama.*

My body stiffened, my cheeks flamed. "No! I won't do it."

"Nyet, nyeeeet!" he railed in Russian.

I stood by and waited until he stopped screaming. I took a

quick peek at Mrs. Tupper and she looked petrified. I thought both of us were in danger of getting fired or smacked by an irate Russian.

I inhaled and locked eyes with Yuri. *Oh, no!* His eyes were glistening in tears and I began to shake in a panic. *What have I done? My career is over.*

"Yuri, I'm sorry. I haven't danced with a man before. Oh, gosh, I didn't mean to hurt your feelings." I touched his chest.

He stepped back in a snit.

"Yuri, show me the lift. I'll do it. Please ... I'm just scared ... okay?"

Not certain he understood but maybe he did. Anyway, he moved towards me and wrapped his arms around me in a warm hug and sang a gentle song.

When he finished singing, he let go and stepped away.

"Yuri, I'll do the lift. Show me but do. Not. Yell. Nyet yell."

"Da?" He straightened his shoulders and took a deep breath.

I moved to the other side of the room and posed. He signaled Mrs. Tupper to play and I ran and leaped into his arms.

He lifted me high in the air, one hand at the small of my back, the other hand across my thigh. Two beats later, I slid around his body then over his right shoulder and slid down his back. His hand guided my torso across his chest. I twisted and slid over his thigh to the floor. In a swift move, his hands lifted my waist, to a pose on pointe in an arabesque finish.

He kissed my shoulder and walked over to his dance bag and grabbed a towel to dry his face and arms. Problem solved but the next issue was our lack of communication.

Yuri knew fourteen words of English and I got to hear them all. "Hell-o, goo-bye... Sa-rah, nyet bebe. Sa-rah, Red Rain-bow prin-cess, danse a gin, danse o-yer and ... shit, shit, shit, nyet goot... crap, crap, crap, nyet. Crap crap shit ... fook it."

These classy words he screamed during the final hour of our beautiful duet. The sobbing could fill buckets. Not his tears, mine.

If this first day had been longer than three hours, I would have drowned in my own waterworks. In defense of my behavior, no one told me the story of the ballet. No one played the musical score written by some esoteric mad Russian living on the streets of the lower Eastside. Or, most confusing, no one explained why the music had odd-ball chords and sounded more dissonant than Igor Stravinsky's "Firebird."

The music was no Swan Lake you could take home and sing to your sister. "It was pure cacophony," said Mrs. Tupper. "To be played by the tubas, the bassoons, the tympani and kettle drums." I recognized only the flute part because according to Mrs. Tupper, "That instrument soloed the Red Rainbow theme in Act I."

While confused over the music and learning this first pas de deux, I tried to follow Yuri's choreography. But, I did everything wrong except the lifts. My new sport of body slamming became my triumph. Performing great lifts was the only ace up my sleeve and a deterrent to being fired. *No more wasting time dreaming of David Katz who never called.* I had to pay attention to my partner.

At this same rehearsal while Alexi took a bathroom break, Yuri directed me in Russian to move upstage, I did a leap downstage to the piano. He screwed up his face and yelled something. Why? I didn't speak Russian and he was too impatient to wait for Alexi's return.

Next out of spite, he pirouetted to the left when I turned to the right, my good side, his glare turned to ice.

Could he strangle me? Yes, if we'd been alone without the pianist to witness my murder.

"Stop it!" I screamed, hands on hips.

The pianist and Yuri froze.

I stomped my foot. "Okay, partner. I can't read your mind. Next time, signal. Blow smoke out your ass."

He glared at me transfixed.

Alexi returned to Studio B and witnessed me pacing back and forth. "I don't have a crystal ball," I fumed and shouted at my mentor. "How can I know? Please, slow down!"

Yuri wrung his hands, mumbled in Russian and yelled at the overhead fans, "Shit, shit ... fook it."

Then during the last half hour, I turned the wrong way for the third time. Yuri stopped dancing and held his head.

"Nyet, mu-sak. Nyet, Sa-rah," and stormed out of the room followed by Alexi. They both slammed the door like an echo apart.

Several alarmed mothers whose young daughters were taking a ballet class in Studio C, rushed into our room. Mrs. Tupper told them, "Mister Yuri is an artist, very temperamental."

One of the mothers chuckled, "I should know, my in-laws are Tartars from Russia. They're madder than Yul Brenner in the movie, *The Brothers Karamatsou*."

Minutes later, Yuri returned wearing a long-tailed, red devil costume over his rehearsal clothes. He waddled in like a circus clown and banged a pitchfork on the floor.

Not knowing whether to laugh or cry, I hiccupped.

Yuri paraded in a figure eight and twirled his tail like a majorette in front of a band. Then he changed direction and leaped towards me imitating a frog. "Ribbit, ribbit."

I swallowed air and hiccupped faster.

Yuri roared, "Ggggggguuurrrrrrrr" making me laugh and guess what? My hiccups stopped.

"Yuri, fix!" he laughed and jumped.

"Thanks, but what are you? A devil or a frog in your ballet?"

He ignored my question or didn't understand and tore off his devil suit and threw it across the room. I ran for a bench, getting out of his way.

Seconds later, he came after me and offered dark chocolate and a drink from his silver flask.

"Blah!" I spit out the nasty liquid and made a face. He snickered and grabbed the flask and swallowed. Guess he didn't know this American teenager didn't swig vodka but I ate the chocolate.

The studio door opened and in trotted Mrs. Pace and an average height, dark-haired, young man in a grey suit and tie.

Mrs. Pace smiled, "Sarah, Mrs. Tupper, Yuri … "This is Alexi Grigoriovitch. Boy, say that name fast three times, you'd win a prize!" She broke up laughing and we stared bewildered.

Mr. Grigoriovitch mumbled, "Could be funny."

"I apologize," continued Mrs. Pace. "For not telling my friend here," she indicated Alexi, "our newly-hired translator about the rehearsal time which was more than an hour ago, right?"

No one answered.

"Alexi will be your constant companion and can translate anything. Use him well starting right now."

I shook his hand, "Hi, I'm Sarah." Mrs. Tupper also nodded, "Hi." But, a grateful and excited Yuri kissed Alexi on both cheeks and on the mouth.

"Yuk," I scowled. Men kissed men on the mouth in public? Not in Brooklyn they didn't, you'd get your ass in a sling. But, in the coming weeks I learned, it was no big deal. Russian men especially relatives and good friends think nothing of it.

And in the days that followed, Yuri tried kissing me on the mouth. I pushed him away and told him in no uncertain terms, "Nyet! No way!" He laughed at my spunk. The girls in the ballet corps adored when Yuri greeted them. They lingered at his lip kisses or returned his kisses in spades. I was the exception.

Although once, he caught me fully on the mouth and tried to poke his tongue down my throat. I slapped him hard and it left a welt. The challenge left him fascinated. After that, he'd sneak up behind me and tap my shoulder and pucker his lips, or jump out from behind the girl's dressing room door and hug me tight. He loved to scare me and play.

Respectfully, he never kissed me again on the mouth. Maybe because Mrs. Pace threatened him or maybe, when I turned eighteen on November 5th, he had a more aggressive plan.

Still, he could be perverse and teased, "Sa-rah, nyet bebe … da, vo-man …"

"You're damn right, I am and don't mess with this woman."

He enjoyed learning English anyway he could and repeated "damn" several times to annoy me.

HOWEVER, A COUPLE days later, there was an incident.

Near the end of our rehearsal, Alexi and Yuri argued in Russian, their hands thrashed through the air emphasizing their screams. It was obvious Yuri complained about me and Mrs. Tupper whom he called "Tuppervare." Alexi had earlier mentioned she was a relative of the inventors of Tupper plastic salad bowls and containers with lids.

So our pianist, visibly frightened, gathered her music, her purse and empty cough syrup bottle and tip-toed out the door. I didn't understand their language but I recognized the harsh tone in their voices.

Sometime later I learned, Yuri told Mrs. Pace to ask the Tuppers to write a check as patrons. He loved to startle Mrs. Pace when he addressed the pianist as "Tuppervare."

Oh, yes, we had a rough rehearsal. No happy campers.

THE NEXT DAY, after the professional class, I bribed Alexi with soft, butter-cream-cherry-centers, Barton Chocolates and he reluctantly told me the truth. He said, "Last night at dinner, you should have seen Yuri have a go at Mrs. Pace. He was a wild man and he leaped on her couch. In a temper tantrum, he bellowed, "Yuri nyet vork wid Sa-rah, nyet vork vid Tuppervare. Miss-take! Yuri jumps off ... Brooklyn Bridge. Yuri kill Yuri-self.'"

"No, Yuri, don't be silly," said a calm and dignified Mrs. Pace.

"Yuri then threatened to fly to the Paris and give the Paris Opera his new ballet if, Mrs. Pace didn't get rid of you, Sarah and the pianist. He wanted Mrs. Pace to throw you both off the George Washington Bridge because the current in the Hudson River moved faster than the current in the East River."

Alexi whispered as if embarrassed, "My friend spends his spare time standing on bridges analyzing the water speed."

"Oh, my God," I held my throat. My heart pounded in fear.

"No, Sarah. Don't be scared," assured Alexi with a smile. "Mrs. Pace is a magician. She pulled a crazy Russian out of a hat and fixed everything."

"How?"

"She made Yuri realize that you are the only one, who can dance the Red Rainbow."

I searched Alexi's face. "Really? So, what about Mrs. Tupper?"

"She's not fired either. Mrs. Pace convinced Yuri to keep you both."

"Wow, thank you Mrs. Pace." I let go of my throat.

Alexi sighed, "And Yuri's happy."

BUT AS I heard gossip in the girl's dressing room later in the week, I didn't know Alexi was only telling half the truth. He lied about Yuri's devotion that flipped overnight and turned altruistic.

Alexi omitted the part where Mrs. Pace gave Yuri lots of money to keep us. She took Yuri shopping, to Saks Fifth Avenue and bought him a new fall wardrobe. If I'd known Yuri had to be bribed to dance with me, I'd have taken the Express BMT to the Court Street/Borough Hall station and quit dancing forever. Home to the Valiant Arms, to Brooklyn College and to satisfy Mama, *this one I almost choked on*, find a husband and have children.

But to continue this soap opera drama … at six o'clock when our rehearsal finally finished, Mrs. Pace flung open the studio door and marched in like a storm trooper. She threw her purse and briefcase on a chair and stood at attention.

"Alexi," she commanded. "Translate every word that comes out of my mouth. My exact words or, I'll cut your balls off with a tweezer."

Alexi's face blanched. Mrs. Tupper's mouth dropped open in shock and I felt a chill.

"As of right now," said Mrs. Pace standing at attention. "I won't cave-in to anyone's temper tantrums or emotional blackmail. I won't listen to complaints about the rehearsals. Don't call me late at night with threats. You'd better get your job done and do it well. Or I'll fire the whole lot of you. All four of you. Am I clear?"

We eyeballed one another and Mrs. Tupper and I nodded.

Yuri looked uneasy and shifted his weight.

"Okay!" she said glaring at Alexi. "Are you translating word for word?"

"Yes, ma'am. Go on."

"To make this happen, you will work together and get this beautiful ballet on its feet." Her jaw tightened. "And, if anyone has a problem with that? If you refuse to co-operate, tell me now and leave. I'll tear up your contract."

No one said a word.

Yuri leaped at Mrs. Pace and kissed her cheeks, kissed Mrs. Tupper, kissed Alexi and tried kissing me. Everyone else looked relieved but not me. I didn't trust anyone or what was professed. My upbringing, my ethnic group had legitimate fears. We trusted no one, ever. *My ancestors had reasons.*

"Well, that makes life a whole lot easier," she clapped her hands together and grinned. "Now on a happier note, Alexi, Yuri, Sarah, Mrs. Tupper … you are coming to my house for dinner."

"What?" I muttered.

"Get your things," she announced. "We're leaving at once."

"Why?" I asked.

"Why not?" she responded looking amazed.

My heart sank. Why tonight? My sister promised my favorite dinner, roasted chicken and blintzes for dessert."

"Mrs. Pace, I can't," I pleaded in almost a whine. I lacked the courage to say no. "Melissa will be worried if I don't come home for dinner."

"Of course, she'll worry. Call her from my house."

DAVID KATZ NEVER *called. Hating myself for guessing the reasons he wouldn't call, I cried myself to sleep after long days of dancing.*

CHAPTER 11

September 9th, Thursday. The dinner at 323 Sutton Place.

WE ALL STEPPED into the waiting limo while irate horn honkers blasted the double-parked limo blocking traffic. Mrs. Tupper waved goodbye as we pulled away. She had declined dinner since she needed to get home to her sick mother.

Twenty minutes later we arrived at Sutton Place, to a brick townhouse on the East River. There Mrs. Williams, the house-keeper, led Yuri and me upstairs to separate bathrooms where we showered and changed.

After shampooing my hair, I combed it loose and telephoned Michelle.

In the dining room, Cook announced, "Serve yourselves. Bon appetite." The aroma of seared lamb chops, buttered lima beans, scalloped cheese potatoes and mint jelly filled the air. We savored the meal and complimented Cook.

Mrs. Pace tapped her wine glass. "Okay, I have demands. Alexi translate every word, verbatim, please."

Alexi cowed, "Yes, ma'am." *Why was she a bitch to Alexi? We knew he'd translate every word including the punctuation and tone of voice.*

"Yuri, darling, no more yelling. That's a waste of energy and your strength and Sarah? No more crying. You both must behave. If you don't, I'll knock your heads together. I can replace a rehearsal pianist but I can't replace my dancers. Opening night must be electrifying. Make it work, you two."

She sipped her wine. "We need standing ovations, flowers by the bushels and curtain calls. That's what we live for, right?"

"Right," we all nodded like sheep. Then Yuri cheered in Russian and I giggled at his response.

Mrs. Pace rose from her chair and raised her wine glass. "Opening night will be Yuri's triumph. To our premiere dancer and choreographer."

"Chin, chin," bellowed Alexi.

"Yes! Way cool!" I squealed.

Yuri sprang to his feet and spoke a Russian response so captivating, it needed no translation. His expression, his hand covering his heart, charged the air. The gooseflesh on my arms, prickled. Such passion I vowed to try to trust after hearing him speak from his heart. When he finished, he bowed to Mrs. Pace.

She toasted "To Yuri and the *Colors of The Rainbow.*" The crystal stemware pinged.

Mrs. Pace inhaled and looked mighty smug ... "I will win the bet. Sarah will do it for me."

All four glasses clinked.

"Great!" she smiled. "'The dye is cast,' said Julius Caesar crossing the Rubican. We will prevail and beat the bastard Karl Kreisler." She took my hand. "Dear girl. When you and Yuri dance with one beating heart, you will be unstoppable. The audience will fall in love with you and him." Her eyes flashed, "You have a sparkle, Sarah Rothman, and a joy like no one else. You will be magnificent!"

I gasped.

Alexi grinned and translated. Yuri nodded vigorously.

With a lump in my throat, *I vowed not to let them down* and swallowed hard watching the serious intent on three faces.

Mrs. Pace released my hand and motioned to Alexi. She insisted he translate every word as gospel and he nodded. Turning to Yuri, she said, "Please, be patient with Sarah. Emphasize every detail. Find her strengths."

Yuri's eyes locked mine. I shifted in my chair feeling the heat from his stare.

"You have five weeks, Yuri," said Mrs. Pace. "Thirty-five days. Make every minute count."

Then, as if prompted by a stage director, Alexi, Yuri and Mrs. Pace downed their drinks in one gulp.

With such bravado, I expected the trio to toss their empty glasses over their shoulders into a raging fire but, *good grief, Charlie Brown,* no fireplace.

WHATEVER POWER MRS. Pace held over Yuri, after her serious speech, he did a one-hundred and eighty-degree attitude change towards me.

Yuri walked over to where I sat and extended his hand to help me up. His demeanor softened like creamery butter. The attention he paid felt weird. I dropped his hand and moved to the other side of the room, he was spooking me out.

Mrs. Pace pushed her chair back and stood tall. "Excuse me, I need to separate a new patron from his bankroll. Stay and visit. I'll be back when I've gotten enough money."

Cook appeared in the doorway. "Everyone, please move upstairs to the sitting room for dessert and tea."

ALEXI AND YURI opted for the beige leather couch and I sat on the brown sofa. A coffee table divided us and on top of the table was a tea set, Smirnov Vodka bottles and plates of marzipan cakes, Swiss light and dark chocolates and fresh fruit. I poured myself a cup of tea, added milk and munched on dried apricots. I avoided the chocolate-covered bees from Bloomingdale's specialty shop. *Oh, the things I give up for the dance.*

Yuri and Alexi, between shots of vodka, reminisced about life back home. Between laughs and private jokes, Alexi translated Leningrad for Yuri and his own working-class family in Moscow. Alexi smoked "Gauloises," French cigarettes, forcing Yuri to open windows, to clear the stinking air. We coughed and laughed and then it was my turn, Alexi translated.

"I grew up in Flatbush and now lived, in Brooklyn Heights. Very different from Leningrad and Moscow."

As I spoke about my family hating my career choice, gradually, a shy trust and camaraderie unfolded between the three of us. An image similar to tiny layers of onion skins, peeled away from its center.

During the next hour, Yuri's eyes lingered on my face. It wasn't a leer or rude. It was as if he was learning how to better connect with me. Maybe how to teach me choreography, without a death threat attached? Was this our director's plan? The blueprint where Anna said, "Mrs. Pace was always scheming."

Alexi translated, "Sarah, Yuri wants you to know. He cast the final deciding vote at your audition?"

"Wha, what?" I stammered, "His was, was the fifth vote?" The hair on my arms stood up and my breath hitched.

"He wanted you and prides himself on never being wrong. His only concern, you looked so young. The judges guessed your age as thirteen or fourteen."

I giggled, "Alexi, tell Yuri, I got into the movies for a quarter, on a child's ticket until I was fifteen. My looks saved me money."

Yuri smiled and stretched out on the couch.

Alexi continued. "Yuri could see potential and compared you to a rough diamond. You danced with a light in your soul."

"Yuri said that?" My skin tingled as he spoke words so amazing.

"And you danced with a fluidity and sensuality that could fascinate an audience. Inherent traits that can't be taught."

I gulped air. "Yuri … said that?"

"Sarah, you were born to dance."

I stared at Alexi in disbelief. "Tell me the truth."

"Yes, you were born to dance."

I jumped up, circled the coffee table and flung myself on top of Yuri.

My slightly drunk hero didn't expect such a physical reaction to his praise. Abetted by Smirnov Vodka and buried under throw pillows, he had to grab the edge of the couch to keep from falling.

He grumbled and Alexi refused to translate. No matter. Yuri tossed the throw pillows over the couch and steadied himself. He reached forward to hug me and laughed.

When I moved to return to my sofa, Yuri pulled me down into a bigger hug. He stroked my hair and played with loose ends the way my dad did when I was a kid.

Yuri murmured, "Sa-rah," (Alexi translated) "Reminds me of my mother, a dancer who died young … in a car crash accident. She had long, blond hair and wore it braided. And like you, she cried a big baby and yelled like a chicken with no head. She had lots of energy and mischief. I loved her more than anything in the world. I miss her every day." Tears streamed down his cheeks.

My heart melted. "Tell Yuri. I'm sorry to hear about his mother's tragic death. I didn't know he voted for me and I will work very, very hard from now on, to make him proud. I promise."

Yuri buried his face in my hair and held me close.

BECAUSE OF OUR attention to Yuri, neither Alexi nor I heard Mrs. Pace enter the room. She threw her purse at a desk lamp to surprise us which worked. She glared at Yuri and me as if, *angry enough to spit wooden nickels as my Uncle Al would say.*

"You two look cozy," she sounded sarcastic. "That doesn't make me happy. Let me be clear."

Yuri and I jumped apart and sat upright on the couch.

"Alexi …," said Mrs. Pace, "make sure your friend understands the seriousness of this situation."

"Of course, Mrs. Pace."

She gritted her teeth. "Sarah is seventeen and still a minor in the eyes of the law. There will be no sex between Sarah and Yuri."

"Sex?" I muttered. My cheeks blushed crimson.

Mrs. Pace stepped in front of Yuri. "Sarah is jailbait. Already in my company, there's too much hanky-panky and sneaking around."

Alexi's expression looked strange when he translated "jailbait" when suddenly, Yuri broke up laughing.

Mrs. Pace slapped Yuri's shoulder. "Not funny."

I bit my lip.

"Nyet, Mrs. Pace," Yuri declared and threw up his hands in surrender.

"No sex, only dancing," she pointed her finger at his face.

I moved to the edge of the couch and hiccupped.

"Da. On-ly danse," declared Yuri. "Grate danse! Too much vo-man."

"Wait!" Alexi interrupted, "He means he's already slept with too many girls in the company."

"What?" I gasped.

"Please understand Mrs. Pace," said Alexi speaking very fast and in earnest. "Yuri wants peace and quiet and to sleep alone.

Some girls try to empty his balls. He needs his strength for this new ballet. Yes, he's like a fighter in training, no sex till the ring, or the stage premiere."

Alexi rolled his eyes at Yuri behind Mrs. Pace's back meaning it was all a lie. But, Mrs. Pace bought into the explanation and heaved a big sigh of relief.

"Thank God," said Mrs. Pace. "That's one less headache. I don't need a pregnant Red Rainbow on opening night."

Mortified, I jumped up from the couch and moved to the far side of the room faster than a bumble bee could fly. My face heated up and my hands shook. I said, "Mrs. Pace, I guarantee that will never happen."

Alexi signaled Yuri it was time to go and said something he didn't translate. The both stood, and made for the door calling "Do svidaniya," over their shoulders. Alexi added, "We don't need the limo. We're taking a cab home. Thank you, Mrs. Pace for dinner. Lovely evening. Bye, Red Rainbow." They hurried down the stairs and out the front door.

Mrs. Pace turned to me. "Plans have changed, Sarah. You're staying with me."

"Huh? Why?"

"You will eat, sleep and live *Colors of The Rainbow*. From now on, all you do is dance."

"I'm fine at my sister's, really I am."

"My driver will bring you to my house after rehearsals. Cook will feed you and no one will bother you when you sleep."

"But, I ..."

"You'll be safer here. Your family will be happier knowing you're protected."

"But, they ..."

"I'll call your father and your sister."

"No, no."

"Yes, Sarah, you're doing this. Fernando will drive you to your sister's right now. He'll wait for you while you pack your things and carry your suitcases."

"I don't think …"

"Do you want me to call your father?" She thumbed through her rolodex on the desk. She stared at me.

"Ah, no …"

"Then I'll call Melissa. Leave now, Sarah. Cook will see you to the car."

I trudged down the stairs and out the front door. Fernando opened the limo door. When we approached the Murray Hill section of mid-town, Fernando said, "Miss Sarah, I'll come up stairs with you and help you pack."

I scowled at him in the rear-view mirror.

He smirked, "Boss's orders."

"Right now, I don't like the boss."

"She wins every time. But, she's good people."

"Yeah? Not if she controls every minute of my day. I'll be under a microscope day and night. I won't breathe."

Fernando laughed, "It ain't gonna be that bad, Miss Sarah."

"Oh, no? My gut tells me otherwise. Not cool. No freedom. I hate it already!"

"Miss Sarah, take it easy."

"Not if I have to bark like a dog and meow like a cat being the house pet."

"The boss lady won't treat you like that."

"She already has."

CHAPTER 12

September 10ᵗʰ, Friday. The watch dog at the gate.

KARL KREISLER, THE evil choreographer who bet I'd be a failure in Yuri's new ballet, turned into a stalker. Wherever I was, he was.

I met him in the lobby, in Mrs. Pace's office and in the rehearsal rooms. Outside on the street, I bumped into him leaning against the building next door. I saw him puffing on a cigarette that he held in a long rhinestone holder. He could be Pepe Le Pew. Or, as in a Noel Coward comedy, he could play the fool, chewing up the scenery or the character who came late to dinner.

Over lunch at the automat, Anna swore she heard Karl ask company members, "How's the new girl? The teeny-bopper? Can she dance?" Anna never heard the answers or so she said.

LATER IN THE girl's dressing room, I overheard the two principal ballerinas, Irina Maya and Sonia Reeves discuss Karl. They raved about his ballets and how he helped their careers.

Irina lamented, "The bet was cruel." And, Sonia agreed. "He deserved better."

"He's a great choreographer," said Irina. "An inspiration to us all in the world of ballet."

Why are they inspired? There has to be something else going on with this bet. Someone had an axe to grind as my Uncle Al would say.

Trembling at this revelation, I tip-toed out of the dressing room and stayed out of sight. But when Mrs. Pace left early, Karl and the two ballerinas popped up like Jack-in-the-boxes.

During the afternoon rehearsal, I flitted around the room antsy as a firefly. Alexi eyed me with suspicion.

"What's wrong?" he asked.

I whispered, "Please ask Yuri, what he thinks of Karl Kreisler? Why does Karl hang around the school?"

Alexi discussed this with Yuri and reported, "Yuri thinks Karl Kreisler is a piece of shit, ignore him and have nothing to do with him."

"I can't. He lurks around the building and when he sees me, he follows me."

Without missing a beat, Alexi repeated what I told him to Yuri. And Yuri ran out of Studio B and screamed for Mrs. Pace. When he couldn't find her anywhere, he went ballistic. Alexi telephoned her home.

"Hello, Mrs. Pace? Alexi. Come to the school at once. Karl Kreisler is upsetting Sarah and you need to get him out of the building. Yuri wants to kick his ass, out the door."

Mrs. Pace arrived sixteen minutes later.

"Yuri, Sarah, darlings! I can't banish Karl Kreisler from the building." Her voice sounded punitive. "He's done nothing wrong. He's rehearsing his ballets for the fall season. Your new ballet and his ballets will be on the same program."

"But Mrs. Pace," I cried. "He stares at me. It's spooky."

"So what? He's harmless. Doesn't have the balls of a goat."

"Please make him leave. He makes me nervous."

"Really?" She looked indignant. "That man has never intimidated anybody. He sucks on a rhinestone cigarette holder from

Woolworth's like a baby on a tit, for God's sakes."

"Can't you switch the rehearsal schedule so Yuri and I don't see him?"

"No, I can't. That wouldn't be fair to Irina and Sonia and their partners. I still pay Karl. His dancers need to rehearse."

"I know but..."

"Sarah! He needs to do his job!"

"But, I, I ..."

"Sarah, I pay you to rehearse not whine. Ignore him. You're a tough cookie."

She stormed out of Studio B and slammed the door.

"Ah, shit!" I yelled. "I'm supposed to say lookie, lookie here comes cookie whenever that bastard's around. What is wrong with that woman? She doesn't listen."

Yuri wrapped his arms around me and purred, "Sa-rah."

Alexi sidled up to Yuri and me. "Ignore her. She's only the boss" and he laughed.

"Grrrrrr," I growled mashing my teeth.

Alexi looked puzzled. "Are you two okay?"

"Da," pouted Yuri.

"No, duh. Do I look okay, Alexi?"

"Can't tett."

Hitting the air with my fists, I snapped, "What if Kreisler tries to hurt me? What if something happens and I can't dance. What then?"

"He wins the bet!" scowled Alexi.

"Yes," I snapped back. "Then my boss can eat her words."

"Sarah, calm down. He not going to hurt you, he's not that stupid. And, he's scared of his own shadow, I've watched. He's chicken shit."

Yuri glared at Alexi. "Chick-ken vhat? Shit?"

"You heard me right."

CHAPTER 13

Sunday, September 12th. The need for Public Relations.

TODAY WAS MY first day off and I planned to spend it with Dad and Bubbe in Manhattan. The three of us would meet Melissa and Leon at Tavern on the Green, a restaurant inside Central Park on West 67th Street and Central Park West. We were set to enjoy a leisurely brunch until Mrs. Pace ruined our plans the night before.

So at nine on Sunday morning, in place of my day off, Fernando drove Yuri, Alexi, Mrs. Pace and me, to a photographer's studio in Greenwich Village. Yuri and I had an appointment with a famous photographer who "only photographed celebrities," according to his interview with the New York Times.

Why the photos on our day off? The PR, our publicity stills were needed ASAP to promote Yuri's ballet. Mrs. Pace and her publicist were getting the word out in a frenzy.

Mrs. Pace announced the photo session during my Saturday night dinner with Cook. "Sarah, cancel your plans for tomorrow. Sorry, dear. We have work to do. You and Yuri."

I telephoned Dad.

"Our day's ruined, Daddy. I know you're disappointed. Me, too. What? You're coming to see me anyway? Okay? The BMT ... changing trains? Right ... Am I excited taking pictures? Yes... this guy's supposed to be famous but I wanna see you. Ten o'clock. What? Uh-huh. Love you, Daddy, bye."

AT THE PHOTO studio, when the buzzer rang for the building's entrance outside door, I quickly signed the release forms to be photographed. By the third buzzer sound, I skipped reading the fine print on the forms and raced downstairs to unlock the front, two doors.

When I saw dad through the glass window of the second door, I screamed, "Daddy, hell-oooo, come-iiinnn," so loud, the people upstairs yelled, "Sarah! Be quiet."

Even Dad scolded, "Hey! They heard you across the river. Dogs are barking in Hackensack you're so loud."

I clung to my dad, "I missed you."

"I missed you, too, honey." His hug as joyful as mine until he chuckled, "Better get this show on the road" and let me go.

Upstairs in the studio, the photographer's assistant walked in from a side door. "Hi! I'm Tony, Mr. Forester's right arm and he should be here in an hour. Let's get started. Mr. Konstantinov … our hairdresser will shampoo and style your hair and Miss Rothman …"

"I shampooed my hair already, it's still damp."

"Make-up for you."

The make-up man, did glamour make-up explaining it would be a natural, subtle look similar to print work in magazine ads. He applied tiny, brown, strands of individual false eyelashes and a smidge of taupe eye shadow. Then with a lip brush, he applied several shades of near red lipsticks and powdered me down.

The hairdresser brushed my hair in a tight bun and sprayed enough hairspray to shellac Aunt Ida Mae's china cabinet. *Yikes!* I had to cover my eyes, my nose and my lips.

Yuri looked pleased at being fussed over. I could see he adored being groomed. Even Mrs. Pace chuckled watching him make faces at himself in the mirror when his hair was being combed and sprayed. She walked up to him and teased, "I'm ready for my close-up, Mr. DeMille."

After Alexi's translation, Yuri laughed with delight.

I blew my partner a kiss from my make-up chair and gushed, "You are my handsome prince."

"Da. Yuri, prince." He lapped up my compliment with a radiant grin.

I also loved the pampering and attention. *My birthright ... a princess to hear my family announce my presence on this earth. And Bubbe would agree having dressed me in ruffles and curled my hair since I was two.*

The photographer maven, Robert Forester, arrived with two Nikon F's hanging around his neck. A third camera with a fisheye lens was held by an attractive blonde secretary, slinking in behind him wearing a white, tight sheath and red stiletto heels.

Dad sat up straighter when the red stiletto heels clip-clopped right past him. She winked at Dad, over her shoulder and he caught his breath in surprise. I giggled to myself.

After moving some white screens and light tweaking, the photographer announced, "Magic time. Let's shoot."

He shot black and white photos of Yuri and me wearing black and white leotards. He suggested I put on a white tulle, knee-length ballet skirt over my leotard and wanted Yuri dressed in all white. We did and he took photos.

Next during the break, Mrs. Pace insisted I change into a white *Swan Lake* costume and tutu with feathered headdress. When I looked in the full length mirror, my breath caught. The costume so classical, my heart fluttered. Having never danced *Swan Lake*, I could only imagine.

The photographer shot various swan poses and when finished, I ran into the dressing room so I wouldn't cry in front of him.

Next, it was Yuri's turn and fun to watch him pose.

Dad and I chatted briefly in between each of Yuri's set-ups. We watched as he donned a white loose shirt, fitted blue-colored velvet vest and tights and became the pirate Conrad in *Le Corsaire*. So elegant and astute, he knew his best profiles and poses. He switched costumes to an odd military jacket with epaulets. He clowned for the camera, his eyes ever alert. Robert Forester adored shooting Yuri and he ate up everything he did.

Because I had no professional pictures, Mrs. Pace insisted I change into various colored leotards for more photos. The hairdresser styled my hair in a figure eight for a few shots then, combed my hair, long and loose around my shoulders. Everyone commented, they preferred the long hair to the upsweep. This half hour turned into crunch time getting many shots for the publicity announcements.

During the next break, when the photographer answered his phone, I noticed Yuri, Alexi and Mrs. Pace conspiring in a corner. When they came out of their half-time huddle, Alexi signaled my dad. "C'mon poppa, Yuri and I are getting coffee next door. Come join us, Yuri's paying the bill."

"Okay with you, Sarah?"

"Sure, Dad ... go."

Daddy nodded, smiled at the red stiletto heels and disappeared with the guys down the front stairs.

Mrs. Pace handed me a small box. "Sarah, do me a favor. Change into this swimsuit and do it quickly. We don't have much time."

I looked at the swimsuit and figured – if I weighed it on a butcher's scale, it might weigh eleven ounces. "You want me to wear this?"

"Yes, dear girl."

I felt a lump in my throat and carried the tiny bit of nothing, as I told Anna the next day over lunch, to the dressing room.

While I got dressed or rather undressed in this beige string bikini, Tony set-up new lighting at the back of the studio loft.

"Miss Rothman, sit over here on this stool."

When I sat on the tiny wooden stool made for a kinder-gartner, several assistants surrounded me with gorgeous bouquets of fresh flowers. Hundreds of yellow and white daisies were tied and hung from a huge metal picture frame (me in the middle) for a cascading effect. *An unbelievable setting!* I mar-veled at the fresh flowers.

But, the Waltz of the Flowers never had daisies and the danc-ers wore bodices with skirts. *Why was I wearing a crocheted string bikini? What was Mrs. Pace up to? I needed a good lawyer. Where the hell was David? Crap, he never called.*

I hiccupped in a panic.

"Get her a sugar cube and a glass of water," barked Mrs. Pace. The make-up man hopped to and handed me both.

Mrs. Pace whispered, "You're a lucky girl. These photos might be for Vogue. Never can tell, or Seventeen Magazine."

"Vogue Magazine? Seventeen?"

"Yes, Robert suggested this extra shoot when he agreed to photograph you and Yuri."

"He did?" My hiccups stopped and I reversed my stance on posing in a bikini.

"It'll be fine. I'm sitting near you. See ..." She pointed to a chair in the corner.

Robert Forester entered the room from somewhere upstairs arriving on a wide service elevator at the back. He greeted me with a cordial smile. "Miss Rothman, are you ready?"

"Yes, I'm ready."

"Good. Me, too." He adjusted the shiny boards and stepped away to check the lighting. He tweaked the boards again, this way and that way until, he nodded to Tony, "Okay."

"All set?"

"Yes."

Mr. Forester stared at me. His hand fisted his chin like the statue of Auguste Rodin's "The Thinker" in the exact way Yuri did when meeting me with Anna. *Men must have similar moves under the same circumstances or maybe I'm wrong.*

The maven held my chin and turned my face from side to side. "Miss Rothman, you have fantastic cheek bones and flawless skin. I can work with that. Tony? I need a key light in her eyes, yes … green eyes … right, tighter focus, good … okay, Tony, get out of the way, get my cameras. And, please … bring me a Coke. Ice, cold Coke. Thanks, man."

He drank the Coke and studied my face and body. He blinked several times and tilted my head and adjusted the shiny boards again.

"You are a beauty, Miss Rothman but I need the right light to show exquisite. I need to take test shots. Tony, get me a Polaroid camera and my portrait lens on the Nikon."

Mr. Forester whistled, "If ever I should leave you" from Camelot while he moved the prop flowers in various positions. He draped the Nikon F around his neck and started taking Polaroid pictures. He and Tony waved the Polaroids in the air saying, "It helps the chemicals develop faster." They liked the results and tossed the black and white snapshots aside.

"Okay, people" said the maven. "We're getting close. Tony turn up the rock music. Blast it, baby. Let's lock and load."

He winked at me and moved his camera to his eye. "Miss Rothman, ready when you are."

"I'm ready."

"Hold your head still and don't forget to breathe." The clicks sounded slow. "Yes, breathing is good, in and out. Turn your head to the left, a little more, look up. Yes, my camera adores you. Can't live without your smile. Yes, smile. No, don't frown ... darling, no."

I swatted a fly near my face and tensed my shoulders.

He grabbed my shoulders and held on tight. "Relax, don't tense up on me. Forget the damn fly." He kissed my nose.

I flinched in surprise at the kiss.

"You are lovely. Show me, lovely. Relax, darling. I won't bite. Only photographs or, maybe ... an occasional kiss on the nose if you're a good girl like I kiss my horse." He laughed. "You know, I own a race horse called 'April Morning' and when she wins a race, I give her kisses on the snout. Anyway ... I'm too old for you and I prefer men for sex. So, you're safe."

Holy moly, did he just say he prefers men? I'm safe! Here goes nothing.

I laughed and wiggled my shoulders. It worked and he gave me a thumbs up. "We're good to go," he roared.

"Great bone structure, no skin blemishes and beautiful, big eyes." The camera clicked a couple more times. "Open your eyes, Miss Rothman, flirt with those gorgeous green eyes, open wider."

He crouched down on the floor shooting upwards at different angles. "The lens is your friend, your lap dog, your sweet pussy cat." He peered into my eyes over his lens. "You are gorgeous. Enjoy yourself and relax your chin. I love looking at you and soon the world will, too."

I flirted and in response, Mr. Forester charmed like no other man I'd ever met. His soft brown eyes mesmerized when he took his camera away from his face. The twinkle in his eyes bathed me in adoration.

"You like having fun, Miss Rothman?"

I giggled.

"Of course, you do. Let's have fun," he cajoled. "Turn up the music, Tony. And, turn on the fans! Make-up," he screamed.

"Flying in."

"Powder her down. Too much shine."

Tony turned on two fans.

"Oh, no," I screeched. "The flowers are flying, my hair is twirling."

"I love it!" yelled Mr. Forester. "Move to the music, darling. Free as a bird. Show me wild and loving life."

I turned sensuous, caught and kissed flowers and danced in uninhibited circles.

"Keep going, don't stop. Camera loves you. Return the love, darling ... open your heart, open your lips," *said Svengali to Trilby*. "Good, keep your head down." *And Trilby did what she was told* hearing the clicks from Svengali's camera moving faster.

"Now," he said. "Slowly raise your eyes and look at me ... stare into the lens. That's it. Good, yes, turn your head, yes ... make love to the lens."

I pushed the hair out of my eyes, "Make love?"

"Yes, to the lens, to the camera. Imagine, the lens is dark, sweet, chocolate syrup. Lick the chocolate with your tongue, your lips. That's it, good. You love fourteen karat gold jewelry? A diamond on your finger? Show me your hands. I see golden earrings glittering in the sun ..."

I laughed and flirted.

"Yes, I'm iridescent, smooth, pearls ... I'm red, overripe, juicy strawberries, you like strawberries, darling?"

"I loooove strawberries."

"Good, bite into juicy, luscious strawberries, ooooo, yummy ... bite your lip ... more pout, wonderful. Who's your favorite movie star?"

"Paul Newman," I swooned. "Tab Hunter."

"Great, Paul Newman loves you, smile for Paul, pucker your lips, kiss Tab Hunter, good ... you're his leading lady in a new film, kiss Tab Hunter on the mouth ... laugh, laugh louder, run your hands through your hair, tilt your head back, yes, shoulder to camera ... perfect!"

Mr. Forester took rapid shots using a high-speed shutter burst. The non-stop clicks that sounded like subdued gunshots, annoyed me at first. But, as I began to trust his directions and he talked me through turns, profiles, lunges and back arches, I ignored the rapid camera clicks.

Mrs. Pace grabbed the photographer's arm and yelled over the music, "Okay, Robert, we're done. That's a wrap." She pointed to her wristwatch. "You said forty minutes and it's been thirty-five. That's enough!"

He chuckled, stepped into me and kissed my nose. "Miss Rothman, it's been a pleasure, thank you, darling." He put the lens cap on the Nikon and told Tony, "Kill the lights. Kill the Rolling Stones. And get Joe and Pete to clean up the flower mess. Good man."

"Come, Sarah," beckoned Mrs. Pace. "Change into your street clothes and hurry. We're finished here."

I walked to the dressing room suddenly drained. All that love making to the camera and pleasing Svengali, tired me out. Or, was it because I didn't sleep last night, *worried and upset over David not calling.* Anyway, I changed quickly into my sun dress and sandals.

DAD, ALEXI AND Yuri returned to the photo studio from the coffee shop next door. Dad touched my cheek.

"Sarah, why is your face so flushed?"

I shrugged and looked up at the overhead lighting grid. "Maybe the hot lights overheated me."

Nope. I was photographed in a bikini the size of three half dollars and now, buyer's remorse set in.

"Did you have coffee?" I smiled.

"Yo, great coffee. Chock Full o' Nuts and a pink icing cake donut. I'm telling Goosey Lucy your dance partner contributed to her divorce settlement."

The buzzer to the front door blasted and kept blasting like someone needed to get in. Tony raced downstairs to see who it was.

Seconds later, heavy footsteps stomped up the stairs and in burst the *Colors of The Rainbow* costume designer and his entourage. They chattered in euphoric chaos and smoked smelly cigarettes. Mrs. Pace and Yuri hurried over to greet them.

At the same time, I observed Mr. Forrester and Tony acting like the dynamic duo, Batman and Robin. They and two others on their staff, scrambled to stash, Nikon cameras, lighting equipment and shiny boards in a walk-in closet. After locking the closet door, Mr. Forester ran down the front stairs and disappeared. Tony announced to everybody, "My boss had to run errands. He'll be back. Carry on Mrs. Pace with your costume designer."

"Thanks, Tony," she smiled. "Kind of you."

Justin Saint Claire handed his designer's portfolio to Yuri. And as Yuri turned the pages of the monogrammed in gold leaf, black leather portfolio, you could see he was over the moon. These were the water color drawings of the costumes for *Colors*. Carefully, Yuri inspected drawing after drawing noting every detail.

"Da, da, grate … rain-bow boot-e-full."

"Sa-rah, Red Rain-bow. Regardez! C'est manifique. Qui?"

"Qui, c'est ca, formidable."

However, minutes later, Mrs. Pace noticed something in a drawing of the Rain Men she didn't like and argued with Yuri. My dad cringed and we moved to another part of the room.

Dad kissed my cheek. "Time for me to go. I'm meeting Michelle and Leon at their place and we're walking over to a hole in the wall restaurant on East 34th Street."

"Yeah, I guess. Thanks for coming, Daddy."

"Wouldn't miss seeing you. We spent a little time together, huh, honey?"

"Sure did." We hugged.

"Call me later or tomorrow when you have time."

"I will. Kiss Mama and Bubbe and give my love to everybody."

"Take care."

Dad circled the back of the room, careful not to get in anyone's way. However, he zig-zagged very close to the red stiletto heels to get a final look. *Hey, buster!* The hair on my arms stood up watching him drool. *Really, Dad?* You're fifty-two years old. *I'm gonna kick your butt next time we talk on the phone.*

"Sa-rah!" yelled Yuri sounding tense.

I hurried over to join him, Mrs. Pace and Alexi standing in front of two long tables. The watercolor drawings were arranged in neat rows of 10" x 13" costume designs.

Yuri pulled me aside and elbowed my ribs.

"Eeeek," I squealed.

"Da, grate cos-tume. Sa-rah like?"

"Yes, I like the costumes. The colors are very vivid and they look easy enough to dance in."

Yuri shook the costume designer's hand. "Yuri like! Sa-rah like. Mrs. Pace like?"

"Yes, Yuri, except for the codpiece on the Rain Men." She

glanced over at the costume designer, "You're getting rid of that horror, agreed?"

"Consider it gone," Justin clapped his hands. "Thank you, Mr. Konstantinov, Mrs. Pace, this is a fabulous honor." He waved his two seamstresses over.

"Girls! Kindly, take Mr. Konstantnov's and Miss Rothman's measurements. Make certain every measure is precise and accurate. Double check each other. These are important costumes for important people." He smiled at us, especially Mrs. Pace.

His female-looking, male assistant named Robin, took flash pictures with his new Kodak Instamatic Flashcube camera. And, the designer's secretary, Dee Dee Le Bon, handed a contract to Mrs. Pace to sign.

How did I know the secretary's name was Dee Dee Le Bon? It was spelled out in silver sequins on her tee-shirt.

And a young man answering to "Jeffery get over here," wearing short shorts and boots, shouted, "Sing out, Louise" to Justin. Followed by, Jeffery and Robin singing "Everything's coming up roses" from Gypsy. Their two part harmony accompanied the sounds of the camera's flash.

Now, an hour had passed and Mr. Forester returned and sat at his studio desk. He eyeballed the group of intruders and resented the flash camera. Reaching for a bottle from a cabinet, he poured and swallowed three shots of Jose Cuervo Tequila licking salt off his fist and sucking on limes. His expression resembled an aggravated tiger about to pounce.

As his face contorted in ugly grimaces at the costume designer and his groupies, he yelled, "This isn't Circus Maximus!"

The costume designer and his people turned around in shock.

"Get out! This is my professional studio. No Kodak shit, Brownie box cameras. Only Nikons, Hasselblad's and Canons enter this sacred place. This shrine to the stars."

"Oh, pardon-moi," said the female-looking, male assistant named Robin. "We're talking Instamatic Flashcube, in the TV commercials? Fourteen dollars and ninety-five cents a camera."

"I don't give a fuck-a-duck!" hollered the photographer. "Get the hell out. And don't leave your TV commercial ice cubes on my floor."

The mice scattered and disappeared down the front stairs.

Mrs. Pace waved for us to leave and we followed.

FERNANDO HELD THE limo door open. *Goody gumdrops,* my day ended. But no, wait, big mistake.

Mrs. Pace had more schemes for today. She insisted Yuri and I, with Alexi, accompany her to a Fifth Avenue split-level co-op. We were to romance a philanthropist and potential backer. She was fund raising and we were the bait.

She cast her fishing pole of charm and collected a sizeable check over Oysters Rockefeller, fois gras on toast, red caviar on deviled eggs, French meringues and gin and tonics. Yuri and Alexi drank gin and tonics like nomads and camels discovering an oasis in the Sahara. Two gin bottles turned into dead soldiers.

IT WAS DARK and late when Fernando dropped me back at Mrs. Pace's townhouse. Exhausted, I tip-toed up the stairs hoping to avoid Cook, but she heard me anyway. What does she have the ears of a bat? I plopped down on the bed.

Cook pleaded, "Please, Miss Sarah, come downstairs. You need to eat. Mrs. Pace will me mad. I made you a lovely Porterhouse Steak, medium well not medium rare."

"Who cares if the damn thing is mooing? Not me! Throw it out."

Cook removed my shoes and wedged a second pillow under my head.

"My dear Cook, do you really think I care what Mrs. Pace thinks?"

"Don't say that, Miss Sarah."

I crashed for ten hours.

CHAPTER 14

Monday, September 13th. It's complicated.

THE REHEARSAL SCHEDULE for *Colors* changed at the start of my second week. I still took Madame's eleven o'clock professional class but the three o'clock rehearsal moved up to two o'clock. Yuri and I rehearsed almost four hours with a ten-minute break every hour or when, he wanted to make phone calls. Which today, totaled three so far.

In addition, on Tuesday and Thursday nights, we rehearsed again at seven-thirty for an hour and a half. And in between the time slots, we ate Madam Wong's Chinese take-out selected from Columns A, B, or C and sat on the lobby couches to eat.

After a while, I got tired of Chinese food and longed for a thick Sicilian crusted pizza, heavy on the cheeses and marinara sauce. *My brothers and I knew a great place on Flatbush Avenue.*

Equally, not only did the additional hours of dancing wear me out but even my late-night shower turned into work. During the showers, I'd wash my leotards and tights and hang them to dry over the curtain rod. I'd done this for years. Every dancer in New York City, taking classes or rehearsing including Broadway gypsies repeated this ritual.

Problem was, September still sweltered "the dog days of summer" as Bubbe would say, hot and humid. To keep dry, sane and cool, I wore three sets of leotards and tights daily. I sweated a lot. And, I left a horrible mess in the postage sized bathroom. My wet clothes dripped on the black and white tiles and my shoes dirtied the floor.

Mrs. Williams, the sweetest housekeeper on earth, couldn't stand the mess I made every night especially finding foot prints on her floors. She decided, for her peace of mind, to launder my dance things. She'd throw them in the washing machine's gentle cycle and stick them in the dryer for ten minutes.

Bless her heart, her Westinghouse Dryer saved my health. No more sniffles and aching joints. No more feeling icky and yucky in damp leotards and tights in class. Especially around the crouch.

AND TO CONTINUE with my changed schedule, another night time addition. On Mondays, Wednesdays and Friday nights, when Yuri didn't need me for the hour and a half rehearsals, Fernando drove Mrs. Tupper and me to Sutton Place.

There following our dinner, Mrs. Tupper played the complete *Colors of The Rainbow* score. I preferred Petula Clark's "Downtown" and the "Beatles For Sale" album but that wasn't to be.

Also, on these same evenings, the skinny Russian composer with tobacco stained fingers and clothes smelling of stale cigarettes and kosher dill pickles joined us. He coached Mrs. Tupper on his musical score and she now sounded pretty good.

So during dinner, the unwashed Russian composer ate like a horse and stuffed additional food in his pockets. We girls never told Mrs. Pace about the stolen leftovers.

But when Cook came to clear the dishes, I whispered, "He's very hungry. Please make him a doggie bag to take home when he leaves."

"Poor man. And do we tell Mrs. Pace?"

"No, no, let's not. It's our little secret."

"Okay," she whispered reaching for my empty plate.

"Oh, and Cook? The steak you usually give me for breakfast, can you give it to him? He needs the protein."

"You're a thoughtful girl, Miss Sarah."

NOW DURING THIS same week, on Tuesday to be exact at 10:35 a.m., a messenger arrived with a package for Mrs. Pace from the celebrity photographer.

Fortunately, Yuri and I had arrived early for the pro class and got to see the contact sheets. *Oh, good golly!* We were both stunned. The photographs were beautiful.

Mrs. Pace grinned, "These are the most enchanting photos ever! He's too damned expensive but worth every cent."

She opened the photographer's letter and read aloud.

"Dear Mrs. Pace,

When I finished developing these contact sheets, my heart soared looking at the results. I hope your reaction is the same. I believe this is some of my best work. Miss Rothman and Mr. Konstantinov were outstanding and stunning models. I'd like to schedule another shoot, preferably in the costumes for their new ballet.

Sincerely, Robert Forrester"

That afternoon, I cornered Alexi while Yuri ran upstairs to change in the dressing room. "Alexi, tell me everything you know about our photographer." I wiggled my clenched fists.

"What? That he's famous and rich or do you want to hear the real dirt?"

"The real dirt and the juicy gossip."

"Okay," he rubbed his hands together. "Robert Forester has a reputation for photographing beautiful women. His notorious black and white photographs of the female body sans clothing emerged in London, Paris, Nice, Cairo and Rome. His photos, exhibited in elitist galleries could be purchased in private by the wealthy and affluent. His work is hidden from the public and discreet buyers have paid thousands of dollars."

I gasped, "Who does that?"

"Somebody with too much money. Why not?"

"Okay," I exhaled. "Answer me this."

"If I can, Sarah."

"Does Mr. Forester prefer men over women?"

"Where did you hear that?"

"He told me during the shoot."

"He was pulling your leg. The man is a womanizer. He's slept with hundreds of women. And married three times so far. And he's still only thirty-eight."

"What?" My voice caught.

"Husbands and boyfriends have chased him over balconies, on rooftops and threatened his life. Stay away from Don Juan."

"If you say so," and I rolled my eyes.

"Sarah! I said so. Stay. Away."

With my curiosity piqued, I'd welcome another photo session.

FOR THE REST of that Tuesday afternoon and evening, I rehearsed with Yuri our first pas de deux.

Now, fast forward to three days later and it's Friday evening at 6:15 p.m. Having finished dancing for the day, Mrs. Tupper and I waited outside, in front of the building for Fernando to pick us up.

Suddenly, Yuri ran out of the ballet school and joined us on the sidewalk. "Nyet go!" He sounded out of breath. "Sa-rah, more danse, Tuppervare … play mu-sak."

"But, Yuri, it's Friday. We're waiting for Fernando to drive us to Sutton Place to eat and rehearse the musical score with the composer."

"Nyet."

"Oh, for Pete's sake, why?" I spun around and faced the other direction. The news pissed me off and I harrumphed very loud.

A taxi stopped at the curb and out stepped Alexi. He carried several take-out bags advertising the Fat Chow Chinese restaurant. He smiled and waved.

Now I'm furious at Yuri's cockamamie request and through gritted teeth I mumbled, "Not tonight, mister. I have a headache. My legs hurt and I'm tired."

Yuri's Ukraine stare pierced my heart watching his forehead drip sweat.

"Guess not, ugh!" I moaned sounding like a brat. "I forgot. Your legs never hurt. You're Superman." I rushed back into the school followed by Mrs. Tupper.

Yuri ran around me and grabbed my arm. He held up four fingers indicating four weeks to rehearse. "Sa-rah, danse, sleep, eat." He flashed a grin accenting his high, cheek-boned face.

"Do I have a choice?"

"Nyet."

Gee whiz, the jungle drums must have been beating because in the next moment, Fernando entered the lobby carrying my dinner from Cook. He opened the box and licked his lips.

"Oh, crap, not steak again," I groaned. "Applesauce, salad and 'sufferin' succotash?' Bugs Bunny eats this stuff."

"Goot, da?" said Yuri, sniffing the steak.

"Nyet, not good," I pouted. "I wanted a Nathan's kosher

foot long, hot dog, a cherry Coke and chili, cheese fries."

Fernando chuckled, "Not Twinkies and Ho-Hos for dessert?"

"Shut-up!"

"Ain't gonna happen," Fernando laughed. "But, I'm with you girl. Give me Bronx bombers. The ballpark kosher dogs any day. Heavy on the onions, ketchup and mustard and keep the beer a comin'. But, don't tell, Mrs. Pace."

"You with hot dogs? I'd kill for a chocolate egg cream with Fox's U-Bet Chocolate Syrup. Yo, babe."

"Hellllll, no! She'll strangle me if she hears you talkin'. I can't dance no Swan bird in a tutu."

"But, hope springs eternal, huh, Fernando?"

"Don't be teasin', Miss Sarah."

FERNANDO, DID ME a favor. He ate the steak before he disappeared. The rest of us gorged on General Tso's Chicken, Dim Sum, Rice, Moo Goo Gai Pan and Baby Bok Choy.

However, oh, dear! Have you ever danced on a full stomach? *Remember your relatives telling you to wait an hour before going in the water?*

Neither of us could move eating all that food. Yuri, now bloated, called it quits after some feeble attempts to jump. Mrs. Tupper laughed and closed the piano lid.

I liked Mrs. Tupper and made a special request, before she left to go home. "Mrs. Tupper, can you join Anna and me for lunch at Horn & Hardart's? You know the automat, the one on West 57th Street not too far from here."

She looked skeptical and put on her pillbox hat. "When would this be?"

"Tomorrow, Saturday. Meet us a little before one, out front. You've worked so hard on the score and you, me and Yuri are a team. I'd like to be friends."

She smiled and relaxed her unsure attitude. "Yes, I'd like that. I have so little invites outside of taking care of mother."

"Okay," I patted her shoulder. "Bring your sandwich from home and if you'd like, buy a drink or a snack. It's pretty cheap. Nickels, dimes and quarters can buy drinks or food in those little glass window boxes. How about it?"

"Yes," she giggled as she gathered her musical score and stuffed it in a weary-looking, leather briefcase. "See you tomorrow at one o'clock."

"Great ... goodnight, Mrs. Tupper."

A sheepish grin covered her face as she scurried out the Studio A door.

I had an ulterior motive for the invite. I couldn't figure out why Yuri never fired Mrs. Tupper. Don't misjudge me, I didn't want her fired, I was curious. As Bubbe said, "You need to know everything. How else can you defend yourself, so snoop and ask." And where did Yuri get his money? *Maybe Mrs. Tupper knew.*

Yuri spent money lavishly on the latest men's fashions, expensive watches and dance bags in various styles. *From what I'd learned, dancers couldn't afford his wardrobe or things. Not without a sugar daddy or sugar mommy.*

At our first evening rehearsal last Tuesday, Yuri arrived with packages. They were "Esprit de France" designer shopping bags covered in Tarot Cards in red, white and black. No store name was on the bags. That's because New Yorkers, recognized a Bloomingdale's shopping bag.

"Shoes?" said Yuri as he paraded around the room wearing new leather loafers.

"Wow," I said. What else could I say? He modeled a black leather shoulder bag and black silk shirt.

Anna had tales to tell about that. The business manager at CCBT refused to tattle and told Anna to stop asking. The girl said, "It was nobody's business who paid the Bloomie's charge card. End of story."

Anna tried again. "Is catnip to a tomcat a credit card?"

"I own a dog," the business manager blew her nose. "And a goldfish."

"But, it didn't take a lame brain," said Anna over lunch, "to figure out why Fernando drove Yuri shopping in the limo. And why? Mrs. Pace went with him wearing Jackie Kennedy sunglasses and a floppy hat in disguise."

I chuckled at the floppy hat disguise.

"You know Sarah, Mrs. Pace had to buy Yuri expensive perks to keep him from leaving the CCBT. They were gifts to keep him on a leash. However, she panicked when the Paris Opera sent him telegrams and flowers by wire. She tried to sabotage the deliveries but failed. Western Union insisted Yuri Konstantinov sign "on the dotted line, in person.""

The following day when Mrs. Tupper met us for lunch at the automat, she confirmed Anna's facts. She said rather shyly, "I caught Mrs. Pace giving Yuri the credit card on the Q.T. and if I promised not to tell, I'd keep my piano rehearsal job."

"Whoa," I reared back. Anna poked me in the ribs and whispered, "Told you so."

WHEN OUR REHEARSAL fizzled out because Yuri and I ate too much Chinese food, this is what happened. Mrs. Tupper and I talked about the automat and then she left for home.

I changed shoes, threw on street clothes over my leotards and dialed Sutton Place on the office phone.

"Hello, Cook? Yep, it's me. Can Fernando come get me at the school? We're finished. Yes … Now … okay, thanks. Bye."

Twenty minutes later, Fernando entered the lobby, picked up my dance bag and grinned, "Ready?"

ON THE DRIVE back to Mrs. Pace's townhouse, Fernando slipped me a chocolate egg cream from a Second Avenue tobacco and magazine shop. "Shhhh, don't say I did nothin' for you," he grinned.

I giggled, "Thanks, I owe you. Hide the cup when I'm done."

"Yes, ma'am."

As the limo headed east, I watched people walk West 57th Street arm in arm in the sultry, nighttime air. I started to cry remembering how David and I walked this same area exactly two weeks earlier.

His dark hair curled over a white starched collar. I wanted to run my fingers through his curls. Why hasn't he called?

Fernando checked his mirror. "You okay, Miss Sarah?"

"Yes, I have to be." I wiped my tears.

"Don't cry. Tomorrow will be a better and blessed day."

CHAPTER 15

Wednesday, September 15ᵗʰ. Day by day by day.

CREEPY KARL KREISLER continued to snake around the ballet school and turned up, at unexpected times. *What a weirdo.* If I caught him staring at me, I kept my distance. I acted the tough cookie but he still freaked me out.

On a happier note, Mrs. Pace true to her word, kept me safe and spoiled at her townhouse. Cook fed me steak and eggs for breakfast and steak and veggies for dinner. Bag lunches were steak sandwiches, egg salads with pieces of steak and yogurt and fruit. Most of the steak, I hid in a napkin and threw in the trash. I begged Mrs. Pace for a chicken leg or a piece of fish. On Friday for her religion, I ate filet of Sole *and cheered for the Catholic Church and the Pope in Rome.*

Desserts and sugar were verboten. "Poison," said Mrs. Pace.

Conversely, when Cook baked Toll House Chocolate Chip Cookies, Mrs. Pace and I ate the cookies. *Okay, so she's human and had moments of weakness. Yes!* If we smelled the warm cookies coming from the oven and there was cold milk in the fridge? What were we girls to do? Plug our noses and walk on by?

"No way in hell," said Mrs. Pace. "Dig in, Sarah."

And when teen girls dreamt of Ricky Nelson and the Beatles, I dreamt of glazed donuts, Sno-balls and hot fudge sundaes. I could kill for a plate of Fettuccine Alfredo or stuffed manicotti but carbs were off limits. My mouth watered for a toasted bagel slathered in cream cheese. Push carbs past me and I'd bite your arm.

At breakfast, I swallowed mega vitamins and Brewer's Yeast. At bedtime, I swallowed calcium tablets and zinc. But, when Mrs. Pace asked her doctor to give me liver and iron shots and vitamin B-12 shots, that's when I called a halt. "No more shots, not unless you let Cook buy me Coke at the A&P!"

"What! Are you testing me?" She screeched baying at the moon. You'd think I asked for a vacation in Greece.

Next, she censored Yuri.

At our rehearsal, I overheard Mrs. Pace scold him for breaking the "no drinking vodka rule for the next thirty-four days … no alcohol until the opening."

Yuri's response to his boss, "Nyet, Enga-lesh."

Alexi joked, "That's like telling an old dog to stop scratching fleas."

She stuck to her guns and demanded Yuri become a teetotaler and she held Alexi accountable. Whenever Mrs. Pace heard her premier dancer fell off the wagon, she docked Alexi's salary, fifty cents."

NEAR THE END of my second week at the CCBT, two red flags went up the flag pole. First, ten more pairs of toe shoes were ordered. I'd have to sew elastic and ribbons on new pointe shoes until my fingers bled. I asked Cook and Mrs. Williams to help.

They both refused. "Not my job, Miss Sarah."

"Not mine, either."

Oh, bippety, boppety, boo.

Second, my body ached in places, I never knew I had muscles

and tendons. Anna gave me bottles of her favorite liniment. "Here, rub it in and use a lot."

Before Thursday's class, I slathered the "Banalg" turquoise liquid, all over my body before putting on tights and a leotard. Allowing the smelly liniment to dry, I walked around stark naked in the girl's dressing room.

"Sarah? Put your clothes back on," chastised Irina Ivanova, the lead principal dancer whom I admired. "We don't like exhibitionists."

"I'm not an exhibitionist."

"Yes, you are, Sarah Rothman. You are disgusting. Always showing off your tits. Well, cows have tits, they give milk. Silly child, you're tits are good for nothing."

I bit my tongue and got dressed.

Then during the company class, Irina Ivanova again criticized my body. She objected to my hip placement when I stood in an arabesque. She complained to Madame who poked her cane in the ballerina's shoulder.

"Stop it, Irina. Yuri taught her the Vaganova Method arabesque."

Not knowing a Vaganova from an egg bagel, I was totally humiliated. I felt more than ashamed for the rest of the class. But my friend, Anna, bless her heart, dragged me into the women's bathroom after the professional class and set me straight.

"Irina Ivanova," said my friend. "Thinks she's hot shit just because she studied the Cecchetti Method in London, at the Royal Academy of Ballet. They taught her the Cecchetti positions and she scored high on their examinations and got a diploma. La-ti-da. She can hang the diploma on her bedroom wall or glue it to her ass."

"Who's Cecchetti?" I frowned.

"A dead Italian."

"What?"

"He started the method in the U.K."

"Why?"

"Exactly. Who cares?"

"At my school, Miss Candy taught us ballet but never said what kind. She studied with Mr. B at the New York City Ballet."

"Mr. B? Oh, my God! He's the greatest! Now you're talking. A genius choreographer and teacher. No dancing for him with a stick up your ass and stupid flicks like the Cecchetti training."

"Irina also criticized how I parted my hair."

"What? You've got to be kidding."

"Irina called me amateurish because professionals part their hair down the middle and I parted mine, on the side."

"She's jealous," shrieked Anna. "She's a thirty-six year old maid with no man waiting in the wings and she doesn't know how long she can dance."

"Why? She's a leading dancer with a famous company. She should be grateful and thank God."

"Bitches are never thankful."

"Anna," I shook my fists, "I wasn't the only girl naked in the dressing room."

"They're not Yuri's partner."

"This auburn-haired girl, what's her name?"

"Which one? Zelda or Francine?"

I held my head, "I'm guessing Francine. She stood naked in front of a full-length mirror and brushed her hair. Irina never looked at her."

"Sarah," Anna grabbed my wrist. "Stay away from Irina. She's evil."

"Evil like scary dangerous?"

"Evil like Halloween scary." She dropped my wrist and reached for a hug. "Hey, are we still eating lunch at the automat?"

"Sure. Gotta hurry. Let's change first then run."

AT SUTTON PLACE the next morning, I dressed and ate quickly getting ready for the Friday pro class. The entire time, my mind spun with the pros and cons of the past two weeks. One of the highlights, made me smile.

Alexi, someone I never imagined could be a friend turned out a friend. He was an endearing surprise. Being raised never to trust anyone, I kept my feelings in check until a person jumped through hoops to prove trust worthy.

Hired in as a translator, Alexi was an unpaid mensch. He defended Yuri and me and even Mrs. Tupper, to Mrs. Pace. He acted as our referee and advocate. He kept Yuri focused and chided him if he turned difficult. He stopped me from whining and teased me "for using my feminine wiles," whatever that meant. And he got the composer to come to Sutton Place to coach Mrs. Tupper to save her job and keep him from starving.

"Sarah! Yuri!" scolded Alexi. "Don't throw things across the room and don't throw things at each other. You frightened the little kids taking ballet next door. They complained."

"Got it," I said. "No throwing old or new toes shoes." *Thank Goodness, no one told Mrs. Pace, the teachers were too scared.*

Alexi explained, "Just like lovers, we couldn't go to sleep mad." He setup rules. (1) At the end of the day, none of us could leave upset. (2) No name calling. And (3) Yuri couldn't tickle Sarah which he enjoyed doing whenever he got the chance.

But rules can be broken. At the second evening rehearsal, Yuri got furious at me for repeating the same mistake. His back stiffened, he bristled and his teeth mashed. Instead of yelling, Yuri marched over to Alexi and in a calm voice, spoke to him in Russian. No temper tantrum, *wow!*

The next day, Alexi told me what Yuri had confided.

"Alexi, I want to kill Sarah. I want to strangle her beautiful neck but I didn't. See, I'm a changed man." He grinned at Alexi with clenched fists and turned to me and harrumphed. "And with your permission," Yuri continued in Russian. "I will spank Sarah until her ass turns beet red for ruining my ballet, and I will kiss her pouty mouth, and suck the air out of her lungs until she's dead."

Alexi looked surprised.

"What did he say?" I asked at the time.

"No need to translate. It's boring."

"But, Yuri doesn't look bored. He's grinning... wait, he's laughing! Why?"

Alexi groaned. "Ah, my dear Sarah... Yuri likes to recite romantic poetry. What can I say?"

"You're not telling me the truth, Alexi. What are you doing?"

Alexi and Yuri slapped each other's back and roared.

"Not fair you guys. I hate you both!"

Then in a heartbeat, Yuri's demeanor changed. He turned sullen and spoke very fast in Russian. He looked agitated and the vein in his neck stuck out.

If that was romantic poetry, I didn't want a translation. Not when Yuri scowled at me imitating a fierce lion. I left the two men to argue and crossed the room to sit by Mrs. Tupper on the piano bench.

"Enough!" screamed Alexi hitting Yuri on the side of his head.

Yuri looked embarrassed.

"It's over, Sarah," said Alexi. "Yuri has nothing more to recite."

"Wow," I giggled and walked back to the men. "That was some poetry."

Alexi shook his head. "Sarah, not my type of verses." He left the room to smoke a Gaulois outside on the street.

Yuri took my hand, kissed my forehead and went back to teaching the pas de deux. Go figure.

AT THE END of Friday's class, Anna and I changed into fresh leotards and did our usual, hurried to the automat for lunch. Now bonded as best friends, our five year age difference didn't matter. She being an only child, I was her new baby sister.

Anna wolfed down a turkey sandwich and talked ballet. "I decided to dance to please my mother," she said. "Mom wanted to be a ballerina. When I turned twenty, I auditioned for the CCBT and was accepted into the corps. That was three years ago."

"Did you ever dance a solo?"

She shook her head and chewed, "No."

"You should. You're talented and commanding enough.

"Let's call it politics. I'm not a favorite of Mrs. Pace's but I did dance the *Four Swans* in *Swan Lake* last season."

"Well done, I'm in awe," I smiled. "That's a difficult pas de quatre. Exacting and precise and the timing? Without bruising each other's legs, how did you do?"

Anna looked smug. "Actually, pretty good and I performed the Chinese Dance in Nutcracker last year and loved it. What about you, Sarah?"

"I saw *The Red Shoes* on my eight birthday, and that was it.

Ballet for me."

"Did your mother want it?"

"No. She hates it. Don't ask."

"Do you have a boyfriend?"

"I wish. I met someone I like and he's sooooo handsome."

Anna laughed, "Well, look at you, you're glowing."

I waved my hands, "It's nothing. He's too old for me and he doesn't know I exist."

"I had a forty-one-year old boyfriend here in Manhattan. We lived together for almost a year and he paid the rent."

I gasped, "Why did you do that? He's old."

"I slept with him, you ding-a-ling, so I could dance. He took me to Puerto Rico after The Nutcracker. He was very nice."

"So what happened?"

"He asked me to marry him but that meant I'd have to stop dancing and be a wife. He wanted children right away but not me even though we're both Catholic."

"Did your mom know?"

"She knew. She made me quit seeing him."

"Anna, I don't know anything about men."

She laughed, "A no brainer."

"Stop it, don't tease me."

"Sorry. What's up?"

"When I'm dancing a duet with Yuri, I slide all over his body and I get these weird feelings, this tingle."

"I would, too. That's a great, sexy body."

I blushed and paused. "Is it wrong to feel tingly like that?"

"No, you're a girl, he's a guy. Bound to happen. But, don't think about men. Concentrate on Sarah and perfect your ballet technique. This is a contact sport lasting for a minute or two. The audience sees the romance not you."

"I worry about my family seeing me dance with a man."

"Don't worry. Partnering happens fast. The non-dancer doesn't grasp the action. If it's spectacular, the audience gets excited. Stand on your head like a monkey and they'll applaud."

I chuckled, "Yesterday, I had no qualms about shoving my body snug into his."

"What? I thought you were afraid of touching him."

"No, I loved it. I enjoyed feeling his muscles and smelling his skin."

"Oh, Jesus, now I'm jealous. You partnering slut! C'mon, strumpet, we're done eating lunch. You have to rehearse."

I wrinkled my nose, "I'm looking forward to it."

"Sarah! Keep your hormones under lock and key and behave yourself."

CHAPTER 16

Saturday morning, September 19th. The last day of the work week and the beginning of the end.

I WOKE UP in the middle of a nightmare seeing Irina Ivanova try to kill me with an axe. I also felt excruciating pain in my right thigh as if a truck ran over my leg. I took a hot shower to ease the hurt.

Slathering Banalg all over my thigh and after allowing it to dry, I dressed in pink tights and a black leotard. The Irina nightmare, I'd have to deal with later and maybe discuss it with Anna. With such a busy day ahead, I'd have to plow through the pain and try my best.

The only thing I looked forward to was lunch at the automat with Anna and Mrs. Tupper and nothing else. Because after lunch, Yuri scheduled a rehearsal for the rainbow girls and the pain in my thigh muscle would be the problem. The scheduled two o'clock time slot was pushed to two-forty-five as of yesterday.

We rainbow girls, Anna included, would meet for the first time to learn our ensemble choreography. We dressed in our newly assigned, rainbow colored leotards. This color hint made blocking easier for the choreographer. *Good golly,* my heart pounded with anticipation. I'd be dancing with the company professionals and finally learn the story of my ballet. I knew the beginning but not the middle or the end. The mystery would unfold … maybe. Since the ballet wasn't a fairy tale or fable, I couldn't peek at the end pages in a book at the library.

In my canvas dance bag, I packed my new, bright red leotard and red pointe shoes and carried my bag and purse downstairs for breakfast.

"Phone call, Miss Sarah," yelled Mrs. Williams. "It's your father. Take it in the hall."

"Hi Daddy, yes, I have tomorrow off… right, I plan to take the train tonight after the rehearsal ends at six … rain? A thunderstorm? Oh, well … I know, I can't wait to see you either. How's Mama? Bubbe? Okay … love you. Bye, Daddy."

"Was it a good phone call?" asked Mrs. Williams.

"Yes, great. I'm going home tonight. I'm seeing my family."

"Wonderful, dear. When you leave for class, take the black umbrella out of the stand at the front door. It rained cats and dogs last night. It's raining now."

"Yes, the black umbrella. Where's Cook?"

"Waiting for you in the kitchen with an omelet and a skirt steak." Mrs. Williams blinked, "Better move."

AT 2:45 P.M. in Studio A, seven excited girls wore their specially designed leotards and new pointe shoes in the seven rainbow shades. We hugged, chatted and giggled for guess what? Seven minutes.

"Nyet," yelled Yuri throwing up his hands. "Vork! Nyet, lafting … ha, ha, nyet."

We quieted down.

"I vant to start … en-trance … Act II."

We girls nodded.

"Tuppervare, play mu-sak, bee-gin-ning." She played and he

waved his hands, "Da, da, da, daaaaa, cres-scendo, loud mu-sak. Da, da! Danse!" His finger pointed to us to start.

We seven girls entered Act II, step, step, pas de bourree, step, arabesque, "Packed in tight, body-to-body like encyclopedias on a library book shelf," translated Alexi.

Yuri's vision, "Was to move as one, to emulate the rainbow formation in the sky." We stepped and held the arabesque for two musical beats and attempted a snug rainbow. But snug as a bug-in-a-rug and dancing full-out caused ripples in the choreography. We fell out of formation. Fourteen feet in brand new, clomping pointe shoes overstepped each other's toes. *Our tits and asses got in the way mouthed Anna, behind Yuri's back. She made faces and pointed to our female parts.*

The Purple Rainbow fell, the Blue Rainbow bumped into the edge of the piano. The Yellow Rainbow screeched, "Ouch, you kicked me, you clumsy, fat green pig."

"I'm fat? Shut up, you five-foot-two yellow walrus!"

"Nyet, tauk-king," yelled the choreographer.

"Sorry, Yuri ... sorry, sir."

We leaped and pivoted and tried our best. But, it just didn't work. Our geometric formations had problems and the pain in my thigh was killing me.

Yuri sulked and paced and finally forced himself to change the opening entrance. No more arabesque-kick-in-your-face-horror. In its place, we girls did a short bourree in a tight little capsule, split apart at center stage and *thanked our lucky stars*. Our choreographer realized we seven girls couldn't dance as one unit any longer than twenty bars of music.

Yuri tried new choreography, tiny jumps but that looked undignified as a group. He tried tour jetes. No, he banged his fist on the wall. Pas de bourrees, eschappes and pas de chats he liked and repeated. His creative juices formed oddball dance combinations making some girls snicker and others, shake their heads in disbelief.

Most pretty faces turned sour looking up at the wall clock. Two hours had passed and not one step closer to a rainbow united front entrance. *I wanted to suggest two simple waltz steps into step, step, tiny jete, twice but I scratched my head and shut my mouth.*

Our translator pointed out to Yuri, the dissatisfaction among the girls. And, Alexi's nature being what it was, kept up the ridicule enjoying Yuri's cheeks begin to burn. Yuri retaliated by ranting in Russian and shaking his fist at his sadistic friend.

Alexi shoved Yuri's fist away and muttered something.

"What did he say?" asked Suzanne, the Blue Rainbow.

"Hell, if I know," said Lily, the Indigo Rainbow, "and I don't care. My feet hurt in these tight shoes."

"Not relevant," said Alexi raising his voice.

FINALLY, AT THE end of two hours and forty minutes, Yuri figured out new steps and looked pleased. He settled on a short variation of pas de bourrees and glissades that ended in a developee, a la seconde by a snug, seven girl ensemble, in a semi-circle. Our right leg then moved en l'air, in a ronde de jambe into an arabesque and ta-da, into a finished pose. The process almost ended in disaster but didn't. We held tight to each other's waist to keep from falling. *Oh, happy days. His creative fever for perfection drove everybody crazy and me, most of all.*

I could certainly eat a pint of Rocky Road ice cream, oodles of chocolate M&M's and Twinkies to calm down right now. And the strain on my legs, trying every step Yuri improvised started to show. When he changed his mind and tried something else, my right thigh cramped up or gyrated in a spasm. The pain ... agonizing.

Not used to dancing so many hours every day, my legs no longer responded to my brain. I lagged behind the other dancers and clenched my jaw getting tense.

Alexi rolled his eyes at Mrs. Tupper, astonished I couldn't keep up.

Anna whispered, "Get it together, Sarah. What's the matter?"

When the girls started the pique turns, I hadn't joined the line. Yuri ran up behind me and yelled in French, "Tournee Sarah, vite, vite, mon dieu."

I mumbled, "I can't," now furious at myself. My stomach churned acid and hurt.

At the rainbow group's exit jump, Yuri ran his hands threw his hair and screamed, "Sarrrraaah!" His eyebrows lifted in horror when I traveled, across the chalk-marked floor representing the stage area. I was late by two bars of music in three-quarter time. The other girls had completed their jumps and stepped back in alarm. Embarrassed beyond anything I'd experienced, this three hours of torture ended on a high note for everyone but me.

My hips and back quit feeling any sensations. Fatigue invaded every cell. I had enough. Bending from the waist and hanging my head, I dangled my arms. When I stood up straight, my knees wobbled and I let out a moan. A couple girls laughed. Hot tears filled my eyes.

If I had a fairy Godmother? Could she smack me with a magic wand and make the pain go away?

I blushed redder than my leotard. *And could the rainbow girls stop staring at me?*

Anna put her arm around my shoulders, "Hey, we're done."

"What do I do now?" I whispered watching Yuri leave the room and slam the door.

"Talk to him and rest for a couple days."

"Five classes a week at Miss Candy's never prepared me for this. Not with all the hair spray I inhaled and fluffy pink tutus I wore."

"Sarah, find a rhythm. We're athletes. You must train mentally and train physically like a long distance runner with a determined mind and a healthy body. We train daily the same way Olympic athletes train to compete. Pace yourself when your energy is high and push beyond the lows, when the mountain gets tough to climb. Got it?"

I leaned my head on her shoulder.

Alexi clapped his hands. "Ladies! It's six o'clock. We're finished for the day. Thank you from Mr. Konstantinov. He appreciates your hard work."

The girls applauded, gathered their things and walked out. Mrs. Tupper waved and closed the door.

Alexi walked over and watched me cry on Anna's shoulder. "This isn't good."

"Yes, we know, Alexi."

Anna hugged me. "If you need anything? Call me. I have to go, get some rest."

"Thanks." I watched her pick up her oversized black bag and leave.

Alexi smiled, "Now, Sarah, you'll rest and feel better."

"How would you know? You dance?" I snapped at him.

"What?"

"I danced six hours every day for six days. How would you know? You sat on your ass and watched."

"I was only ..."

"I danced on pointe, broke in new shoes. My feet swelled, my toenails bled, my thigh hurts like hell. I'm done."

He wrung his hands, "You're an artist."

"Right. And you're the king of Siam." I limped towards my dance bag in the corner and didn't care how fast Alexi ran out of the room. He banged the door shut.

"Good!" I yelled.

Minutes later, Alexi returned with Yuri.

Yuri stared at me which made me tremble at the knees. *Oh, crap, he hates me I'm sure* but maybe not. His eyes showed concern. He took a step towards me and said in a soothing tone, "Nyet, Sa-rah, stop-ping."

"I'm sorry. Yuri. I can't dance your ballet."

Yuri's nose twitched and he wrapped his arms around me.

"I can't do it." My shoulders shook starting to sob. "Everything hurts, my right thigh the worst and I'm numb."

Yuri said something in Russian and Alexi left the room. I stepped away from Yuri now afraid. *What were they planning to do? Why is Yuri looking deep in my eyes?*

I bit my lip and got defensive. "Oh, that's just peachy keen. I need to talk to you and there's no translator."

Yuri simply frowned, "Da."

"Right, duh ... I'd like to apologize to you but now I have to wait for Alexi. Is he coming back? Oh, crap. This is the worst day of my life," I shrieked. "I've ruined everything."

Yuri gestured then responded in English, "No sheet, Sure-lock."

"What!" I reared back in surprise. "What did you just say?"

Yuri laughed, "No sheet, Sure-lock."

He squeezed my upper body and whispered, "Yuri fix Sa-rah. Nyet, ruin ball-let."

"You understood me?"

"Da. Yuri a ... speak. Yuri knowth Enga-lish."

Alexi opened the door and hurried in. I yelled at him before he could speak, "Alexi! Yuri understands English."

"Of course he does, he speaks and know more than he lets on."

"You liar!" I glared at my mentor, "All this time."

He nodded. "Lit-tle. Study ... Moscova School. Lauf-ting on me."

I turned to Alexi, puzzled.

"He had this one girlfriend, a British girl dancing with the Kirov. She taught him verbs in English and he taught her the positions from the Kama Sutra."

"No shit, Sherlock," I screeched in his face in a not-so forgiving tone. "What is the Kama Sutra? Another form of ballet technique like Vaganova and Cecchetti?"

Yuri hid his face while Alexi chuckled. "I guess you could say that in your dreams. If you danced in bed?"

I gasped and felt my cheeks burn. "Sex."

"Never mind what I just said ... Yuri understands most English but gets embarrassed if he has to answer in English. He won't tell Mrs. Pace he knows what she's saying because he doesn't trust her. He learns more by listening."

Yuri grinned. "People think stu-pid. 00 sev-ven, mar-teen-ee, shake... nyet stir." He pointed to himself. "Bond."

"What?" I winced.

"James z Bond z," he grinned.

"You're a movie spy?"

Alexi looked apologetic. "We should have told you earlier but Yuri loves secrets. He's wired that way."

"Dou-bble a-gent, yuk, yuk," Yuri laughed.

"No, you're not. James Bond tells the truth. You lied to me. You know English."

Yuri looked offended, "Nyet." He reached for a hug.

I stepped back. "No, hug!"

Yuri frowned.

"Asshole," I muttered.

"Da," he muttered back. "Ass-a-hole."

"You pronounce asshole pretty good. Must have heard it a thousand times."

"Da, a lot," he chuckled.

"Ouch," I felt a stabbing pain in my right leg.

"Sa-rah?" Yuri grabbed my wrist.

"It's my thigh." I yanked my wrist away. "You know what?"

"Vhat?"

I threw my hands in the air. "I quit ballet, your ballet. I'm through. Done."

Yuri's hands held his head in agony.

I turned and limped away. "I'm sorry," I said over my shoulder. "I failed you and Mrs. Pace."

Yuri swooped me up into his arms. He carried me to a bench and laid me on my back.

"No, no, please, I just wanna go home."

Alexi shoved a chair next to me but Yuri blocked the chair. "Go. Alexi … leave-it. Smoke Gaul-oise."

"Why? It's raining."

"Go! Smoke sis-sy cig-ga-vette, smoke a-pot."

Alexi grunted and left.

My mentor, hovered like a helicopter and gently massaged my right thigh.

"Ouch, damn it, that's agony."

"Da, Yuri fix."

He swung his leg over my ankles and sat over my legs on the bench. He massaged both thighs, deep into the muscle sheath. He worked the length of both legs.

"Whoa …that's it … oh, gosh," I mumbled and bit my lip when he hit, "Oowwww," a tender spot.

"Goot? Sa-rah?"

"Aaahhh."

Alexi burst through the door and Yuri yelled at him in Russian. Alexi huffed and ran back out.

"What did you tell Alexi?"

"Fernando … car."

Yuri got to his feet and helped me up. "Sa-rah. Get dance bag … Sa-rah go."

"What?"

"Yuri a-part-ta-ment-ta."

"No, I quit, remember? I'm going to Mrs. Pace's house to tell her and pack my bags." I sat back on the bench and removed my toe shoes. Putting my street clothes over my leotards, I slipped on my sneakers.

Alexi opened the door. "All arranged. Fernando will drive us."

IN THE LIMO, Alexi frowned while Yuri and I argued.

"Sa-rah, danse."

"No, it's over. I messed up everything."

"Sa-rah!"

"I made up my mind, please stop."

I leaned forward and tapped on the limo's glass partition. "Fernando?"

He slid the window open, "Miss Sarah?"

"After you drop the guys off? Please take me home."

"Sure, Cook has dinner ready."

"No, home to Brooklyn. I quit ballet."

"Is that so? Does the boss lady know?"

"I'm gonna tell her now."

"Oh, praise the Lord and pass the collection plate. I ain't

gonna hear her scream. No, sirree, no how. See ya."

"Fernando, not fair!"

"Miss Sarah, yes, fair enough."

CHAPTER 17

September 18th. Fifteen minutes later.

AFTER MAKING AN impossible U turn in heavy traffic, Fernando parked on West 57th Street. The limo pulled forward a few feet past Seventh Avenue heading west.

"We're stopping here? In front of the Osborne?"

"Da, Yuri live here."

Oh, crap, if David knew this, he'd be nice to me and telephone.

I faced Yuri. "How can you afford the Osborne? It's a historical landmark and there's Tiffany windows."

"Mrs. Pace pays the rent," said Alexi.

"Da," nodded Yuri.

"We have a two-bedroom sublet. It's furnished and a pretty Cuban maid cleans our rooms twice a week." He grinned and shot his eyebrows up and down.

"How nice to be so close to the school and the theatre."

Alexi exhaled a huff. "Yes, but the radiators bang and hiss at night and last week we didn't have hot water on Monday. Sometimes Yuri has trouble sleeping when a fire truck passes by blasting the sirens."

Fernando howled, "Damn! You guys don't know what rough is. I live in Spanish Harlem. Nobody has hot water. Single light bulbs hang in the hallways, gun shots day and night, barking dogs and husbands and wives scream and curse screwing or fighting, all night long. Kids and pimps sell drugs and there's hookers in the alleys and on the streets. Stop your belly achin' you fools!"

Nobody dared say a word after that. We sat in silence and listened to the thunder and the traffic.

I watched the rain streak the rear limo window. The lights of Carnegie Hall glistened diagonally across the intersection. And next door, people gathered under the canopy at the Russian Tea Room holding umbrellas. My heart flip-flopped and tears blurred my vision. *The best lunch ever with David Katz and then nothing. He never called, why did he say he would?*

"Vhat?" said Yuri tapping my shoulder. "Nyet, cy-ing."

"Never mind," I sniffled and blew my nose with tissues Alexi stuffed in my hand.

"Sa-rah ... hun-gary? Tu as faim?" Yuri smiled. "Moi, aussi."

"Really? You're speaking French now?" I shook my head. "You'll try anything."

"Da, Yuri, goot."

"Okay, oui, j'ai faim." I glared at my idol.

"Alexi, get take-out, da."

"I know, we can't walk in the rain to Madam Wong's."

Yuri touched my arm. "De quoi avez-vous faim?"

"Duck lo mein, ya happy?"

"Tres bien. C'est ca, quack, quack."

"Fernando, please unlock the door. I'm gonna wait in the lobby. See what it looks like."

"Let's all get out," said Alexi. "I'll use the pay phone on the corner. What do you want, Sarah?"

"I just said, 'Duck lo mein, quack, quack,' duh."

"I don't speak French. Okaaaaaay, everybody out."

"No, wait," hollered Fernando stepping out of the driver's

side. He disappeared around the back of the limo and opened an umbrella and my door.

"Miss Sarah, c'mon and move under the doorman's umbrella. Stay inside the lobby. I'll call Mrs. Pace. If she doesn't need the car, I'll drive you to Brooklyn."

"Can I take my dinner with me?"

"Sure, why not?" Fernando smiled, eyeing Yuri and Alexi shake their heads "no" behind my back.

He extended his hand, "Watch your step, Miss Sarah. The pavement's slick."

INSIDE THE LOBBY of gold gilded mirrors and creamy marble wainscoting and carved recesses, I watched the doorman do his job. The thin, old man dashed back and forth greeting visitors in his damp, grey uniform and cap. When outside in the rain, on the sidewalk, the doorman opened his over-sized, black umbrella to escort residents. But once inside, he'd shake out the rain on the carpet. The idiot had it backwards. No wonder he looked wet and disheveled and wore a sourpuss expression.

At the sound of the elevator door sliding open, I turned and nearly choked, "Oh, shit."

Out stepped Karl Kreisler, tall, elegant and dressed in a tuxedo. He sported a paisley bow tie, cumber band and paisley handkerchief, folded "just so," in his breast pocket.

"A little dab will do ya," I muttered seeing his Brill Cream slicked back, grey hair.

He hit my leg as he brushed past me. I staggered and almost fell. If I'd been a wooden soldier in the Radio City Music Hall's Christmas Show, I'd be on the floor by now, on my ass.

"Son-of-a-whore," I hissed, knocking into Yuri.

"Aha!" heralded Karl Kreisler. "What have we here? Nijinsky and his teeny-bopper protégé, Miss Barbie Doll." His laugh resounded in the 19th century lobby.

Yuri mumbled in Russian, probably swear words.

Karl nodded, "Good evening," to an elderly couple that just entered the lobby and stepped up to the elevator. He spoke to the two, tiny, old people standing at my side. "Aren't you going to introduce me to this wanna-be, ballet dancer?" His bony finger, pointed at my face.

"What? Huh?" They stood like matching salt and pepper shakers and wondered if the gray-haired man dressed in the tuxedo was talking to them. The old man adjusted his hearing aid.

At the elevator bell, Yuri reached for my arm and pulled me inside. He spun me around fast to face the door which started to slide shut. I was trapped.

"Rouski refugee?" shouted Karl.

Yuri's hand stopped the door. "Vhat, bass-turd?"

I pushed the open-door button.

"Prince Siegfried, you won't win the bet. Everybody's got money on me." He switched his focus, "And you, Twinkle Toes."

"Oh, crap," I muttered.

"Don't have a snowball's chance in hell. If you think you can win the bet, Miss Barbie? Think again."

I bit my tongue watching him shake his head.

"Why don't you marry some Jew boy and have a dozen kids."

"Bigot!" I screamed back at him.

Yuri leaped from the elevator and grabbed Karl by the throat.

"Stooopppp!" yelled the doorman.

Yuri twisted Karl's tux lapels into knots and he shook him hard. Karl jerked back and forward and banged into Yuri's head.

"Stop. Please, stop it," shouted the doorman as he blew his whistle several times.

Karl and Yuri clawed and punched. Karl yanked and curled Yuri's hair. Furious at the hair move, Yuri landed an upper-cut-hit at Karl's cheek. He staggered.

Fleeing the elevator, I scrambled past the men and the elderly couple. The panicked doorman and I ran outside to the sidewalk and huddled under his umbrella. The rain came down in torrents and we got soaked and wind battered.

We heard Karl yell, "Get your friggin'... your hands off me."

Yuri threatened something in Russian. I heard my name.

The doorman again blew his anemic whistle for help. People on the street, being typical New Yorkers, walked on by and minded their own business.

The old couple stood like statues against the lobby wall. They clung to each other, too scared to move.

Blood sprayed everywhere when Yuri connected with Karl's nose. The doorman saw Karl's blood and yelped, "Help! Anybody!"

Karl got in a couple good punches, but in the end, Yuri slammed the final blow, right on Karl's jaw. Serious blood splattered on their jackets and the back wall near the elevator.

A guest entered the lobby and seeing the bloodied men, hollered, "Call the police! Help, somebody, call the police," as he ran back out to the street.

Alexi and Fernando ran past us and in the lobby. Alexi pulled Yuri off Karl and Fernando grabbed Karl, twisting his arm behind his back. Karl continued to struggle even though Fernando held him in a strong grip.

Yuri ran for the elevator and yelled my name. I responded

like one of Pavlov's dogs.

Alexi held the elevator door. "Yuri, go upstairs, I'll get dinner. Sarah, push number ten and change those wet clothes."

I fixated on Karl watching blood drip from his nose and chin. I was glad he bled. Nothing else mattered except the evil things I wanted to do to him. *Blood should drip from a stake driven through Karl's heart.*

Yuri shouted, "Ten, Sa-rah. Le dixieme etage."

Still staring on Karl, I did nothing.

Yuri reached across my chest and pushed the ten button and the door slid shut. The elevator lurched and jerked upwards. I stopped trying to stab Karl with a pitchfork in my mind and considered Yuri. Oh, dear God, my mentor's face and chest were stained with blood. Shivers ran up my spine.

I touched his face. "How bad are you? Should we call the police on Karl?"

"Nyet. Bad to Mrs. Pace. Nyet pub-bliss-city. To-morro, Yuri ... talk ... Karl, Mrs. Pace."

"Should we get you to a hospital emergency room?"

He shook his head. "Nyet. Hot shoa-ver. Vodka."

"Vodka?"

"Karl, cra-zy fook. Jell-louse bass-turd."

I fidgeted suddenly overwhelmed with anger. *Did the other dancers share Karl's opinion of me? Was I the Barbie Doll? The laughing stock of the company?*

Tears rolled down my cheeks. I hiccupped.

"Nyet, Yuri fix."

The elevator door slid open and Yuri nudged my elbow into a dimly lit hallway. The hair on the arms stood up. "Yuri, what Karl said about me to my face just now," I snapped. "He hated my dancing."

Yuri's eyes narrowed. "Karl old man ... Karl jell-louse ...

allez." Yuri waved his hand to follow.

"I was his joke!"

"Nyet ...allez!"

We stopped at Apartment 10A.

Yuri spun me around. "Karl see Sa-rah danse ball-let?"

I hesitated and thought a moment. "No. Never."

"How Karl know?"

"Nooooo, he doesn't know. He never saw me dance."

"Nyet, problema," chuckled Yuri and unlocked his front door.

"Huh? No, that can't be right. It's too simple."

Yuri grabbed my shoulders and yelled, "Nyet, problema." He nudged me inside his apartment, turned on the lights and shut the door. He looked me in the eye. "Sa-rah, grate danse-sing."

"Not today, I ruined the rainbow," Uncontrollable tears gushed down my cheeks.

Yuri's eyes blazed. "Von day, Sa-rah famm-mousse."

"I don't think so." My shoulders shook. "Bubbe said I had chutzpah; no common sense. Right on, grandma. I won the battle but not the war."

"Da, chutz-pah... grate. Allez avec moi." He waved his hand to follow.

IN THE BATHROOM, Yuri ran hot water in an old-fashioned porcelain white tub, with four claw feet. He threw in handfuls of Epsom salts and jasmine bubble crystals.

"Is this bath for you, Yuri?"

"Nyet. Yuri shoa-ver ... Alexi bat-room."

He pointed to me. "Ici. Here. Take off clothes."

"What?"

"Take off clothes," he repeated in a softer voice.

"Wow, you speak good English."

"Take off clothes, Sa-rah."

"No, I won't." I stepped back against the towel rack and folded my arms across my chest.

"Nyet, bebe," he scolded. "Take bath. Yuri fix."

I shook my head, "No."

Yuri grinned. "Irina tell Yuri. Sa-rah na-ked at vo-men. Sa-rah like vo-men?"

"What? Irina told you that?" I blushed. "Someone should tape her mouth shut."

Yuri opened the cabinet door and took out a bar of soap wrapped in black tissue. A lady flamenco dancer in a red dress was on the seal.

"Voon-der-ful soap ... Sa-rah, pree-sent."

"Oh, gosh, it smells good. Is it lavender or jasmine? Where is it from?"

"Bar-cel-lon-a."

Goosebumps broke out on my arms. I gazed up at Yuri, "It's very nice, thank-you."

Yuri looked wistful. "A tout a l'heure" and closed the door behind him.

Soaking in a warm, bubbly jasmine, orange and lavender scented bath, defined soothing and delicious. I lathered the Maja soap and inhaled the fragrance. Every sore muscle and bone in my body relaxed in the soothing warm water. I closed my eyes and shut out the bad things. *Life can be beautiful in a bath.*

The next thing I knew, Yuri pulled me out of the tub and yelled, "Sa-rah! Open eye ... nyet sleeps!" In a panic, he had rescued me out of the tub after peeking-in first. I dripped water all over the floor and on him.

Drowsy and incoherent, I felt a towel drying me off and a

big, blue tee-shirt pulled over my head. Men's briefs, moved up my legs. In a stupor from sleep, I didn't grasp what happened until minutes later. Feeling Yuri's toweled hands drying my hair, I suddenly woke up.

"You saw me naked?" I screeched. "How could you?"

"Da. Boot-ti-full." He smiled with admiring eyes.

"How?"

"Sa-rah drown-ding. Sleeps." His eyes flashed in fear.

"You saved me?"

"Yuri fix."

"Oh, my God, you saved me. I could have drowned."

"Yuri goot?"

"I'm sorry. I shouldn't have yelled. And, look at you, my hero. You showered and changed. You look nice."

"Da, Alexi bat-room."

"I'm a brat, huh? Firemen could see me naked and dead in your bathtub but you saved me."

Yuri looked away as he moved behind me. He unpinned my barrette and brushed my hair long and loose down my back.

We both faced the mirror over the sink and he still averted his eyes. I smiled an awkward smile and mouthed the words, "Thank you."

"Da … Yuri fix." His face grinned like a boy winning a prize. *He was Prince Igor, Prince Siegfried and my Sun Prince.*

"Yuri? Is the Chinese Food here?"

"Nyet. Big rain."

IN THE LIVING room, we heard knocking and Yuri answered the door. In strolled a body-builder guy wearing blue sweatpants, a tee-shirt, basketball high-tops and a Yankee baseball cap. He carried an athletic sports bag, a bottle of wine and a large, black cat with amazing green eyes.

Yuri introduced, "Jay-son, Yuri friend … the mass-sewer."

I giggled, "You mean masseuse?"

"Sounds like I'm not paid enough when Yuri says it," chuckled Jason.

"And," Yuri stroked the feline. "Fat cat … Lu-ci-fer."

"Hi, Jason. Hi, Lucifer. Wow, what amazing eyes."

"Oh, thanks, I get that a lot," said the masseuse.

"I meant the cat."

"Jason, mass-sewering, Sa-rah," explained Yuri as he took the Chablis from his friend and set it on the living room table.

"Not until after we eat, I won't," he said. "You promised Chinese take-out. Sarah, how about you? Kung Pao Chicken and Moo goo whatever?"

"Every Christmas and Easter."

Knock, knock, bang, bang!

Yuri, Jason and I froze. The cat scrambled in a frenzy over the couch.

"Yuri, Alexi?" yelled a woman's voice. Bang, Bang! "I know you're in there. Where's Sarah? Fernando said she quit. Quit what? Her father called me all upset." Bang, bang!

Yuri grabbed Jason's arm and my wrist. "Nyet, tell Mrs. Pace, Yuri speak Enga-leesh. Alexi need vork. Need … monneee, pas de monaie."

Jason whispered, "Okay, I won't tell her."

My heart raced and I whispered, "I won't say anything, I promise."

"Daaaaa," yelled Yuri. "Com-ming."

Geez, facing my boss made my throat go dry and I inhaled counting to five.

Yuri opened the door and Mrs. Pace marched in like Napoleon going to battle. "What are you doing here, Sarah?" (She looked surprised but knew all along Fernando had to have told her.)

"Sarah, why didn't my driver drop you off at my house? And by the way, Fernando didn't know a damn thing about you or anybody else!" She looked past me. "Where's Alexi?"

I shrugged and hiccupped.

"Sarah? Answer me."

I sat on the couch next to Lucifer and stroked his back. Changing my focus to the cat, slowed my hiccups but not much.

Mrs. Pace turned to Jason. "And you are?"

"Hi! I'm Jason, the masseuse." He extended his hand. She didn't take it.

"Sarah, let's go. Fernando is waiting downstairs. Cook made a Chateau Briand for you. Very rare and yummy cauliflower."

"No, thank you," I hiccupped. "My dad called?"

Mrs. Pace sighed, "She speaks! Yes, he's worried about you taking the subway in the storm. Call him ASAP." She squinted at her watch. "I need to go, Sarah. We'll discuss this quitting nonsense in the car."

I didn't answer or get up but I did hiccup again.

She glared at me. "Stop being childish. Get your dance bag and ... what are you wearing? A blue tee-shirt? Where the hell are your clothes?"

"I got soaked in the rain." I smiled at her, and patted Lucifer curled up on my lap and purring.

"Now!" demanded Mrs. Pace pointing to the door.

A key turned in the lock and in walked a rain drenched Alexi carrying several bags of food.

"Alexi," smiled Mrs. Pace. "Someone I can talk to but we need to talk fast, I'm late."

"Yes, we can chat. Sorry, the food is late. I couldn't get a cab, what a surprise?" Alexi handed the food to Jason. "It's raining so hard we should find Noah and get on his ark. Oh,

Yuri, did you tell Mrs. Pace you gave Karl Kreisler a bloody nose?"

Mrs. Pace flashed her eyes at Yuri. "What? You hit that old fart?"

"Da. Lit-tle bit." Yuri waved his hands like it was nothing and grabbed Alexi's wet raincoat and umbrella and ran to the bathroom.

Mrs. Pace snickered, "Did he scream like a girl?"

Alexi chuckled, "No, he pulled Yuri's hair and hit him back."

Mrs. Pace shook her head watching Yuri return. "Okay, I don't have time for you boy's fighting. Is it over?"

"Da," Yuri grinned at Alexi.

"But knowing Karl, he'll call Sutton Place and leave twenty messages for me with Cook. I'm glad you guys warned me in advance."

"Mrs. Pace," smiled Alexi. "Let's walk to the elevator." He opened the front door. "Be careful. I left my wet shoes in the hall."

"Yes, I see the shoes." They both exited the apartment walking into the hall.

A few minutes later, Mrs. Pace came back and hugged me. "Sarah, stay and eat Chinese and in one hour, Fernando will pick you up. Please call your dad and tell him you'll see him tomorrow morning. Too much rain tonight for traveling." Alexi patted my shoulder as if to agree.

Relieved, I pointed to the phone on the desk. Yuri nodded. "I will, Mrs. Pace."

"And don't forget, Monday, two o'clock rehearsal with Yuri in Studio B."

"Nyet!" snapped Yuri and Alexi quickly translated, "Yuri needs to teach the Thunder and Lightning Bolts their choreography on Monday and Tuesday. He doesn't need Sarah for two days."

Mrs. Pace looked confused. "Sarah? Taking two days off?"

"Yes," answered Alexi. "She needs to rest her legs."

"And why so soon with the men? Don't they learn faster than the girls?"

"Really? Those queens learn fast?" Alexi took a Superman stance, hands on hips. "Don't make me laugh."

Yuri shot him a dirty look.

"Sorry, I meant, Yuri is teaching them some difficult and unusual choreography. Lots of jumps and gymnastics."

"Well, if Yuri thinks it's best, fine but remember all of us must spend our time wisely. It's a big production. Okay, got to go. Goodnight."

Alexi took Mrs. Pace's arm, "I'll take you downstairs."

"Ciao, Mrs. Pace," waved Yuri and he shut the door.

Jason grinned, "Whew! She's a nightmare. I have to eat, I'm starving!"

Yuri looked frantic. He took a chilled bottle of unopened vodka from the top freezer of the fridge. He poured two shots and drank both.

Jason opened cartons of food and unwrapped his chopsticks. "Bon appetite," he told himself and dove into the Sweet and Sour Pork over white rice.

I telephoned Dad and apologized. "Yes, Daddy, I'll take the subway in the morning. Right ... safer ... love you, bye."

Fifteen minutes passed before Alexi returned. He sat at the table and looked forlorn. "You know," he said. "Mrs. Pace drilled me like a root canal. She asked about Sarah wanting to quit. God damn, she's a barracuda. Never shuts her mouth."

"Eat, Alexi," said Yuri. "For-get mon-ster vo-man."

"Yeah, man, the food's great," grinned Jason. "MSG works

for me."

"I do strength to discuss that sharp-edged and ferocious woman," chuckled Alexi, "I'm eating." He reached for a plate.

"Vodka?" asked Yuri holding up an empty glass.

"Or white wine?" said Jason picking up the bottle of Chardonnay and popping the cork.

"Vodka," answered Alexi.

"I'm having wine," said Jason pouring himself a glass.

"What about me?" I asked. "I'll be eighteen November 5th"

Jason added ice cubes to another wine glass and poured. "For you madam, enjoy" and we toasted, "Cheers."

I sipped and envisioned the cast of characters. Mrs. Pace, the barracuda, Karl the snake, Yuri the fox, Alexi the bear, Jason the dove, Lucifer the cat. And, who was I? A pink flamingo standing on one thin leg with its head under a wing?

Okay, fine but *should the pink flamingo quit ballet or continue with the rainbows? And what about David Katz? Damn it, he should be forgotten and omitted. I still agonize over why he never called.*

CHAPTER 18

September 18th. Later that same Saturday night, I recalled what my French Club president said, "Oh, saints preserve us." Only when she said it in French, it sounded wiser than me repeating in English.

I HAD DOWNED two glasses of Chardonnay. I felt tipsy but not tipsy enough for what was happening. Yuri and Jason lead me into Yuri's bedroom.

"I'll massage you in here," Jason said. He pointed to the king-size bed.

My face went crimson wearing Yuri's skimpy briefs and a tee-shirt. "On the bed?" I swallowed hard. "I think we should go back to the living room for the couch."

"Think nothing of it," said Jason. "Pretend I'm not here. I'll be right back. I'm getting my massage oils from my bag on the chair."

Yuri stood admiring himself in the full length mirror rocking back and forth. "Jason, goot ... fix you. Grate mas-seuse," he mumbled. Having drunk most of the bottle of Smirnov Vodka, he'd probably have a hangover headache in the morning. His glassy, blue-grey eyes rolled around in his head.

"Yuri," I said watching him sway in the mirror. "I don't wanna take my top off for Jason. He's a man."

"Da. Take shirt off." He grinned a devilish leer. "I take off Yuri shirt."

"What? No! Not your shirt. Put it back on, Yuri! No! My shirt."

"Okay ... Jason like boy... nyet girl."

"What? That doesn't make sense. You and I like boys."

"Jason like boys ... more! Yum-Yum!"

Jason entered the bedroom. "Ready? Take off your shirt."

"Do I have to?"

He flipped his wrist at me. "Don't worry, Sarah, I'm a professional. I only massage muscles. No extra treats."

"Treats!" I giggled and again flushed red in the cheeks.

"Yuri, she's embarrassed and adorable."

Yuri's eyes bugged out. "Sa-rah, grate dan-ser. Sa-rah, Red Rainbow prin-cess."

"Right and Yuri is drunk."

"Da," he wobbled and grinned.

Jason unfolded a bath towel and placed it on the bed. "Okay, great dancer. Get rid of the shirt. Lay on your stomach."

"Okay, here goes nothing" and zip, went the blue tee-shirt and landed on top of a lamp. I laid on my belly and rested my head on my arms.

Yuri leered.

"Behave yourself, Yuri," yelled Jason moving closer to me to block Yuri's view. "She's seventeen. Some respect."

Yuri laughed.

"Alexi," yelled Jason.

Alexi came running in the room. "What?"

"Make him strong coffee."

"Is Yuri misbehaving?"

"No more than usual but take him with you and sober him up. Thanks. Shut the door."

Bang, the door rattled as it closed.

"Sarah," said Jason. "Move close to the edge of the bed so I can work." He coaxed my arms to my sides and I closed my eyes. I don't know how long Jason massaged my sore body. However, at the finish, I floated on a sleepy cloud of relief.

"Thanks, Jason. That was awesome."

"Your welcome, princess". He moved away and smiled, "Goodnight."

When I found the strength to move, I put back on the blue tee-shirt and strolled in the living room. "Where's Alexi?"

"In his room." Yuri pointed to a door off the kitchen.

"And Jason?"

"Go home... second floor. Sa-rah goot?"

"Yes, thanks Yuri. Jason's great."

Watching him sip tea in a glass, with a sugar cube between his teeth reminded me of grandpa. *Only grandpa hated Russia, the Cossacks and pograms whereas Yuri loved his Tartar roots and welcomed any chance to tell stories.*

"Yuri? How do I get home? Is Fernando coming?"

"Nyet. Left Sa-rah."

I looked at the clock on the table. "Eleven o'clock." I yawned, "What do I do?"

"Sleep, ici."

The idea sounded ... "okay, I guess, maybe on the couch?"

"Nyet. Yuri sleep, couch. Sa-rah sleep, Yuri bed."

"Are you sure?"

"Da."

"Goodnight." I strolled back into his bedroom and shut the door.

But, being overly tired, I tossed and turned and couldn't fall sleep. A problem I'd had since childhood. There was only one solution. So, I woke up Yuri.

"I can't sleep. Can you rub my back? Please?"

He followed me into the bedroom, laid down and started a

gentle massage.

"Daddy and Bubbe always ... when I couldn't ..."

"Shuush ..."

I don't remember anything after that.

CHAPTER 19

Sunday, September 19ᵗʰ, 9 a.m. Cloudy with a chance of rain.

I OPENED MY eyes when I heard Alexi's knuckles, "Knock, knock," on Yuri's bedroom door. "Breakfast is ready. Hurry up you two."

I looked down and saw an arm across my chest. "Nooooo," I screeched and pushed the arm off me. "Yuri? Did I do anything stupid last night? You know, anything?"

He raised his head and laughed. "Sex?"

"Not funny." I elbowed his chest.

"Nyet. Sa-rah sleep."

Relieved, I jumped out of bed, picked up my dance bag and ran to the bathroom. Like every dancer in New York City, my bag contained everything I needed if aliens attacked, a snowstorm stopped the city or, I crashed at someone's apartment.

I put on the beige pedal pushers, a wrinkled cotton blouse and my sneakers. Ready for breakfast, I met Alexi, Jason and Yuri drinking coffee at the dining area table. Lucifer slept all curled up on the couch.

"Hi, good morning," I tried to act nonchalant but felt embarrassed. *And how did Jason get back here?*

"Blueberry pancakes," asked Alexi. "For Sleeping Beauty?"

"Yes, please."

Jason pulled out a chair. "How do you feel, Sarah?"

"Much better. Thanks to your healing hands."

Lucifer strolled over and rubbed his body in a figure eight against my legs. "Meow."

"Sarah, did you get any sleep with Rasputin?" Alexi made the sign of the cross before spooning blueberry pancake batter onto a sizzling hot skillet.

"Yes, and nothing happened if anyone wants to know."

"Jason and I placed bets."

"You bastards. Who won?"

"We lost," chuckled Jason.

"You lost? Why?" The blood rushed to my cheeks.

Yuri looked disappointed. "Sa-rah... vir-gin. Nyet sex."

"Oh, great." I threw my napkin down on the table. "You had to announce this to the world. Why?" I snickered. "Am I the only virgin in the company?"

"Yes! At the last count." Alexi winked at Yuri. "So, don't wait a hundred years for a prince. You'll be too old and wrinkled."

"Kiss frog," laughed Yuri between pancake bites.

"But only straight frogs for you, young lady," warned Jason.

"I prefer toads and fireflies," said Alexi flipping pancakes.

"We know," said Jason. "You hang out Tuesday nights at that Second Avenue bar with special clients. Right, Mr. Flap Jack Queen?"

Alexi gave Jason a dirty look and reached over and bopped him in the head with the spatula. "How would you know?"

"I go with you."

"What are you guys talking about?"

"Never mind, Miss Goody-two-shoes," smiled Alexi as he set blueberry pancakes, dripping in butter in front of me.

I sniffed the pancakes. "Awesome. I haven't tasted pancakes in months."

"Only twelve thousand calories, me pretty," said Alexi imitating his favorite witch. "All carbohydrates turn into glucose and then what?"

"Fat," grunted Yuri and handed me the maple syrup.

I shoved my chair back and jumped up. "Okay guys, all kidding aside. Please, don't tell anybody I slept here last night. You have to promise. Don't tell Mrs. Pace. Don't tell my family, don't tell anybody. Got it?"

"Nyet." Yuri squeezed his lips together with his thumbs.

"What's to tell?" said Jason. "I only massaged your back."

"I could get in trouble with my dad. He'd kill me."

"We get it, Sarah," said Alexi patting my shoulder. "It's okay. We promise. Lucifer won't talk. His furry lips are sealed."

"Thanks." I sat back down.

Yuri frowned, "Yuri take shower" and left.

I smacked my lips. "Mrs. Pace and Cook would strangle me if they saw me eating blueberry pancakes smothered in maple syrup."

"Why?" asked Jason.

"This breakfast would disgust them. No protein."

Jason swatted a fly. "There! Protein."

Alexi added, "Just stick a spoon down your throat and throw up."

"Like everybody else? I can name two principals who stick their heads in the toilet and throw up. Irina and Sonia."

"Ow, that's disgusting," moaned Jason.

"It's a way of life," I said. "At first I was shocked but now when the girls do it in the bathroom, I just run out."

"Oh, I know." Alexi agreed. "If you gain an ounce you get hysterical and your partner complains. He has to pick up a sack of potatoes at the next rehearsal."

Alexi looked sad. "Some dancers visit Dr. Fix-it on East 74th Street and get uppers and downers."

"Anna never told me that."

"Ask Mrs. Pace. The doctor prescribes little greenies ... Bennies, Benzedrine diet pills to lose weight and boost your energy and to sleep, he prescribes Placidyls and Seconals.

"Is that why Irina put a doctor's scale in the dressing room?"

"Yes, that's why and according to Yuri, she's a frequent patient. Her age is against her metabolism but not you."

Jason smiled, "A quarter says you weigh a hundred pounds."

I tapped his wrist, "A hundred and three but after this breakfast probably a hundred and ten."

"Not to worry. Throw up in Yuri's bathroom and here's a quarter."

"Vhat is go-ning on?" announced Yuri as he walked in the living room after taking a shower. He sat down with us.

"How bass-turd Karl feel-ding taw-day?"

Alexi rolled his eyes. "I'm sure he's in pain. You walloped him good, Yuri. You probably broke his nose."

I looked at Jason wondering if he knew.

"Yes, Sarah," Jason said picking up on my thoughts. "I know. Yuri told me about the fight last night in the lobby. You were in the bedroom getting dressed for breakfast."

I blinked several times and swallowed.

"Yeah, too bad it happened."

Alexi scoffed, "Jason, let's not talk about it, okay? Yuri, are you still hungry?"

"Da. Grate."

Alexi served him two more pancakes and some scrambled eggs. He laughed, "Yuri burns calories faster than anybody I know. He eats four times a day and never gains a pound."

"Good golly," I said. "If I ate like him, I'd be a blimp."

Yuri laughed. "Sa-rah, nyet fat."

I leaned into Yuri's face. "You smell so good after a shower?"

Alexi answered seeing Yuri's cheeks bulge like a chipmunk full of food. "Estee Lauder," grinned Alexi. "Aramis pour l'homme from Saks Fifth Avenue. Mrs. Pace gave him a credit card and he used it."

Yuri chuckled, "Alexi, jal-loose."

"Are you jealous? Is that true, Alexi?"

Alexi's face scorched red.

Yuri rose to his feet. "Sa-rah ... Yuri talk."

"It's okay. I'm not quitting your beautiful ballet. I apologize. You were right."

"Da?" Yuri grabbed me in a bear hug and picked me up.

"Please, Yuri," I struggled. "Put me down" and he did after a twirl in a circle.

"Da, rehearse, Wed-nes-day."

"That's perfect. Thank you, Yuri. I owe you everything. I'll be very ready Wednesday and no more crap out of me."

Yuri kissed me softly on my lips and smiled.

"SORRY KIDS, THE weather's clear so I'm putting a leash on Lucifer and taking him outside for a walk."

"Your cat walks on a leash like a dog?" I giggled.

"Yeah, I was shocked, too", said Alexi, but somehow Lucifer behaves on a leash like a well-trained dog."

Jason scooped up Lucifer in his arms and stroked his back. "Okay, my buddy, Lucifer and I are off. Thanks for breakfast. Nice meeting you, Sarah. Bye, bye, everybody."

Yuri opened the front door. Alexi hugged Jason and nuzzled his face in Lucifer's tummy and sneezed really loud from the cat hair. The frightened feline, jumped out of Jason's arms and ran out the door. He leaped and scooted down the hall.

The four of us stood mesmerized until Jason yelled, "Come

back here, Lucifer!"

The cat ignored him and hopped and bounced along the dark, carpeted corridor, past the elevator.

Yuri leaned against the door frame. "Yuri, nyet chase cat. Yuri chase vo-man." He walked back inside and sat at the dining table.

Alexi sneezed again and his eyes watered. "Oh, shit, I forgot. I'm allergic to cats. If I catch Lucifer," Ha-chew. "I can't pick him up." Ha-chew.

"You two are no help," I mumbled and ran out the door. I chased Jason who chased Lucifer and we all doubled-back to the elevator. Jason and I watched the cat crouch in wait.

The elevator door slid open and out stepped a tall woman. As the door closed, Lucifer slithered through the last bit of narrow open space.

The elevator door slammed shut and shook. Jason and I were left without a cat. We stood dumbfounded looking up at the golden needle indicator on the wall, above the elevator. The needle stopped on the number two indicating the second floor.

"Lucifer!"

"Ya think?" Jason ran to the end of the corridor and stopped under the exit sign. "Sarah, I'm taking the stairs to the second floor."

"Wait! What if the cat didn't get out of the elevator?"

"Lucifer hates elevators," assured Jason and he opened the stairwell door and disappeared.

I pressed the down button and minutes later, the elevator arrived. When the door opened, guess who?

"Lucifer, you bad boy!"

I stepped inside and bent down and picked up Lucifer but I didn't press the keep door open button in time. The door slammed shut and the elevator moved. This time with me and the cat.

"Wait, waaait," I yelled at the elevator as if it had ears. "Oh crap, Lucifer. We should have gotten off."

The lift ascended and stopped at the fifteenth floor, the penthouse. The door slid open and Lucifer leaped out of my arms and *geez Louise, no surprises,* he ran down the hall.

"Damn you, Lucifer," I groaned and chased after him. "Here kitty, kitty, you dumb cat ..." But the hyper cat ignored my calls. *Now I know why mama never let us have cats. Mama was smarter than I gave her credit for.*

I ran after Lucifer, trying to grab him and missed. He jumped away from me and scooted inside Penthouse 1502 which had its door slightly ajar.

I knocked on the door. "Hello? Anybody home? Yoo-hoo ... Hell-oooo?"

No answer.

I elbowed the door open and entered the tiny entry room. I peeked in the living room and stopped short. The room looked like a tornado swept through and turned everything upside down. Shattered lamps, broken chairs and end tables were trashed on the floor. Throw pillows and couch pillows were ripped apart and slashed. Feeling uneasy and now scared, I mumbled, "Dorothy? Toto? Auntie Em?"

I panicked seeing Lucifer's head and paws pop up in a corner across the room. He played with the shredded ends of a window drape.

I called out, "Hello? Anybody here? Hello? People?"

No answer.

My stomach turned queasy at an awful smell. I didn't know what the odor could be. The cat stopped in place. I made a dash to grab him but he jumped too fast over several broken glass picture frames. And ... I almost slipped on scattered papers and torn up books and plays. So much stuff strewn on the polished floor, I had trouble trying to zig-zag to Lucifer.

"Here kitty," I whispered. "Kitty, kitty."

In a flash, he moved and I rushed forward and ended up in the corner. The cat leaped up and over the couch.

I turned around and screamed, "Oh, my God!" Clutching my throat, I shut up fast and grabbed hold of a chair.

Behind the couch, a man laid spread-eagle on floor, on his back and fully clothed in a tuxedo. A pool of blood surrounded his head and upper body and his chest resembled a fountain of blood and the smell. I hiccupped. *What if someone heard me scream?*

"Mr. Kreisler. Please, don't be dead," I shivered sucking in air. I covered my mouth to stop the sound. My throat closed.

Creepier than a nightmare, there was blood splatters on the wall and the parquet floor. And the odor? Death smelled beyond rank. Too intense to describe. I trembled as I yanked a hankie from my pocket and pinched my nose. The urine stink and I'm not sure but I'd heard of rigor mortis on Perry Mason, could this be rigor mortis?

My heart pounded. My brain said, "Run, get out of here, run, you're in danger." The message thumped loud and clear. My skin started to itch from hives breaking out on my chest.

But curiosity did not kill the cat or me at the moment. Instead, I studied the body with a morbid curiosity. His eyes were wide open, he must have died in fright. And there was so much blood covering his body, I couldn't tell if he was stabbed or shot with a gun. But, hey, I'm no cop. Unlike the fake TV drama, this was the real thing. Murder piqued my interest more than I cared to admit the fascination. Like fire in a fireplace, I had to watch. I leaned in. *Who killed Karl?*

Did Yuri sneak out of his apartment and murder Karl? Yuri

had motive and opportunity as Perry Mason would tell the jury.

I stared at the dead man. His face looked grey and waxy and a tiny piece of ruffle and skin rested on his sleeve. Suddenly, I choked, "The cat! Where the hell is the cat?" *No wonder Mama hates cats.*

I hurried back to the tiny entry room and saw Lucifer run into a second room, an office. He frolicked on pillows and leaped under an antique desk. I chased him and trapped him with pillows at the back of the Rolltop relic.

"Meow."

"Schuss." My heart raced.

I pulled my long sleeves over my hands and covered my fingers. Moves I'd learned on TV crime shows to avoid leaving finger prints.

I crawled under a large antique desk into a pile of statements, canceled checks and letters. The papers scattered. The cat frolicked in the mess and pawed at anything that moved. He loved playing with a dangling blue velvet ribbon above his head.

Following Lucifer's gaze, I saw taped to the bottom of the desk, the blue ribbon tied a bundle of letters. I yanked them down. The top envelope was addressed to Yuri with no return sender. But the rest of the letters had Anna's, Sonia's and Stephanie's return addresses and were mailed to Yuri at the Osborne Apartments. My mouth went dry and I had a gruesome, uncomfortable thought. *Why were hand-written letters hidden in an undetected place in Mr. Kreisler's home? What was he up to? Dealing with emotions and secrets in personal correspondence? My mind assumed blackmail; I'd watched Perry Mason TV shows with Bubbe.* I stuffed the letters inside my blouse and grabbed the cat.

I ducked down and crawled out from under the desk trying not to touch anything. Rushing to the tiny entry room, I lost my grip and the cat leaped off my chest. He bounded into the living room and into a corner. *No! Not again!*

Lucifer crossed Mr. Kreisler's legs then stopped and crouched near his shoes. I held my breath. *I couldn't watch. He's gonna leave paw prints. And prints on the body and in the blood.*

"Nooooo," I mumbled under my breath. "Don't, yikes. We gotta go." The cat ran to chair.

"Forget it!" I quickly exited the tiny entry room and stepped into the fifteenth floor hallway leaving the door exactly as I found it.

As if God answered my prayer, Lucifer rushed out of Penthouse 1502 and made a tun for me. Like an old friend, he rubbed my pants leg in a figure eight. I scooped him up and we ran to the elevator. Pressing the down button, the door opened and we got in.

"Okay, you fur ball shit. You'd better keep your mousey mouth shut. This is our secret."

Lucifer purred and closed his eyes. I pressed the number ten button.

Endless minutes later, I returned the Lucifer to Apartment 10A to a relieved and thankful Alexi and Yuri. "Alexi, call Jason and return the cat. I don't know his apartment number."

"Sure, Sarah."

The cat hopped on the couch and curled up.

"And Yuri," I picked up my dance bag from the chair and ran to Yuri's bathroom.

"Are you okay, Sarah?" yelled Alexi.

"Uh-huh!" I lied and shut the door.

Inside the John, I grabbed the letters from inside my blouse and tucked them in my overloaded bag. Leaving the room, I hurried to the front door. "Yuri, I can't stay. My dad gets worried. Forgive me, I love your ballet. Truly, I do. Sorry, I'm such a brat. I'll work harder, I promise, I love you."

"Goot!" He grabbed my face and kissed my cheeks. "Yuri valk, Sa-rah subvay?"

"No, I'm okay. Thanks, you're a dear man. Bye."

ON THE RIDE home, I sweated bullets. *What will Mrs. Pace do when she hears Karl died? Will she replace me with Sonia or Irina cause there's no more bet?*

"Is my career over?" I said out loud. "Is this the end?"

Three passengers looked up and stared at me like I was crazy.

Right now, could I be? What if the theatre stopped the premiere over the murder? Would the public refuse to buy tickets? My mind spun in circles. *Did Yuri kill Mr. Kreisler?* I grabbed my neck and gasped. "Don't even think such a thing."

My stomach churned acid. I felt nauseous and wanted to puke. "Brooklyn College? I hate math and science." The old man seated a few feet away, stared at me. *I didn't care.*

Anyway, he got off at the next stop. *So what!*

CHAPTER 20

Same Sunday, September 19th. Brooklyn Heights, home sweet home.

WHEN I UNLOCKED the front door to my family's apartment, I nearly fainted. Every relative sat or stood in my living room drinking coffee. Michelle and Leon the jeweler were the only two missing. Didn't my family clear up Mama's problem with the psychiatrist? What more was there to discuss?

The shock of Karl Kreisler's bloody body still active in my imagination caused me to jump a foot at the chorus of "Hello, Sarah." That and the screeching subway made me yearn for a quiet afternoon.

"Hello, Sarah. How's by you?" greeted Uncle Louie looking way too comfortable in Dad's plastic covered Naugahyde chair.

"Hi, yourself, Uncle Louie."

"Who's the young man in the kitchen? He brought flowers for your mother. Why is he here?"

"Huh?"

"He brought roses and carnations from a florist, very nice, you get my drift?" grinned Bubbe rolling her eyes. "He came in with Jeff. Aunt Lucy said ..."

"Wait, I'll tell her," said Lucy jumping up from the couch in a near panic. "I think he's going to ask you out Sarah, you know, on a date."

"What? Who?"

"You'd better say no!" She wagged her finger under my nose. "He's too old and too sophisticated."

"Why?" said Aunt Sophie. "You date now, Sarah? Since when? Nobody tells me anything."

"Keep your wig on. She doesn't date," said my brother Max.

"I'm not wearing my wig, Max. This is my natural hair."

"Ya could have fooled me, Sophie," laughed Uncle Louie. "But, you look marvelous."

Aunt Sophie giggled.

Uncle Al leaned forward in his chair. "So tell me, Sarah? How did you meet this young man? Who's his family? What does he do?"

"I don't know. Who said I met him?"

"Go look, Sarah," said Aunt Ida Mae pointing towards the kitchen door. "He's having coffee with Ben and Nessie." She turned to her husband. "Al, who knew? Looks like a nice boy."

"A boy?" said Al. "He's a man, Ida Mae."

I ESCAPED TO my bedroom and looked in the mirror. *Yikes!* I looked like crap. I can't meet anybody even if it is "Oh, God, David," I squealed.

Nah, can't be him. He would have called.

I grabbed my dance bag with the letters inside and shoved the whole thing in the closet. I hid it behind stuff and piled loose clothes and magazines on top. "Yes," I whispered. "I made a wonderful mess."

Aunt Sophie, my forced-upon-me roommate, hated messes and she'd never clean up anybody's mess not even her own. I shut the closet door and checked myself in the mirror. *Holy cow, I needed help! Where was my fairy Godmother?*

I fumbled with various shades of lipsticks trying to hide my pale face. After choosing several, I decided on the coral but the color didn't hide the dark circles under my eyes. I put the lipstick on anyway, added a touch of rouge and brushed my hair in a ponytail. I looked in the mirror and I still looked like crap, only coral crap.

Could I hide in the closet? No, not an option. *Way too crowded and a mess.* Besides, my family knew where I was and they'd yell my name until the cows came home. *Oh, shoot a moose, what else could go wrong today?*

I took several deep breaths and tip-toed down the hall. I peeked around the kitchen door and gasped. My hands flew to my throat. My heartrate spiked.

What if he told my parents we met already? I jerked my head back from behind the door but Mama caught me.

"Sarah? Come in. We have a visitor." She looked ecstatic. Her face showed thoughts of talking to the rabbi and discussing wedding invitations with the neighbors.

"Hello, Sarah," said David pushing his chair back and standing up. "I'm David Katz. I met you at your sister's wedding two years ago. I was wondering …"

I shrugged and looked down at my sneakers, "Wondering? What, wondering?"

"Yes, wondering. If you would like to go out with me sometime?"

I hesitated then looked up at Dad's face and Mama's face. I bit my lip. "Oh, sometime wondering … like when?"

"Like now, tonight?"

"Tonight? That's a lot of wondering," I giggled a nervous reaction. He was playing it straight, acting like this was innocent.

You have to admire a man who can lie.

"Forget it, David," said my brother Jeff. "She's too young. Besides, you two are not a good fit. She's a ballet dancer, you're a lawyer. You guys have nothing in common."

David snapped, "That's an asinine assumption."

"It's my opinion."

David turned to me, "Sarah." His expression softened. "You're eighteen aren't you?"

"Almost," said Mama faster than anybody else could speak.

"Yes," I chirped covering my mouth in embarrassment. "Soon," I nodded. "I mean soon."

"Would you like to go to a party with me?"

"What?"

"Tonight? It's my boss's birthday. It starts at seven."

I blushed and looked down at the linoleum floor and counted the soup stains around my sneakers. *What do I do? He didn't call. He never mentioned the reason. Whew! Now, I'm mad.*

"I have a car," David said looking at me hopefully. "We would drive into Manhattan."

I glared at him, my nostrils flared.

"You hear that, Sarah?" Mama wore a grin the size of Florida. "He has a car. No subway ride for you-who."

Mama touched David's arm. "Does your car have air conditioning? I hear that's the latest thing."

David nodded.

Mama grinned, "You hear that Sarah, air-conditioning."

"Where in Manhattan?" asked Dad.

"Upper East side. A co-op on Park Avenue. I can give you the address when I pick your daughter up."

"Yes, I'd need the address and the phone number."

"Of course, sir." David took another look at me, smirked and sat down in his chair. He sipped his coffee.

Mama pushed the plate of raspberry and apricot Rugalas in front of her guest. She picked out the biggest Rugala in a napkin and held it under David's nose.

He chuckled, "No, thanks."

"What time would you bring my daughter home?" asked Dad.

"Depending on traffic, maybe eleven? Certainly not later than midnight."

"Sarah, you should go," said Mama looking at Daddy for approval.

"Sister, no, you shouldn't go," scoffed Jeff. "He's too old."

"Schuss," warned Mama.

"Look, Sarah. David was my friend in school but ..."

"But what?" interrupted David.

"You disappeared until Michelle's wedding. Where were you?"

"Law school and the DA's office."

"Yeah, but out of the blue, you ask for my sister's phone number? What for, man?"

"Jeff, I tried calling you for two years to shoot hoops, go to a hockey game, a Yankee game anything but, you were busy with some girl."

"You mean Selma Stevens? I almost married her. We were living together."

"Okay, Selma Stevens."

"She left me, the fucking bitch!"

"Hey, watch your mouth." Dad slapped the side of Jeff's head. "There's ladies present."

Mama rolled her eyes at me.

David cleared his throat. "Sorry about the girl." Then he focused on me. "Sarah?"

"Huh? What?"

"I asked for your number and called you several times. I left messages at the ballet school."

"I never got any messages," I pouted and fisted my hands on

my hips.

"Some guy named Alexi and a lady, I guess, the school secretary kept saying 'you were rehearsing with the choreographer.'"

"Right. That's what I do."

"Did they give you the messages?"

"No," I shook my head. "I'm gonna ask why not?"

Dad grumbled, "Sarah? Do you want to go to this party with David or not?"

"I'm not sure," I shrugged watching the cuckoo clock on the wall. *Gosh. He did call but I look like crap.* I dropped my hands to my sides.

Dad glared at me. "What's it to be, Sarah?"

"I can't go, Daddy. I'm too tired. Sorry, David. Thank you for asking me but it's been a long week."

David rose from his chair.

"Please, excuse me" and I left the kitchen and ran to my room.

Mama knocked on my door, barged in and closed it behind her in four seconds but who's counting?

"Sarah, bubbela," she said sitting on the edge of the bed. "Can't you reconsider? He's a nice boy. A lawyer, a professional man. He wears a suit and a vest, a nice tie. He has starch in his collar and cuffs."

"Really Ma, starch?"

"And gold cufflinks and leather wingtip shoes like Daddy wears to a funeral. They're very expensive shoes. Could be Tom McCann?"

"No, please, I'm exhausted."

"Baby, listen. Take a nice nap, a warm bubble bath. You'll feel like a million dollars. Then you go out with Mr. Lawyer." She rubbed my back, knowing my favorite spots and started singing the "Margery Daw" song.

"Mama, you don't understand. I've had a rotten day and a busy two weeks."

"Sarah, you dance professionally for a year, maybe two years then what?"

"I keep dancing."

"Oye vey! No wedding? No babies? You want I should never be a grandmother? Your daddy never a grandpa? We'll die without a family tree? No branches? No leaves?"

Mama glared at me and sent Jewish guilt by the truckloads. I ignored her witchcraft. Instead, I switched my brain to a phone call I made at a pay phone near the subway. I dialed the NYPD and reported the murder as an anonymous caller. *I hoped I did the right thing.*

Mama shook my arm to get my attention. "Sarah, please think. After dancing for years, what will happen to you? Where will Mr. Lawyer be?"

I shrugged.

"He'll be married to some other nice girl and have children. Do you want that?"

"No."

"Well? Don't be masuganah. Say yes to the party and then take a long nap."

"Mama, what if I don't go?"

"I'll kvetch for a month making you crazy."

"Oh, geez Louise, okay, I'll go."

Mama grinned, "Such a smart girl" and pinched my cheeks.

"Ooowww!"

"You needed color."

"Rouge works better."

She grabbed my hand. "C'mon Sarah. Let's go tell Mr. Lawyer in a suit and nice tie you're going."

"Oh, God."

"A car owner in Brooklyn?" Mama grinned, "How lucky can a girl get?"

Bursting into the kitchen with me in tow, Mama announced, "It's settled. Sarah's going to the party. I changed her mind."

"Yes, David," I smiled. "I'll go to the party, thank you for asking. Is it still okay?"

"Yes, of course, it's fine." His eyes twinkled, "Pick you up at six o'clock." He shoved his chair back and stood tall.

"You'd better treat my sister right," said Jeff. "You know."

"Why wouldn't I?" snickered David.

"Stop it, Jeff," said Mama. "David's a gentleman." Her eyes glazed over seeing a bride and groom under the Huppah. "Sarah's happy to meet David. And maybe they'll be friends."

"Yes, maybe," I blushed.

David excused himself and left the kitchen. The next sound we heard was the front door closing gently.

"Sarah," grinned Mama. "Go take a nap."

BUT, BEFORE I closed my eyes, I needed to sort out what I should do. Since I decided not to tell anyone I discovered the body, my lips were sealed.

I threatened Lucifer not to talk, as if he could go out and blab the news. Plus, I shouldn't have spent the night in Yuri's bed. My dad would strangle me if he knew. Using the rainstorm as an excuse not to come home wouldn't be a real reason. New Yorkers ride subways in all kinds of weather, it's underground.

However, regarding the murder ... should I tell David and ask his advice? As a criminal prosecutor in the DA's office, he works with cops and he'd know what to tell me ... maybe? I ... oh, gosh, I should probably leave out the parts about the bathtub ... the massage ... the two drinks ... and Yuri's bed, duh!

CHAPTER 21

Again Sunday, September 19ᵗʰ. 4:45 p.m. Ready, set, go!

AUNT LUCY KNOCKED on my bedroom door and woke me from my nap. She declared a truce. "If you're dumb enough to start dating an older man, I'll make you look so beautiful he'll have a heart attack and drop dead. Then you'll have to date someone your own age."

"Aunt Lucy, that's not very nice."

"Well … a successful attorney like David has egotistical demands and shameless ambitions. He's just like you. Things in common. You'll get along just fine or kill each other trying."

"Mama's right. She thinks you're weird."

"Never mind what Mama thinks. Your father, my ever-loving brother, thinks David is honorable and could be important to your future."

"How do you know?"

"Ben just informed me, he approves of the young man so I'd better be nice."

"Really? Daddy likes David?" My jaw dropped.

"Seems to think he's a decent sort and Ben is pretty good at reading people."

"Auntie, I'm nervous. Look, my hands are shaking."

"Forget shaking. Get in the bathroom and let's get you showered and ready."

I slipped on my furry pink slippers and headed for a toothbrush and shampoo.

When I stepped out of the shower, Aunt Lucy towel-dried my hair and kept talking. "You know, Sarah, an attorney with money can be the best guy to start with. That's better than some poor schmuck working in a factory."

"Is he rich?"

"Bingo. Very wealthy. I telephoned a few friends and they asked around."

"What?"

"David Katz is smart, eligible and graduated top of his law school class. He's a successful prosecutor and inherited his late grandfather's fortune."

"A fortune? Geez."

"His grandfather invented a few things and owned the patents. The money keeps rolling in."

"It goes to David?"

"None other."

"Oh, dear," I gulped.

"Rich is good, Sarah, believe me."

"Auntie, but you married for love."

"I did, with dollar signs dangling before my irises. Here ... put these panties on and the nylons with the garter belt."

I gave her a dirty look and took the underwear.

"My advice young lady? Stay as sweet as you are and don't let David talk you into anything. Play hard to get. He wants a respectable woman. No sluts or tarts need apply."

"Ick! You mean say no to sex?"

"Sarah! I mean say no to sex! You're not a hippie. No free love in the park. Put a ring on your finger then spread your legs and do what he wants."

"What he wants? What are you talking about?"

"With this type of professional man. He wants a lady in the

living room and a whore in his bedroom."

I stumbled putting on a stocking and began to tremble. "I don't understand."

"You heard me. But that's a discussion for another night."

I shook my head. "Mama told me not to listen to you many times."

Aunt Lucy snickered. "That's because I'm a Gemini and talk out of both sides of my mouth. She gets confused. She's a Virgo."

"Huh?"

"Never mind," said Lucy. She reached for the stool under the dressing table. "Sit down. Face the mirror." She plugged in the curling iron and worked the ends of my hair. Then she applied eyeliner and mascara.

"Red lipstick," she emphasized. "Gets a man every time."

"You should know," I smirked. "Three husbands and a tango dancer at the Roseland Ballroom."

"Antonio Hernando Rodrigo?" She sneered. "Old news."

"Since when?"

"He has a wife and four kids in Staten Island. When I found out? Goodbye Mister Fancy Dancer and Tricky Dickie. No more three to tango."

DAVID ARRIVED AT six o'clock driving a pale yellow 1965 Bentley S3 Continental Coupe. He parked the car in front of The Valiant Arms. How did I know the car's make and model? My brother Max telephoned two minutes later.

"Funkin' A, the car is a classic. You'd better marry the guy."

Wow, no pressure. And in the living room, Mama and Bubbe hung out the front windows.

"Sarah," yelled Mama. "He's here. Come see the car." Then Mama called to a neighbor across the street, "Yoo-hoo, Mrs. Orenstein, the man in the fancy car is dating my daughter."

"Oh, God, no."

OUT FRONT, ON the sidewalk, David greeted Dad with a handshake and a business card presumably with Mr. Loeb's address and telephone.

Across the street, the neighbors in brownstone rowhouses, sat on high stoops and ogled the expensive car. Other neighbors rubbernecked or sat on ledges. My relatives watched through binoculars out their living room windows. Max still excited over the Bentley, shouted the make and model, to the neighbors.

And as far as the Valiant Arms and my family?

Only a Rothman could lease the street side apartments facing the morning sun and the lilac trees. Outsiders were stuck leasing the dark, rear apartments facing back yards, the clotheslines and stray, screaming cats. They all saw the car.

"Sarah!" Mama raised her voice from the living room.

"No, Mama, you and Bubbe meet us at the elevator. I should leave."

"Hold on, I'm getting Daddy's camera."

"Okay, David can wait. Aunt Lucy just said so. Take your time."

Mama met us holding Daddy's instamatic camera. "Ready?" She held the camera to her chin. "Stand like a model selling a washer machine on television."

"I like Amana refrigerators on TV," smiled Bubbe.

I posed. "No, Mama. You're cutting off my head. Hold the camera up higher."

Mama raised the camera. "Okay, say Kraft cheese."

"Camembert, Brie."

Aunt Lucy opened the elevator door. "Remember what I told you."

"You told me so many things, Auntie."

Bubbe kissed my cheeks. "A thousand kisses."

"Bye. Love you, ladies."

I WALKED OUT of my building wearing a long sleeve, teal blue, crepe de chine mini-dress and high heels in the same teal blue. My blonde hair now slightly curled, hung long and loose around my shoulders.

Aunt Lucy lent me her sapphire and diamond pierced earrings which had to be, the most gorgeous earrings in all five boroughs. Her parting words, "Sarah, walk slow ... then you can show off my hard work getting you ready. You're gonna knock the socks off Mr. Katz, I guarantee it."

As her words bounced around in my head, "Don't rush, Sarah. Make him wait. Let him come to you." I had the biggest urge to chicken out and run as fast as I could, back upstairs and hide in my room until ... I saw David's face.

With such wonder as if appreciating a work of art at Sotheby's Parke-Bernet, he admired my face and body. His expression sweeter than cherry pie in the window of Steinberg's Bakery on DeKalb Avenue.

Both terrified and excited, I stopped in place and giggled feeling my heart flutter. I'd always remember the moment. "Badda bing" as Uncle Al would say. Me with a lawyer?

But my giggle turned to guilt. *Should I forget Mr. Kreisler? That poor man? Yes, maybe just to keep sane. I would try for tonight.*

Both men walked towards me and smiled.

Daddy kissed my forehead. "Behave yourself and David, take good care of her."

"I will, sir."

My dad did the honors and opened the passenger door. I sat inside, surrounded by the color beige and the faint smell of new, soft leather.

The neighbors gawked watching David check his rearview mirror and pull away from the curb. Feeling embarrassed by the nosey yentas seated on brownstone stoops, I fidgeted with the thin shoulder strap of my tiny beaded evening bag.

At the stop light, David looked over and smiled. "I'm glad your mother changed your mind and you both decided to join me."

I blushed.

He chuckled at my shyness. "You look lovely." The clef in his chin deepened.

"Thank you for not telling my parents we met at the zoo."

"I figured ..."

"They're old-fashioned."

"Not an issue."

I watched David drive, seated in a smart three piece black suit. He had fine, handsome features and looked unflappable but couldn't that be a cover-up for something else? Underneath, I suspected a hunger and true grit. My pulse quickened. *How did Aunt Lucy describe him? Passionate and ambitious like me.*

In the blink of an eye, *I realized the blue in his tie matched the blue ribbon tying the letters I stole.* I chewed on my lip. *Why were they taped and hidden under Karl's desk?*

"Sarah, why are you staring at me?"

"Was I? Sorry." I turned my head away and *wondered did*

Anna write love letters to Yuri? Did Sonia and Stephanie also pour their hearts out?

"I can help ... try me?"

I looked back at him and smiled. "No, I'm good."

His concerned expression softened to a smile drinking me in with his eyes. *Such a charming smile. He could melt Barton chocolate at fifty paces.*

In Manhattan, cruising uptown on the FDR Drive, the traffic suddenly picked up speed. Police cars blasting sirens took off like "bats out of hell" as Uncle Al would say. And vehicles, headed in our direction, turned vigilant as black and whites swerved in and out, changing lanes. I flinched and grabbed the door handle.

"Sarah, relax," chuckled David. "They're not after you."

"Sirens scare me."

"No shit. With all the alarms in your neighborhood?" He turned left catching the end of the light.

My mind flip-flopped. *What if someone saw me enter Karl's apartment and told the cops? What do I say?*

We crossed mid-town Manhattan and while waiting at a red light, David reached for my hand. He murmured, "I'd like to kiss those red lips, that sweet pouty mouth."

I swallowed hard and couldn't look at him after that. *Shame on you, Aunt Lucy. You got me in trouble and I'm upset enough thinking about poor Mr. Kreisler.*

AT THE PARK Avenue party address, David stopped at the curb and I watched the valets open car doors. Assuming a parking attendant would open my door, I turned and looked the valet in the eye but oops, I assumed wrong. It was David's dreamy, ocean blue eyes that sank into mine. The chemical tension between us sent sparks. I caught my breath.

His eyes gazed into mine as he reached for my arms and pulled me to my feet. He whispered, "Sorry. I shouldn't have made such an intimate comment. I didn't mean to startle you."

"Well, you did," I snapped and stepped aside catching my heel in a pavement crack and stumbled.

David blocked my fall by wrapping his arms around my waist. "Careful ... are you okay?"

"Yes." *Mostly embarrassed.*

"Then you won't slap me? I'm forgiven?" His eyes flashed.

"How can I, Mr. Katz? You've got me in a wrestling hold and I can't move."

He dropped his arms and stepped back looking uncomfortable. "Hey, lighten up. I'm teasing you, Miss Rothman."

"Why? Because I'm young?"

"No, because I'm old and I can."

"Really? I think it's because you know how but be on guard, I'm a fast learner, I will get even."

His arrogance softened to a delighted grin. "I certainly hope so. I love a challenge." He cupped his hands and signaled "bring it on."

Crap, I just threatened a gun fight at the O.K. Corral. "Okay, smarty pants, you won round one."

He reached for my hand and kissed the back. "I'm looking forward to round two."

WE ENTERED THE lobby and stood waiting for one of the two elevators. In a large gilded mirror, I noticed David had a devilish grin on his face and a glimmer of light in his eyes.

I wondered, what was he thinking? I poked his side with my elbow, "What!"

He bent down and brushed his lips across my mouth. He smelled of lemons and mossy woods and *I dare say,* way too delicious.

"To tell the truth," he whispered. "I'd like to kiss you right now, right here, long and hard. I won't apologize for my intentions but I'll mind my manners. You're safe."

No, I'm not safe. *Not if you smell that crazy good. I'll kiss you first.*

"David," I tried to shut my raging hormones down and sound cool. "You have no idea what kind of a morning I've had."

He brushed my cheek with the back of his hand. "Try me."

"No, too dangerous."

He reared back and gave me a defiant look. "Miss Rothman, I live for danger. You have my undivided attention."

"Not tonight, Mr. Bond." A hint of perspiration dampened my spine.

CHAPTER 22

Same Sunday, 7:15 p.m. The Party. Quid pro quo, this for that.

At the penthouse, the elevator doors opened to a high-ceiled elegant co-op. Oil paintings hung on damask walls and furniture from another century decorated the rooms. In the foyer, two well-dressed, young men approached David.

"Well, well, the ambitious Mr. Katz has arrived with a trophy date," said one of the men. "'The first thing we must do, is kill all lawyers.'"

David snickered, "Kill all lawyers? Shakespeare's play *Henry VI?*"

"Dick the Butcher said it best."

"Everybody knows that. Can't you do better than a cliché?"

"How about Hail, Caesar?" said the second man raising his arm. "Veni, vidi, vici." He bowed in jest.

"Cut the shit guys. I'm not happy to see you, either."

"Why? Competition's a bitch?"

"Not when I win," crackled David.

"Aren't you going to introduce us to thy fair maiden?"

"No."

David took my arm and we moved past the men faster than I could ask, "What was that all about?"

Better, I didn't ask.

WE WALKED INTO a room of gold fixtures, oriental rugs and crystal chandeliers. A swarm of chic people chatted and drank cocktails. David didn't know anybody so we moved on to the next room.

David pulled my hand past waiters carrying trays of roasted beef kebabs and broiled shrimp hors d'oeuvres. Inhaling such lovely smells made my nose dance the samba. I hadn't eaten in hours and could bite any hors d'oeuvres on a waiter's tray.

At the third room, a circular mahogany bar spanned a corner near several enormous picture windows. But the large windows seemed silly since our view across the street was more large windows. Only they were housed in grey stone, without trees or flowers. At least the bigger than life-sized windows in the "Dakota," on West 72nd Street had a view of Central Park. An extraordinary view worth watching in any season, snow, rain and spring time trees and tulips.

"Shall we?" asked David. He pointed at two open spots at the bar.

"Why not?"

We sat on bar stools and I grabbed a handful of pistachio nuts and munched. People around us gazed out windows. They commented on the last rays of the September sun, settling over the Manhattan skyscrapers.

I agreed with the couple next to us and added, "Yes, it is an amazing view, but it ain't Brooklyn."

It must have sounded inappropriate because David reared back. "Damn, did you just say that?"

The couple harrumphed and got up and left.

Oh shit, they thought I was rude. My underarms dampened and my face felt hot. I chalked one up for my big mouth.

David sat upright and snickered, "You don't give one iota, do you Sarah?" He leaned in and kissed my cheek. "You just say what's on your mind."

"Why? Is there a problem?"

"Some people might think so but I find it cool."

The bartender moved over and wiped off the countertop. "What are you and the lady drinking?"

David studied my face. "Orange juice or a Coke?"

"Champagne."

"Yes, Madam, Dom Perignon or Piper-Heidsieck?"

"Dom Perignon."

David furrowed his brow.

Stop it, fancy pants. Orange juice can't compete with a dead man, a screeching subway and my nosey family.

"And you, sir?" asked the bartender.

"Cutty Sark on the rocks."

The bartender placed our drinks on napkins, on top of the marble counter and left. David picked up our glasses and walked away with them. I followed. He then literally, backed me into a corner like Fred Astaire leading Ginger Rogers dancing backwards, in high heels.

"What's with the Dom Perignon?" he smirked.

I giggled taking my glass in hand. "I recognized the name from a magazine ad."

"Yes?"

"The ad read for the most romantic night of your life with that special someone."

David stared at his drink.

"And during my senior year in the French Club, we talked about champagne and I wanted to taste Dom Perignon. That's the vintner we discussed the most in French."

"Anything else at the French Club I should know about? French kissing? Naked postcards?"

"What?"

"Ménage a trois? French ticklers …"

I batted my eyelashes and he stopped talking. He took a swig of Cutty Sark and murmured, "Not amusing?"

I matched his swig with my champagne. "You'll have to do better than that, Mr. Katz."

"DAVID? MISS ROTHMAN?" Bernie Lieberman sidled up. "Glad you could make it." He glared at the champagne glass in my left hand.

"Is she old enough, David?"

"No."

"I will be in two months."

Mr. Lieberman remained unsmiling. "Miss Rothman, only one drink for you tonight."

"But it's yummy. Maybe, two or three more?" I scrunched up my nose.

"No, not tonight. And Sarah, don't tell anybody your age. Oscar Wilde once said, 'Never trust a woman who tells her real age. A woman who tells her age, will tell anything.'"

"My Aunt Lucy lies about her age."

Bernie looked amused. "Why?"

"She's had three husbands and several boyfriends. She gets younger every year because the boyfriend's get younger."

"Well, if she needs a divorce attorney?" Bernie chuckled. "We have a good one in our office."

"Oh, no, Mr. Lieberman, all her husbands died and left her money. She owns our building and a whole lot more."

"I think I like Aunt Lucy."

"Everybody loves Aunt Lucy."

"Sounds like most of New York."

"No, silly." I shook my head. "Just Brooklyn and a part of Queens."

"Oh, God!" Bernie laughed. "Where did you find this treasure, David?"

"At the zoo," I answered. "In front of Edgar the Gorilla."

"No kidding?"

"Yep."

"David, don't let this one get away. But, Miss Rothman?" Bernie took hold of my elbow. "Most of these people are conservative Republicans. They supported Barry Goldwater. So, don't tell these old goats anything. You hear me? Say nothing."

"Why?"

"Simple. It's not the theory of relativity."

"Why are you sarcastic? I didn't say anything wrong."

"No, sweetheart. You're a breath of fresh air. I only meant don't tell these people about your family and nothing that goes on between you and David."

"I love my family."

"They don't need to know. But for me?" He patted his heart. "I love when you talk. You can tell old Bernie anything." He rolled his eyes and dropped my arm. "But at this event? We're going to shut your mouth and subdue your effervescence."

"Huh?"

"Good talk, Miss Rothman."

Bernie turned to David. "Keep her in check and her mouth closed. We don't need an albatross" and he waved at someone and stepped away.

"An albatross?"

David whispered, "I'll tell you later. Never mind."

"Whatever."

Following my intense desire to choke Mr. Lieberman, several colleagues asked to meet David so Mr. Lieberman brought them over to join us.

Bernie the snake charmer, held court. He introduced "David

Katz as our newest addition to the law firm, a successful prosecutor for the D.A.'s office who's never lost a case and ... the
lovely Miss Rothman."

Yada, yada, yada.

The group discussed a high-profile legal case, currently vili-
fied by the press which bored me no end. I skipped faking
interest and played Monopoly in my head "passing go" and
questioning what I found.

*Why did Karl have other people's personal mail? Blackmail?
Do I tell Anna I have her letters? I've got to read them. Aunt
Sophie better not snoop in my closet.*

My musings halted when David abruptly turned and faced
me up close. "You look distracted. What's up?"

"Nothing." I averted his eyes.

"No, not nothing." His lips narrowed to a thin line.

Silence.

He latched onto my elbow and guided me through the French
doors at the end of the bar. We stood on the balcony in the
warm, muggy night. "Sarah, forget what Lieberman said. The
man's an asshole."

I stared at the clef in his chin.

He held my upper arms. "Let's enjoy the party. Forget my
boss." He pushed a strand of hair away from my eye.

"Did I embarrass you?" I sniffled starting to tear up.

"No, you didn't." He dabbed my eyes with a monogrammed
handkerchief. "You love your family." He pocketed the hankie
and took my hand.

"Yes."

He kissed my fingertips and brushed his lips against my palm.
I gasped a startled "Aaah."

WE RETURNED TO the air-conditioned bar where the birthday

person, Mr. Loeb came over and introduced himself and his wife. Like magic, David produced a tiny blue box tied with a white ribbon and handed it to Mr. Loeb.

"David, you shouldn't have."

"Yes, I should. Happy Birthday, sir."

Mr. Loeb's thin lips quivered, "Most thoughtful." He patted David's back and he and Mrs. Loeb moved on.

The crowd turned quiet as we heard someone singing. In paraded a teenage boy, dressed in a chef's uniform. He held a small brass gong in one hand and a mallet, in the other. In a falsetto voice, he announced, "The buffet dinner is served." He hit the gong, bang, bang. He sang again, "The buffet dinner is served." Bang, bang. He moved on and into the next room and again vocalized. "Ladies and gentlemen, your attention please. The buffet dinner is served." Bang, bang.

"They sing for their dinner?" I laughed nervously. "Where do we eat, David? I'm starving."

The man behind us answered, "Two rooms over, heading south. In the ballroom."

"Nooooo," I cooed. "Who has a ballroom in their apart-ment?"

David whispered, "Evidently, Mr. Loeb. We'd better hurry." He grabbed my hand, "C'mon.

We hurried through two more rooms like starving immi-grants entering Ellis Island. Near the head of the line, we slowed down and joined the others. I cheered along with the noisy guests.

Following dinner, David and I chatted with a young couple around David's age when the wife asked, "What do you do, Sarah?"

David smiled. "Sarah is the new soloist for the City Center Ballet Theatre. The lead in Yuri Konstantinov's new ballet."

His announcement spread fast and guests who enjoyed ballet, sought us out. Many had read the New York Times and New York Post's interviews and saw the photos of Yuri and me.

"Miss Rothman," asked a red-haired woman. "What's it like dancing with a famous Russian? Is he temperamental?"

"No, he's very nice and it's exciting," I replied. *If I told the woman the truth, I'd be fired. Mrs. Pace doesn't approve of opinions other than her own.*

Questions aimed at me kept firing like bullets from an automatic weapon. "How many hours do you rehearse? What do you eat to stay thin? How much do you weigh? Why did the City Center Ballet choose you? Can Yuri speak English? How do you communicate? Does dancing hurt your toes? Can you stand on your toes without toe shoes?"

Facing exuberant strangers holding cocktails, zapped my energy. In contrast, my date thrived on the Q&A like "a flaming comet" as Uncle Al would say. More people entered the room and joined us. I yawned looking at the crowd and whispered in David's ear, "Please, let's go. No more questions."

He looked surprised. "Why? These people love you."

"No, they don't," I spat. "They just want a piece of me. I should rip up my dress and throw them each a square."

A middle-aged woman pawed my arm. "We're season ticket holders and we can't wait to see the *Colors of The Rainbow*. Can we come backstage and visit you?"

"Why?" I answered. "I don't visit you at your work."

David nudged my side. "Be nice, Brooklyn. She meant well."

No, she didn't. She wanted to smooze and suck my energy after performing for her in a full length ballet.

I tried to be civil and chewed my lower lip listening to guests imitate cackling hens and crowing roosters. Overwhelmed by the poultry chorus, my fingers twisted my hair and I fidgeted. David grabbed my hand to make me hold still. He smiled and pointed to the next person, "Yes? What is your question?"

"Miss Rothman? Is your Russian dance partner your boy-friend? I mean I see you with this man tonight but, there's marriage rumors circulating by the press regarding you and Mr. Konstantinov."

David squeezed my hand and looked curious.

"The rumors are false," I said straight away. "Whatever you've heard or read is not true."

The next question, came from a man at the back of the room. He yelled, "Miss Rothman, does your carpet match the drapes?"

A hush silenced the room.

"What did you say?" yelled David.

"I asked the fair maiden, 'Are you a natural blonde or a bot-tle blonde?'"

"Don't answer him, Sarah." David brushed his lips against my neck. "We're done." His arm pulled me flush against his body. *I closed my eyes and savored his citrus and musk scent. He smelled sexy.*

His arm moved and his hand gripped my forearm pulling me forward. No more sexy smells as he forged ahead and parted the crowd. I guessed his intention was to push his way through the next two next rooms and head for the elevators. But, we didn't get far.

Bob Strauss the firm's third senior partner, stopped us. His wife Myra trilled like a magpie, "Aren't you Sarah Rothman? The girl dancing with the Russian defector?"

"What?" I stood dazed.

"I studied ballet and I can't wait to see you dance. I should host a luncheon in your honor. Please say yes?"

I stared at David for help.

"Thank you, Mrs. Strauss but Sarah is busy rehearsing."

"You know, honey," said Myrna. "You look younger in person than in the newspaper. Oh Lord, you're the seventeen-year-old. The baby ballerina!"

Hearing her shriek, I sidled behind David's shoulder. He whispered, "Age is only a number. Deal with it."

I took a beat then stepped a little forward. "Thank you, Mrs. Strauss." I smiled, "Yes, a luncheon would be nice, maybe on a Sunday? Arrange it with David."

"Wonderful but call me Myrna. We're birds of a feather, Odette and Odile." She laughed at her quip.

David kissed my cheek and winked.

Bob cleared his throat. "I'm afraid I stole Myrna away from any career. It was love at first sight. We met in college and one month later, we were engaged."

"Must have worked," smiled David. "You two look happy."

"Forty years we're married. Don't listen to your head when it comes to love. Business, yes. Romance, never." He winked at his wife. "My advice, David. When you find the girl of your dreams? Marry her."

"I'll keep that in mind, sir."

He pointed to David's hand holding mine. "Don't let go. It's a bumpy ride but worth it. Good night, kids."

David and I hurried to the elevators where he spotted Bernie Lieberman and waved. While waiting, David whispered, "Did you see Bernie's face when the crowd gathered around you?"

"'Je m'en fous,' dit Pierre."

"What?"

"'I don't care,' said Pierre."

DRIVING BACK TO Brooklyn, David said, "Sorry about my boss.

The man's a nightmare."

"He didn't like me."

"No, he liked you alright. Treated you like an errant child. I'll fix that."

"Nah, forget it. Not worth it."

"Sarah, you were my date. He needed to respect you, no matter your age."

"But I ..."

"You're with me. End of conversation."

I yawned, "I guess you know best" and relaxed into the seat. Closing my eyes, I welcomed the arms of Morpheus.

Later, I heard David's voice. "Wake up, sleepyhead. We're here."

"Did I nod off?"

"Let's say, all the way home. Forty-five minutes." David extended his hands and helped me out of the car. He planted a quick kiss on my lips and took my hand.

"Sarah, I should take you to the beach."

Tasting his kiss, I perked up, "What beach? Why?"

Dad opened the front door. "Home at eleven, good. Did you have a nice time?"

I glanced up at David, "Yeah, I think so."

"Ben, tomorrow, I'm driving to the Hampton's to visit my aunt and uncle at their beach house. I'd like to take Sarah with me if, it's okay? We'd stay overnight and come back late Tuesday night. Sarah would have her own room upstairs, next to my aunt and uncle."

"If she's spending the night?" said my dad. "I'd need to check with your aunt first."

"It's too late now, but, we could call her in the morning when I pick up Sarah."

"As long as I can talk to her first."

Dad turned to me. "What do you think? I'm working. Mama and your aunts are off to Grossinger's in the morning at six. You'd be home alone."

"I don't ..." I looked up at David. "I don't have a bathing suit."

"We could buy one," he said. "There's shops and boutiques in Southampton Village."

Dad nodded. "Okay, bathing suit solved. What's it to be?"

I yawned, "Sounds nice but, David, I warn you."

His eyes widened, "What?"

"I take naps. I'm exhausted."

"You can sleep on my aunt's sun porch. Anything else?"

Dad and I looked at each other and smiled, "No."

"It's settled. See you at nine in the morning and Ben and I will call Eleanor."

"David? What was in the blue box you gave Mr. Loeb?"

"Cuff links."

"Why didn't he open it?"

David grinned. "He didn't have to."

"But, that was rude."

"Good night, Sarah ... Ben."

CHAPTER 23

Monday, September 20th. By the sea, by the sea.

I SLEPT SOUNDER than a possum playing dead until Jeff picked up Mama, Bubbe and my three aunts. Their noisy chatter woke me from a dream. I could hear them in the kitchen discussing their vacation. And worse, Dad told them of my date with David to go to Southampton to visit his aunt and uncle.

Each of their voices pitched higher and faster and they all talked at the same time. Most of it was positive, *thank my lucky stars*. Otherwise, I'd be miserable the rest of the day.

My dad raised his voice above the babble. "Ida Mae? Don't make a second pot of Folger's drip coffee. No time and no more discussing my daughter's date."

"Killjoy!" Ida Mae ran the water in the sink so loud, I heard it. *Guessed, she rinsed out the coffee pot to take more time to irritate Daddy.*

"Jeff? Where's Jeff?" Dad's boots sounded down the hall to the bathroom door. "Get downstairs and unlock the car."

Next Dad shouted so the neighbors could hear, "Hey, ladies? Time to go. Grab your things. I'm opening the front door."

JEFF DROVE THE whole gang upstate, to Liberty, New York, in the deli station wagon, to Grossinger's. A two hour trip to the famous hotel resort in the Catskill Mountains driving through the gorgeous, red, autumn trees.

According to Uncle Al, "Singers, comedians and musicians loved to play Grossingers, the jewel of the Borscht Belt."

"And that's where a lot of them got their start," said my dad.

"So, what's not to enjoy?" chuckled an excited Bubbe. "We dress up fancy each night for dinner and on weekends, we see shows. Imagine, Steve Lawrence and his adorable wife, Eydie Gorme singing on the stage. So charming, you wanna pinch their cheeks."

And because this yearly exodus followed Labor Day, the timing suited the ladies just right for a month-long stay. The hotel rates dropped to their lowest price after the summer rush making the weather in the mountains affordable.

"Almost wholesale," said Aunt Ida Mae.

And to sweeten the deal, Uncle Al finagled an additional twenty percent off the room rate from his lunchtime CPA customer. This made the whole vacation kosher in Al's mind. His customer's "lean pastrami on rye, hold the mayo, use horseradish instead," knew a friend of the owner's first cousin. This friend did the billing for the lodging, meals, ballroom dancing and entertainment but not the beauty salon. "Hair appointments cost extra."

"And so on and so on, oye!" said Uncle Al scratching his head.

But not to worry. My aunts being card sharks would win cash prizes and free spa visits to cover shampoos and acrylic nails.

My uncle talked a salesman's lingo, "What can I say? I know business, I can afford to be generous" but when Grossinger's demanded payment at check-out? Aunt Lucy paid the bill with her new American Express Card.

As Bubbe said later, "So much for a big mouth. Talk is cheap."

DAVID SHOWED UP around nine and just like he and dad agreed to last night, they called David's Aunt Eleanor. Satisfied that his little girl would be in good hands, Dad approved my trip to the beach.

Within minutes, we were in the car, driving towards the Long Island Expressway.

Two and a half hours later, in the quaint and charming Southampton Village, we stopped at the Surf and Turf Boutique on Jobs Lane.

David held-up a one-piece navy-blue swim suit with a sailor collar and a pleated white skirt. "How's this?"

"I don't think so," I grimaced. "I want something like my girlfriends. They wear bikinis."

"Are these the girls in the French Club?"

"Yes, why?"

"French women go topless on the Riviera."

"You're teasing me," I blushed recalling the string bikini I wore in the photo shoot.

"No, a fact according to Brigitte Bardot in the Paris Match."

David eyed the street from the shop window while I thumbed through racks of bathing suits. Finding something I'd wear, turned into a scavenger hunt until … "Oh, jeepers," I swooned. "This color is amazing. It's the same as the …"

"The what?" David asked as he watched a fender bender through the window.

"Never mind. Don't know what you call it."

I hurried to the dressing room before David could see the suit and tried it on. Inside the tiny cubicle, I could hear him pacing on a squeaky wooden floor outside the door.

"Sarah, how long is this going to take? Are you coming out

to show me the suit?"

"No," I raised my voice, looking at myself in the mirror. "It fits fine."

Yep, it's good. Boobs and a butt like the movie stars in "The Girls on the Beach." I loved the color.

"I'll pay," said David waiting outside the dressing room door.

"No, you won't."

Truth was, Daddy gave me cash but I said instead, "I'm a working girl, I have money."

"You worked two weeks," he chuckled. "You can't spend your money like a drunken sailor. What do I do with you?"

How do I answer that and behave myself?

NOT TOO HOT, a sea breeze and sunshine, Eleanor and Harry greeted David and I with warm hugs. Their two story house, straight out of the pages of "House Beautiful" was white clapboard, blue trim, very Cape Cod and as inviting as they were.

Their beach house, huge by most anyone's standards, was probably the smallest in square feet, in the playground of the rich and famous. Southampton ranked, the wealthiest area in Long Island.

"Eleanor, I smell licorice and peaches. Is that you?"

"Quadrille Perfume by Balenciaga? Do you like it?"

"I usually hate licorice but you smell wonderful. Yes, I like it."

Eleanor hugged David. "You rascal. You know how much I love the ballet. And, you bring me Sarah Rothman? Why didn't you tell me? I would have planned a party, a dinner."

"That's why I didn't tell you. She needs to rest."

His aunt moved closer. "I'm on the board of directors for the CCBT and a patron of your company."

"A patron?" I mumbled. "David never mentioned ..."

Eleanor took my hands, "And you pretty girl are Yuri Konstantinov's new partner."

"Yep," I winced. "I'm the girl. Full of bruises and aches and pains to prove it."

David shot me a startled look. "You never mentioned you hurt?"

I wiggled my shoulders and twisted my neck, "Still do."

"David can help with a massage," said Uncle Harry gesturing for me to sit on the couch.

I sank into a cushioned, rattan couch and smiled at David. "Could you?"

"I can."

"But Sarah?" said Eleanor. "I should warn you."

"Huh?"

"No, don't," said David. He threw a red, hibiscus pillow to another couch and sat next to me.

"Yes," said his aunt. "For the record, David," she glanced from him to me, "loves to keep secrets."

"But not today," he looked smug. "I brought her."

"Yes, we see secret Sarah," said Harry pushing David aside and sitting next to me.

"David?" said Eleanor. "Take Sarah's suitcase upstairs to her room, last door on the right."

"That's her room?"

"Yes. And put your things in one of the two small bedrooms downstairs, off the kitchen."

"Would you rather I slept in Vermont or Rhode Island?"

"Oh, hush up. We bought a new bed from B. Altman's. We

want her comfortable in the pink room."

Harry patted David's shoulder. "You get a twin bed in the maid's room with the parrot, 'Ole Blue.' That damn bird spits sunflower seeds. Or, sleep in the other room with the smoke alarm that chirps like mating finches."

"Why can't I stay upstairs in one of the five bedrooms?"

"Because you can't. Now please take Sarah's bag to her room."

David left.

"Young lady," said Harry gazing out the glass wall of windows. "How's the view of the Atlantic Ocean?"

"Oh, wow, breathtaking. I sighed, "You must love the summers here, Harry."

"And the fall and winters until the weather turns cold." Harry sounded wistful. "Four feet of snow drifts in paradise, can be alarming in gale force winds."

David joined us from upstairs.

"Well, son," said Uncle Harry. "The chess board's ready. Shall we play?"

"After I stash my bag and say hello to Ole Blue."

"I'll get the drinks," said his aunt.

David joined Harry at the chess table and Eleanor served lemonade and sat by me. "Sarah, tell me everything about the Russian. All the juicy gossip."

"Gossip?" I laughed. "I don't know any." *Mrs. Pace would fire me if I gossiped.* I needed to change the subject. I jumped up and circled the coffee table. "David? Let's sunbathe or walk on the beach? Anybody mind?"

"No, feel free," said Eleanor. She looked baffled as I flitted like a butterfly.

I ran upstairs and found the beautiful pink room with my bag on a chair. I changed out of my seafoam green sundress and returned to the living room. I posed standing barefoot, wearing my new blue bikini and my hair combed long and loose.

David glanced up and dropped his jaw.

His Uncle Harry chuckled, "Well, the girl means business! Take her some place and show her off."

"I have the perfect place," smiled Eleanor. "Take her to Congressman Ernie's. He's having a barbeque."

David frowned, "I don't think it's appropriate."

Harry grinned, "Sure it is. You two go play. The chess game can wait."

"Please," I giggled at David. "Let's go."

"Okay, but, put on shorts and a blouse over that swim suit and wear shoes."

Eleanor added, "I'll give her Coppertone and a sun hat."

"No, no Coppertone, Eleanor."

"Why?"

"Dancers can't get sun-burned or sun-tanned if we're dancing on stage. Body make-up can't hide strap marks and tan lines. And body make-up rubs off on costumes."

"Then Sarah," said David walking towards me. "You should do as the French. Sunbathe totally nude or go covered from head to toe." He bent down and kissed my lips.

"Which would you prefer?" I giggled.

Eleanor snapped, "Don't answer that. I'll get her a terrycloth robe."

"A naked woman," pronounced Harry. "Is beauty. Take the late Marilyn Monroe. When asked, 'What do you wear to bed, Miss Monroe? She answered ... Chanel No. 5.'"

Eleanor scolded, "Harry! You're embarrassing, Sarah."

"No, I'm not. She's laughing and David's making a mental note to buy Chanel No. 5 at Macy's."

WE PASSED SEVERAL sprawling mansions as David drove the Montauk Highway and turned somewhere off Dune Road. The mansions left me speechless. Some resembled French Chateaus and others, Italian villas from postcards.

When I finally spoke, I said, "I never knew people lived like this. Imagine cleaning all those bathrooms and buying five hundred rolls of toilet paper at the A&P." I scratched my head. "Not my idea of comfort."

David pointed out the congressman's Southampton mansion as it came into view. A rambling, fifty-two room estate overrun with gardens. David turned onto a private tree-lined drive. "Besides twenty bathrooms," he snickered. "Ernie has an indoor movie theatre, an over-stocked wine cellar and a bowling alley."

"I don't bowl but I love the gardens. The roses are beautiful and there's yellow roses, my favorite. Wow, two white gazebos, how pretty."

David pointed just beyond, "And three guest cottages."

"I could live in one of those cottages."

David smirked, "Only if the maids cleaned the bathrooms."

"That's right."

Around the side entrance, David parked near a large swimming pool displaying a blue grotto. Inside the pool were mermaids spouting fountains and a winding, s-shaped water slide.

Bikinis, diamonds and luminous sun-tans seemed everywhere except for me, the whitest person outside of Stockholm. I'd definitely tell Bubbe and Aunt Sophia this mansion was the perfect setting for a soap opera.

The aroma of steaks and ribs sizzling on barbeques filled the air. Guests in sun suits or Caribbean casual beige or white linen, sat on the lawn at lace covered tables. They ate and drank among the tabletop covered with vases of orchids.

We entered the mansion through the front doors and felt the floor vibrate under our shoes. The music came from inside, a large ballroom where a ten piece, live, rock band played amplified music. The chandeliers shook and the windows rattled but some guests danced and loved it. We looked at each and laughed and retraced our footsteps.

Back outside, in the blue grotto, we chatted with nearby guests and found a small table. We sat and watched the swimmers in the pool.

A waiter approached. "Sir, madam? Drinks? And, can I get you plates of ribs or steak?"

"Sarah?"

"No, steak, thank you but, I'll have a lemonade and a dish of ice cream."

"Ma'am? Chocolate, vanilla or pistachio."

I smacked my lips. "All three," I giggled and watched another couple join us at our table.

The waiter referred to David. "And you, sir?"

"A steak, medium-rare, baked potato; hold the sour cream and chives on the side, corn on the cob and a lemonade."

I sat forward, "Waiter? Where's the restroom?"

He pointed to poolside.

"Excuse me," I smiled at the couple now seated and ran off towards the restrooms.

A few minutes later, I returned. "David, I have to pee. The bathrooms are full of people changing into bathing suits."

"Hang on."

"I can't wait." I stripped to my bikini throwing off the blouse, shorts and shoes.

"Well, don't do it here," he laughed and pointed to the stairs at the side of the house. "Second floor, there's bathrooms in the bedrooms."

I ran.

He yelled, "If you're not back in ten minutes, I'm sending the sheriff."

ON THE SECOND floor, the mansion was a labyrinth of corridors and funny open spaces filled with modern art. At the first bedroom suite, I found a private, small bathroom.

When I came out of the toilet, a dark-haired man, maybe mid-thirties, stumbled around the bedroom acting drunk. He was clean-shaven and dressed in a starched white, button-down shirt and slacks.

"Oh, hi." I tried to act nonchalant.

"This is … mm, my room." He slurred his speech.

"Sorry," I giggled a little too high-pitched. "I just used your bathroom. Hope you don't mind."

He stared at me, bleary-eyed.

I moved to get past him but he grabbed my arm pushing me up against the wall.

"What the …?" I said in alarm.

"Sex-y in yur, yuuur blue bi-kini." His other hand went for my breast and he moved his legs up against mine.

"Get your hands off me," I screeched and slapped him. But he moved fast using both hands and gripped my forearms even tighter. He pushed his face against my neck.

"Let go!" I struggled to break free.

He laughed, "I got you pret-ty, sex-y girl." His mouth came down hard on mine.

I turned my head and spit. "Let me go or I'll scream."

"No, you won't. I'll hurt you if you scream."

"Try me. I'm seventeen. Underage. Jailbait!"

"Prick teaser ... bitch!" His hands shoved me hard against the wall.

I fell off balance and yelled, "Seventeen," and kicked him in the shins.

He yelped, "Fuck!" and released my arms and pushed me aside. He opened the door. "Get out."

I rushed out and bumped into David carrying my tote bag over his shoulder. He stepped back. "What's going on?"

The stranger pushed past me, stopped and extended his hand to David. "I'm Leo Des-siglia. Howdy-doody part-ner." He slicked back his greasy hair with his other hand.

David didn't shake hands. "Sarah, who is this?"

"I don't know," I shrugged never making eye contact with him. "I used his bathroom and when I came out, he was standing in the bedroom." I glanced over my shoulder, "Thanks for the bathroom, Leo."

The man nodded and walked down the hall and disappeared around the corner.

David touched my cheek. "Are you okay?"

"Yeah, sure. Just a drunk guy. I get them all the time on the subway."

"Did he try anything?"

"Nah," I shook my head and smiled as I lied. "I'm fine." David handed me my tote bag.

You think I'd tell David the man attacked me? It's not something we girls talk about or tell. Just like my brothers, he'd beat the guy up, lock me in my room and blame me later.

"Sarah, cover up. Put on your blouse and shorts."

"Right."

"And sandals." He smiled watching me dress. He took my

hand and we turned the corner and ambled along a corridor. We stopped and looked at several paintings of modern art hanging on walls. From an adjoining corridor, an older man dressed in a dark blue suit walked up to us.

"Excuse me, I'm Aaron Newman, Chief Counsel for the owner of this house and you are?"

"Why? Is there a problem, Mr. Newman?"

"Only if the young lady is underage at an adult party serving alcohol."

David reached for his wallet and handed Mr. Newman his business card.

Mr. Newman smiled. "And the young lady is?"

"Her name isn't important. Several witnesses at poolside saw her drink lemonade and eat ice cream." David caught my eye and squeezed my hand. "We're leaving."

"Mr. Katz, allow me to show you a prudent way to exit the premises. There's a particular guest I'd like you to avoid."

"Why?" asked David.

"He accused the lady of soliciting."

"Excuse me," David almost growled.

The hair on my arms stood up. "That man attacked me!"

"Attacked you?" David's jaw clenched. His eyes narrowed in fear.

Mr. Newman raised his hand. "Mr. Katz. This man is a houseguest. He made the formal complaint and has powerful associates that could make life unpleasant."

David's chin pushed forward. He squeezed my hand tighter and glared at Mr. Newman.

The Chief Counsel turned and took a step. "We need to leave now."

David and I followed Congressman Ernie's attorney to the maid's quarters and down the servant's hidden staircase. We escaped the prying eyes of the barbeque staff, swimmers, sunbathers and Leo Dessiglia and his powerful associates.

Once in the Bentley, David started the engine and drove zero to eighty in less than a sixty seconds.

"Slow down," I hit his arm and hugged my knees.

But he didn't slow down. Not until he drove the entire Southampton Village to the end of Main Street where he pulled over. He parked in a secluded area. Cutting the engine, he banged the steering wheel with his fist.

"We shouldn't have gone to that house, God damn it."

I froze. Then my lips moved. "Your aunt suggested …"

He interrupted, smacked the wheel and yelled, "My aunt believes Congressman Ernie helps people. She buys the bullshit. The truth is, he snorts cocaine and his friends are celebrities and mobsters that do bad things. Shit!" He exhaled and ran his hands threw his hair. "It's all my fault."

"No, it's not. Thank you for not telling my name."

"For fuck's sake, I gave him my card."

"Why did he complain? I've been to weddings where adults drink alcohol, so what?"

David glared at me. "What did you say? He attacked you?"

"No, what I meant." Heat rose up from my chest and my cheeks burned.

"You're lying, Sarah."

"Please, don't get mad."

He snapped, "Don't get mad! Criminals lie to me every single, fucking day. You can't!"

I trembled a whisper, "I'm sorry."

He ran his hands through his hair again and blew out a deep breath. "If anyone hurts you or touches you? I, I, ah …" He looked away.

I moved closer to the door.

He turned and stared at my eyes. "Don't you ever ... lie to me again? Do you understand?" His lips narrowed to a thin line.

I nodded and dug my nails into my palms.

"What did he do to you?"

"Nothing."

"What did I say about lying? Not nothing! The man was pissed off enough to make a formal complaint on two counts."

My lips trembled. I couldn't look at him.

"Start when you first saw the man. What happened?"

I told David everything. He listened with a cool head. When I finished, I waited for a reaction. None came. He stared at the sea and focused on a seagull picking up something from the beach.

"Was it my fault?" I mumbled.

"You were in the wrong place at the wrong time." He reached for me and pulled me in tight. "There's bastards everywhere," he murmured. "They want sex and don't care how they get it."

I pulled away. "Aren't men supposed to be gentle and kind? I know from seeing Rock Hudson and Doris Day movies."

His eyes squinted. "You know better. Movies are make believe."

"But my parents are gentle and loving."

"What do you mean?" He locked my eyes. "That can't be real."

I trembled at his intense stare.

He caressed my face. "What do I do with my naïve and sweet girl?"

"Hey, don't make fun of me," I hissed. "I know ballet and family. That's it. I'm not sophisticated like you!"

His eyes saddened. "Sarah, don't do this."

"I never went to a prom. Never went to parties. A few movies, three Yankee games. Dad taught me sex. He said, 'Don't let boys touch you. If you come home pregnant, I'll kill you.' That was my sex education."

"Sarah," he lifted my chin. "It's okay."

"No, it's not okay!" I shrieked. "The man called me a prick teaser. I don't know what that means. My first date was last night. With you."

David whispered, "Come here, I want to hold you."

"No, don't touch me." I sat up and gripped the passenger door feeling stupid, out of my league and screaming mad. I watched the sea gulls fight over things on the sand.

"Sarah, do you want to go home? Back to Brooklyn?"

I opened the car door, "Maybe," and stepped out of the car. I kicked off my sandals and walked to the water's edge.

David followed, kicked off his loafers and ran in the water ahead of me. The ebb and flow of waves pulled at our ankles. Our feet sank in the wet sand as the water receded. I shut my eyes.

"Sarah, say something," David urged. He touched my shoulders then dropped his hands. "Is it back to Brooklyn?"

I wondered what to do? The waves washed over our feet.

"I don't want to." His tone softened to a plea. "Sarah, I can't leave you alone and upset in your apartment. It would kill me." He moved closer.

His words "kill me" sent my mind back to the crime. I turned away so he couldn't see my tears. *Karl's glassy eyes stared into space. The blood. The letters. The stupid cat. How do I get rid of the images?* I started to tremble. *How would I explain the last twenty-four hours to my dad? To the police? To David?* I wanted a nice day at the beach with David. My heartbeat pounded what to do, what to do.

David's hands turned my face around. "Please, don't ask me to drive you home. I'll work at more tolerant."

I laid my head on his chest. "There's so much going on."

"Talk to me."

"I can't," I whimpered. "Not yet and I'm worn-out." I cuddled in closer. "Could I take a nap at your aunt's house?"

His strong arms wrapped me in a safety net. His heartbeat matched the throb of my rhythm. No need for Brooklyn.

CHAPTER 24

Later that Monday afternoon at the beach house. Cozy and warm.

IN THE ENCLOSED porch, I slept on a daybed covered in nautical sailboats on a patchwork-quilt. David laid beside me making notes on legal briefs. His Uncle Harry read the Times in an easy chair while Eleanor, whom David dubbed "Nervous Nellie," circled the wagons and hovered over me like a crow on a carcass.

When David left to get more files, Harry took his wife aside and whispered. "David and Sarah will do whatever. We can't stop the laws of attraction and hormones. They care for each other."

Harry and Eleanor didn't know I heard them discuss David and me. They thought I'd fallen asleep. My eyes were closed but my ears were wide open.

Eleanor answered, "But, I promised her father …"

"Honey, these two can blow up a chemistry lab there's so much combustion. Go bake cookies."

"Cookies at a time like this?" She whined.

"Or, study Quantum Physics if you'd prefer. Make a choice."

"Right. Chocolate chip cookies."

"Wise decision."

I heard a kissing noise and then it got quiet. Combustion? What does that mean? Never mind, David returned and laid down next to me.

A couple hours later, David shook my arm. "Hey," he smiled standing alongside. "Does your body still hurt?"

I stretched my legs. "Yes, I ache. Yep, all over."

"Take off your blouse and bikini bra and lay on your stomach."

I hitched, "What?"

"Yes, take the tops off." His eyes narrowed.

"Psst, you mean undress in front of your uncle?"

"Why not?"

"I heard that," chuckled Harry. "I'm six feet away."

"Sarah, he's a doctor at Mount Sinai."

Harry glanced over at me. "Mammary glands? Nothing new. I've seen hundreds in my practice."

I flinched.

"He's a cardiologist. He's seen a few."

I stuck my tongue out at Harry behind his back.

David held out his hand, "Clothes off."

I undressed.

Eleanor appeared in the doorway. "Oh, my Lord. Good night!" She choked in surprise seeing my breasts.

I plopped down on the daybed and snuggled on the quilt.

"It's okay, honey," assured Harry. "It's a massage."

"A massage?" she crossed her arms.

"Eleanor, what do you want?" coaxed Harry with a grin. "We're all ears."

"Obviously more than ears but I came to say, I made dinner reservations for the four of us at the club, seven o'clock."

I lifted my head and smiled at her.

"We should take two cars so the kids can stay longer and swim. No danger of sunburn under the stars for our Sarah."

David touched my arm. "Okay?"

"Yes, sounds great. What should I wear? Eleanor?"

Nervous Nellie frowned. "I think a dress is more appropriate than what you're not wearing now." She harrumphed and went back to the kitchen.

David brushed his hand against my cheek. "Why did you make a face when Eleanor told us about dinner?"

"It was nothing."

"You say that but every now and again, your eyes cloud over and show fear."

"Sorry," I tossed my hair and laid my face on the daybed.

He was right. I had sudden visions of the ransacked apartment. A dead body. And blood splatters on the wall and furniture.

David whispered, "Talk to me I don't bite. Well, at least not yet."

"You bite?"

"Yes, and you'll like it," he chuckled straddling my back and sinking his frame onto his knees and ankles. He moved my long hair further to the side.

"You're teasing."

"No, I'm serious."

I exhaled, "Too much."

Harry got out of his chair, walked over to a tall armoire and opened a drawer. He handed David a small, purple glass bottle. "Use this. It has healing properties. The queen of England swears by holistic medicine."

"We'll try it."

David unscrewed the black cap and sprinkled a few drops down my spine.

"Ah-ha," I squealed at the coolness of the drops. David gently massaged the lavender scent into my skin. The pads of his fingers sank deep.

I squirmed and said, "Harder, David, yes, better … a little

more to the right ... go along the shoulder blades, massage lower yes, ah, near the cocci's."

David slapped my butt. "Shut up, Sarah."

"Ouch!" I jerked my head up.

"I studied Qigong and Tuina in China."

"China? No way," I sassed.

"Yes, I did and I learned acupressure without needles. Japanese call it Shiatsu." He touched my shoulder. "Put your head down."

Harry chuckled. "You'd better behave, Sarah. David means business. He mastered Qigong in Hong Kong and Shanghai."

I pouted and laid my head on the daybed. When I peered out of the corner of my eye, I caught the top half of David in a long, oval, wall mirror. He was rubbing his hands together, his eyes were closed. (He later told me the hand rubbing created heat and energy.)

So when his eyes opened, he instructed, "Take one, slow, deep breath to the count of eight. Hold it, four counts ... exhale for eight counts."

I did.

"Now repeat the breath and count again and again."

I did and a calmness streamed through me.

"Use your mind's eye and relax every part of your anatomy. Start at the top of your head ... move slowly downward ... through the seven chakras, into your toes. Let your body go limp ... light as a feather ... float on air."

I sighed on the exhale and traveled to a lovely place.

The next touches of David's long fingers and strong palms took on its own sensuous energy. A sorcerer, he rubbed and kneaded deep into muscles and aggravated nerves. He used light touches to pressure pushes. His healing energy slowed my heartrate.

He changed his straddled position and turned to face the other direction. His hands massaged my feet and toes. The sensations so amazing, my mind swooned, *I'm yours body and soul*.

Stroking the soft pads of my feet then moving to my ankles, my hips squirmed in delight.

David shifted his straddled position and groaned.

"What?" I murmured.

"Don't ask," he laughed and his uncle laughed.

David judiciously climbed off me and the daybed and disappeared from the porch.

Uncle Harry handed me my bikini top and blouse and he left.

FOLLOWING DINNER THAT night, at the Southampton Bath and Tennis Club, David and I swam in the club's Olympic size, outdoor pool. Under a full moon and starry sky, we played water volleyball and raced each other swimming laps. When David beat me, I sulked and bitched. We raced again and I won. A third race, I won.

"Enough, Sarah," he sounded amazed reaching his arm around my shoulder. "You're a fighter. I like that."

"So, you aren't?"

He didn't answer.

"Right. You let me win."

"I did ... why not?"

We climbed out of the pool and grabbed guest towels to dry off and take a break. David reached for my shoulders.

"Sarah?" He looked concerned. "What's the matter? You're making that face again. Talk to me."

"David, stop." I pulled free from his shoulder hold, my hands trembled. *I was chasing that damn cat, hoping no one saw me or, could describe me to the police or, recognize my voice on the NYPD phone recording as the anonymous caller reporting a murder.*

Suddenly, a stranger interrupted the moment. "David Katz! Hello, man," said a voice at David's side.

"Well, hi Marv," responded David shaking the man's hand.

"Marv, this is Sarah … Sarah, this guy's an old college friend."

"Hi, lovely lady. Can I steal him away and we'll bring back drinks from the bar?"

I smiled at the two of them, "Sure."

David grinned, "What are you drinking?"

"My usual."

He walked away laughing. "I should know."

I sat in a lounge chair and watched his six foot, one inch muscular frame walk away. Wearing an abbreviated red swim suit from his former swim meet days, not much was left to the imagination. His body could be chiseled in stone including the dimples above his butt.

I people-watched then stared at the stars in the night sky. Some fifteen minutes later, I spotted David at the far end of the pool and he started to move towards me. He took confident strides, comfortable in his own skin. His eyes focused on my lounging self the entire length of the pool. My breath caught. The man oozed gorgeous. *I wanted to touch and feel every inch of him.*

He grinned holding two drinks. "Cutty Sark neat for me and for the lady, a tall, frosty glass with an umbrella." He leaned down and planted a lip kiss. "Sorry," he murmured. "They were all out of your usual, Dom Perignon."

I laughed, "It could happen," and reached for the raspberry

lemonade. "Where's your friend?"

"He met a woman at the bar."

"Good, I have you all to myself."

"Be careful what you wish for."

My heart did a somersault watching his perfect lips and the deep clef in his chin. *I melted wondering how his mouth and lips would feel in certain places.*

Using the club's Men's and Women's facilities, we showered and changed into our evening clothes.

On the beach, we danced to a live band on the water's edge and strolled barefoot in the sand. Stopping to watch a lighthouse signal, David kissed me under the full moon, in a slow, lingering taste. Couldn't be more romantic for my first, real kiss. Giddy and feeling the rush, I kissed him back.

Oh, gosh. He brushed his lips across my face and planted tiny kisses along my neck. Nipping at my earlobe, he sent chills down my spine. The clench in my stomach scared me.

"It's been a long day," he murmured. "Better get you back to the house and into bed."

"Bed?" I swallowed.

"Yes, your bed but I'd rather have you in mine."

"Ah, ah, wait," I stammered. "Just like that."

His teeth tugged gently on my upper lip. "Ever since I met you at the zoo, I've had have to fight real hard to stay away from you." He laughed a throaty response. "My aunt would kill me."

I slapped his shoulder. "We girls stick together."

"Don't hold out too long. I won't make it."

My cheeks flushed the color of my rose-colored dress.

Sensing my embarrassment, David tightened his arms around me and kissed my head and neck. He murmured, "I could love you."

"No ..."

"Yes," his hands moved to my face. His lips parted my mouth allowing his tongue to slowly caress my tongue and mouth. Our throaty kiss deepened and we both trembled into each other's bodies. A heat started to build as we continued to kiss until David stopped the hotness.

He stepped away and rubbed the back of his neck stretching his face to the sky, "Right." He shook his head. "We can't do this, I want to keep on kissing you and not stop until the sun comes up. Not good, baby ... definitely, no good."

We returned to each other's arms and I listened to his heartbeat in rhythm with mine. The waves pounded the surf against our breathing as it slowed.

I buried my face in David's chest inhaling his skin of musk and citrus. I loved his scent and when the aroma passed through me, I went weak at the knees. The other man in my life had an invigorating scent. *Yuri's face appeared in my mind saying goodbye at his door.* I needed to get back to him and rehearse.

"David? Can we leave early tomorrow morning?"

His eyes flashed. "Something I said? Did I scare you?"

"No, you said to talk to you so here goes."

He tilted his head and smiled.

"I had a terrible fight with Yuri Saturday night and I told him I quit dancing."

"You quit your career? Why didn't you tell me?"

"Wait ... no, I, I didn't quit. I was in pain and exhausted and feeling sorry for myself."

"Okay, so what? Is it cool?"

"Yes, we talked and we're good."

David caressed my cheek and took my hand. "What time do you want to leave in the morning?"

"Eight, eight-thirty."

"We'll stop in Brooklyn to get your things then drive into

Manhattan."

"When I get home, I'll just take the subway."

"Sarah, I live in Manhattan."

"You do? I thought you lived in Flatbush."

"I stay with a friend."

I marveled, "I don't know you at all."

"Soon," his eyes shone bright. "We'll know each other well." He kissed the inside of my palm and brushed his lips against my fingers. "I'll learn every intimate detail. Better than you know yourself," he winked. "And you'll know a man."

"You scare me."

"No, I don't. You're a risk taker and you thrive on challenge." He kissed the inside of my other palm. "We're the same."

I locked his eyes and saw the same glint he shared the night of Loeb's birthday party.

He held tight to my hand. "C'mon, I hate to say it but, we need to leave."

"Maybe one more kiss?"

"Tease me and you'll never get home."

CHAPTER 25

Tuesday, September 21ˢᵗ. Time to say goodbye.

$\mathcal{E}$LEANOR KNOCKED ON the guest bedroom door where I slept. She popped her head in and called out, "Rise and shine, dear girl. It's seven o'clock."

I yawned, "Good morning."

She entered the many shades of the pink frou-frou room and smiled. David followed on her heels, freshly showered in a light blue Ivy League shirt and tan slacks. His dark towel-dried curls missed the comb and he looked adorable.

His eyes took a sweep of the flower fantasy room in rosy pink hues then rested his gaze on my face. "I see," he laughed referring to the floral nursery gone wild. "My aunt put you *Through the Looking Glass* and sent you down the rabbit hole."

"I slept like a princess," I giggled and batted my lashes. "Everything is pretty and colorful."

"Sarah has good taste," smiled Eleanor. "We girls stick together."

"I know," he chuckled. "She said those same words regarding you last night."

"And what was that?" Eleanor threw a look.

I blushed and shook my head.

"Hopefully not on everything." He winked and stole a kiss on my mouth. "Hurry, Sarah, we leave at eight. Do you need help in the shower?"

"No, she doesn't need help in the shower," chided his aunt.

"Just asking? Always the gentlemen like you taught me, Aunt Eleanor."

"Who needs to behave himself?"

I hid behind the blankets in a flirt with David then stuck my head up in time to catch Eleanor push him out the door. I hopped in the shower and dressed quickly.

When I joined everyone downstairs at the kitchen table, they had finished breakfast. I sat down to orange juice and a cheese omelet laid out before me on a lovely placemat. Harry sipped his second cup of coffee. He stopped drinking and peered over the top of his folded New York Times. "Sarah, did you know Karl Kreisler?"

"What a shame, Karl Kreisler, may he rest in peace," said Eleanor putting dishes in the dishwasher. "This isn't a topic for breakfast, dear heart."

"But, did you know him, Sarah?"

I froze in my chair staring at David.

"It's a simple question," he said. "Yes or no?"

I stammered, "No, I, I ah, never met him."

"Too bad, my dear, he was a talent," lamented Eleanor. "Such a beloved choreographer."

"Obviously, not that beloved," replied Harry in sarcasm. "The LAPD is treating his death as a homicide investigation. And not justifiable homicide … seems he died from multiply stab wounds to the back and upper chest."

"Who's covering it?" responded David grabbing the paper and reading the front page. "Sarah, look at this. He lived at the Osborne in a penthouse apartment. Remember, I pointed the building out to you? Across from Carnegie Hall?"

I took a forkful of eggs, "Yes, you did." *Holy crap, how do I get through this breakfast?*

"How timely. I've always wanted to go inside the Osborne and see what it's like. Maybe, I can get the detectives to get me in."

Eleanor patted my shoulder. "Are you okay, dear? You've lost all color in your face like you've seen a ghost."

I smiled, "Sure. I just need to eat."

David kissed my cheek, shoved his chair back and stood up. "I'll put our suitcases in the car. Enjoy your breakfast."

I nodded with a mouthful of food.

WHEN DAVID RETURNED and sat at the table, he leaned in and squeezed my thigh. The scent of his citrus aftershave made me tingle. *What is it? I'm an Alaskan Wolfhound with an acute sense of smell. Sniffing David takes on a whole new meaning to forgetting a not justifiable homicide.*

"Sorry, Aunt Eleanor, Harry," said David. "We're running out the door. Sarah needs to rehearse. Two days away from the new ballet makes her ..."

"Antsy and nervous," I swallowed the rest of my orange juice.

"Quite right," said Harry. "What's the driving plan, David?"

"Direct into Brooklyn and Manhattan but maybe, if we have time ..." He looked at me.

"What?"

"A quick stop to visit Vinnie and Carol Balducci in East Patchogue."

"I rehearse at three. You figure it out."

David caressed my cheek. "I was best man at their wedding and he mentioned they have news but he wouldn't tell me over the phone."

"Lunch at their restaurant?" asked Eleanor.

"No, we'll do it another time. Sarah, when you're ready?"

"Ready" and together, we rose from the table.

I kissed Eleanor's cheek. "Thank you, Eleanor for a lovely visit and thanks Harry ..."

Harry patted my shoulder. "Don't be a stranger."

Eleanor clucked, "Oh, Sarah? I just realized why I love your hydrangea patterned dress. You match my pots on the front porch."

"Your pots?"

David reached for my hand. "Lucky you. She can hang you in a picture frame on the wall in the blue room."

"Oh, stop," scolded Eleanor.

On the front porch, I noticed that I did match the lavender-blue hydrangeas. And for additional Brownie points, my dress wasn't backless, low-cut or mini-skirted and covered my chest to the throat. My baby blue sandals complimented her lawn swing which David quickly pointed out. At least, I matched the décor.

We waved goodbye and drove the Sunrise Highway.

YES, WE STOPPED and visited Vinnie and Carol Balducci at their restaurant in East Patchogue, Long Island. David explained who I was.

Vinnie shook my hand. "Ballet? I know zilch about ballet but I can name almost every make and model American car manu-factured in Detroit since 1910. Can you?"

"No." The lump in my throat made me cough.

His wife Carol knew. She squealed, hugged David and came at me with excited high-pitched chatting and opened arms.

Vinnie gave David a manly hug. "Stay, my friends. The food! Vatta voom!" His Italian gourmet fingers blew a kiss from his lips. He smacked his mouth, "Delisioso."

Carol elbowed Vinnie. "My Neapolitan husband's favorite gesture is blowing kisses among us Sicilians and speaking with his hands."

Vinnie's cousin, the waiter Anthony, flung a red and white checkered tablecloth across a large table. We watched and stood on floors covered in sawdust reminiscent of Henry's in the Village.

"Sorry, Vinnie, we ate breakfast a couple hours ago and we don't have time."

"C'mon, Daaa-vid, a little this, a little that." His hands circled the air and never stopped gesturing. "Steamed Little Neck Clams? Linguini? Broiled lobster? Look your girl is too thin. She needs meat on those bones."

I laughed and shook my head at Vinnie. "My dance partner would kill me if I gained weight and it's not even lunchtime."

Vinnie punched David's shoulder. "Hey, paesano. Eat! Mange! Make me happy for Christ's sakes."

"What can I say?" David aimed the question at me.

"Sarah," Vinnie pointed his finger. "You know my family is Mafia."

"What?"

Carol laughed. "Vinnie! Stop it. Don't scare the girl."

"Sit down, Sarah." He pulled out a chair. "Or, I'll have to kill you!" *No way could he have seen me in the penthouse?*

I cried, "Murder me?"

"Yes!" Vinnie rushed to stop me from fainting, "I meant noooo!"

David caught me in his arms.

Vinnie yelled, "Anthony, bring ice cubes."

David propped my head up and whispered, "Vinnie made a joke. He didn't mean it."

I exhaled a staccato breath and felt tears in my eyes watching

Vinnie wrap ice in a napkin. "Oh shoot, Vinnie didn't mean it did he? Sorry, I got dramatic."

David refused the ice from Vinnie. "Hey, she don't need it. Everything's cool. We're okay."

Carol waved her hands and danced in a circle. "The rabbit died. That's our news." She kissed her husband.

"What does that mean?" I wiped my eyes with David's hankie.

"A baby."

"A baaaby?" I cooed. "How wonderful! Congratulations!"

Vinnie made the sign of the cross, "Jesus, Mary and Joseph, a miracle. Salvatore? Anthony? We're starving in here!"

"Mazel tov, mom and dad," shouted David. "Anthony? Bring your best bottle of champagne!"

Anthony and his helpers brought the bottle, plates of antipasto, anchovy salad, warm breads and small dishes of olive oil. I kissed the expectant mothers cheeks. We laughed sharing her wonderful news.

David toasted Carol and Vinnie, "L'chaim v'l'vracha."

"Speak English!" roared Vinnie.

"To life and to the blessing, L'chaim." We clinked and drank.

Vinnie's turn. "To David. To the Godfather."

"What Godfather?"

"You, you bastard!" he roared.

"What? A Jewish Godfather to a Catholic kid? Are you serious?"

"Yes. Our child would be blessed. If something happened to us, you're the only one we considered."

David's eyes glistened. "I don't know what to say."

"Say, yes. A la famille," chuckled Vinnie.

"Okay, yes! A la famille. It's a mitzvah," toasted David. We clinked and drank.

Vinnie smacked his fist on the table. "It's settled."

And soon the feast appeared. Salvatore served the steamed Little Necks, broiled lobsters, Linguini with white Alfredo sauce and spaghetti with Marinara sauce. I couldn't inhale enough, the deliciousness; garlic, onions, rosemary, Italiano Basil and fresh oregano.

Vinnie raised his glass, "Salut! We eat! Buon Appetito."

"Buon Appetito," and we dug in. David fed me lobster dipped in warm butter tart with lemon.

"Well, Sarah? What do you think?" He furrowed his brows in concern.

I sighed, "It's wonderful. But, don't tell my family. I'll never hear the end."

"Why? Because lobster isn't kosher so what? How is it?"

I licked my lips, "Yummy, I want more."

BACK IN THE car and driving the Long Island Expressway, David confided, "I don't understand why it took Carol so long to get pregnant? They went at it like rabbits."

I giggled. "Rabbits?"

Yes, they fucked a lot. He's twenty-nine, she's twenty-seven. They'd been sleeping together since Carol was seventeen."

"Seventeen? She couldn't wait until eighteen?"

"No. They were in love."

"Because I'm seventeen and I can't have sex."

"Why not? If you love someone. Go for it."

"What do you mean? Mrs. Pace told Yuri not to touch me because I'm jailbait."

"Why would he touch you?" David turned and glared.

"No! He's not touching me," I blushed. "Mrs. Pace was making a point. I'm too young."

"Bullshit. You're not jailbait. And why did she have to make a point?"

"I guess because he sleeps with a lot of girls in the company."

"Well, stay away from him."

"He doesn't touch me that way, David. We only dance together."

"Right," he brooded.

"So, why am I not jailbait?"

David's jaw tightened. "According to New York State law, the legal age for consensual sex for a female is seventeen."

"Really?"

"But, if the female is under seventeen and the male is older than twenty-one then it is considered a crime of statutory rape."

"Mrs. Pace is wrong?"

"Very wrong. She probably lied to protect you from Yuri. Does he touch you in rehearsals?"

I looked down at my folded hands. "He kind of has to. I mean, we dance a duet together. Oh, gosh."

"What? Say it."

"This means I can have sex if I want to … maybe with you even, I can …"

"Make love, yes, however, both parties must be willing and of sound mind."

"Of sound mind? Are you teasing me?" I laughed a nervous twitter. "Who? You or me?"

"No, don't joke, Sarah." He reached over and squeezed my thigh through the dress.

"Ouch!"

"Listen to me."

"Okay, okay."

"The law has varying views if someone is disabled or incompetent. And some counties can differ in laws as well as states. Crossing a state line is tricky. In some instances, it is statutory rape."

"But, Mrs. Pace convinced my dad, I had to move in with her and he called your aunt?"

"He's being a protective dad and my aunt never left the nineteen fifties. She believes in fairies and Peter Pan. If I said 'sexual intercourse' in front of her, she'd faint."

I flopped my head over my knees and pretended to faint.

"Oh, really? I can't say sexual intercourse in front of you?"

I shook my head, "No."

"But I can say, I'd like to fuck you, Sarah."

"Oh, good night," I gasped. "That's not romantic."

"What?"

"Do girls actually jump into bed with you when you say that?"

David rubbed his fisted hand on his forehead then placed it back on the steering wheel.

I gave him a dirty look, then stared out the passenger window.

"Babe, do you have any idea what I'm thinking right now? The sexy things I could do to you?"

"Shut up, David."

"No? You don't want sexual favors?"

"You're rude."

"May I approach the bench and ask the court for a pardon and grant me immunity?"

I looked at him sideways. "You're a bad boy, counselor. I should spank you but you'd probably enjoy it."

David dropped his jaw. "You catch on fast. Admirable."

I shook my head, "Really."

He chuckled, "Madam Judge? I plead stupidity in the eyes of the law. Can I lay my head in your lap?"

"You are shameful."

"I throw myself on your mercy, Madam Judge."

"Not acceptable, counselor. You're full of crap."

"I know," he grinned. "But, is it working?"

"No. But, you can appeal."

"I will. I never stop. Not until I get what I want."

I watched the passing scenery.

ONCE IN BROOKLYN Heights, we stopped at Al's Deli to say a quick hello to Dad and after that, we drove two more blocks to my apartment. I packed my dance bag and threw clean clothes in two suitcases. Next stop, mid-town Manhattan.

Turning onto the FDR Drive, David said, "Sarah, I won't see you for a few days. I need to work overtime at the office to clear out my desk and fly to L.A. to finish details on a case."

I felt a lump in my throat. "Okay."

He smiled a slight upturn of his lip. "And, you'll be busy rehearsing, right?"

DAVID DOUBLE-PARKED NEAR the ballet school while I jumped out and grabbed my suitcases from the trunk. A cab driver shouted obscenities and the #104 bus driver honked repeatedly trying to pull away from the curb.

The Bentley drove away so the bus could move. My heart sank watching the car drive east on West 57th Street out of sight. It was hidden by the bus. No kiss goodbye, no nothing. I picked up my things and started for the door and stopped cold. No one was near or at the door. The whole front of the building looked deserted.

"Crap!" I bit my lip. "Should I even be here?" The murder ended the bet. *Did I have a job?* I'd been wrapped up with Prince Charming. I could face a firing squad, literally. *What if Mrs. Pace or Yuri chose another girl to dance the Red Rainbow?*

In a panic, I opened the school's front door, hurried to the bathroom and threw up in the toilet.

CHAPTER 26

Ten minutes later, September 21ˢᵗ, whatever ... if Doris Day sang, "Que sera, sera."

I BRUSHED MY teeth and walked to Mrs. Pace's empty office and stored my two suitcases under her desk. The clock read 2:30 p.m. I ran upstairs to the girl's dressing room and changed into leotards and soft toes shoes.

When I returned to the lobby, Yuri arrived with Alexi. "Sa-rah," he bellowed from across the room. He took long strides heading my way.

"Two days, Sa-rah, nyet danse." The look on his face meant he might yell.

"I missed you, Yuri," I teared up. "I missed dancing."

His high cheek bones, typical of the Tartars of Mongolia, relaxed into a gracious smile. His slanted, blue-grey eyes shone brighter than the sun's reflection from the windows up above.

"Da," he kissed my cheeks and hugged me tight.

"Well," pouted Alexi. "Did you miss me, Sarah?"

I chuckled, "Yes, a little but not enough to kiss you."

"Well, thanks for nothing."

Yuri pointed to a corner and moved us out of the way of the group of dancers now entering the lobby. "We talk," he whispered making us huddle like football players. "Po-lice vant you, vant me, vant Alexi, Jason ... vant Lu-ci-fer."

"They want the cat?" I gulped. "Why?" My voice trembled.

"Da," Yuri laughed. "Yuri make joke on Sa-rah, ha, ha. Cat nyet talk. Meow, meow, meow."

"Yep, that's funny but what are you talking about?"

"Police come ball-let." He pointed to the floor. "Here. Ici."

Several dancers joined us and a girl who never spoke to me since day one said, "Sarah, Karl Kreisler died. Did you know that?"

"Yes, I heard. How awful." *I agonized an Academy Award response and look.*

Her girlfriend pushed forward. "It was murder!" The idiot girl gushed gory details.

I wished she'd shut-up and interrupted her gushy gore. "How terrible," I mumbled. "My condolences to his family."

And condolences to me. Did I still have a job? Forgive me God for asking? Did I pack two suitcases for nothing?

In strode Mrs. Pace, parting the crowd who hushed and backed away. She saw me with Yuri and nodded.

"Everybody, please," she clapped her hands and raised her voice. "Move into Studio A. I'll make announcements in there."

Anna and Mrs. Tupper rushed over and looked relieved I was back. "I'm so happy, to see you," squealed Anna. "I was worried. Yuri wouldn't tell me where you were."

"Anna, don't hug me so tight. My ribs ..."

"Sorry," she let go.

Mrs. Tupper smiled and patted my arm.

Anna played with the ends of her ponytail. "Only thing Yuri told me was you'd be back tomorrow. What's that about?"

"I'll tell you later. What will Mrs. Pace announce?"

"A lot. Let's hurry and get a seat inside. Mrs. Tupper, stay with us."

WE THREE GIRLS elbowed our way inside Studio A and milled

around with the other dancers fighting for a bench. No such luck. We sat on the floor.

Anna whispered, "What a shock! Karl's death."

"Yeah."

"Mrs. Pace will probably talk about him and discuss the fall and winter schedule. Maybe a few notes from the Board of Directors." Anna shrugged as she glanced around the room. "There's probably fifty dancers here. I recognize some former company members."

"Could this be my last day with the company?" I rubbed my eyes feeling the moisture blur my vision.

"Maybe." Anna crossed her legs. "Who knows?"

My heart skipped a beat. "I'm fired, right?"

Anna locked her arm in mine and whispered, "Act cool. People are watching."

"How can I?" and started the waterworks.

"Pavlova, stop it, Sarah. Don't cry. Jesus, I can't take you anywhere."

"As if? Ha, ha. Where do you take me? Horn & Hardart's?" I sniveled and wiped my nose on my leotard sleeve. "Can't we always have Paris?"

Mrs. Pace entered Studio A trailed by three men dressed in business suits. She moved in front of the piano, reached for a hand-held microphone and introduced the men as members of the CCBT Board of Directors.

The audience applauded as the men sat on folding chairs.

"Ladies and gentlemen," began Mrs. Pace. "We are saddened by the death of Karl Kreisler. We mourn the loss of a true artist and a member of our company."

Applause erupted in the room.

"The funeral will be held this Friday, in Fort Lee, New Jersey at the Holy Trinity Parish Catholic Church. On the desk in my office, you'll find printed hand-outs giving the time and place. There's also information for the Port Authority busses, car-pool instructions and a map. The church hall will serve a courtesy dinner following the internment. I hope you will attend and represent the company and our love of Mr. Kreisler."

"As some of you know, Mr. Kreisler and I had a serious bet regarding Mr. Konstantinov's new ballet. Karl's death ended this bet. However, nothing will change. The dancers already cast in this ballet are still dancing their parts. The composer's music, the rehearsal pianist, costumes, sets, props, publicity, all remain the same."

I grabbed Anna's hand feeling my eyes smart with happy tears. Mrs. Tupper exhaled a noisy sigh of relief.

"The world premiere of *Colors of The Rainbow* will be pushed forward to Saturday, October 23rd."

Mrs. Pace looked to the back of the room and waved at Yuri seated on a bench, next to Alexi. "Mr. Konstantinov, I'm thrilled to announce advance ticket sales for opening night are selling in record numbers."

Yuri shouted, "Grate!" and the dancers laughed and clapped.

"And," continued Mrs. Pace, "Since the New York Times reported Karl Kreisler's death as a probable homicide, there's been a run at the box office from the curious to buy tickets for Karl's ballets. We will respect and honor Mr. Kreisler's choreography by performing his ballets exactly as they were originally conceived. Our dancers will interpret their best to make him proud."

"And I have a delightful surprise. On October 23rd ... we will celebrate an opening night gala party, at the Plaza Hotel, following the world premiere of *Colors of The Rainbow*. Generous patrons from the Metropolitan Museum of Art will sponsor the gala event."

I grinned at Anna and Mrs. Tupper. "A gala party?" My heartrate made a delighted leap. "Sounds exciting."

"Yes. We dress up and eat and drink too much."

"Can my family come?"

"Of course, invite the neighbors."

"Also, ladies and gentlemen," said Mrs. Pace. "As a special tribute to Mr. Kreisler, we will open the 1965 fall season with his *Variations on Bach* and *Eight Etudes* on Thursday and Friday, October 21st and 22nd. Please check the bulletin board for your performance dates and rehearsal times. And on December 2nd, *The Nutcracker Suite* will have its first performance. Our subscribers love this time of year. And like always, the role of Clara will be danced, by a student from the ballet school. The fall and winter seasons will extend to the end of January. So, mark your calendars. And the spring season begins the third Thursday in March, 1966."

Applause, laughter and chatter resounded around the room.

"Anna, what's going on?"

"It means we have additional weeks of work to pay the rent. She sang, "Deck the halls with boughs of paychecks. Fa, la, la, la, la," and laughed.

"Quiet, please," said Mrs. Pace into the microphone. "I have another announcement."

The crowd hushed to a whisper and the dancers who were standing, sat quickly on the floor.

"On a happy note, Frederick Borgen of the Copenhagen Royal Ballet, will be flying here tomorrow from London. He will take over the rehearsals for Mr. Kreisler's ballets. Frederick Borgen danced Karl's ballets for several years in Copenhagen, Paris, Stuttgart and London."

At the mention of his name, several dancers made comical faces. I wondered what that meant and elbowed Anna.

"Later," Anna's lips mouthed the word.

"Mr. Borgen," said Mrs. Pace. "Will rehearse *The Nutcracker Suite* using the same choreography as in previous years. Okay, ladies and gentlemen, that's it," she paused. "We …" she smiled at the three board members, "anticipate a successful season. Break a leg and thank you."

Some dancers whooped and clapped hands. Others gathered their things to leave.

The office secretary entered the room and whispered something to Mrs. Pace.

"Excuse me," said Mrs. Pace into the mic. "May I have Mr. Konstantinov, Alexi and Sarah Rothman, come join me in the lobby?"

She placed the microphone on the piano and tugged at her pearl drop earring. She exited the room and wouldn't take questions.

Minutes later, Yuri, Alexi and I met Mrs. Pace in the lobby. She spoke in a quiet voice, "You three go right now, to my private office in the back where I sometimes hide."

Alexi furrowed his brow. "You mean the tiny one couch room, next to the kitchen and bathroom with the shower?"

"None other." She lifted her shoulders and exhaled a huge sigh. "Ugh! The things I have to put up with."

Alexi and Yuri exchanged funny looks.

"And Sarah?" She straightened her shoulders and checked her wristwatch. "Fernando will drive you and your suitcases to my house when we're done."

"Nyet," interrupted Madame Madyaslavic whose nosey ways earned her a reputation for upsetting intentions. "Sarah should danse. My advanced girls meet at four o'clock. Sarah should take class vitt teen girls."

"Fine by me. Use her to demonstrate." Mrs. Pace stepped

aside to let her join the circle.

"Yes, Madame, four o'clock," I muttered.

She pinched my cheeks like Bubbe.

"Ow," I wiggled.

"Sarah, upstairs, Studio C."

That was the end. We five participants dispersed as if we heard the school bell on the playground.

In the next moments, Yuri, Alexi and I stood in the tiny back office, one minute before Mrs. Pace entered. With her, were two men whose faces looked serious.

Homicide Detective Brendan O'Malley and his assistant, Detective Connor Lynch of the NYPD introduced themselves. The lead detective asked to interview each of us separately in the tiny office.

"The others can wait in the hall." He sounded gruff.

The phone rang.

Mrs. Pace answered. "Yes? What? Detective O'Malley? Yes, he's here." She gave him the phone.

"O'Malley ... copy that. We're on our way." He handed the receiver back to Mrs. Pace and she hung up.

"Sorry, folks. We need to leave. Emergency... we'll have to meet another time."

Detective O'Malley tipped his hat, "Mrs. Pace" and he and his assistant hustled out the door.

I harrumphed feeling thrilled they left while Yuri and Mrs. Pace looked pissed. The detectives invaded their work and time. An unhappy Yuri announced, "Yuri late. Rehearse men, Studio B."

I got out of his way to let him pass.

Following the hour and a half advanced class, Madame worked with me alone for another hour. She had specific suggestions to improve my grande jetes so I'd jump higher and perform a perfect mid-air split. Her teaching methods and broken English were hard to follow. I struggled but finally, she banged the floor with her cane and yelled, "Jumper frog. Goot!"

"Yes," I laughed. "I did it! I can jump higher and longer."

"Sarah, vork. Madame, coach."

"Yes, I needed help. Thank you, Madame." I gave her a quick hug and ran to the girl's dressing room to change my damp leotards.

In the lobby downstairs, Fernando waved, "Miss Sarah, ready to go?"

"Oh, wait my suitcases."

"In the car." He smiled a toothy grin. "Welcome back."

"I'm happy to see you, too." He escorted me out and opened the limo door.

AT SUTTON PLACE, Cook met me with a grin, a medium-rare steak, steamed cauliflower and carrots. And yes, I greeted her like she made a hot fudge sundae. *Bubbe didn't raise no fool.*

Cook and I sat at the kitchen table while I ate dinner and she sipped chamomile tea. On the table were fresh flowers in a glass vase. I played with the tiny flowers and rearranged the baby's breath into a circular fan. Now satisfied with the display, I sat back and sighed, "I wished somebody sent me flowers like that, boy-oh-boy."

"Someday, Miss Sarah, they will."

"Cook, what do you call the bouquet?"

"It's a nosegay of miniature tea roses." She pointed to the underneath doily. "See, how they're tied with a tiny, satin yellow ribbon to match. That's typical in British flower marts and street sellers where I grew up in London."

"Yellow is my favorite color rose. I'd like to get a yellow nosegay from someone special."

"They were delivered an hour ago. Mrs. Pace asked me to put them in water and she left."

"Who sent them?"

Cook looked sheepish. "Mrs. Pace took the card. Maybe she has a new admirer."

"Well, she should be admired." I chomped on the steamed carrots. "Look how nice she's been to me. And you and Mrs. Williams are kind and help me."

She chuckled, "We enjoy a young girl to fuss over."

LATER THAT NIGHT, I took a long, hot shower and washed my leotards in the shower. Too tired to break an old habit, I hung the dripping wet leotards and tights, over the curtain rod to dry. I forgot, Mrs. Williams would be upset. *Oh, shoot.*

I telephoned Dad for my nightly five minute call. As I said, "Goodbye," Mrs. Pace peeked in my room and opened the door. I hung up the Princess phone.

"Sarah, you should know. Yuri fought like a raving lunatic insisting you not be replaced with an experienced ballerina. That charming Russian thinks you're a pot of gold at the end of his rainbow."

Feeling a heated rush of gratitude, I leaped out of bed and started for her. "I love that man."

"Yes, we all do."

I flung my arms around her neck and squealed, "He thinks that much of me?"

"Yes, he does but I'm a bit nervous."

I dropped my hands. "You're worried about me?"

"Bet or no bet, he wants to keep you. So, I guess I shouldn't worry."

"Oh, Mrs. Pace, thanks for telling me. I promise, I'll work very, very hard."

"You'd better. His neck is on the chopping block. He was the deciding vote at our meeting yesterday with the Board of Directors."

"Just like at the final audition."

Mrs. Pace raised an eyebrow, "How did you know?"

"Alexi told me."

Her lips thinned to a narrow line. "Some people can't keep their mouths shut."

I stammered, "No, no. Don't, don't get mad at Alexi."

"Good night, Sarah." She pivoted in a rear march out the door.

My stomach turned queasy.

CHAPTER 27

Wednesday, September 22ⁿᵈ. Three steps forward, two steps back and flick, a side step. Tango, anyone?

ARRIVING AN HOUR earlier than my four o'clock call time with Yuri, I knew from the bulletin board, he'd be working with the male dancers in *Colors*.

The five Rain Men and three tall, Thunder and Lightning Bolts were scheduled to meet at two o'clock for two hours. All eight men were strong, impressive dancers but not today. *Egads!* They moved like frantic wildebeests.

Yuri couldn't make up his mind whether to lead with his right foot or his left. He changed the direction on jumps and inverted steps three times. No one was happy.

Watching this torture made me nervous. Half way through the hour, I craved Barton's chocolate walnut creams and Rocky Road ice cream. Too panicky to sit still and too afraid to leave and get noticed.

Yuri screamed obscenities in Russian. Swear words I'd heard before and could pronounce quite well and parrot the meanings. The male corps swore in English. Both languages revealed a colorful vocabulary reserved for sea captains and longshore men. *If my dad heard them swear in front of me, he'd make me quit the CCBT. So, I never told.*

At the end of the rehearsal, Mrs. Tupper looked frazzled. Two empty bottles of cough syrup sat atop the baby grand and she never coughed. Her pillbox hat slipped over one eye and her short, cropped hair needed a hairbrush. I guessed playing the forty-eight bars of thunder pounding music, over and over could distress anyone. My heart went out to her.

Valiantly, I stayed throughout the whole ordeal. When it was over, the Thunderbolts and Rain Men didn't exactly thunder out the door with their long faces, and stinky, dirty, sweaty clothes. *Yikes! My nose needed an oxygen mask.*

Yuri ran over but halted, two feet away. "Yuri sha-ver ... clean cloth-ed."

"Yes!" I mugged. "Please!"

Would I be grateful for "cleanliness is next to Godliness?" Right on, sister.

I limbered up getting ready for my turn at bat.

Mrs. Tupper came back from the ladies' room, having adjusted her pillbox hat. Alexi returned from smoking outside the building and Yuri charged in, invigorated and revived. He babbled at Alexi who translated, "Time to make love!"

Holy smokes, he was ready to work on our final love pas de deux, at the end of Act II.

Last week, he had marked the basic choreography but hadn't settled on the lifts. According to Alexi's translation, "This romantic duet was still fluid, a works in progress." *Okay, fine, I get it.* If only my pulse didn't rock around the clock doing the jitterbug and I could calm down enough to learn the steps.

Yuri helped me stretch my legs and back. He held my arms overhead and pressed his back into mine. Satisfied I was warmed up, he pointed to the exact bar of music where "Tuppervare ... start here, ici."

She played the intro and I performed a series of grande jetes entering the stage in a semi-circle. The Sun followed, dancing as a shadow. We plowed through the beginning movements until my double piquette turn, fouette, double piquette turn, fouette moving across the stage when suddenly ... a different idea popped into Yuri's head.

He yelled, "Nyet." I stopped turning.

I tried his new idea. The Sun again followed the Red Rainbow, dancing as a shadow. Not liking this either, Yuri stopped the dancing. Ten minutes later, he asked for last week's entrance and choreography, both versions.

"He needs to experiment with the look," according to Alexi's translation. "Did I recall last week's variations?"

With four different ways to actually dance the pas de deux, I got confused. He also inserted new lifts that were difficult. *Even daring for a circus performer on a trapeze with a net. And greater still for the Flying Wallendas on a tightrope.*

I executed the lifts almost to his liking except for a lift following the second combination. He stopped the action, put me down and screamed in frustration. In fear, I ran to a corner.

Alexi and Mrs. Tupper consoled his temper with sweet words and a swig from Alexi's hidden flask filled with vodka.

I watched and chewed on the insides of my mouth. Alexi, bless his charming ways, got the maestro under control.

Yuri looked uncomfortable. "Yuri, so-rry."

I punched his shoulder angrier than a mad dog. The punch surprised us both.

Yuri staggered. "Da? Bet-ter?"

"Yes," I shook my stinging hand. "Right, better."

After a short break, we returned to the duet and worked on each lift separately. In one of the lifts, which I named the "treacherous spiral," my throat closed. I couldn't swallow and asked for a moment alone. *I wanted to run.*

Yuri was to toss my body in a complete turn in the air, horizontal with the floor, my arms folded. He was to catch me as I slid across his back, looping around his torso to an arabesque on pointe. The scariest eight musical beats in the score. *Oops, a fork in the road.*

Following the arabesque pose, should Yuri clasp my thighs together and lift me over his shoulder? Or, through his legs?

Shoot a moose! Make up your mind, Yuri. I can't hold this pose forever. My big toe just went numb.

The pas de deux being a love attraction meant continuous body contact and difficult transitions. I ran to him or, stepped backwards into his chest or, stood alongside and became a Caesar salad toss. I twirled, slid, did somersaults and landed in poses on pointe or, in split legs en l'air or, on the floor. I spun, whirled, posed above his head as an eagle or, arched my back, on his left shoulder. *Whew! I need a nap.*

The most dangerous lift followed the treacherous lift. Yuri swooped my frame into the air, lifting me by one hand, his right hand at my waist. I held a stiff body, mid-air for two musical beats. My heart stopped at the count until his hands guided me in a quick wrap around his body, to the floor and back into his arm around my waist in a front attitude on pointe.

During our ten minute break, the secretary walked in carrying plates of fresh, cut-up oranges. "I thought you guys needed something sweet and healthy," she smiled.

"Sweet? Yes!" teased Alexi. "I'm exhausted from translating, thank you." He kissed the secretary's cheek. "You are kind."

Yuri grabbed a handful of orange pieces and paced the floor. The rest of us lapped and slurped oranges until Yuri hollered, "Goot!" He jabbered in such a fast Russian stream of consciousness, Alexi had trouble translating. But, he did the job.

"Yuri has the complete pas de deux. The vision just came to him from start to finish and he nailed it."

"What?" I looked at Alexi in disbelief. "You're kidding."

"No, he's got it. That's it, Sarah. All done."

"Until he changes it." I slid into the splits on the floor and stretched by back forward.

"Da!" Yuri squealed in delight. "Fini!"

He bent down and pulled me to my feet from the floor splits. He hollered across the room, "Thumb-a-up, Tuppervare."

Bless his genius. The man told the truth. We rehearsed the same variation a couple more times by marking the lifts without changes until ... the key word here was "until" the so called dramatic ending.

Everyone got quiet including the secretary who sensed something was up. She begged to watch and Alexi allowed it only if, she sat next to him and wouldn't tell Mrs. Pace. But, and here comes the "big but" and I don't mean a big butt tush. I hadn't a clue why their faces looked tense and why Yuri hugged me before he explained.

Alexi translated, "Starting with the final thirty-six bars of duet music, the Sun ... who is filled with a heartfelt adoration for the Red Rainbow ... expresses his love by kissing her with a mighty passion. Unfortunately, the heat from his fiery, hot body kills her. She dies instantly. She melts dead on the stage."

"Oh, noooo," I moaned. "How sad."

"Da," laughed Yuri. "Yuri kill Sa-rah. Ha-ha."

"Oh, get out of town. It's not enough you throw me around like a beach ball but now you have to kill me?"

"Da!" he snorted.

"Yes, Yuri kills you," said Alexi. "You die in front of a sold-out audience. And if you're a great actress, the audience will be devastated. You'll break their hearts and they'll love it."

My hand covered my mouth.

"Tuppervare," yelled Yuri. "Play mu-sak."

"Huh?" said Mrs. Tupper as she reached for a quick swig

from the cough syrup on the piano.

"Yes, Mrs. Tupper, please play the final, thirty-six bars before the coda," said Alexi.

"I'm counting, give me a minute."

"It takes thirty-six bars to die?" I mumbled. "What's the hurry?"

Mrs. Tupper played the music when suddenly, Yuri grabbed me. He bent me over backwards in a deep, passionate kiss pushing us both to the floor. He held my shoulders down, his head on my chest.

But, I struggled and jumped to my feet, a trembling eager beaver. The wallop of renewed energy from Yuri's kiss, hit me strong.

Alexi's jaw dropped, Yuri glared and the secretary giggled. Mrs. Tupper saw me stand and stopped playing.

"Woweeee," I giggled seeing my nipples hardened through my Danseskin leotard. "That was some kiss. Definitely not goodbye. It was hello, how are you, dinner at my place?"

"Sa-rraaah!"

"You wanna do it again?"

"Sa-rah! Die! Dead!" Yuri yelled pulling his ponytail. He laid down on the floor pretending to be dead.

"Alexi! Tell him. His kiss felt invigorating. How can I melt and die?"

"I can't tell him that."

"But, he has too much electricity and passion. How am I supposed to play dead? I wanna jump up and down and sing the national anthem."

"Sarah, you must die in this ballet.

"Why?" I pointed to the floor, "You mean play dead."

"Yes! That's the plot. The Sun kissed you and you drop dead. Any actress would kill for this part. It's Shakespeare. It's

Tolstoy. It's Madame Butterfly at the Metropolitan Opera!"

I cried, "God awful!"

"What's the matter now?" Alexi clenched his jaw and showed his teeth.

"Such a sad and depressing ending to a ballet," I sobbed.

"It's make believe!" yelled Alexi.

I shook my head and saw Mr. Kreisler lying in a pool of blood. *His glassy eyes stared into nothingness.*

"Sarah, please, co-operate."

"Oh dear, forgive me." I inhaled a deep breath and wrung my hands. "I didn't expect to feel distress at the sorrowful finish. Give me a moment." I ran out of the room.

Minutes later, after throwing cold water on my face in the bathroom, I ran into the lobby. The secretary met me with strong words. "Give em hell, Sarah. Do it for us girls, sister!"

I giggled, she laughed and I went back into Studio A.

Yuri looked puzzled. "Sa-rah? Okay? Sa-rah die?"

I sighed, "Yes. I'll die for you. I'll be the dramatic actress."

"Dying acc-tress! Goot!" He roared and grabbed me in a tight hold. He kissed me with the energy of a tornado in a big smooch.

I came up reeling and trembling. "See, Alexi," I rolled my eyes. "Too much passion. How am I supposed to play dead after a hot kiss? Don't believe me? You kiss him. You try a sexy kiss!"

Yuri shook his finger. "Goot for love, Sa-rah." He furrowed his brow, "Bad for danse." He stepped closer and screamed, "Die. Red Rain-bow!"

I jumped a foot in fright. "Okay, okay, I'll die, I'll do it!"

After we all calmed down, my heart melted.

I liked kissing Yuri. I liked kissing David. I liked kissing.

"Moving on," announced Alexi "to Sarah's solo variation."

"My solo?"

"Da," answered Yuri thumbing through the musical score. "Tuppervare, play here. Ici!" He hit the page with the back of his hand.

"I love this theme," smiled Mrs. Tupper. "It's beautiful and suits Sarah."

"Da," and he walked over to me and took my hand.

Yuri taught me the solo and I loved the choreography. The movements were simple, lovely and lyrical. However, knowing Yuri's track record, I was ready for any changes but there weren't any. *Knock me over with a feather but don't call me late for dinner.*

Alexi told me after the rehearsal. "Yuri had envisioned your lyrical solo weeks before."

"How come?"

"The Red Rainbow must radiate an innocent, seductive spell over the hot and fiery Sun when she dances. Her beauty and charm so intrigued the Sun, he falls madly in love and lust and must possess her."

"Wow, all that in one dance?"

"Yes, and if performed with great passion, your solo could be the highlight of the ballet."

"You don't expect much, do you?"

"Not me. Yuri expects a standing ovation."

Chills and fears put on the back burner, I threw myself into the choreography and worked hard at perfecting every nuance. The progression of steps became second nature but I couldn't get my timing in sync with the tempo.

Yuri looked worried. He paced back and forth.

I chewed on the ends of my ponytail. Alexi sucked on the end of an unlit cigarette. What to do?

In an abrupt move, Yuri stopped pacing and yelped. "Da, Tuppervare? Nyet, mu-sak. Nyet, play."

"Why?" she sounded surprised. "The composer worked with me on these pages."

Alexi translated. "You know the music. Sarah does not."

"What do you mean?" I stared at Alexi confused.

"Sing Sa-rah," said Yuri waving his arms like a conductor in front of an orchestra. "Sing et danse."

"At the same time?"

"Da!"

"I can't do both together."

"Yes," said Alexi. "Yuri wants you to feel the Red Rainbow's theme song in your bones. You are the flute playing her song with your feet and body."

"How do I do that?"

Yuri tapped my skull, "Mu-sak in head."

"Hey, warn me first."

He slapped my rear, I jumped a foot. "Mu-sak in bod-dy. Sarah sing, da, da, daaaaaaaaa."

I sang and danced. Or rather, I tried and stumbled.

The brise voile combinations were impossible to sing and flick my ankles together en l'air. But the pas de chats and pas de bourrees were simple to sing in sync and fun.

"Holy smokes!" I laughed. "It's working." My singing and my steps meshed.

"Tuppervare!" yelled Yuri. "Play mu-sak."

My pulse soared to the tempo. The music and I danced as one.

Yuri yelled, "Spot turns! Head up! Hands soft!" At the finish, he grinned, "Goot, Sa-rah. Goot ball-let!"

My heart pounded with joy hearing his praise. He grinned a lascivious leer. "Next ... Yuri teach Red Rain-bow sex."

"What?" I gasped.

Alexi yelled at Yuri in Russian then turned to me. "Sorry,

Sarah," he said looking embarrassed. "Yuri meant to say ... at the next rehearsal, he'll work on getting you sexy and using your charm to entice the Sun."

"You mean, I'm not attractive enough?"

"No, you're not. Not by a mile."

I faked a half-assed smile watching Yuri's face lit up with another idea.

"Sa-rah, danse solo ... tree times. Nyet stop."

"What?" My eyes bugged out. I looked up at the clock on the wall. Six o'clock and another half hour to go.

"Tuppervare! Play mu-sak. Over, over ... tree times. Un, deux, trois ... nyet stop."

"I can't," I snapped. "You think I'm Wonder Woman?"

"Tuppervare, play!"

Mrs. Tupper played the intro and I ran to the chalk-marked line on the floor and began. Three times, I danced my solo non-stop and at the end, hungered for air.

Last double pirouette into a pose, I dropped to the floor and stretched my arms and legs like a snow angel without the snow.

Alexi translated. "Sarah, in the Kirov-Leningrad Ballet re-hearsals, soloists dance full out three times with no breaks. When the time comes to perform only once before an audience, they are strong and confidant."

Yuri eyed me lying on the floor. He chuckled at my chest expand and contract. Extending his hand, he helped me up. "Sa-rah nyet sing-ger."

"No kidding."

"Goot danse," he grabbed my hands. "Goot vork."

"Really?" My heartbeat quickened. "Thank you and Yuri?"

"Da," he looked suspicious.

"A little while ago, I punched you in the shoulder. Sorry, I don't know what made me do it. Please, forgive me.

He searched my face and didn't answer. After a minute, he grimaced. "Sheet hap-pen ... may-be da, may-be nyet ... da."

I threw my arms around him and planted kisses on his cheek.

THAT NIGHT, AFTER Yuri's afternoon kiss to make me die, my mind focused on my first real kiss with David. I missed him. And wondered if he missed me. I remembered the romantic moments on our dates; dancing under the full moon on the beach, the glimmer in his eyes when he looked at me, and how my skin tingled at his touch. And he was tolerant of me after we argued and explained things. But why didn't he ask for my phone number?

Maybe, he didn't wish to disturb Mrs. Pace or, start something he couldn't finish. He blew me off. Too busy with work; a polite way of saying goodbye.

My sister Melissa always complained about her dates. She said, "Men are weird. You think you had a great time on a date? And the guy thanked you for a nice evening and then, he never called."

Aunt Lucy and Bubbe said Melissa waited by the phone for several years for a nice fella to call back. But, a nice fella never did. The one guy who did call back turned out to be Leon the Jeweler. It happened during the spring of her last year of college. She got so excited at her luck, she got engaged at graduation. "No way," she told Dad "will I let this man get away."

Maybe my brother, Jeff, had it right. "We were not a good fit," and David realized it.

"Say goodnight, Gracie," I muttered into the pillow then the waterworks followed.

CHAPTER 28

Thursday, September 23rd. The news radio predicted a cool and cloudy day.

I WOKE UP in a cold sweat and biting my thumb nail obsessing over David. My immediate reaction? *Stop it, you idiot.* No more wasted energy on a make-believe prince who doesn't care about me.

I would (1) get out of bed, (2) dress in my favorite V-neck, burgundy leotard, (3) eat a protein breakfast and (4) perfect my dance technique. If I focused on my Red Rainbow job, I'd get more done and make Yuri and Mrs. Pace happy. In turn, I'd be happy.

So when I entered the ballet school and read the bulletin board, my heart leaped over the footlights. I was, "rarin' to go," to quote Aunt Lucy.

ATTENTION ALL DANCERS IN COLORS of THE RAINBOW. A NEW RE-HEARSAL SCHEDULE FOR MONDAY, SEPTEMBER 27TH, WED. 29TH & FRI. OCT 1ST. PLEASE ARRIVE FIFTEEN MINUTES EARLY TO WARM UP. BRING A LIGHT SNACK and DRINK IF YOU THINK IT'S NECESSARY. NO ABSENCES WILL BE PERMITED. NO EXCUSES. THE COLORS NEW BALLET WILL PREMIERE SAT. OCTOBER 23RD. 8:30 PM CURTAIN, 2ND BALLET ON PROGRAM.

2PM – 3:30PM Yuri Konstantinov & Sarah Rothman REHEARSE – Studio B

3:55PM – 6:30PM 7 RAINBOW GIRLS REHEARSE with 2 breaks – Studio A

Sarah Rothman – Red

Anna Ekaterina Zvyagintsev – Orange

Marta Escuella – Yellow

Natasha Pashkova – Green

Suzanne Meade – Blue

Lily Mandrake – Indigo

Marisa Catalina Albanese – Violet

7:15 pm-8:45 pm 3 ECLIPSE OF THE SUN GIRLS REHEARSE – Studio C

Arianna Hunt, Belle Charmaine Delon and Carol Voss.

ANY QUESTIONS ASK MRS. PACE OR OFFICE SECRETARY. THANK YOU.

I muttered, "Ready, Freddy," and turned to walk away when a short, stocky man stopped me.

"Miss Rothman, is it?"

I recognized his brooding expression and the rumpled, dark brown suit. "Why are you asking?" Hiccup.

"I'm Homicide Detective Brendan O'Malley of the NYPD and this is my assistant, Detective Connor Lynch."

Hiccup. Detective Lynch nodded.

They both flashed their badges at the count of three.

"Right." Hiccup. "You were here Tuesday." Hiccup. "Yes, I'm Sarah Rothman." Hiccup.

"Ma'am," said Detective O'Malley in a poppa bear tone. Hiccup. "There's a drinking fountain on the wall over your shoulder."

"What?" Hiccup.

"Use it."

"Huh?" Hiccup. "Oh, right." Hiccup.

I turned the handle and gulped icy cold water slurping the high spray. All the while, I focused on Detective O'Malley out of the corner of my eye. When I stopped drinking, "Aaaaaaah," I slurred the 'a' sound and waited … nothing.

"Better?" the detective looked smug.

I wiped my mouth with the back of my hand. "Yeah."

"Miss Rothman, we need to speak to you. Come with us." They headed for Mrs. Pace's office, escorted me inside and shut the door.

I glanced out the window at the corps de ballet girls staring back at me from the lobby.

Detective O'Malley looked at the girls and then me. He furrowed his brow. "You look nervous, Miss Rothman. Any particular reason?"

"No, you startled me first thing in the morning."

"Well, it's hardly the first thing in the morning. We start at six and by all accounts it's half past ten."

I bit my lip. "It's the start of my day."

"Miss Rothman, take a seat."

I moved to a folding chair and settled in. The men sat on office chairs behind Mrs. Pace's desk and took out small notepads. They borrowed pens from the secretary's empty coffee cup.

"Miss Rothman, how well did you know Karl Kreisler?"

I tucked the canvas dance bag under my chair. "Know him? Not at all."

"Did you ever speak with him?"

"No." I looked at the file folders atop Mrs. Pace's desk and wondered if they were bills for my toe shoes.

"Let me rephrase the question."

I shifted in my chair and stared at the white phone with gold trim. *That's so Mrs. Pace. She loves gold jewelry and gold trim in clothes and picture frames and furniture.*

"Ma'am," he harrumphed. "I understand there was a disturbance last Saturday night in the lobby of the Osborne Apartments. You were with a Mr. Yuri Konstantinov when Mr. Kreisler exited the lobby elevator. The two men had words."

"Yes, but I didn't speak to Mr. Kreisler. I'd never been introduced to him."

"What was the altercation about?"

"Altercation? They punched each other in the face. They fought."

"Why did they punch each other in the face, Miss Rothman?"

"Mr. Kreisler said some mean, awful things about me and Yuri's new ballet."

"And this caused them to physically fight each other?"

"Yes," I nodded. "Uh-huh."

"What did you do?"

"I got out of the way."

Detective O'Malley scribbled something in his tiny notepad, looked up and narrowed his eyes. "Miss Rothman, do you think Mr. Konstantinov murdered Mr. Kreisler?"

"What?" I screeched. "No, of course, not. Yuri, I mean Mr. Konstantinov had no reason to murder Mr. Kreisler. Why?"

"However, and I quote your words, you did say 'Mr. Kreisler said some mean, awful things.'"

"What? Like sticks and stones can break my bones but names can ..."

"Really?" interrupted the detective.

"Detective O'Malley, Yuri has everything going for him. He's the star of this ballet company. His beautiful new ballet will have a world premiere. Why would he ruin his career by murdering someone? Doesn't make sense. Mr. Kreisler was old. His career was over. Just like on Perry Mason, the person who did this had to have a motive and Yuri didn't have one."

I glanced at the assistant detective taking notes. "Perry Mason, you said?"

"My grandma and me love his television show."

"That's all, Miss Rothman. Thank you," said Detective O'Malley. "You may go."

I EXITED THE office and headed for the stairs. My hands trembled and I grabbed the rails. *What if the detectives didn't believe me? Could they tell I was hiding something? Crapola!*

Running up the stairs, I hurried in the girl's dressing room, changed into dance clothes and returned downstairs to the lobby. When Alexi and Yuri came over, I put on a happy face and locked my arms with theirs. We three paraded into Studio A ready for Madame's class.

"Sarah," whispered Alexi. "Yuri has something serious to tell you. I'll translate but keep it quiet."

"Sure." I faced my mentor.

"From now on, at every company pro class, Yuri wants you to stand next to him at the barre and in the center. Unless he's asked to perform alone, he wants you by his side."

I fluttered my eyelashes at both men. "Why? Is Yuri afraid I'll run away with the Thunder and Lightning Bolts?"

"That's never going to happen," laughed Alexi.

"Why not?" I looked startled.

"They prefer men, not women."

"Oh, not that stuff again. Egads." I grimaced at Yuri. "Say it's not true."

Alexi translated his answer. "Never mind, you don't party week-ends at Fire Island." They both chuckled.

Yuri mumbled something then ran out of the room to look

for someone or the bathroom.

I grabbed Alexi's arm. "Fifteen minutes ago, the homicide detectives questioned me in the office. Detective O'Malley asked me if Yuri killed Karl Kreisler."

Alexi looked surprised. "What did you say?"

"I said no. What would I say?"

"Don't mention this to Yuri. It would upset him."

"No kidding? Of course, I won't."

AT HORN & Hardart's, Anna and I ate lunch without Mrs. Tupper who had errands to run for her mother.

"Hey you," said Anna sitting at our usual table. "What happened to my friend, Sarah? The laughing, silly girl I used to know."

"She's here. Just tired from dancing."

"I don't believe you. What's up?"

"Ah ...," I hesitated and felt her eyes bore holes in my closed eye lids. I'd better tell her something and it can't be about the detectives asking questions. I cleared my throat ... "Since you asked, there is this guy."

"I knew it," she squealed dropping her purse on the floor. "Holy shit! Tell me everything. Wait, I have to get my purse. Okay, start talking."

My cheeks burned.

Anna chuckled, "Your face is red. He's got to be drop dead gorgeous."

"He is and a little dangerous."

"I love it. Tell me everything." She wiggled her hands and feet in the air.

"He's twenty-eight, very cool, a lawyer and rich."

"Bingo! The perfect man except for the lawyer part but go on."

"Ah … well."

"Is he married?"

"No, of course not."

"I dated a married man once but that's my story not yours. Go on."

I inhaled a breath and blew it out. "His name is David Katz and I met him at the zoo and …"

I told Anna about lunch at the tea room, his boss's birthday party, his friends Vinnie and Carol and how he kissed me under the full moon in Southampton.

"He sounds a dreamboat. When do you see him again?"

"That's the problem. He hasn't called. He said, 'he'd call' but he doesn't know my number."

"Anybody can call the school. The number's in the yellow pages."

"Yes, but …," I sniffled and she handed me a tissue.

"Stop blubbering, I can't stand it. And don't drag your sorry ass around like you're half dead, you're not."

I made a face.

"He's one guy and there's a hundred more."

"What?" I blew my nose. "I want him."

"Really, Anna Karenina? You want Count Alexei Vronsky?"

"Are they ballet dancers?"

"No. Don't you read books?"

"I love reading. I know a Count. I read the *Count of Monte Christo*."

"Look! Here's how I see the big picture. David digs you and from what you've described, he likes you a lot."

"You think so?"

"Yes, blockhead. He'll call."

"That one I know. Charlie Brown in the Sunday funnies."

BACK AT THE school, when Yuri and I finished rehearsing, we stayed an additional hour to get more time in. His facial muscles tensed up when he spoke about losing our tomorrow's rehearsal.

"You know, Sarah," whispered Alexi. "Yuri is going to the funeral to keep up appearances. He doesn't want anybody to suspect him of murder."

"Huh?" I gasped. "That's awful."

"He plans to arrive late and leave early then return to Manhattan. He's rehearsing the Eclipse girls at five-thirty."

"I'm sorry he has to go but not me."

"That takes courage." Alexi sounded surprised. "Why not?"

"I didn't know him. No love lost."

Alexi stared at me. "Well, we're stuck. Fernando has to drive us with Mrs. Pace but the one saving grace. She has to get back to the city early. She wants to wine and dine new patrons at the Rainbow Room."

"Good luck," I shuddered at Alexi, kissed Yuri goodbye and waved to Mrs. Tupper. "See you guys in the morning."

I never changed my damp leotards. Instead, I threw on pedal pushers and a jacket and scurried out the front door. At the curb, I stepped into the parked limo and sunk my exhausted body into the black leather seat.

"You're very sweet for waiting, Fernando. Thanks."

"For you Miss Sarah, the moon."

THE NEXT DAY, following the Friday morning pro class, dancers took the bus from Port Authority to Fort Lee for the funeral.

I took the subway home to Brooklyn and surprised Dad. And

since the women were at Grossinger's, I spent the afternoon and evening with Daddy, Uncle Al and Max. The men put me to work waitressing at the deli. I made twenty-two dollars in tips, yippee!

Uncle Al telephoned the girls long distance and I spoke to Aunt Sophie and Bubbe. Aunt Sophie told me "not to do anything she wouldn't do." And Bubbe cried, "She missed me but she loved the room service and the floor shows at night. What? Who's this? ... Oh, hello, Aunt Lucy ... what murder? Ah, the newspapers ... yes, oh, that Mr. Kreisler. No, I didn't know him ... I know, his funeral was today ... Jersey, somewhere. How's Mama? Good! She's playing bingo in the card room and Aunt Ida Mae? ... The beauty salon? She won another hundred dollars at Canasta and she's dying her hair to blonde?" Hold on, Auntie."

"Uncle Al did you hear that?"

"No. So tell me already?"

"Your wife is becoming a blonde at the hairdressers."

"Tell her I prefer redheads. Hang up the phone, Sarah. This is costing me a fortune."

"I have to go, Aunt Lucy ... love you, too ... and tell everybody I love them. Bye."

I hung up the wall phone. "Thanks, Uncle Al for the call."

"Anytime, Sarah."

THAT NIGHT, I slept in my own bed, in my old room without Aunt Sophie and I loved it. Dad snoring down the hall made it even better. Too bad, Mama and Bubbe stayed in hotel rooms in the Catskills. We could all be under the same roof.

How do I stop being homesick? I don't like sleeping at Mrs. Pace's house.

CHAPTER 29

Saturday, September 25th. A little bit of this, a little bit of that.

fORGET THE LAST two days of cool and cloudy Thursday and mild and sunny Friday. The 6:15 a.m. news radio announced a drastic change in the weather. Today would start a record setting heat wave.

I dropped a token in the slot and boarded the early morning BMT express on the last Saturday of the month. The weatherman got it right. Hot air blew through the train's open windows and searing metal wheels screeched on metal tracks. Tunnel travel aggravated several commuters. It showed on their faces as they fanned themselves with the Daily News or Racing Form. Droplets of perspiration dripped off my forehead on the dance bag in my lap. I sure as heck didn't want to take the pro class at eleven. What excuse could I give?

MADAME MADYASLAVIC MARCHED into Studio A swinging her silver-handled cane. She greeted the Russian pianist who looked ready for an ambulance ride to Roosevelt Hospital. She dabbed the sweat off his brow with her hankie. He finished the job with his white shirt sleeve and coughed.

Anna leaned her head on my shoulder. "What if our piano player drops dead like old people do in the heat?"

"Stop it, Anna. I love Chopin."

"Chopin loves you. You could date him if he was alive but

he'd be too old for you and couldn't get it up."

I slapped her arm, "Stop."

"No shit. Our accompanist has played every waltz, etude, polonaise, and mazurka Frederic Chopin wrote since the age of ten. I'm sick of it." She dropped to the floor in the splits and extended her chin to her shin bone.

I tapped Anna's shoulder. "Lookie, lookie, cookie. The secretary is giving him orange juice and chocolates. He's returning to earth."

"Damn it! He won't die. I was hoping for Aaron Copland, Tchaikovsky and Stravinsky played by a young, starving, concert pianist Mrs. Pace could hire for fifty cents an hour."

"Anna, you're a bitch."

"I know, I dance at the CCBT. You'll be a bitch, too."

"Nope," I shook my head. "Hey, why are there so many dancers taking class? What gives?"

"Oh, sweetie, you're in for a treat. Watch your back, toes and feet. I'm a poet and I know it."

"Shut-up, Anna. There's Yuri." I waved my hands. "Yuuuriii, over here."

My partner rushed through the open door and ran in between Anna and me at the barre. He kissed my cheeks and her lips.

Alexi fast on his heels, analyzed the crowd. "Today I see former members of the defunct Marquis de Cuevas Ballet Company of Monte Carlo. Did you know their final performance was in 1962? But since they arrived in town, they're performing at the 92nd Street Y. Go figure."

"So much for defunct," chuckled Anna. "You know dancers never die."

"They fade away." Alexi pinched Anna's arm.

"Da. French ad-dor Svetlana Madyaslavic."

"They do. They pleaded with Mrs. Pace to join Madame's company class. They know her teaching reputation and our scheming director probably charged them double."

I made a quick head count. "There's fifty-two dancers in this room. That's a hundred and four arms and legs. We won't be able to move."

"Nyet move, nyet danse." Yuri eyed several French females stretching their bodies on the floor and slicked back his hair admiring their effort.

Anna placed her leg on the barre and slid her ankle to the side as far as the leg could go. Her foot startled a Marquis de Cuevas girl who jumped out of the way. Anna chuckled, "Oops, I just bumped one of the twelve dancers lucky enough to travel the globe from the south of France."

The French girl mumbled, "Merde," and turned away.

Anna whispered, "They're esoteric gypsies."

Madame clapped her hands and pointed to the clock on the wall. "Il est tard!" Vous etes prets?"

Several dancers shouted "Qui, Madame," and scrambled for places at the barre.

The ballet mistress nodded to the Russian pianist and he played an arpeggio.

"Bonjour et bienvenue, Madames et Monsieurs, mon aimes de Monte Carlo," grinned Madame. The music started and Madame banged her cane. "Allons-y maintenant."

Anna tugged at my ear. "He's playing Chopin."

"Son of a gun," I giggled, "we're having fun ... Ouch!" A slap on my back between the shoulder blades slammed me forward into Anna. *Oh, God,* Yuri had spoken. I shut up for the next hour and a half.

Madame screeched, "Allez ... seconde position!" She clapped her hands and banged her cane again. "Seconde position. Dos bien droit ... Eeeeeee, grande plie, un, deux, trois ... lentement, eeeeeee ... releve ... port de bra ... eeeeee ..."

We performed barre exercises packed in rows like sardines in a tin. There were too many dancers, too much kinetic energy, too many cooling fans and very little space. Extending one's leg higher than the hip could result in bruises, temper tantrums and frayed nerves.

Of course, the dancers spoke French which wasn't a problem. French is ballet's universal language around the world. The problem was the dancers themselves who refused to follow the dress code. Our Russian pianist came alive during the frappes-tendues at the barre. He hollered at the foreigners in his Ukraini-an lingo which Alexi later translated.

The pianist called the French dancers, "A freak show and disrespectful to the arts." Madame threatened, "Quiet" and hit him on the shoulder with her cane. He never spoke after that.

The French women, hating the heat and humidity of New York City wore bikini bottoms and sheer tank-tops emphasizing their protruding nipples. Half of the men refused to wear tights and their hairy, naked legs looked gross. And a couple guys, didn't wear jock straps. Their man parts thrilled a few of our male dancers but disgusted others. Yuri made snide remarks.

We girls tried not to look at the men and if we did, we twit-tered like parakeets. Madame yelled, "Arrete!" if she heard tweets and giggles.

As a consequence, some of our own corps de ballet member's undressed to their undies once we left the exercises at the barre. Or, they returned from the bathrooms wearing skimpy, two piece bathing suits more suitable for the Rockaways.

Madame was furious. "This is not a beauty pageant," she declared slamming the door as she stormed out to complain to Mrs. Pace. But, have a heart Madame. It's too hot to suffer. And who could blame us for wanting lighter attire sans tights? Most dancers were frightened of air conditioners and preferred open windows and fans.

Anna stripped with the rest of the girls. "I'm dying in this stagnant air without air conditioning. "C'mon Sarah, get naked."

"No, thanks."

Yuri, also, stuck to tradition. He kept his usual tights and shirt on but following the barre exercises his damp tee-shirt bit the dust. Nothing out of the ordinary there. Except, he became intrigued with a petite, red-haired French girl with perfect breasts that never jiggled when she jumped.

Anna assured us. "She had a boob job. I'd bet on it. Tits don't act like that in real life."

As if the fake tit discussion wasn't upsetting enough, my partner Yuri, left me and moved to the other side of the room. Acting the feral tomcat, he strutted his stuff, trying to attract the French girl. When he touched her face and whispered something in her ear, my teeth mashed.

"Look at that jerk! Who's sticking to whom during class? Where's his common sense?"

Anna grunted, "In his pants. It's called lust."

"Seriously?"

"Yes! Men think with their dicks. Watch his next move."

Yuri pranced and posed. Anna poked my ribs. "See! He's smoothing back his hair and ballooning up his chest."

"Salope!" I stamped my foot. My green eyes turned greener.

"Jesus, Sarah. Don't just stand there you twit. Go get him. He's your partner."

I tore across the room and hissed at the red-haired bitch. "Salope! Il est a moi, il m'appartient."

The girl picked up her bag and mumbled, "I no want. Bad

man." She ran out of the room and slammed the door.

"Sarah, qu est quil ne va pas?" seethed my partner yanking on my wrist.

"De rien. Et toi?"

The studio door banged open and in returned Madame Madyaslavic stomping her Cuban heels. She nodded to the pianist and sang out, "Allons-y maintenant."

It was obvious, her complaint fell on deaf ears.

LATER THAT DAY, at my two o'clock rehearsal with Yuri, Mrs. Pace surprised us with a visit. She tip-toed in, sat on a bench and observed.

As I posed on pointe at the finish of our pas de deux at the end of Act I, Mrs. Pace applauded. My heartbeat moved up the charts seeing her face flush.

"Your performance ..." She dabbed her eyes with a white handkerchief, "beyond amazing. Alexi, translate ... I saw a joyful Romeo and Juliet. A chemistry so enchanting and uplifting and spectacular technique." Her eyes opened wide. "Like Olympic gold."

My hands flew to my heart. Yuri bowed his head.

"The choreography? Nothing like it on the American stage. A little jazz and the lifts?" Sarah ..."

"Da, goot?"

"Yes, Yuri more than good. The way Sarah twists around your body. A virtual circus performer and a snake. One difficult lift after another."

She stepped towards me and took my hand. "Sarah, I won the bet. You exceeded Karl's expectations, may he rest in peace."

Alexi mumbled, "He should rot in hell, the bastard."

"Alexi, let's not bad mouth the dead," admonished Mrs. Pace. "And Yuri? My genius? You must choreograph another ballet."

"Da? Ball-let?

"For you and Sarah. Ten maybe, fifteen minutes long. A short, complete piece."

Yuri whispered to Alexi and Alexi shouted, "Yuri wants to know when? For what?"

"Now! I'd use it now. A new, short piece in the divertissement program on the nights when *Colors of The Rainbow* isn't scheduled."

Yuri and Alexi spoke in animated Russian until Yuri exhaled a loud, "Da!"

"Yes! Yuri has a duet. He and Sarah would portray Monarch butterflies discovering love. He thinks the music of Frederic Chopin's *Prelude in D flat Major, op. 28 number 15 'Raindrop' music would be ideal.*"

"Wonderful!" Her eyes lit up. "I need it yesterday."

"Da, daaaaa, da." Yuri hummed the first few bars.

Mrs. Pace laughed. "You don't have to sell me. I adore the music."

My happy heart rocked my chest watching the two of them agree on the music and theme. The flickering in my partner's eyes expressed his excitement. But Chopin? I loved the raindrop prelude but I wouldn't tell Anna. *No, someone else gets to handle that pleasure.*

And would there be enough hours in the day? Enough energy in my head and legs to make it through two ballet premieres? I'd heard of Dr. Fix-it's magic for actors and dancers. Should I ask Anna if he could give me uppers? Irina and Sonia lived on little greenies so why not me?

CHAPTER 30

Monday, September 27th thru Friday, October 1st. Why isn't life a walk in the park or a bed of roses?

ON MONDAY, FREDERICK Borgen arrived from Copenhagen as the new resident choreographer. Kreisler's dancers were already contractually cast in Karl's ballets so Borgen had no say if he didn't like a particular dancer. The only exception was *The Nutcracker*. He could switch out a few soloists if he didn't like last year's line-up. And, Kreisler's rehearsal pianist would remain on board to help the new hire with his music.

The gossip swirled pro and con. Male dancers who worked with Borgen in Berlin and the Stuttgart Opera, hated him while two girls who traveled to London at his request, adored him. And no one knew his sexual politics. He kept his private life private which infuriated some because there was talk of a marriage but no one actually met or saw pictures of a partner. The company dancers only knew he dressed in white dance clothes and drank beer with a whiskey chaser.

On the new choreographer's first afternoon, he rehearsed *Themes and Variations of Bach* using six dancers. Anna's friend, Marie Larson was one of the ensemble. Marie had a few things to say over lunch at Horn & Hardart's the following day.

Marie told Anna, Mrs. Tupper and me, "The Bach ballet went duh for three and a half hours. If you like to whisper and dance in a library. I was bored out of your skull and just my luck, God damn it. Borgen's rehearsing more of Karl's ballets tomorrow."

"I know," said Anna. "I saw your name on the bulletin board. His schedule for the week is posted."

"Are Sonia and Irina's names on the schedule?" I gave a furtive glance at Anna.

"Of course. They're both dancing leads. Especially Irina who's the soloist in most of Karl's ballets."

"Yeah," whined Marie. "She probably licked his ass and kissed his balls."

Mrs. Tupper shocked at the remark, spilled her tomato juice.

"Hey, Marie, take it easy," derided Anna. "Mrs. Tupper has virginal ears."

"How? With Mrs. In front of her name?"

And earlier that Tuesday morning, in Madame's professional 11 a.m. class ...

The Monte Carlo French dancers joined us for their final pirouettes then flew to Chicago to perform at the Blackstone Theatre. Anna never said if Yuri slept with the pretty red-head over the weekend. But, she suspected he did and screamed obscenities at him at the bus stop. Several of us girls heard the argument and watched Yuri console her with kisses. I wanted to ask? How did you know he cheated and what was your love and sex life? *Darn it, I never got up the nerve.*

And even earlier on Tuesday, at the ungodly hour of 9 a.m. ...

Mrs. Pace held a press conference on the stage at the City Center Theatre on West 55th Street. The reporters from the New York Times, the Post, the Daily News, two theatrical magazines and television's entertainment news were all on deck. They stood in the front three rows.

Yuri wore a suit and I wore a dress and heels because Mrs.

Pace insisted we tag along and look presentable. We sat behind a long table, on stage in bright lights for the interview.

Mrs. Pace, dressed in a cream-colored Chanel suit with navy blue/gold braided trim and shiny gold buttons, smiled at the journalists and waved.

"Good morning, ladies and gentlemen. Happy to see you made it on such short notice. Thank you for coming. I have exciting news." She turned her head away from the mic and coughed.

"I am pleased to announce, a new ballet choreographed by Mr. Yuri Konstantinov for our evenings of short programs. The ballet is called *Monarchs In Spring* and will be danced by Mr. Konstantinov and his seventeen year old partner, Miss Sarah Rothman, our debut soloist."

Our boss turned to both of us and gestured. "I've brought my two lovely artists along with me to share my news." She turned back to her audience and grinned, "With all of you my esteemed members of the press and television news."

Some reporters chuckled and others mumbled things we couldn't hear. *Just as well.*

I tried to act cool under the glaring, hot lights. My cheeks heated up and I wiggled in my chair. Flash bulbs popped and my vision blurred. Yuri reached for my hand and held on. Grinning as the proud teacher, he leaned in and kissed my cheek. The reporters ate up our interaction and shouted questions. Yuri seized the moment, answered questions and milked the crowd. He winked at me, "Boot-ti-ful Red Rainbow, da."

My lips responded on auto pilot, "I love you."

A TV newsman shouted, "What did you say Mr. Konstantinov? Miss Rothman? And please speak up!"

"Boot-ti-ful Red Raaain-bow! Daaaa!" Yuri kissed my cheek again. "Yuri love Sa-rah danse-sing, da."

"Da's," replaced questions from the front rows and cameras captured our facial expressions. Yuri kissed my hand and Mrs. Pace dabbed at her eyes with a lace hankie. Her acting display directed at a nomination for a Tony Award. She emoted and Yuri and I waved. Mrs. Pace then took a dramatic pause before picking up the microphone to continue. But continue, she did.

"Mr. Konstantinov's new, full-length ballet, as you know, *Colors of The Rainbow*, will premier Saturday, October 23rd at the City Center Theatre. This two-act ballet promises to fascinate and delight. I was fortunate enough, to observe a recent rehearsal. Mr. Konstantinov and Miss Rothman performed a spectacular pas de deux from Act I. Their dancing so unique, it took my breath away. Uncommon moves and lifts too difficult to describe. I'd never seen anything like it. I'm humbled by their talent and I can't wait to show you and the world our City Center Ballet Theatre artists."

Her announcements and photos taken by photojournalists including publicity stills by Robert Forester appeared the next day in all three New York papers. The late night TV news was also, all a buzz. The mention of the spectacular pas de deux among balletomanes spread like wildfire. Many of the CCBT patrons, former dancers, backers and board members asked to watch our rehearsals. Mrs. Pace declined all requests with honeyed apologies.

Aunt Lucy called to tell me she saved a copy from each of the three newspapers. Her voice hit high notes sounding in awe.

However, the thrill of recognition and sweetness came to a halt. The next day, Wednesday, Mrs. Pace delayed the start of Madame's professional class. She spoke to the company dancers in an abrasive tone and listed her demands much like my high school gym teacher. The only teacher I hated because of her holier than thou attitude.

"No, visitors! No company members dropping in for five minutes! All rehearsals are closed and off limits for *Colors* and *Monarchs*. No admittance unless you participate in one of these ballets. And please keep your opinions to yourself. I hate gossip. There's been much, too much talk concerning everybody's business except your own. It's got to stop. Now. Today!"

"Da," nodded Yuri curling his upper lip.

A not-so-receptive Mrs. Pace shot him a look of disdain. "Please, Yuri, say nothing to no one about your ballets. And don't discuss anybody else's ballets. Alexi can explain."

Mrs. Tupper took a swig from her cough syrup and Anna and I poked each other's ribs and choked back giggles.

However, from then on, life turned into a fish bowl and I became the attraction. A goldfish ogled by female sharks. I discovered how nasty and jealous dancers could get. Sure, I'm Brooklyn born and raised and can handle shit. But this professional envy, I never imagined. Especially when I discovered ground-up Coke glass in my toe shoes before jamming my feet inside the tight fit, size 3 Pavlowa.

I ran screaming to Mrs. Pace who held a company meeting and threatened to fire the person who did it. She questioned several suspects but no one confessed. Ever thankful I noticed specks of glass shining in the linings, I now inspect my shoes, my underwear and my leotards for razor blades, sharp objects and straight pins.

On a positive note, I hunkered down and danced harder than ever. My New York attitude kicked in and yes, I considered the bitch angle. My upbringing encouraged tough but not evil. *I said no to bitch.*

YURI STARTED CHOREOGRAPHING our fifteen minute piece, *Monarchs In Spring*, to Chopin's *Raindrops* music. This began on

Wednesday following lunch. On Friday, we rehearsed the ballet again, towards early evening.

Tuesdays and Thursdays, Yuri rehearsed the five Rain Men and the three Thunder and Lightning Bolts. Which meant, Madame Madyaslavic worked on my technique on the days away from my partner. Madame fancied herself my new, overly protective mentor and a pain in the ass for detail. She insisted I was a jumper and could levitate. "Ha! Really?" I shot back at her wax-filled ears. She ignored everything I said.

And Madame was creepy. She locked the door to Studio C when we worked together and told me again and again, "Tell no one Madame teach Sarah." Of course, I bobbed my head up and down like a Cupie doll hanging in the back of Jeff's station wagon. No, I wouldn't tell but Mrs. Pace knew.

She refused to give Madame her tape recorder unless she knew what it was for. "Ransom," yelled Madame and stomped her Cuban heels out of Mrs. Pace's office and up the stairs. She schlepped the recorder wrapped in sweaters so no one would guess it was music for a purpose. *But if you're carrying a square box into a studio? What else could it be?*

Regarding job security?

Anna and I were thrilled to learn, Mrs. Tupper was Yuri's only choice to play the rehearsals for *Monarchs In Spring*. He trusted her diligence and if she was late to rehearsals, he'd panic.

"Vhere Tuppervare?" he'd holler.

And when the studio door opened and Mrs. Tupper would appear, she'd scurry past Yuri like a frightened mouse. Her head bent down in fear of ridicule. But he never reproached her. He'd run after her and give her a hug.

"Don't kiss me," she'd squeal and squirm. Her cheeks red as autumn apples.

The next day, Thursday, Yuri insisted Madame, "Vork on

Sa-rah arm." So, Madame devoted two hours to softening my hands and lengthening my arms. I improved the fluidity and when we finished, Madame rushed out of Studio C.

Left in an awkward silence, I walked across the hall to the girl's dressing room and changed clothes. Downstairs, I asked the secretary to call Fernando to pick me up. As I sat and waited on the lobby couch, dancers walked past me and talked and laughed with one another. I tried to say hello but I was shunned. Partnering a prince wasn't all a fairy tale.

I SAT WITH Cook, in the kitchen eating roast beef, a baked potato, corn and green beans. Cook said with a twinkle in her eyes, "Guess what?"

"Is this a riddle?"

"Kind of. More flowers arrived this afternoon. They were delivered by the same man from the Madison Avenue Florist."

"Why are you telling me this?"

"Mrs. Williams and I … well … we think Mrs. Pace is hiding something."

"You mean like a boyfriend? Oops!" I giggled.

"Don't get weird, I don't know."

"Well, she's not the romantic type." I wiped my chin with a napkin. "Imagine her holding hands with a man. She'd tell him how to do it and then say, next?"

"You know, this is the third flower delivery and Mrs. Pace filled her own vase with water and the bouquet. She carried the whole thing upstairs to her room."

"Okay, so what?"

"After she left, I peeked in her bedroom and saw the bouquet on the bureau next to the other two flower vases."

"Miniature roses like before?"

"No, yellow lilies and pink carnations."

"Where's the card?"

"That's just it. She grabs the card, shoves it in her pocket and no one can read it."

"A secret admirer?"

"Can you imagine, Sarah?"

"No, I can't … not by a mile."

DURING FRIDAY'S SHORT piece rehearsal, Justin Sainte Claire walked in Studio A unannounced. He carried his black leather portfolio of watercolor drawings for *Monarchs In Spring*.

This time, he didn't schlepp his chattering, cigarette smoking entourage. He escorted one lady seamstress and his female-looking, male assistant Robin.

Around Robin's neck was his Kodak Instamatic Flashcube camera. The seamstress carried two butterfly detachable, mechanical wings.

"Vhat?" Yuri laughed and grabbed one of the wing contraptions and tried it on. He wobbled flat-footed like Charlie Chaplin in *The Great Dictator*. He scoffed, "Cir-cus an-ni-mal cost-tume?"

Robin took flashcube photos, Alexi and I bowled over laughing and a furious costume designer chased Yuri around the room.

"Nyet," teased Yuri. "Nyet catch Yuri."

Justin screamed, "Miss Rothman, tell your partner to stop jumping so I can explain."

"Why? Because the silly Monarch wings work better hanging on trees with baboons?"

"They're not silly. They're made of silk!"

"This isn't an opera. We don't stand downstage and sing."

"Why the sarcasm?" The designer's jaw tightened.

"Why not? You built wooden sticks on Yuri's back waving back and forth and Velcro on his sleeves. He could poke my eye out or his."

Alexi translated in Yuri's own words. "Mr. Sainte Claire, the wings don't work. I lift, spin and twist Sarah around my shoulders, my chest and down my legs. The wings are no good and crazy as shit. Sarah and I looking like bats flying blind, upside down and not graceful butterflies. Very dangerous. We could stab each other with the sticks."

Yuri turned and leaped across the room demonstrating the dangers. "Nyet ... nyet goot."

"But, but ... look how beautiful the flowing silk gossamer wings flutter when you turn. Think of shimmering sunshine on a lake when the water ripples."

"Yuri dances on a stage, not a lake." Alexi fisted his hands on his hips.

"And I don't ripple."

Yuri attempted several pirouettes wrapping himself in a co-coon. He fell to the floor. Acting as a mummy unable to get free, "Help! Bad boy cost-tume." He tore the wings off and broke the wooden sticks.

Alexi shook his finger at Justin. "Go back to the drawing board and design proper wings, or?

"Or what?"

"Yuri can choose someone else to design his butterfly."

Justin packed up the broken wings, drawings and his two assistants. He left in a huff.

BECAUSE I WAS rehearsing in a bubble, my only feedback regarding Frederick Borgen came from Marie Larson. She continued to join Anna, me and Mrs. Tupper daily, at Horn & Hardart's and kept us informed.

"I like Freddy's coaching, it's precise," explained Marie biting into a tuna salad.

"Freddy? No shit." Anna glared at Marie. "First rehearsal you were bored out of your skull. Now, he's Freddy? Not sweetie pie or snookum's?"

"Okay, wise ass, but everybody deserves a second chance."

"Right," agreed Mrs. Tupper eating peanut butter and jelly.

"And even with his weird Danish accent, we understand his directions. Freddy apologizes if he makes a mistake."

Anna laughed, "Can you imagine? A choreographer that apologizes?"

"You mean they don't?" I wiggled my shoulders in a fake surprise.

"No, they don't," replied a bitter Anna. "Karl Kreisler was a horse's ass. I'm happy for you Marie. You're finally working with a choreographer who cares about his dancers."

CHAPTER 31

Saturday, October 2nd. A day of reckoning and drama.

IT WAS ELEVEN days since I'd seen or heard from David Katz. Anna was wrong. He never called. Maybe, his intentions were figments of my imagination and he'd let me down using time instead of a letter or words of goodbye over dinner.

To soothe my sad self. At bedtime, I read Edgar Allen Poe's "The Raven" which I loved in school. And to my surprise, I wasn't the distraught lover falling into madness after all.

"Let my heart be still and this mystery explore ... Quoth the Raven, Nevermore.'"

I ate, slept and danced ballet determined to improve. No more what's his name. I worked on my hands and arm gestures, a turn of the head and triple turns instead of doubles. I convinced Mrs. Pace to hire an acting coach to teach me pantomime and nuances for the Red Rainbow role. But, the road to success had potholes.

At this afternoon's two o'clock rehearsal in Studio B, Yuri arrived excited and hyper. He had dreamt up, two more dramatic lifts for the end of our love pas de deux, Act II.

When I died on stage, Yuri insisted through Alexi's translation, "The moment should be more dramatic and meaningful. He knows of a newer, perfect lift for your death scene."

I inhaled to the count of five.

"Together," translated Alexi. "You two should soar and dare to do what other dancers never attempt."

The hair on my arms stood up. "Tell my partner in Russian not fair! He promised no changes to his choreography."

Yuri snapped, "That … then, now … now."

"But, you set the final lifts in stone. You said it yourself to keep me safe. To keep us both confidant."

Alex spoke Yuri's words, "I changed mind. Why to be safe? Artists should constantly create. Take chances."

"Tell him he lied!"

"No, he changed his mind. Not a lie."

I chewed my nails and glared at the two men.

"Sa-rrrrah, pleez."

"No! Every time, you catch me in a new lift, I get hurt. I get bruises."

But Yuri had a bug up his ass. He soothed, smiled, kissed my hand, cajoled and tried to cuddle.

"Don't hug me, you cheater." I shoved him away.

Geez, did I just shove my mentor? The man who cast the deciding vote? Goodbye Red Rainbow, hello, Brooklyn College. I'm an idiot!

But I wasn't fired. Yuri scoffed then laughed.

I tried the scary lifts twice and fell once. On the third try while throwing me in the air, he almost missed catching me by a slip of the hand.

"Oh, good God!" I screamed. "See!"

"Yuri, soar-ry." His face blanched, his fingers dug into my skin holding me tight against his muscular torso.

"I hate new lifts. I'm scared."

Yuri let go and stepped back in thought. Several minutes later, his face relaxed and his eyes flickered. "Yuri catch Sa-rah bet-ter. Idea bet-ter. Trust Yuri."

"No. Nyet."

"Nyet, Sa-rah try." He touched my cheek and waved at Mrs. Tupper to start the music for my entrance.

But, I didn't run to the corner in preparation for a fast, running leap into his outstretched hands. I stayed in place frozen like an orange-flavored Popsicle.

"No, I can't do this. Please, don't make me."

"Da ... une fois, s'il te plait, pour moi."

I glared daggers at the man.

To soar in the air like a seagull, switch to a semi-prone arabesque, held by one hand ... his other hand, the right palm pressed into my left thigh. One beat later, my legs switch, I snake his neck and chest and drop to the floor. His arm takes me by the waist and pulls me up, above his head into a back-arched pose, my hands crossed my chest, my extended legs tight. He turns and sets my left leg on pointe, I pirouette three times, maybe four, into attitude pose.

I whimpered a reluctant, "Okay, I'm stupid, I'll try."

"Da! Tuppervare, play mu-sak."

I ran to Yuri's outstretched hands and forgot to breathe and lost my balance. The second try, I jumped seconds too early and slipped and never soared into the air. The third try, I soared but was too late on the snake wrap-around.

The fourth attempt, I soared in the air, switched legs as choreographed and continued the lift. At which point, Yuri was thrilled his new lift worked, he tried something not discussed. He held me by one hand and paraded in a circle as if I was the winner's trophy.

I panicked and fell but not to earth. Yuri caught me inches from hitting my head on the wood floor.

He clung to me and stood my body upright. "Sa-rah broke?"

"No," I shivered. "Yuri, stop! You're making welts on my

skin."

He let go and massaged the red imprints on my arms. When I winced, he stopped and moved away.

I took his rejection and walked over to the barre and stretched my legs. Alexi screamed something at is friend and they fought. I covered my ears and wished we were done for the day.

The yelling stopped and Yuri joined me at the barre. "Sa-rah, new lift. Da?"

"No, new lifts." I turned and headed for the door.

"Sa-rrraaah!" His eyes flashed and he grabbed my waist and lifted me in the air. I squirmed in a backbend over his head. "No! I protested. "I won't do it. Not ever, oh, God."

I saw in the mirror people enter the room. The trio of visitors froze. Hearing my gasp, Yuri returned my frame to a standing position and I faced the three adults.

Mrs. Pace, Eleanor Katz and David Katz stood transfixed. They'd heard our lunatic screams. In fact, everyone in the building heard us screech.

Being a trooper, Yuri performed several pirouettes and took a bow. Our audience looked baffled. Should they applaud? Or, leave the room?

They chose to applaud and Mrs. Pace exclaimed, "My solo-ists have artistic temperaments, isn't that so, Alexi?"

"Yes, ma'am," he mumbled, red in the face.

I hyper-ventilated watching Mrs. Pace urge her guests to sit on a bench in front of the wall mirrors. Eleanor waved but David stared. His icy, ocean blue eyes fierce. I turned away and focused on Mrs. Tupper fumbling with her music. But curiosity didn't kill the cat, I glanced back at David and he caught my glimpse. The intensity behind his eyes, darkened his expression.

I hate you, David Katz, what chutzpah. No word for eleven days and you show up unannounced. You ass ... I wouldn't say the rest of the word, not in front of Eleanor.

My blood ran hot as I paced in the same frantic way Edgar jumped back and forth in his cage. A worried Yuri stopped me pacing. He whispered, "Sa-rah ... who care dees peoples come in ... for-get peoples, is fleas on dog ... bite peoples, da!"

The professional in my partner shone bright. Who cared if we had visitors? He was right. Even my dad, the ex-Navy sailor would d*amn the intruders, full speed ahead.*

I prayed and counted past five determined to pull myself together. "Okay, partner," I inhaled. "I'm ready ... let's do it, to it."

Yuri and I broke apart and moved to either side of the room. He signaled Mrs. Tupper to start the music.

At the appointed musical cue, I ran from stage left leaping into Yuri's arms in a swan dive. The guests gasped seeing my head barely touch the floor and like a cavalier, my partner raised me up, to an attitude on pointe. I pirouetted four turns and ended in a "develope a la seconde." A slow turn of my hip into an arabesque ... Yuri grabbed my inner thigh and up I went, high in the air.

Seconds later, after a series of chasing grande jetes, Yuri lifted me above his head by my hip bones. Arching my back, I posed as an eagle in flight.

The music changed to a legato, three-quarter waltz. A romantic-themed melody defined our roles. Yuri, "The Sun" expressed his love to me, "The Red Rainbow." We danced, soft and sensuous. A lyrical style I took to "like a duck to water," according to Mrs. Pace.

My body slid down Yuri's back, a languid action snaking around my partner's shoulders and front, to his back again. The result, an arabesque penche at his side, dropping my head to my knee. Yuri, holding my hands in his, turned my body inside out and into an embrace on pointe.

The music changed to a brisk two-four beat. Yuri's lips brushed my neck and torso in a loving touch. I danced a brise, glissade, eschappe sur les pointes, entrechat and repeated. Yuri executed three double tours en l'air and ended, in a pose on his right knee.

At the musical key change, Yuri stood up, grabbed my shoulder and spun me around. This move wasn't part of the choreography but I wasn't afraid and followed his lead. He whispered, "Trust, Yuri."

"Okay."

"Allez! Jump Sa-rah!"

I leaped into Yuri's arms fully in control and fearless with a heartbeat hitting overdrive. I did the lift we attempted earlier; a half body twirl in the air and ended in a handstand atop my partner's shoulder. Whoosh! To the floor in a swan dive then to an arabesque pose en pointe.

The two of us separated in a traveling glissade, pas de chat and ran to opposing corners. We posed and seconds later, when the music surged, I ran to my partner determined to jump upwards. A series of body acrobatics, a leap of faith and I finished triumphant in the air.

Our three-person-audience rose to their feet. "Bravo, bravo, beautiful!" Applause, applause.

Yuri and I took a slow bow, out of breath.

David's surprised expression, a picture of joy, sent my ego into orbit. I giggled at his face-splitting grin, lit by the sunshine streaming in from the ceiling windows. His eyes glistened and locked mine.

Doggone, he was gorgeous.

Yuri, aware of David's flirt, narrowed his Tartar blue-grey eyes and pulled me in close. He kissed my cheek a little too long and David's demeanor stiffened. The pissing contest was on.

David stepped towards me but, Mrs. Pace stopped him. "Yuri and Sarah," she said. "A beautiful performance. Please, let me introduce my guests."

"No need," said Eleanor bypassing Mrs. Pace. "This is my darling girl." Her hands held my shoulders and she kissed my cheek.

"I'm sweating, careful, Eleanor."

"Yes, your cheek is damp," she laughed and moved aside.

David stepped forward. "Hey," his eyes smiled. "You're stunning. I had no idea."

I blushed.

"Did you like my flowers?"

"Huh? What flowers?"

"I sent you three bouquets while I was in Los Angeles. The last bouquet had my hotel number asking you to call collect."

"I never got any flowers."

Mrs. Pace cleared her throat and looked at me then focused on David. "This is embarrassing, Mr. Katz. The bouquets arrived and I naturally assumed they were for me from backers and patrons. It's the new season."

"The flowers were addressed to Miss Rothman."

"My housekeeper must have … I'm sorry."

David lunged at me, his hands held my face. Wet leotards didn't stop this man's trembling, ardent lips kissing my mouth. His chest pushed into me.

Tears filled my eyes. I missed him and I didn't care who knew. His aunt tugged at both our arms to stop the kiss.

Clasping my hand, David glared at Mrs. Pace. "You will excuse us."

Everyone nodded except Yuri.

We exited Studio B and hurried into a costume room at the

side of the lobby. No one was in there and David shut the door.

The perspiration covering my skin hardly mattered. His mouth was on mine and time stopped still. "I've missed you," he murmured. "I'm fighting not to kiss you all over."

My heart went into a tailspin when his teeth nipped at my bottom lip. Happiness washed over me in quivering waves until his deep, wet kiss stopped.

"I'm taking you to dinner."

"What?" I pulled away. "I can't. Mrs. Pace... I have to leave with her. How can I shower and change?"

"What time do you finish?"

"At six, but she won't let me go. Fernando drives me to her house every night for dinner."

David grinned, "I'll handle it."

WHEN WE RETURNED to Studio B, we listened to Eleanor plan a fund-raising dinner to honor *Colors*. To say, Mrs. Pace and Yuri were thrilled was an understatement. Yuri saw free publicity. "Invite press? Photo-tog-raphers? Goot."

Mrs. Pace gushed. "Sarah? Aren't you excited? Eleanor's giving you a party."

I winked at Eleanor feeling David squeeze my hand knowing I could throw up any minute. *I hated any gathering that authorized strangers to ask my weight, my diet, my romantic life and how I brushed my teeth.*

A live-band, catered, Texas style barbeque fund-raising dinner complete with bronco busting at her beach house sounded silly. Investment bankers and Wall Street tycoons riding a mechanical bull in her patio? Not twenty feet away from the Atlantic Ocean?

Eleanor looked at her listeners. "How about Saturday, October 16th at five o'clock? Is everyone available?"

Mrs. Pace answered fast. "Sounds perfect. October 16th. Drinkers, diners and money welcome. Let's print those words on the invitations."

"Let's not." Eleanor bit her lip. "Save that surprises when you greet the guests at the door."

"You know, I will." She glanced up at the wall clock. "It's five thirty. If it's alright with you, Yuri. Can we stop for the day? No more rehearsing until Tuesday?"

Yuri glanced over at me for approval. "Da?"

"Okay," I nodded.

"That's it. Two days off to rest up." She looked around. "And tonight as a treat, I'm taking everyone to dinner. Four Seasons. Eight o'clock. I'll make reservations. Who's coming?"

"Da," sang out Yuri and Alexi in unison.

Mrs. Tupper smiled. "My neighbor can watch my mother. Yes, I'm coming."

"And yes, for Harry and me," echoed Eleanor noticing her nephew shake his head no. "However, David and Sarah won't be joining us."

"Why not?" said a surprised Mrs. Pace. "Of course, Sarah will come with me, isn't that so. Sarah?"

David winked at me. "Miss Rothman?"

"I don't think that's going to happen," said Eleanor holding my hand and eyeing David. "My nephew prefers a candlelit dinner alone with his girl and so he should. They both need some quiet time together."

"Yes, we do," David responded matter-of-fact. "Please, accept our apologies, maybe another time." He turned his head, "Babe?"

I picked up my dance bag from a chair and we left. In the girl's dressing room, I changed shoes, stripped and put on street clothes and my sneakers. Gathering my things, I ran downstairs and joined David and the others waiting in the lobby.

Fernando tipped his hat, "Miss Sarah."

"Fernando, meet David Katz."

"Yes, ma'am, we already met. Mighty glad he's your friend," he chuckled. "You needs a strong man friend, Miss Sarah. I do believes."

My cheeks flushed.

Fernando winked at me behind Mrs. Pace's back. *Fernando, stop teasing me you stinker.*

Alexi joined David and me and asked to walk us out. We stopped at the curb, in front of the Bentley, parked several doors down. Alexi whispered, "Sometimes, it takes a rat to kill a snake."

"Yes, but it has to be a clever rat," agreed David.

"What does that mean?" I eyed them both.

Alexi looked sheepish.

"Maybe a Russian fairy tale?" replied David tongue-in-cheek.

"Or, not," said Alexi. "Maybe New York reality. David strong arms Mrs. Pace and wins."

"Oh, no."

"Not to worry. You love danger." He opened the passenger door and waited as I got in.

DAVID DROVE ME to Sutton Place where he double-parked while I packed a dinner dress. From there, he drove us to his East 62nd Street townhouse and parked the Bentley in front. Every house on the tree-lined street looked identical being stuck-together like red-brick Lego pieces.

"We're here."

We carried my things and climbed the nine steps to his front door. He used a key to the brass deadbolt and in we walked. Turning on the entrance foyer lights, David set both our things down and took me in his arms.

"I've missed kissing you," and he meant it. When he finally stopped exploring my tongue and throat, I felt every one of his eleven days of longing. I trembled so hard, I felt embarrassed and apologized.

"Don't apologize for your feelings," he murmured. "You missed me and that's a sincere response. C'mon, let me show you around."

In the living room, David turned on lamps. Family photos in silver frames glistened atop a baby grand piano. Three Chinese antique pieces, two leather couches, paintings, drawings and books filled the room. And as I followed him through three more rooms, books lined many shelves on walls.

Beige and brown drapes covered windows while mahogany furniture dominated several rooms. I giggled to myself ... besides leather and corduroy fabric sofas, *did David have Naugahyde couches covered in clear plastic?*

"Oh, wow, the kitchen."

"Yes, it's happy. I like it."

White appliances stood in front of red poppies on a white background wall paper and a tiled, dark, red floor. Dishtowels and the tablecloth carried smaller sized red poppies.

"Would you like something to drink?" he asked leaning against the fridge.

"No, thanks," I opened several cabinet doors. White china dishes decorated in tiny red poppies were trimmed in gold. *No Melmac dishes? See, Mama, some people prefer China.*

"David, do you have any plastic Yankee cups?"

"No, why?" His face lit up, amused at watching me snoop.

"My brothers collect Yankee things."

"C'mon," he switched off the lights and I followed him into his office/ study.

"I inherited this house from my grandfather."

"What a nice man." My fingers ran along the edges of the smooth leather couch facing a large, heavy desk. *No lace doilies underneath plastic covers on chair arms or couches? Bubbe and Mama might have to tat or crochet extra doilies to help this room.*

"He died when I started law school and never saw me graduate."

"That's sad."

"Yes, it was. He took great care to secure for me, a quality education. Through his attorney, he insisted I have my own trust fund following his death. That trust maintains this property by annuities from blue chip stocks and several patents. He invented a ballcock with a special feature and several other plumbing things."

"A ballcock?" I giggled, covering my mouth.

"Not what you think, Sarah. For easy flush toilets. Indoor plumbing not outdoor plumbing."

I blushed. "Oops a daisy, I was raised with brothers."

"Lucky you and I always wanted sisters."

He took my hand and we moved to the entrance hall. "I was an only child. I'll show you the upstairs. There's five floors but I use only three. The basement is for storage."

"How many people live here?"

He held up a finger. "One ... me. Except for my housekeeper. She has a bedroom if she needs to sleep here otherwise, she comes in for the day."

I took a moment to rethink. "Ah ... is there a bathroom I can shower and change in?"

"Yes, second floor in the master bedroom. I'll show you."

I hesitated.

"What's the matter?"

I shrugged. "It's your bedroom?"

"Yes. So?"

"Ah, so." *Yikes! What did I get myself into? I can't be willing to use a man's bedroom shower? What will he think? Worse, what do I think?*

David picked up my garment bag and overnight bag. I gripped my purse and dance bag so tight, my knuckles showed white. *What should I do? Crap, it's too late.* I followed him up the stairs.

Inside the black and white tiled bathroom, David pointed to the linen closet. "Towels in there." He stared at me through the double sink mirrors. "You okay?"

I mumbled, "Yes, fine." *My heart pounded to beat the band. Alone in a man's house, naked in a shower, changing my clothes, I hadn't thought this through.*

"I'm happy you're here." He smiled and placed his hand on the door. "I'll give you some privacy." He left and I heard the bedroom door close.

Too nervous to stay long in the shower, I dried off and dressed in a hurry. I put on my favorite periwinkle blue dress, beige strappy heels and gold loop earrings. Wanting to appear older, I brushed my long hair into a twisted figure eight at the nape of my neck. Princess Grace Kelly wore this style in Vogue magazine and after trying the twist, I did look older and a little more polished.

Not wanting to give David any silly ideas like I would spend the night, I trudged all my things downstairs. Next to the front door, I set my three bags against the wall. I heard voices; low tones of David and another man coming from off the hall.

I entered the living room and both men stopped their conversation and followed me with their eyes. David smiled and reached for my hand. "You look beautiful." He gave me a quick kiss on the lips. "I'd like you to meet my cousin, Edward Katz. He's a doctor at Mount Sinai Hospital."

I extended my hand and smiled, "Hello."

"Miss Rothman."

I noticed his blue lapis and shiny gold cufflinks then his wingtip shoes. *No, definitely not Thom McCann Mama, had to cost a lot more. He had an air and nonchalance that spelled money. His grey suit and tie and white starched shirt appeared too well pressed and tailored to be sold in Brooklyn. I heard Aunt Lucy's sarcasm in my head. What else could a Jewish doctor at Mt. Sinai on Fifth Avenue wear? It's the upper Eastside, you idiot.*

He spoke. "Eleanor, my mother, visited your rehearsal today with David."

"That was your mother?"

He nodded.

"She's a lovely lady."

"And she's a real fan of the ballet and so is my wife. We live next door. Do you think you could come over and meet her?"

I glanced at David. "I guess?"

"Yes, we can visit." His eyes traveled from me to Ed. "We're going out to dinner. It'll be quick."

"Great. Rebecca will be thrilled. She reads everything about the ballet and especially about you and the Russian."

David chuckled, "She'll call me 'what's his name' after meeting you, Miss Rothman."

"And if you marry her?" said Ed. "You'd be called Mr. Rothman."

The heat rose from my cheeks to my ears. "Stop it, you guys."

"Why? Because you're the best at what you do?" David slid

his arm around my waist and kissed my lips. "I'm a lucky man."

"Enough," said Ed. "Let's go meet my wife."

David's smiled, "Ready, babe?"

"Yes, my things are at the front door."

"We'll get them later."

"Not now?"

The three of us left David's townhouse and walked next door. We climbed the nine stairs to his cousin's cookie cutter townhouse.

ED UNLOCKED HIS front door. "Rebecca? Sweetie, I have a surprise."

"You brought me flowers?" She waddled into the entrance hall and stared at me.

"She's too big to put in a vase. She has to be trimmed."

"Remember my mom talked about the new ballet at the City Center Theatre?"

"Yes, so?" A very pregnant Rebecca yawned and looked as pretty as a porcelain doll.

"Well? Meet Sarah Rothman. She's dancing with the Russian guy. My wife, Rebecca Katz."

Rebecca came alive with chatter. Instant fireworks over the Hudson. Forget shaking hands. She bull-dozed in for a hug. Now, I've never had contact with a pregnant belly before, so I moved back not wishing to hurt her. She thumped forward at me again.

"Oh, great Scott," she squealed. "I'm meeting the famous rising star. Everybody is buying tickets to see you dance. Scalpers are asking a hundred dollars for orchestra seats."

"What? How outrageous! Yes, I'm happy to meet you, too."

"Ed? Honey? How did you meet Sarah Rothman?"

"David's taking her to dinner. That's how."

"Oh, you rascal, David," laughed Rebecca. "Always full of secrets."

"She's no secret, she's right here," chided David hugging Rebecca and kissing her cheek. "You look beautiful and radiant."

"Like a blimp," she sighed.

"No, svelte and lovely like an expectant mother. My beauty queen cousin-in-law."

"Glad someone thinks so."

"I know so," grinned her husband. "You're beautiful and I love you."

"Love you, too, honey. Your mom and dad were here an hour ago."

"I know, mom called me."

"She and David saw Sarah dance today." Rebecca touched my arm. "Mom couldn't stop talking about you and when she learned Yuri called you 'his muse and inspiration for his choreography,' she choked up and cried."

David leaned in and kissed my mouth. My heart raced hearing the remark and David's impulsive kiss.

Seeing me blush, Rebecca saved the moment. "Hey everybody. Come in my kitchen." She pointed towards the open door and we followed. "I'm making stir-fry. Do you like shrimp?"

"We do, but not tonight," replied David. "We're going out to dinner."

"Where?"

"The Sign of the Dove. Come join us?"

Rebecca looked up at Ed, who shook his head. "I've had a long day and my mommy-to-be needs to get off her feet. She'll need a warm bath later and rest."

Rebecca leaned into me. "You know, I love the yellow restaurant. Have you eaten there before?"

I shook my head.

"It's chic American food and there's no prices on the menus."

"Sweetie," said Ed. "The prices are on the men's menus. They know who pays the bills."

"Hey, babe?" David reached for my hand. "We need to go. We have reservations."

"No, let her stay, please," cooed Rebecca, her infectious smile a delight.

"Yes, a few minutes?" I said smiling at Rebecca.

"Ed and I will be out front on the sidewalk."

Minutes passed and Ed returned to the kitchen. "Time's up, girls."

We giggled in surprise and Rebecca sighed, "So soon?"

"Way too soon," I agreed.

"Miss Rothman, David's waiting."

"Yes, well. Hope to see you again. Bye, Rebecca."

She dropped my hand. "Bye."

CHAPTER 32

Two hours later, on the Eastside where real estate is very expensive. Why? The better side of Central Park and off Fifth Avenue that's why.

$\mathcal{W}$E LEFT THE Sign of the Dove Restaurant on Third Avenue and walked East 65th Street towards Second. Having eaten a mouth-watering, rack of lamb and rice Pilaf, we decided to take a stroll.

In an abrupt move, David pushed open a wrought iron gate and pulled me inside the private garden of someone's townhouse. I nearly tripped over a water fountain.

"Stay with me tonight."

"What?"

His lips brushed my cheek. "Sarah, come home with me and stay the night."

"I have to go back to Mrs. Pace, to her house."

"Why? She knows you're with me. My aunt and uncle are dining with her. She's probably hitting them up for more money for her company."

I looked at him in surprise. "She'd do that? After Eleanor suggested a fund-raiser?"

"She's well aware how much my aunt adores you. I don't think she cares where you sleep, if you dance like you did today which was astonishing."

"What if she calls my dad?"

"Would she be that stupid? He'd make you quit the company."

"Yes, he might."

"What happens to her new ballet then?"

"I don't know."

His ocean blue eyes darkened, "Sarah ..."

"I don't ..."

He kissed my open mouth gripping my face in both his hands. I tried to speak tasting warm cognac on his breath. I tried again to say, "I, I can't ..." when he pressured me with his tongue. Such persistence startled my senses and turned my mind inside out. My blood ran hot and I tingled.

"I want you, Sarah," he murmured smothering me with kisses. "I want you ..."

The man taunted arousal the same way he prosecuted in court. "Direct, unyielding and winner take all" in the words of his boss, Bernie Lieberman. "David's modus operandi transcended the norm and he wielded it like the Sword of Damocles."

Quite right, David's unyielding effort did a number on me. My heartbeat pounded crazy feeling the heat in his loins. I wanted what he offered and it scared me.

"Stop it, David!" I shoved him away, out of breath. "You're not playing fair."

His lips tightened to a thin line. "You're right. I don't play fair."

I folded my arms, blocking my chest. "Don't back me into a corner."

"It's not entrapment, Sarah."

"No? You expect me to lie down?"

He looked at me in awe. "Why yes! Lie down, roll over and beg."

I laughed.

"What's so funny?"

"Me on my knees begging."

"Oh baby, I'd love you on your knees." He moved closer and peered down the front of my dress.

Oh crap, cleavage. Why didn't I button my sweater?

David spoke in a low, husky tone. "Sarah … come home with me." He gingerly touched my breasts and tweaked a nipple through the soft fabric.

"Ow," I hitched at the pinch.

"Let me love you," he murmured nuzzling my neck. "It's time."

"Damn you, David."

He kissed my lips, tenderly, eager to please. Sensations again, too lovely.

"Really, not fair," I lamented.

"Say, yes," he pleaded nipping at my earlobe. His hands stroked the length of my neck.

"Daaavid," I squirmed.

"Your decision," he murmured moving his hands to my lower back massaging the pain from days of rehearsals.

I cooed, "That's sooooo nice."

Should I call a cab and hurry to Mrs. Pace's house?

He kissed me hungry yanking fistfuls of my hair. My heartbeat raced pushing me bothered. "Aaaaaah," I moaned wanting him to never stop his delicious mouth.

Would my family kill me if they knew? Would it be worth it?

"Yes," my lips trembled. My knees knocked.

He stopped the kiss. "Yes, to consensual sex?"

I gazed into his eyes, "Yes."

He clasped my hand, pulled me out of the garden and into the on-coming traffic. "Taxi!"

CHAPTER 33

Twenty minutes later. Did I make the right decision?

$\mathcal{D}$AVID FUMBLED WITH the lock to his townhouse, shoved the door open and kissed me with a command as if launching the Queen Mary. He broke away, leaving me breathless and hurried to the living room and dialed the phone.

"Ed? Can you come over? Yes, alone ... bring birth control pills. Yes, I'm serious ... you owe me."

My facial muscles twitched. Furious and too stunned to speak after hearing David's request, my cheeks burned.

During dinner, he never mentioned telling his cousin about us, especially that. I glanced at my low neckline and saw hives breaking out in tiny red spots. Soon, I'd be itching.

The phone hit the cradle and I hissed, "What are you doing?"

"He hung up."

"I'd hang up, too. In fact, I'm leaving. Help me call a cab." I spun around and hurried towards the hall entrance.

David grabbed my wrists. "Sarah, please, don't go." He pulled me in close. "Let me explain. I want you here."

"No," I huffed and wiggled away. "You bastard!"

"Hey?" he snapped. "What's happening?"

"Birth control pills? You want a sex slave?"

"What? No, of course not. Who said?"

The doorbell rang.

His hand caressed my face. "Sarah, be fair. Talk to me. I

mean I have to answer the door." He struggled, "Ah ... stay ...ah, fuck, it's Ed, please wait." His shoulder jerked.

"Okay," I fumed. "Answer the stupid door."

The doctor entered the living room wearing a serious face. "Sarah, good evening."

"Doctor Katz ..."

Silence.

"Well?" said the doctor. "This is awkward. What's up?" He looked at David. He looked at me. "Yes, Sarah, you first."

I'd never talked to a man or doctor about this subject. I exhaled, "My sister's on birth control pills and her husband demands sex every day. She hates it. I can't be a sex slave like her and dance six hours a day, I'll die."

Ed and David looked flabbergasted.

"What?" I glared at the men. "Say something. What are you not telling me?"

David plopped down on his leather couch, rubbing his hands over his face. Ed cleared his throat. "Sarah, as a doctor, I can tell you if a husband makes proper love to his wife, it's a pleasurable experience for both."

"Is that so?"

"Yes, making love should be nurturing."

"My mother told Melissa it's her duty. Close your eyes and open your legs."

Ed looked amused. "No, sex is not a duty. I hope someday, a considerate man shows your sister the rewards of physical love."

I half-smiled hoping he was right.

"So?" said Ed. "Why am I here? David, you wanted birth control. Sarah, how old are you?"

"Seventeen," David answered immediately "but I know the law. She has consented."

"I know the licensing board. She's too young."

"Ed, just give her something for tonight so she doesn't get knocked-up."

The doctor looked uncomfortable. "It doesn't work that way. Use a condom."

"You know that can back-fire. Listen, I'm flying to Hong Kong on Wednesday."

"Wednesday?" said Ed.

"You're leaving again?" I gasped.

David rose to his feet and within the next beat of my heart, his arms slid around my trembling frame. "I'm sorry, babe. I have to go on business. I'm not thrilled about it either." He kissed the side of my head and turned to Ed.

My hands clutched his arms and I started to cry.

"Ed, do me this favor ... for Sarah, please."

"Damn it, David.

"C'mon, man."

He grumbled. "When do you turn eighteen, Sarah?"

"November 5th."

"When was your last period?"

"Mama said it's nobody's business."

Ed's back stiffened. "This is a medical question. I'm a doctor. When, Miss Rothman?"

"I don't know." I shrugged wiping my eyes with David's hankie. "Maybe three months or four months ago. It happened at a Yankee game."

"What Yankee game?" snapped David. "Don't you write it down like every woman on this planet? If not, why not?"

"Hey!" yelled Ed. "Stop it!"

David ran his hands through his hair. "I meant to say, is she normal?"

"Yes and no," answered Ed. "She's overactive physically. Some female athletes go months without a menses. I can help the problem by prescribing birth control pills to regulate the hormones."

"Even if underage?"

"Yes, no matter the age. I can prescribe the pills but I need to see her in my office."

David touched my face, "When, Sarah?"

I turned away.

"Sarah!"

"Ah, a," my lips quivered. "I, I guess Monday? I don't rehearse with Yuri until late in the day."

"Bring her in two o'clock and don't tell Eleanor. Sarah, did you hear me? Don't tell my mother."

"No," I mumbled. "I won't tell."

"David, use a condom for a while."

Ed reached in his jacket pocket and took out a pink wheel with numbered days. "Each slot contains a pill. Take one pill every night at bedtime until ..." He continued with detailed instructions including the negative side effect of weight gain.

"What's the matter, Sarah?"

"Weight gain? No!" I shook my head.

"A few pounds can't hurt. You're thin."

"I'm a dancer. I can't gain an ounce. Girls I know, stick spoons down their throats and throw up after every meal."

"Barbaric. Then, we'll try something else later." He shoved the wheel in a tiny box and handed it to me with his business card. "Any questions? Call me, I'm your doctor."

"Call you," I swallowed hard. "Thanks."

"And give David credit for taking care of you. I wanted to wring his neck at first. I have patients who accidentally got pregnant."

David accompanied Ed to the front door and the men spoke in hushed tones for several minutes. When David returned to the living room, he extended his hand. "Let's get you a drink, orange juice?"

"Dom Perignon."

"You're kidding."

"I'll never tell."

DAVID TOOK MY hand and led me upstairs to the second floor, to his master bedroom. We set my things on an armchair and David put his keys and wallet on a nightstand. He smiled a catbird grin, pulled me in close and kissed me silly.

"Your lips are soft," he murmured. "I like kissing you."

"Me, too," I sighed a little anxious. "Oh gosh, I meant to say I liked it."

David lit several beige candles on top of a bureau then flipped the light switch off. He turned the radio dial to a soft piano jazz and glanced over his shoulder, "Okay?"

"George Shearing is more than okay."

"Good call."

"My dad plays the tenor sax in a jazz band on week-ends. Bar Mitzvahs and weddings, stuff like that."

"Cool," he mumbled clearing books and papers from his bed. He turned down the bedspread and covers to clean, white sheets.

I coughed. "Sometimes dad plays the trombone."

"Trombone and sax?"

"Uh-huh." I acted nonchalant but seeing David set the scene for romance gave me a queasy feeling in my tummy.

He opened the closet door and hung up his suit jacket and vest. When he unzipped his pants and stepped free, I knew he meant business. He hung up the pants and smiled.

"Come here, Brooklyn."

I hesitated then stepped forward. He kissed my upper lip. "Turn around."

His long fingers unzipped my dress. It slid off my shoulders and dropped to the carpet. David's mouth brushed my neck and I shivered scooting to the side. He picked up my dress and hung it next to his suit. *What a sweet thing to do.*

He removed his tie, shirt and socks and threw them on the armchair. Around his neck, a tiny Mezuzah on a gold chain sparkled in the candlelight against his tanned skin. My heartbeat quickened watching his perfect body.

He stood naked except for abbreviated boxers, slung low on narrow hips. I tried to avert my eyes so I wouldn't know what was in the boxers. I did stare at his tight abs and an accentuated muscle line that made me wonder where it ended. He set his watch on the nightstand then ogled me.

Feeling a rush, I imagined myself a hunted animal seeing how fast his expression turned intense. I sucked in air watching him decide his next move. *Aunt Lucy was right. She said he was dangerous. Butterflies swirled in my tummy and I told myself to keep breathing and not act stupid.*

Extending his hands, David urged me forward as he moved backwards and sat on the bed. I stood a little wobbly in between his legs.

"I want your hair down." His tone sounded husky and deep.

Oh, gosh, I obeyed the macho voice and stared at the clef in his chin. One by one, I removed the hairpins and placed them on the nightstand.

His fingers ran the length of my hair and urged the locks to fall long and loose down my back. He tucked a few strands behind my ears. His eyes narrowed, "There, much better. Now, for the bra."

I shuddered at the light touch of his fingers trailing my back as his tongue tickled my neck. Then, like a magician's sleight of hand, my bra left my body. For the first time, a man kissed my breasts and the intimacy made me giddy.

I shivered, "That feels nice."

"It should."

His lips thinned to a straight line and he shifted his sitting position. "Moving on."

The next snap was my garter belt and thigh-high nylons. They fell to the carpet and he tossed them to the pile. His hands lightly explored my skin, until his thumb, *Oh, good night ...* I slurped a quick intake of air when his thumb, in an unhurried move, slid inside my bikini panties along the elastic band. His fingers inched downwards to ... I hitched, "Ah!"

He savored my reaction with a smirk.

His fingers strummed and I choked a frightened, "Uh-oh" at the rapid discharge of dampness. I blushed and tried to back away from his hand.

"You're wet, babe. That's natural," he whispered. "Don't be afraid." He licked my dampness off his fingers. "You taste fine, Sarah. Did you know that?"

Too shocked to respond, I turned my head feeling naughty. But David wouldn't allow any distress. His hand, gently turned my chin to meet his smiling, charming eyes and the naughtiness kind of seemed less.

His mouth parted my lips, in a deep, lingering kiss. During the insane blur, my panties disappeared. Naked never bothered me but being in the buff and feeling sensual sensations did. I trembled.

David's hands continued to roam. He massaged the ache in my hips until his furtive hands moved lower.

"David, not there!" I stiffened when his index finger ... my hands covered myself. "That's nasty."

He lifted my hands gently away. "It's not, Sarah, it's beautiful between a man and a woman," he murmured oozing charm from every testosterone pore. "Close your eyes. I'll make you feel good."

I closed my eyes and felt his hand caress my breast while his other hand moved in between my legs. For a moment, it seemed reassuring until he applied pressure and I winced.

He growled, "Let me" in a masterful sound from the back of his throat and I did. Minutes later, he surprised me by removing his hands.

I shook my head, "I, I ... don't ..."

He took my hands and placed them on his shoulders.

"Shhhh," he said softly. "Easy, Brooklyn. I will pleasure you."

"Oh," my lips formed the letter "O."

CHAPTER 34

Okay, David Katz, the balls in your court. Tell your side of the romantic night. You're the Attorney for the Defense, state your case and appeal to the jury.

"That's right, Sarah, I'd like to please you and win you over."

Her pale green eyes widened in surprise.

I held her face in my hands and cuddled her full and luscious, naïve lips with my trembling mouth. I yearned to be inside her. To make her come until she screamed. But I quickly switched thoughts to Section I, Article I of the Constitution to stop *horny me, counselor*.

"God, you're beautiful," I said matter-of-fact.

She blushed, "Don't say that."

"Can't help it. It's true."

Her mouth opened and our tongues connected in a sudden juicy arousal. Encouraging her to go further, I stroked the moist loveliness between her thighs. The results promised the moon.

But she stopped any promise. Her abrupt squeal and facial expression was that of a frightened deer caught in the headlights of a car. My pleasuring fingers touched a nerve startling my beautiful virgin.

I knew experienced women, willing and able, or at least willing and ready, forget the able. Sarah was an anomaly and I had no precedent. Only Edward's advice, coming from an OB/GYN's education when handing me a prescription ointment.

"If she's tender, Romeo, use it on Juliet. It's a numbing, analgesic ointment to ease pain."

"Thanks, Ed" and I slipped the tube in my pocket.

"David," said the doctor. "You've slept with a lot of women. This one is young and naive. She needs to feel safe. Don't make her another notch on your bedpost. Don't scare her."

Well, damn it! I just did.

In a conciliatory move, I picked her up gently in my arms, her weight almost nothing and placed her on my king size bed.

She stretched her body lengthwise and wiggled her toes. "What a comfortable bed," she sighed and snuggled into the mattress. "Must have cost a lot of money, huh? Betcha can't buy this at Gimbel's or Abraham & Strauss."

I frowned.

"Okay, so don't tell me where you bought it. It's still a soft, fluffy cloud."

"B. Altman and Company."

"Just like your aunt's new bed?" she giggled sounding shocked. "The one I slept on in the flowery pink room?"

"You got me there." I laid down beside her.

"I love this bed. I have to visit B. Altman and Company and see what's so special."

"I'll take you."

She bit her lip and smiled. "I'd like that."

Feeling I earned her trust, I leaned in and traced her sexy lips with my index finger. "You have a sweet, lovely mouth."

Her candid eyes followed my finger moving down her neck and across her shoulder.

"Ooooo, very nice," she inhaled. "It almost tickles but not quite." She wiggled a little.

I leaned closer and where I had moved my finger, I planted light kisses. "Still very nice?"

She hummed, "Uh-huh." Her fingers stroked the side of my shoulder, brushing the top of my skin.

Hot damn, counselor, she's responding.

I continued with the tiny kisses. My lips trailed her breasts, circled the navel and stayed at her belly. Her legs flayed and she grabbed hold of my hair.

"Easy, baby … you're okay."

I stopped for a moment then soothed her stomach with the palm of my hand drawing circles. When she let go of my hair and moaned, I planted more kisses down her belly until I reached my destination. "Oh, David. That feels good." Her breathing hitched but she allowed me to continue until her body exploded.

"Oh, God," she recited pleasurable responses. Her shoulders lifted and she reached for my arms.

CHAPTER 35

Minutes later. Could he be the man of my dreams?

WHEN DAVID'S BOXERS flew to the chair, I didn't dare look lower than his shoulders. So when he reached for something from the nightstand drawer, I peeked but all I could see was his back.

He knelt over my legs and held a small packet. I stared into his eyes and the penetrating results sent shivers down my spine. He ripped open the foil and I watched him take something out. Putting the wrapper between his teeth, he carefully rolled the ... *oh, my ...*

He spit the wrapper out of his mouth. "No more mystery, huh, Sarah?" His mouth curved in a sly smile.

My cheeks heated up.

He sank his baby blues into my irises with a soulful tenderness and held my gaze. "It's your first time, you could feel discomfort."

I swallowed hard and nodded.

"I'm not sure ... maybe?"

"Maybe," I mouthed the word.

He covered me with his hard body and kissed me tender. His quivering lips now moist moved with more aggression parting my lips. Surprising pent-up passion charged through the both of us startling my pulse rate and my mind. He wanted me. My young years never suspected how much.

His wet lips left my mouth and skimmed my neck leaving lovely, light kisses. My back arched anticipating his sweet breath and I got my wish. His lips and tongue teased my breasts with heated kisses and lovingly, sucked on my attentive nipples. The erotic sensations sent luscious signals to places never imagined.

"Yes," I uttered a soft moan. I wanted more. "Don't stop."

Then without warning, David's teeth bit my nipple and yanked. My other nipple felt his fingers pinch and twist. So alarmed, I screeched, "Ow" feeling my groin clench.

He said nothing pinning my wrists to the bed. His eyes flashed watching my reaction like a cat toying with a bird. Captive, I was caught in his paws and just like the bird, I wiggled and tried to escape.

"Baby," he growled and eased himself in. I shut my eyes feeling my heartbeat thunder into his. Holding the reins, he rocked his moves and coveted my body and soul with the speed of an avalanche. Taking possession, he grabbed fistfuls of my hair and tugged. I whimpered. He growled. The scent of his skin ripened to a musky odor. I tasted spicy on his lips.

He murmured against my face, "You're tight." I opened my eyes. He lifted his head as his lower body thrust deep and hard.

I screamed, "Stop!"

A sharp, burning pain cut through me. David stopped. A look of alarm crossed his face.

"Don't move." I tasted blood biting my lip.

"God damn it, I hurt you." He murmured in alarm.

"Wait."

He rested his head against my forehead. "Should I quit?"

"Ah ... wait," I inhaled a silent count of three.

"Baby," he tensed up. "I just can't wait." He hovered, "I have to ..." His eyes rolled upwards.

"I'm ...," I started to cry.

"Not your fault. Mother Nature." He cringed in horror and was about to ...

"Okay, move."

Tenderness warmed his eyes and his lips embraced mine. *God help me,* I surrendered.

David moved easy and thrust until his body bucked and his breathing sounded rough. When his body calmed, he reached for me, "I'm sorry."

"YOU HURT ME! I need to go" and scrambled to the other side of the bed.

"No!" David tackled me at the edge. "You need to stay!"

Screaming, I fought. "You hurt me! Dancing hurts me. I'm sick of getting hurt."

He tightened his hold. "Sarah, you lost your virginity. That pain will never happen again. It's over."

I glanced at the bed. "Is that blood on the sheets?"

"Yes, it's a manifestation."

"A what?" I trembled gulping air in a panic.

"Sarah, don't hyperventilate. Breathe normally."

"I, I ..."

David scooped me up in his arms and set me barefooted, inside the shower. He turned on the faucets and stepped in. "Calm down, you're alright."

"That was my blood."

"Congratulations." He held my face and kissed my forehead. "That's a milestone." He reached for the Pantene Shampoo.

"What are you doing?

"Washing your hair."

"Why?"

"Shhhh, it's healing."

He shampooed my hair and his. He was right. The scalp massage did relieve some of the anxiety. And, with a Swedish loofah, he lathered us both in bubbles. My "aaahhs" filled the steamy shower. Between the soapy shiatsu massage and the orange blossom soap smell, I almost forgave him.

When he turned off the shower, I smiled up at him.

"What?" he looked puzzled.

"Nothing" but it wasn't nothing. As much as he hurt me, I believed him when he whispered, "Give me a chance, I'll make it up to you."

David dried me off and took another towel for himself. He dressed quickly in pale blue pajama bottoms and handed me the top. He left and I used the hairdryer on the wall. When I finished and walked in the bedroom, there was no more radio or candles only light from a lamp. And, David had changed the soiled sheets and put them in a pile by the door.

My hands flew to my mouth. "How humiliating."

"Brooklyn, it's okay."

"No, it's not. How do you explain blood to your maid?"

"She's not my maid. She's my housekeeper and a friend. Mrs. Yee raised me since I'm a kid."

"Mrs. Yee?"

"Actually since birth, my nanny."

"But your mother?"

"No mother. Both parents were killed in a car crash on my tenth birthday."

"Your birthday? Oh, God," I whimpered. "Poor child."

"Never had another party." He sounded bitter.

I rushed into his arms and buried my face in his chest.

"Sarah, don't. It's a bad memory."

I raised my head, "Sorry."

He nodded towards the bed. "Lie down. I'll make you feel better."

"What?" I withdrew my arms. "I don't think so" and stepped back.

He grabbed my wrist. "Smarty pants, lie down."

"I'm not wearing pants, you took 'em."

"Sarah?" he bellowed. "Now!"

"Geez Louise, if it means that much," I sulked and laid down on the bed. He applied the analgesic ointment and finished with clean bikinis he'd taken from my overnight bag.

"Well?" he gloated.

"Better," I mumbled.

"I didn't hear you."

"Okay, much better and thank you."

"You're welcome."

David switched to lawyer mode and explained how men and women make love. He defended his sexual actions and my pain. In closing he smiled, "Okay?"

"Okay to what? Perform everything you just told me and dance Salome and the seven veils?"

"I'm David, a lawyer not John the Baptist." He didn't sound amused.

I climbed off the bed, "Now what?"

"Stay here. I'll be right back" and he picked up the pile of soiled linens and left. His bare feet clomped down the stairs.

Holy smokes, I didn't see this coming.

DAVID HELD A chilled bottle of Dom Perignon, two glasses, a bag of popcorn and a grin from ear to ear. "Don't you think we should celebrate?"

"Yes." My cheeks warmed.

He popped the cork and poured the bubbly. Handing me a glass, he smiled, "L'Chaim."

I murmured an embarrassed, "L'Chaim" and our glasses

clinked. "Doesn't popcorn go with beer?" I asked opening the Zabar's bag of popcorn.

"Could be, princess, but the kitchen was fresh out of caviar and strawberries." He leaned down and nibbled popcorn out of my hand and poured us a second glass.

We curled up in bed and talked about my work schedule and the latest movies. After David finished his drink, he set it down and leaned against the headboard.

"We need to talk about my trip."

"No, I'm happy. Don't spoil the mood."

"Yes, Sarah."

I exhaled a bratty, "Ugh."

"Wednesday, October 6th, I fly to Hong Kong for fifteen days and return, October 20th. That's three days before your premiere on the twenty-third."

I swallowed my champagne and reached for the bottle.

He stopped my reach, moved the bottle further away and took my glass. "I don't know if I'll be able to call you or when."

I stared at my blue dress hanging in the closet where the door was partially open.

"Sarah," he snarled. "Look at me, not the closet, damn it."

"Yeah, sure." I turned back.

"Now ... how do we communicate with the time difference? I think eight hours. It takes a letter ten days air mail to get from ..." He stopped mid-sentence.

"What?" I locked his eyes. "That's it? Your serious talk?"

"Not exactly. I'm asking Eleanor and Harry to look after you."

I hissed, "I don't need Eleanor and Harry."

"Sarah, you're making it difficult. I don't want to leave you. I don't want to go."

"Well, you are. I hate you and I don't wanna talk about it."

"Hey," he grabbed my wrist. "I get it. You're mad."

"Ha! Yeah, I'm mad," I yelled jumping up on the bed. "You're leaving me and you're the only one I can trust making decisions."

"Like what?"

"My contract!"

"It's not up for five months. What else?"

"Well, ah, ah, who do I invite to the premiere?"

"Your family, my family, what else?"

"Ah, ah ... lots of other things, you know, Mrs. Pace and Yuri and what do I do about things I don't know. Oh, crap!" I threw myself on the mattress and buried my face in a pillow. "I don't know how to open a bank account for my paychecks."

He laid down beside me and rubbed my back. "We'll get you a bank account on Monday."

"You'd do that?" I sniffled.

"Baby, I don't want to go, it's my job."

I grabbed a second pillow, "I hate your job."

"Sarah, stop it. Try to understand."

"Why?"

He yanked the second pillow out of my arms, "Because we're grown-ups."

"Not me. Not yet."

He threw both pillows at the wall, "God damn it" and wrestled me into a hug. "I need to kiss you."

"No! You don't deserve a kiss."

"Yes, I do. I brought the champagne."

"Oh?" I raised my head and let him kiss me then pounded my fists on his back. He stopped my fists.

"I hate you, David Katz."

"No, you don't. You like me more than you fully understand. I have feelings for you, too. Deal with it."

"Bullshit!" I bit his arm.

He rolled away from me in surprise. "Two drinks and you're Cat Woman?"

Feeling the champagne buzz, I rose to my knees and kissed him hard on the mouth.

"Hey, tiger, slow down."

"You're going to miss me, Mister Fancy Lawyer. I'll show you" and rubbed my breasts up against his chest.

"No ... Sarah. Don't do this. Your body is tender."

"Not anymore."

"Babe, really, don't do this."

"You're leaving me."

"Not right now, not if you're asking for it" and he reached in the nightstand drawer.

Seeing the packet and the analgesic tube in his hand, I recited, "He pulled out two plums, little Jack Horner."

"Baby."

I grabbed a hunk of his hair.

"Ouch! Stop it. It's not a fight. We can make love but gently."

"Not if I can help it." My eager lips crushed his mouth again.

He reared back. "Enough, Sarah. Stop it!"

I threw my hands in the air and he caught my wrists and held me at bay. "Tonight," he said sharply. "My rules, my way." He stared me down until I relented and apologized.

"Better."

He applied the ointment then kissed me, a lover's gentle caress. "We'll take it easy, one move at a time."

His eyes flashed and his pupils darkened. I wondered what he meant.

But his easy did take time until my hormones reacted and writhed under his unrestrained passion. "Oh, God!" I found out.

The tornado met the tempest and my body convulsed.

"Daaavid," I screamed. My heart pounded, my nails dug into his back experiencing a roller coaster ride.

"Baby," he growled raspy and impatient grasping my hands in a firm hold. His body jerked several shakes. Then, as if the lights went out, he sank on top of me. Exhausted, he tried to move but couldn't.

I held him in my arms and floated like a leaf on calm waters. I smoothed his wet curly hair and stroked his forehead; damp and warm. Seeing him vulnerable, I discovered the power of women.

Tis a pity, Salome danced her seven veils to seduce and sever the head of a man.

CHAPTER 36

Sunday mid-morning, October 3rd. A closing argument from Attorney Katz to the jury.

I WOKE UP to Sarah's head resting on my chest sleeping the innocence of a child. Her cool, quiet beauty disarmed me. She snuggled her creamy white body against my tanned frame, naked and soft. A heartbreaking lust gave me a fierce hard-on. I ached to be inside her.

But my brain screamed stop it counselor, she's a babe in the woods. Last night, she drank enough alcohol to put you to jail.

I gritted my teeth and called myself an asshole for thinking of my needs above hers. I scared her and used her but she used me, too. A hundred-and-four-pound body on two drinks, spun her out of control. I took stock of how she behaved.

Ten years my junior is a big chunk. Fuck that sounds weird. Put her in a taxi, counselor. Send her back to Mrs. Pace but hang on, let's examine the facts.

I took her to Loeb's birthday party at the request of my boss, Bernie Lieberman. I told myself not to get involved although at the zoo, I'd become smitten. I wanted to hold her hand or put my arm around her within the first ten minutes.

She was smart and alert like a wolfhound. She picked up on nuances other people missed. I thought my male ego could chance a young mare. Enter, Miss Rothman, mine to break in and train.

But the joke was on me. Her body and spirit responded like and open and shut case. The young woman proved uninhibited and raw once I uncorked the champagne.

Having a trained dancer's body, Sarah responded sexually like she danced; intuitive, exciting and fearless. She expressed passion more erotic than any woman I'd made love to, even wanton Laura.

I felt the same way at yesterday's rehearsal. Sarah amazed me with her dance talent. The fire and determination in her eyes as she leaped into lifts over her partner's head. Sensuous as a lioness stalking her prey, she blew me away making athletics look easy.

How fast she could turn. How high she could jump. I don't know ballet but I know karate and soccer. It's damn difficult to get it right, never mind excel.

I watched her sleep and heard her moan a tiny kitten purr. She sighed at the touch of my fingers when I pushed several strands of blond hair away from her face. She opened her eyes and gazed into mine.

"Hey, sleepyhead," I murmured.

She stirred and puckered her pouty mouth.

I kissed her lips.

"Good Morning," she smiled and tugged at my heart.

Oh, shit, she had me at pouty mouth.

But, hear ye, hear ye, counselor ... stop any desire to crawl down her pelvis and perform the discovery phase. Court wasn't in session and I needed to behave.

I had hard evidence but no lovemaking case to file an appeal. Therefore, I reluctantly reached for my pajama bottoms. I covered my burden of proof. And, as I headed for the bathroom, I said over my shoulder, "I'm taking a shower."

"Okay, I'm next in the bathroom and then I'm taking the

subway home."

"Give me a few minutes, okay? We'll talk." I shut the bathroom door.

Fifteen minutes later, after I'd showered and shaved and started to dress, I watched her sleep.

"Sarah? Baby? Wake up."

"Huh?" she smiled a lazy yawn. The sun through the venetian blinds caught the glint in her luminous green eyes.

"Hey, beautiful," I grinned. "Your turn in the shower. Towels on the bathroom shelves."

I watched her roam around the room, naked and nonchalant, picking up strewn underwear and her dance bag. She carried her things to the bathroom and I heard the shower spray.

When I returned to the bedroom from downstairs, I found Sarah dressed in a wrinkled beige blouse and pedal pushers. She had brushed her hair in a ponytail and was throwing things in an overnight bag.

"Almost ready," she squeaked running over for a good morning peck on my cheek. "Help me carry my stuff to the front door."

"Wait, a real kiss and let's discuss this."

"What? I'm going home to Brooklyn. My dad, remember? I'm taking a cab to the BMT."

"I'll drive you home."

"What? No!"

"And you need to eat. Mrs. Yee made breakfast."

"Oh?" she stopped short. "That Mrs. Yee? Oh, dear."

I grabbed her and kissed her with a longing in my heart. She kissed the same. She was mine and we could make love all morning but it wasn't in the cards. Sarah had plans with her dad and she needed to go home.

Remembering the dinner dress, I reached in the closet and threw the periwinkle blue dress over my arm. I picked up her overnight bag and raced down the stairs.

"Wait for me, David, I'm coming!"

Reciprocity, Miss Rothman, jurisprudence.

WHEN SARAH AND I met up in the kitchen, I introduced her to Mrs. Yee. For a moment, neither of them spoke only regarded one another across the table. Then, as if the bell sounded at a wrestling match, the two women shook hands in a timid attempt at good manners. I guessed Mrs. Yee questioned my motives and Sarah's face, turned rosy pink recalling the soiled bedsheets.

But when Mrs. Yee asked, "Miss Sarah, what would you like for breakfast?"

Sarah replied, "Sarah. Call me Sarah. No Miss."

Mrs. Yee smiled, "But …

"Two scrambled eggs. Juice. Half a toasted bagel nothing on it, thanks."

Mrs. Yee nodded and glanced over at me, raising an eyebrow.

I winked. "My usual, red onion, sliced tomato, cream cheese and lox on a toasted bagel. Thank you."

"You have lox, Mrs. Yee?" Sarah's green eyes sparkled.

"Yes. Would you like lox?"

"Would I?" she giggled. "Yes, the works! Lox, cream cheese, red onion and sliced tomato, please. We eat this every Sunday morning and read the newspapers. Nobody goes to work until eleven. Then Bubbe and I do the laundry and ironing."

Mrs. Yee rolled her eyes. "Well, today is Sunday. Should I bring you the New York Times from the front hall?"

"No, ma'am," Sarah shook her head. "I have to get going. I'll just eat the best breakfast ever and say thank you." She grinned at Mrs. Yee and me.

I glared at Mrs. Yee when she threw me another questioning look I thought inappropriate. I asked her fifteen minutes earlier, "Would you make breakfast for two? I have a guest and she needs to eat."

As a rule, my housekeeper never prepared breakfast for any of my dates that spent the night. She made a pot of coffee, observed the woman drink a half cup and scamper out the front door.

But this morning, there was a new sheriff in town, a charming threat. And knowing Mrs. Yee, she'd have something to say when she got me alone. The guardian of my keep was neither reserved nor stoic. To others, she appeared inscrutable but to me, she had opinions and argued as well as any trial attorney.

DRIVING TO BROOKLYN, Sarah stayed quiet and so did I. The Hong Kong trip weighed heavy on my mind. If I mentioned any detail, I'd be shot down. She could be childish and stubborn. Definitely, a drawback.

Hence, when we waited at traffic lights, I took questioning glances in her direction and sought motives for our chemical attraction. Okay, the beauty part went without saying but I had dated beautiful women before. The magnetic pull to Sarah? No, I never experienced the hypnotic. That was pure crazy. And why was I anxious to protect and cherish her above all others? Too black and white. And yes, Miss Rothman, I admired your competitive drive. We're one in the same. But could that drive sustain us? Keep the fires burning for more than a few nights in bed?

The jury was out.

CHAPTER 37

Sunday, October 3rd. Brooklyn Heights. Jack and Jill went up the hill and I met surprises going up and alarm bells, coming down.

DAVID PARKED IN front of the Valiant Arms and helped me carry my bags upstairs. He took my key, unlocked the front door and placed it back in my hand.

"Thanks, David, for driving me home. You were right. Much nicer than the subway."

"I know," he puffed out his chest.

"I'm gonna put my things away and walk to the deli. Can you leave? I mean go home to your house? In Manhattan?"

"Fine."

I kissed him goodbye but he didn't walk to the elevator.

In a New York minute, he had stored my bags in my bedroom and returned to the front door. My mouth fell open in shock.

"Well?" he tilted his head. "You're staring. Shut your mouth, you'll catch flies. C'mon, I'll walk you to the deli and say hello to your dad."

"Oh, no. How can I explain you and me together?"

"Simple, the truth. After you visit with Ben, I'm taking you to the advanced screening of 'Doctor Zhivago' at the Paramount Theatre in Times Square."

"Holy crap!" I squealed. "Doctor Zhivago? But, the picture doesn't open until New Year's Eve."

"I know. A client gave me an invitation to a special preview. If we see Bernie Lieberman tonight, smile and wave."

I HUGGED DADDY so tight, I made him laugh. "Honey, I'm happy to see you but you're killing me."

David shook Dad's hand. "Good to see you, sir." He shook Uncle Al's hand and nodded, "Al." The workers stood around and gawked.

"So, David?" harrumphed Uncle Al. "Tell me. Why would you drive Sarah all the way to Brooklyn Heights just to drop her off?"

"I wouldn't. She's taking me to the movies later."

"So, you two are dating?"

David said, "Yes."

I said "No."

"Which is it? Yes or no?"

We repeated the same answers.

Uncle Al crossed his arms and harrumphed.

"Al, leave the kids alone and Sarah, I got bad news."

"No, Daddy, you're not gonna …"

"Yes, I'm gonna … your brothers just telephoned. They're moving a friend to Staten Island. They can't work the delivery truck. I have to deliver a large order, to the opening of a new store."

"We can't spend the day together?" I reached for his arm. "We're not going to the Bronx zoo?"

"Sorry, I can't, Tootsie Roll." He kissed my forehead. "And tonight, I have a dance band gig playing for a twenty-fifth anniversary party. You'd be all alone in the apartment."

"But, I've missed you, Daddy."

"I've missed you, too." He looked at David. "Would you mind driving her back to Mrs. Pace? A little later? I'd feel better."

"Sure, Ben, I can do that."

Daddy tucked his arm inside mine and I laid my pouty face on his shoulder.

"Sorry, honey." He glanced at his wristwatch. "I need to drive the deli truck to Red Hook. I'm delivering one hundred Jerry Lewis Pastrami and Don Rickles Corn Beef ... fifty pounds of potato salad, forty pounds of coleslaw and twenty pounds of kosher dills." He rolled his eyes, "Oy, gevault, as Mama would say."

"Daddy, can't someone else do it?"

"No, I should be cloned and turned into an octopus. I have to schlep all this shit. Damn it, don't know how I'm gonna do it." He screwed up his face and hollered. "Hey, Al? Hey! Yo! I need help!"

Uncle Al pushed the kitchen door open and stuck his head out. "Don't look at me. Who runs this place? Who handles the cash register? Who makes the decisions?"

"I don't know. Who does that?"

"Hey, funny man, you're a regular Alan King. But, you ain't taking any of my cooks, busboys or waiters with you."

"Which adds up to five employees and the place is empty. You're a smuck, you know that?"

"So, what else is new?"

David tapped dad's shoulder. "Hey, Ben, I know Red Hook, I'll go."

"Get outta a town, you're joking."

"No. In high school, I played ice hockey at the rink in Red Hook. I know the area."

Daddy chuckled, "No shit. You're willing to help me cater?"

"Why not? I can schlep with the best."

"Son-of-a-bitch, Sarah. This guy's a diamond. You'd better marry him. If you don't, I will."

My cheeks turned crimson seeing the surprise on David's face. Dad also saw David's face and quickly apologized. "Sorry, honey, I didn't mean to embarrass you or David but the man is a keeper."

"Yeah Dad, but can he throw pots and pans in a fight?"

"What does that mean?" said David looking uncomfortable.

"My daughter has a smart ass mouth. Let's get the truck."

I WALKED HOME and the first thing I did was find the letters tied with the blue ribbon I'd hidden in the basement. After reading the first two from Anna to Yuri, I stopped. They were personal and described every sexy thing Anna would do to Yuri. After my experiences last night and Anna's graphic details, I put the letters back in hiding.

Why were Anna's letters hidden and taped to the underbelly of Mr. Kreisler's desk? Blackmail? Money? Jealousy? What was he after? Gosh darn, didn't make sense.

I took the elevator back upstairs and did laundry and took from Bubbe's closet, an additional suitcase. I packed warm clothes, long-sleeved leotards and my navy blue car coat with the wooden buttons. I changed into a soft grey and white dress for the movie. From the hall closet, I reached for my dress-up coat. A black wool, midi-length, cloth; straight-line with simple black buttons. I found a grey neck scarf and I was ready for the night-time air of Times Square.

"Hi, Aunt Lucy? It's me ..." I dialed the phone in Mama's bedroom. "Great. Yes, everything's good. I'm busy. Yeah, what?

David? Huh-uh. We're going to the movies later ... don't know ... Mama? You won at Bingo? Ten dollars? Wow! How's Bubbe? No, don't wake her. Mama, this is a short call. I'm home calling on your phone ... okay ... Mama, I love you ... okay ... bye."

Mama sounded nice and she never complained once. I guessed because I didn't let her talk long. Her warmth and Aunt Lucy's concern, sweetened my visit home.

Knock, knock.

I looked through the peep hole in the front door and saw Daddy's smile.

"Honey, I knocked like a visitor so I wouldn't scare you with a key."

"Good thinking. Everything went okay?"

"Great. C'mon, sweetie. We're eating lunch at the deli. David wouldn't let me pay him so I offered the deli's star attraction."

"You mean the Irving Berlin tongue on rye, macaroni salad to die for and pickles out of the barrel?"

"And, pineapple cheesecake from Junior's."

"Is Uncle Al paying for this?"

"Of course. He'll bitch and moan, I don't care."

I hugged Daddy and David laughed.

"Son," said my dad. "Anytime you need a job, you've got one catering with me."

"I'll keep that in mind, sir, attorneys are a dime a dozen."

WE SAT AT the center, big table joined by Uncle Al and neighbors and kibitzed and schmoozed over a late lunch. I ate the Sophie Tucker Turkey Sandwich and David, prodded and poked, succumbed to Daddy's suggestion. He ate the star attraction; the

Irving Berlin tongue on rye and enjoyed. "What's not to love?" he joked.

Uncle Al bitched about the cost of Junior's fresh pineapple cheesecake and having to pay the delivery charge. But when we all thanked him many times over, he admitted, "Okay, okay, alright, already. I live in poverty, so I'll die a poor man."

"Al's got a big heart," boasted Dad. "It just takes a kick in the pants. Hey kids, I'm looking at the clock on the wall. Better get going. Don't wanna miss the big movin' pitcha."

"No, we don't," I jumped up and hugged Daddy. "Love you, forever."

"Love you, too, but stop hugging me so hard. I'll have to go on workman's comp. You're strong as an ox, kid ... David, does she hug you that hard?"

David chuckled and winked at me.

"Take care of my daughter, will ya? She's my ever lovin' pain in the ass. Smart mouth and all."

David patted Ben's shoulder, "Goes without saying, sir. Goodbye."

"It's Ben and take care. Yo?"

MY HEART MELTED when David, after the lights dimmed at the Paramount Theatre, held my hand. He never let go during both parts of the three hour and seventeen minute private showing of "Doctor Zhivago" starring Omar Shariff and Julie Christie. Near the end, I curled up close to him and shed a few quiet tears. I loved the movie and loved seeing it with him.

Picking up the car at the parking garage, David reluctantly drove me back to Mrs. Pace's townhouse. He parked a few houses away, out of sight.

"Wouldn't you reconsider?"

"No, Daddy never figured us out. I'd better keep it that way and sleep here."

Fernando recognized David's Bentley and got out of his parked limo. "Miss Sarah, Mr. Katz, good evening. I'll get the suitcases."

I smiled, "Thank you."

David unlocked the trunk.

"Cook and Mrs. Williams," he gestured to the house. "Had the day and night off. Mrs. Pace is home and I'm sitting out here in case she wants to go somewhere."

"Then I'll be quiet. She might be sleeping."

"Yes, she could be or watching TV." He carried my suitcases up the front steps, unlocked the door and put my things inside.

"See you in the morning, Miss Sarah." He tipped his hat.

"Yes, good night." I turned at the top of the stairs and waved goodbye to David.

I CARRIED MY things up the stairs and heard tiny murmurings coming from Mrs. Pace's bedroom. When I reached her room, the door was open. I peeked inside and saw glowing candles, smelling of apples and cinnamon.

Mrs. Pace was in bed, naked and not alone. She was kissing another woman's exposed breast. At first, the situation didn't register as I watched in fascination. Yuri told me about men attracted to men but I never imagined a woman could make love to another woman.

I must have made a noise, a gasp, or my clothes rustled because Mrs. Pace stopped the kissing and sat up. "Sarah?"

Embarrassed that she caught me spying, I rushed to my room

and slammed the door. Minutes later there was a knock but before I could answer it, Mrs. Pace burst into the room dressed in a beige, chenille bathrobe. She stood against the wall and folded her arms.

"Sarah, you saw me with a friend. I'm sorry you witnessed a … us. I thought you were staying with your dad in Brooklyn. What happened?"

I backed up, bumping the bed, not able to make eye contact. "Um, you see, he had to work, ah, I'd be all alone. Oh gosh, Mrs. Pace, I'm sorry I, I, peeked in your bedroom. I don't understand. Um, a, what a, were you doing? I mean were you kissing a woman?"

"Everyone loves differently, Sarah. Yes, I happen to love a woman. My kind of loving is frowned upon and not accepted in our society. You can't tell anyone what you saw, I beg you not to tell. I could lose everything. My ballet company, my reputation, my charitable organizations. Please, this has to remain our secret."

"Our secret?" I blushed and shifted my weight from one foot to the other.

"Yes, our secret. You can't tell anybody what you saw." Her eyes rolled upwards. "If this got out, my backers would no longer support my company. There'd be no money to pay the City Center dancers. Do you want that to happen?"

"No, of course not." I smoothed my hair back.

"So please, Sarah, don't speak about me or my friend. She's a physician at Mt. Sinai Hospital and a good person."

"What could happen to her?"

"She could get fired. Lose her job and good reputation."

"I see." I studied the fear on her middle-aged face and felt a pang of regret. "Right, I won't say anything. But how can people get fired over sex stuff? Wow! People sure are mean."

"Yes, they are."

I took a deep breath. "Mrs. Pace, I can't stay here."

"What?" She stepped towards me in alarm. "Why not? She'll leave if you want her to."

"No," I waved my hand. "Don't make her leave, I'll go."

"Where?" Mrs. Pace barked. "It's late."

"I'd feel more comfortable with my boyfriend."

"What boyfriend? Oh, Jesus Christ, don't get pregnant."

"No, David Katz and I aren't that stupid. Can I call him and see if I can stay with him?"

Mrs. Pace started pacing. "Is this blackmail? He's an attorney."

"No, I'd rather stay a few days at his place. But, you can't tell my family or my dad. He'd kill me. And don't tell anybody else."

Mrs. Pace stopped pacing and looked me in the eye. "No, I won't tell anyone. But in return, you can't tell anyone you saw me in bed with my friend. Especially, don't tell, a former prosecutor from the DA's office, David Katz. Do you promise?" She grabbed my upper arms and squeezed.

"Yes, I promise."

Her nails dug deep and I squirmed. "Please, Mrs. Pace, I'd never hurt you. I love my ballet company and I'm grateful for everything you've given me and done for me."

She dropped my arms. "My darling girl, thank you."

"Mrs. Pace, one more thing ..."

"What?" Her voice trilled.

"If I stay three nights with David Katz? Can I come back on Wednesday? Can I live here? Stay with you?" *After I think through this madness and come to terms?*

She looked confused hearing the question. "Why? Yes, do live with me. I'd like to nurture your career. Groom you for leading roles."

"Good," I exhaled. "Thank you."

"Now make your phone call and I'll tell Fernando to drive you." Her eyes filled with tears.

"Don't cry, Mrs. Pace. It's our secret. No one will know."

"You're right." She kissed my cheek and left.

AS I WALKED downstairs to use the kitchen phone, I puzzled ... *how can a woman have sex with a woman? What parts of the body can she use? I watched Doctor Zhivago kissing Lara and I know how David made love to me. Geez, I've experienced too much. Sex, murder, jealousy. If, I'd stayed at home and gone to Brooklyn College maybe, life would have been simpler.*

"HELLO, DAVID? CAN I come over? ... Right now ... I wanna stay three nights ... No, nothing's wrong. What? No ... don't come get me. Fernando will drive me to your house. What's the address? Okay ... between what streets? ... Now."

CHAPTER 38

Just past midnight, October 4th. Nothing is certain for my people except change and death. An expression of Uncle Al's.

ON EAST 62nd Street, Fernando opened the limo door and extended his hand. David took my other hand. He'd been waiting at the curb and probably did a happy dance before I arrived.

Fernando set my suitcase and bags at the curb and chuckled watching the two of us lock lips. He guffawed a few times until we stopped kissing.

"Excuse me, Miss Sarah?" he grinned. "I'll pick you up at this address at ten-fifteen, tomorrow morning and again on Tuesday and Wednesday mornings."

"Alright." I covered my face as if the sun were shining, our smooch lasted too long. "Ten-fifteen. I'll be here, waiting out front."

"Mr. Katz, should I put Miss Sarah's suitcase and bags at the front door?"

"Yes."

"Also, will Miss Sarah need a ride at night to this address?"

I looked at David for the answer.

"No, thank you, Fernando. That won't be necessary. I'll pick her up."

"Good enough, sir. Leave a message at the school if there's a change."

"Yes, I will and Fernando? This address and why and where you dropped Miss Rothman off, is nobody's business. Are we clear?" He handed Fernando two crisp, hundred dollar bills.

"Very clear and generous, sir, but I can't take a bribe."

"Why not? Everybody at City Hall does."

"In that case, Mr. Katz, I'll just slip these two crispy C-notes in my pocket and I don't know nothin.'"

"You keep Sarah protected and we're even. I need her safe."

I smiled up at David. "He bird dogs me already."

"I do keep a sharp eye, sir. I've worked as a bodyguard for important people. And Miss Sarah is precious cargo."

"Good ... and, I'm going out of town on Wednesday for fifteen days. Nobody needs to know that either. It's between you and me, man to man."

Fernando chuckled, "Yes sir, Mr. Katz. The boss lady would strangle me if I didn't keep my mouth shut. Fernando has lots ole skeletons in his closet. He goes to his maker jangling dem bones."

David shook Fernando's hand. "We're agreed."

I watched the chauffeur carry my suitcase and bags up the steps and took David's hand. When Fernando returned to the car, he tipped his hat.

"Goodnight, Miss Sarah, Mr. Katz" and he started the engine. The black Cadillac limousine edged into traffic along the tree-lined street and drove out of sight.

ELEANOR AND HARRY exited the taxi immediately behind the limo when it took off. They saw us holding hands and kissing.

Eleanor stormed out of the cab as furious as a wet hen. "David? What's all this? Sarah and her suitcases at your front door?

Are you crazy?"

Harry jumped out of the cab. "Honey, calm down. People can hear you in New Haven."

"Don't patronize me, Harry Katz. You know I'm right. David are you out of your mind?"

"No, Aunt Eleanor, I'm not out of my mind." David straightened his shoulders. "I know the law."

"I bet you do but that doesn't make it right. And for God's sakes, don't get her pregnant."

David put his arm around me and kissed the side of my head.

"Quit kissing her David, she's seventeen."

"Sarah consented."

"Consented to what?" hollered Eleanor. "She has an overly protective father who probably owns a shotgun which would serve you right!"

"That's it everybody," said Harry. "This discussion is over. Come on Eleanor, you're not going to change their minds."

"Aunt Eleanor, please," said David touching her arm. "Don't be upset. I care for Sarah, I'll protect her."

"Who protects you? And, by the way, who knows about this arrangement? This, this affair?"

"Eleanor," I said moving towards her. "Nobody knows with the exception of Mrs. Pace. We've told no one. This is our business. No one at the ballet company knows. Not Yuri. Not anybody in my family. Not my dad. We have to keep it quiet."

"Well, young lady, at least you used your head for more than a hat rack. And for damn sure, Harry and I won't tell a soul. I'm too embarrassed."

Harry nodded, "Let's say goodnight, dear."

"I won't sleep!"

"Yes, you will, dear. You always do even though you threaten the stars above, you always sleep."

"Aunt Eleanor, please, don't be troubled," said David in a quiet appeal. "I love you."

Harry reached over and patted David's shoulder, "Goodnight, son" and he kissed my cheek.

Eleanor shrugged in defeat then reached out and gave me a hug. "I'm calling Edward to put you on birth control."

David grinned. "Thank you, Aunt Eleanor but Doctor Ed's already taken care of that."

"Oh, good Lord," she huffed. "Well, at least you two aren't stupid. You're crazy about each other, I can see that but not stupid."

Embarrassed by her observation, David ran his hand through his hair and I chewed on my lip.

"Goodnight kids," said Harry taking Eleanor's elbow.

David's hand, on the small of my back, gave me a small shove up the steps to his townhouse door. His other hand jangled a key from his pocket.

"Whew, we just dodged a bullet," he mumbled.

HEADING IMMEDIATELY UP the stairs to David's master bedroom, fatigue washed over me in waves. At the door, I swayed and David caught me.

"Baby needs sleep."

"Yes, please. Salome can't dance seven veils. Take a rain check."

He took off my coat and unbuttoned my dress. "Raise your arms." He changed my clothes into my ankle length, cotton nightgown covered in blue roses.

When he stepped away, he laughed.

"What's so funny, jackass?"

"You look about as sexy as a rag doll in a flour sack. Sailors would not jump overboard to save you."

"You're mean," I pouted. "Mama and Bubbe buy my clothes at Korvettes."

"No shit, but that's a nightgown for a grandmother. You'd never get molested that's for damn sure."

I threw my bedroom slippers at him.

He ducked, I missed.

"I'm saying you deserve better, Sarah. Silks and satins and tailored clothes. I'm taking you shopping when I get back."

"I never knew men shopped," I mumbled in sarcasm brushing my teeth. "The women in my family buy clothes for the men."

"Some guys don't shop but I do, and so does Mrs. Yee."

I climbed into bed and snuggled into the pillows.

David hurried into pajamas, brushed his teeth and slid under the covers. He kissed me in such a loving cuddle, I returned the kiss with an eager response.

He pushed me away. "Keep that up baby, neither of us will sleep."

"I'm not tired anymore."

He yanked my granny nightgown over my head and threw his pajamas to a chair. "I'll make it a quickie, you need sleep."

"What's a quickie?"

"Many roads to Rome. Tomorrow, I'll explain."

FOLLOWING THE QUICKIE, David gently turned me on my side and drew my body in, against his chest. His arm reached across my shoulder holding my hand in his.

"What are you doing?"

"Spooning."

"Really? Bubbe would call it, "Snug as a bug in a rug.""

"Sarah, why did Mrs. Pace let you leave her house? How could that happen? What did she do?"

I murmured, "Nothing."

"No. Not nothing. You're here and just like Newton's laws of physics every action has an equal and opposite reaction."

"It's no biggie and I don't know Mr. Newton."

"Right."

I sighed and closed my eyes, "I thanked God."

He kissed the top of my head. "You told God and not me?" He squeezed my hand and chuckled. "Goodnight, Brooklyn."

"Goodnight, Gracie."

CHAPTER 39

Monday, October 4ᵗʰ. A little confusion at best.

$\mathcal{F}$ERNANDO PICKED ME up at ten-fifteen on East 62ⁿᵈ Street and drove to the ballet school. I ignored Yuri and Alexi's smart remarks. Those two attack dogs snooped into my Saturday night date with David. Alexi chomped at the bit. "How long have you known this tall, dark and handsome man?"

"Oh, gosh, was he actually tall, dark and handsome? I hadn't noticed. You wanna ask him out? Be my guest."

"No, I just stated a fact. Where did you meet him?"

"Oops-a-daisy, can't talk now."

Madame Madyaslavic burst through the Studio A door and I ran to my place at the barre. We dancers watched her meet and greet the Moscow pianist. They waved hands, handkerchiefs and kissed each other's cheeks. Then, with a sudden bravado, she turned to us.

"Bon jour, Madames et Monsieurs."

"Bon jour, Madame." We sounded the Greek chorus.

"Allons-y." Her eyes scanned the room and she clicked her heels.

We straightened erect as ramrods and held the barre with our right hand. Madame banged her cane on the floor to cue the music. Thus began an hour and a half of sweat, grunts, groans, pained expressions, swear words, competitive floor exercises and exhausted and over-stimulated muscles.

However, a weird thing happened just before the class ended. When a diagonal line of dancers turned on two feet across the room, in a series of Chaines turns, the office secretary stormed in the room. She waved to Yuri to run over to join her and she whispered something to both Yuri and Madame. The three, high-tailed it out of Studio A and we dancers stood with egg on our faces.

Minutes later, the secretary returned. "Ladies and gentlemen ... Mrs. Pace just received a phone call from the U.S. immigration office. They need to see her, Yuri Konstantinov and Frederick Borgen right away. Madame and Alexi Grigoriovitch will go with them."

Murmurs sounded in the room.

The secretary signaled her hands. "Listen. Please. If you don't need to be here, leave the school. Now! All rehearsals are canceled this afternoon and evening. Tomorrow resumes a full schedule as usual. Thank you."

SO, OFF WE trotted, Anna, Marie, Mrs. Tupper and me to Horn & Hardart's. We sat at our favorite table and Anna started a verbal tennis match. I was the bouncing ball.

"Your boyfriend is gorgeous," salivated Anna over a thirty-five cent ham sandwich using nickels in the glass slotted windows on the automat wall.

"How do you know?"

"On Saturday, Borgen rehearsed us in Studio A and when the rehearsal ended, I sat in the lobby to cool off. In walked David Katz, his aunt and Mrs. Pace who kept referring to them by name. All three entered Studio B to visit you and Yuri."

Mrs. Tupper sighed, "He's so good looking and tall. Black

curly hair, blue eyes ..."

"Did you get his red blood type, Mrs. Tupper?"

"Huh? She blushed and I tried not to giggle which kept me on guard. I didn't want the girls to find out we had sex. But, Anna sure tried.

Marie sat bug-eyed. "Who's David Katz?"

"Sarah's new boyfriend and she had a hot date with him Saturday night."

My nerves bristled watching Marie's eyes shine.

"C'mon, Sarah," Anna badgered. "We're dying to know. Did David kiss you? Did he get to first base? Second base? Did he touch you in the infield?"

"Why are you discussing baseball? You think he had a bat?"

"I know he's got a bat," she laughed. "It's probably a big bat. You know, big feet?"

"Speak English, Anna."

Mrs. Tupper nearly fell out of her chair laughing. She whispered, "He's got a big penis if he's got big feet or big hands."

Anna roared, "Why Mrs. Tupper, you know your dicks. I bet you buy fifty cent paperback romances at the A&P."

"I do. I like the medical romances."

Damn, they were too nosey. I cleared my throat. "Hey, I'm making this a fast lunch. I need to open a bank account and do some errands."

Marie looked woebegone. "Don't run and hide, Sarah. Inquiring minds wanna know. My life is dull as mashed potatoes."

I shut her up fast making her and the girls admit, they had things to do just like me.

I TOOK TWO busses and arrived at two o'clock. Doctor Ed's

office was one block away from Mt. Sinai Hospital and the Madison Avenue bus dropped me off at the corner. Five minutes after I sat down, David walked in the waiting room while I filled out paperwork.

Oh, God, no. "What are you doing here?" I squirmed.

"Moral support." He leaned in and kissed me. Then right on his heels, a young couple walked through the same door. The woman looked very pregnant and her husband looked very anxious. The couple sat next to us.

The husband spoke. "Looks like you two are just starting the process."

David didn't respond. I did a double take.

The husband tried again. "Just like you, we saw the doctor once a month in the beginning but now, we visit him every week. It's a pain in the ass to get off work."

David regarded the man but again said nothing.

I leaned in and whispered, "David, tell him I'm not pregnant."

The husband raised his voice. "Good thing our women have the babies. You look as nervous as I did at the start."

David turned around. "We're not having a baby."

"Oh, man, that's too bad. Fertility problems, huh? That's gotta be a bitch. Could cost two grand to take tests."

Just then, Doctor Ed and his nurse opened their office door. "Hello, Sarah ... come in."

I jumped up out of sheer relief and moved ahead of Doctor Ed and his nurse. I rushed down the hall. David followed the nurse and we all paraded into the examining room. Ed, stuck his hand out to block David.

"Hey! This isn't a family gathering. This is a doctor's office."

"I know but it's her first time."

"Yes, I know how to handle a first exam. I went to medical

school."

David frowned and returned to the waiting room. *Oh, my heart went out to him! He*'d have to face the repugnant father-to-be badgering my sweetheart's manhood. *But what about me? I'm facing humiliation; clothes off, shoes in stirrups?* So, in an attempt not to look at the stirrups, I told Doctor Ed about David and the husband sparring in the waiting room.

Ed's reaction? "Knowing my cousin, he'll probably demand a sperm count and compare the findings. He's damn competitive."

Whew, fifteen minutes later, was I ever relieved to climb off the table and get dressed. "Thank-you, Doctor. Yes, I have your phone number. Bye."

But, David had other ideas. "Wait a minute, babe. Can't I ask how it went?"

Ed and I answered together, "No!"

IF DAVID HAD told off the jerk in the doctor's waiting room, he didn't say. We took a cab to Chase Manhattan Bank on West 57th Street and Sixth Avenue. He introduced the two of us and requested a savings account be opened in my name. David, representing his law firm would co-sign which impressed the bank rep who turned us over to the new accounts manager. To thank us for choosing Chase Manhattan, the woman offered a free gift. I could choose an electric blanket, an iron or a crock pot.

"I'm your electric blanket," David whispered. "Mrs. Yee is your iron. Give the crockpot to your mother."

"Why? I'd like to learn to cook."

David grabbed my wrist. "If you need to cook, I'll send you to cooking school. We're not using a crock pot."

"Goodness, you are a snob."

"I prefer copper pans. The food tastes better."

"Yeah, really?"

"And stop saying 'yeah' when you answer me. The word is 'yes' or don't answer me."

The reprimand in front of the new accounts manager so infuriated me, I kicked David's ankle. He flinched and I finished signing the paperwork.

The new accounts manager handed me the Chase savings book for recording entries and smiled a sly turn-up of her lips. "By the way, Miss Rothman."

"Yes?"

"You do understand you can't open a checking account until you're twenty-one. Mr. Katz can remind you when it's time and he can show you how to write numbers."

"She won't need reminding," he snarled. "Or how to write a dollar amount. At twenty-one, she'll be investing in real estate while you're still working at this bank."

The woman chuckled. "You expect me to believe that? She can't pick out a free gift."

He clasped my hand. "Let's go. Leave the crock pot."

THE CAB DRIVER dropped us off on East 62nd Street and I thanked David for his help. Now, as a woman of independent means, I waited for David's reply. None came.

He climbed the steps, unlocked the front door and walked in first. I followed him inside and hurried behind, climbing the stairs two at a time. My breath caught. "What! David, talk to me."

We entered the bedroom, he slammed the door and faced me.

Scrunching up his eyebrows, he turned into lawyer mode. "Sarah, you need to behave more appropriate when we're out in public."

I swallowed hard.

"People judge you on how well you speak, how well you dress and your manners."

"Yes, I know I'm uncool and opinionated."

"At times, yes."

"I'm from Brooklyn. I have a smart-ass mouth. Who cares?"

He grimaced, "I do … that can't happen. Not with me!"

"You know what? Get over it. Take a last look mister. I'm out of here." I opened his bedroom door and ran down the stairs.

David caught me in the hallway and pulled me into his chest. "Hey, wrong attitude."

"You're the ass not me."

"People are shits. I'm older and wiser, take advantage of what I know. The bitch in the bank belittled you every time you opened your mouth. She made me fucking mad."

"I didn't …"

"No, you didn't. You were excited depositing your checks. You missed her snide remarks concerning how little you made at your job. How she had children as customers half your age with ten times as much money."

"I heard her say 'peanuts.' But I thought Charlie Brown."

David reared back. "You mean the comic strip?"

"Yeah, yes, I mean no." I covered my face and peeked out.

His mouth fell open.

I banged my head on his chest a couple times gripping his arms.

He kissed my head. "Sarah, I'm sorry I corrected you. I shouldn't have done that."

"No, you shouldn't."

"At least not in public. Next time, I'll correct you in private when we're alone."

"Is that so?" I pitched his cheek.

"Ow!"

"Good! Then, I'll correct you when we're alone when you scowl ... when things don't go your way ... when you screw up your big, bad face like a bear."

He laughed. "I guess we're even. Touche."

I cuddled into his chest. "Touche. Can I call my dad?"

"Sure, after you kiss me first."

"HI, DADDY ... good ... Guess what? I have a real bank account. David helped me ... How's that? Yep ... I'd like to give you and Mama some money ... No? You don't need my money? Why? ... Put it in the bank ... shopping ... Korvette's? ... Daddy, I prefer Bloomingdale's and I'm gonna try Saks Fifth Avenue ... no? ... Okay ... fine ... Uncle Al? ... Goodbye."

David's eyes smiled, "What did he say?"

"Shut your smart-ass mouth. Keep your money in the bank. No shopping at Saks Fifth Avenue with shiksas. Uncle Al will take you to the garment district on Seventh Avenue in Manhattan. Jews never pay full price. I raised you better. Buy wholesale. Ugh!"

"Sounds reasonable."

"Not to me."

He held my chin and kissed my upper lip, "Are you okay?"

I sighed, "Yeah ... oh crap, I meant, yes!"

"You'll live."

"No, I won't. Not if I have to shop with Uncle Al. He has the first dollar he ever made."

David wrapped his strong arms around me. "Baby, do you have any idea how long I've wanted to kiss you? I mean really kiss you."

I shook my head.

"Since early this morning." His hands moved to the sides of my face. "You interrupted my work with prurient thoughts of mouth to lips."

"You're teasing me."

"Like hell I am." His expression turned serious. "I don't mind-fuck."

I bit my lip.

"Hey, let's go to the kitchen. Mrs. Yee made dinner."

"She's here? No, I'm not going. She heard us."

"Believe me. She hears only what she wants."

IN THE KITCHEN, Mrs. Yee stood at the stove making stir-fry chicken and veggies in a wok. David greeted her with a quick kiss on the cheek. She smiled and nodded. Not wanting to interfere, I hung back.

Mrs. Yee stopped stirring, walked over to me and extended her hand. She smiled a warm grin. *What happened to her evil and cold looks?* I tried to return the smile but only gave it a forty percent try.

From the moment I met her, she treated me like David's plaything, "his tsatskela" as Bubbe would say in Yiddish. Or, as Aunt Lucy called her boyfriends, "The Carvel ice cream flavor of the month."

Anyway, I was surprised at Mrs. Yee's friendliness. I looked at David for help and mouthed the words, "Why is she so nice? What's her problem?"

His eyes locked mine and he didn't answer.

She next apologized for not having dinner ready in time. "Maybe, ten minutes? Everything's ready."

"Can I help?" *The words flew out of my mouth like a Pavlov conditioned dog without thinking.*

David touched my shoulder. "No, Mrs. Yee doesn't need your help, I'm certain."

But, she did help and she pointed to the table. "Yes, Miss Sarah. Take those dishes to the dining room and set two places."

"Why only two?"

"Go."

I did what she asked and returned to the kitchen. "Aren't you eating Mrs. Yee? And my name is Sarah."

"No, I need to go home but before I go, can I do anything for you?"

I glanced at David and crossed my eyes.

"Sarah, she knows you launder your dance clothes at night. They drip on the bathroom floor."

I covered my mouth and giggled, "Oops, sorry."

"Miss Sarah, I'll wash your things on the gentle cycle and hang them to dry on the back porch."

"But, I'm used to washing my own things."

Mrs. Yee gave David a strange look then glared at me.

"What!" I pouted.

Neither of them spoke.

"Okay, okay, I'll get the leotards." I ran upstairs and emptied my dance bag and returned with two leotards, two pairs of tights, a dance belt, two bras and two panties."

"There!" I stuffed the things in a brown paper bag from the broom closet. "I have no more secrets! Might as well tell the New York Times."

David laughed. "You never had secrets from me. Don't flatter yourself."

My cheeks burned. "I hate you."

"No, you don't," he chuckled. "You admire Mrs. Yee and you like me even more. Yes, I went too far. Sorry, Brooklyn. I apologize. So sue me."

"I would if I knew a good lawyer."

I hid my face from Mrs. Yee and put the drinks on the table. I carried in the salad, stir-fry chicken, rice bowl and lit the candles as decoration.

David grabbed me from behind the door and kissed me gently. "I've been rude and hard on you today."

"Yes, you have."

"You push my buttons baby, and get under my skin."

I tilted my head. "Try a kind word for a change."

"That's it?" he winked. "I can do a lot more. Bon appetite."

We started eating while Mrs. Yee did laundry and cleaned up the kitchen. When she finished, she joined us ready to leave. Dressed in a wool coat and scarf, she smiled. "Goodnight, Miss Sarah."

"Please, call me Sarah. The dinner was yummy. Thank you."

David pushed his chair back and walked Mrs. Yee to the front door. Minutes later, the door banged shut and he returned.

"My aunt showed Mrs. Yee your newspaper interviews and pictures from the New York Times and Post. She's making a scrapbook for you as a surprise. She plans to give you the book at the premiere."

"How thoughtful," my heart turned over, "and kind." I shook my head. "Am I supposed to know?"

"No, I think you'd better squeal in shock."

"I can do that," I giggled. "Uh-huh."

"Mrs. Yee is awed by you and shared my aunt's joy. She wants a ticket to see you dance on opening night. That's six tickets for my family plus another nine for my associates and their wives."

The warmth from my core rose to my cheeks. I didn't know what to say. I picked up chopsticks and took another bite then got the courage to smile into David's twinkling blue eyes.

"There's cut-up watermelon in the fridge."

"That's my favorite. How did Mrs. Yee know?"

"Probably from Eleanor ... remember dinner at the South-ampton Beach Club?"

UPSTAIRS, DAVID LIT the candles on the tall bureau and we showered together. When he offered a massage, I couldn't leap on the bed fast enough. Lying on my tummy, naked and willing, I exhaled a delicious sigh.

David straddled my legs and applied a peach scented massage oil dripping down my spine. After meditating faster than I could count seven chakras, his soothing hands went to work.

"Aaaaaahh, yes," I cooed relaxing into the bed. Negative energy shot out my pores and happy vibes floated in. Pain and tightness fought against David's hands but slowly, his hands won. He mastered my tense muscles and strained tendons. His amazing, healing fingers kneaded and manipulated deep. My body responded and the hurt sailed away.

So grateful for his magic touch, I mumbled, "Amazing" and drifted into a lovely tropical place. Dreaming of clear, turquoise-blue waters that ebbed and flowed on a sunny, white beach. *Warm air and beautiful, swaying palm trees ...*

Suddenly, David slapped my butt.

"Ouch!" My eyes popped open.

He roared, "Damn! That's a beautiful ass."

And like a crouching tiger, he flipped me over on my back

and straddled my hips on his knees. His lips, trembling and moist, kissed me hungry. The heat from his loins startled me fully awake.

His gaze deepened. "Are you my Brooklyn?"

I languished trying to lick my lips to respond.

A mischievous grin crossed his face. "I like you trying whatever you're attempting to do. Keep licking those lips and I'll howl at the moon." He laughed a throaty growl.

I didn't have the courage to say anymore.

He pressed his body into mine and his skin smelled of citrus. My mind went wild with pleasurable ideas and I tingled in anticipation. *How can hormones know when to sit up and beg?*

David made unconditional love that night with a full heart. *I couldn't help but fall a little in love but I kept the secret to myself.*

CHAPTER 40

Tuesday, October 5ᵗʰ. Changes take tiny steps.

DURING THE MORNING class, Madame demanded perfection at the barre exercises. Then, when we left the barre to dance in the center, she screamed the variations and made us repeat and repeat the same thing.

Anna punched my ribs, "I hate her."

"Shut-up."

Madame must have heard us because she moved towards Anna but when Anna smiled, Madame backed away. However, it was obvious, our Ballet Mistress had an axe to grind and she treated the class as the enemy.

After an hour and a half of torture and abuse, most of us could use a hot tub, a quart of strawberry ice cream and a psychiatrist. We girls couldn't change our wet leotards and tights into dry leotards and tights fast enough to escape the building. We jogged to the automat to shake the criticism thrown our way from the evil witch in Cuban heels.

Thankfully, the lunch conversation didn't center around Madame or David but on "who would dance the specialty dances in *The Nutcracker*." According to Marie, Frederick Borgen announced his plans.

"He's holding open auditions for certain roles. Wait a minute, girls." She rummaged through her purse and pulled out a white steno pad. "I wrote this stuff down." She flipped some pages. "Yes, he's auditioning the Spanish, Arabian, Chinese and Russian parts and … no, not the Shepherdess, the reed flutes, the male dancer playing Mother Ginger or the Buffoons. Those characters will be performed by the same dancers this season as last year."

"Great," I said. "Mr. Borgen sounds pretty fair and …"

"And, what?" Anna stopped me mid-sentence. She turned her back and spoke to, "Marie? What about the Sugar Plum Fairy? And the Snow Queen/Dew Drop Fairy?"

"Freddy did mention auditioning the understudies who might perform the fairy roles on matinee days."

"But how? Irina Ivanova always dances Sugar Plum."

"I don't know." Marie shrugged. "On Saturday, Irina criticized his coaching on the *Eight Themes*. And yesterday, she told him to his face, 'If you don't stick to Karl's original choreography for the Sugar Plum Fairy, like you're refusing to do on *Eight Themes*, I won't dance in *Nutcracker*.'"

Anna jumped up from her chair. "I love in-house fighting but I need orange juice. Girls, I'll be right back. Don't discuss *Nutcracker* until I buy a drink."

Marie shook her head. "I don't like Irina threatening Freddy. It stresses me out."

Mrs. Tupper agreed. "You know, a few days ago, Irina shouted in the lobby that somebody stole her lunch from the kitchen refrigerator. She accused almost everybody in the lobby acting like a crazy woman."

"Did she find out who took it?" I opened my lunch bag.

"Nope. I don't think so cause Mrs. Pace bought her some Chinese take-out."

Anna returned with her glass of orange juice. "I hope Irina quits or gets fired. Karl Kreisler would turn over in his grave if someone, hurt Irina's feelings."

My hands flew to the top of my head and I stared at my cold, meatball sandwich. Hearing Mr. Kreisler's name *sent a chilling visual seeing him sprawled out on the hardwood floor in a pool of blood; his eyes staring into space.* The red tomato sauce covering my meatball sandwich didn't help either.

I dropped my hands and sucked in a breath of air.

"Oh, fiddle-faddle. I upset you, Sarah," lamented Marie. "You're whiter than a sheet."

Mrs. Tupper leaned over. "What is it, sweetie?"

"Huh? Oh, nothing," I shook my head and made light of the situation. "Get out the dueling pistols. I never dreamt I'd sit here and listen to bickering in a ballet company."

"It gets worse," warned Marie. "I remember the soloists fighting with Karl over costume malfunctions and taking too many curtain calls. Even wearing diamond stud earrings on stage which he was against, imagine? Mrs. Pace said it was acceptable because she gave the girls the earrings."

"Did the dancers complain?" I blinked.

"Yes," said Anna. "But never Irina. For some weird reason, Irina followed Karl around by the nose. She was his poodle dog on a rhinestone purple leash."

"Why? Were they lovers?" I mocked a fake laugh.

"Karl? No way. Sex with men, the younger the better."

Mrs. Tupper almost choked on the last bite of her peanut butter and jelly sandwich. When she recovered, I stuck out my tongue. "Ha! Better keep reading your romance paperbacks. More fun with the male doctors and female nurses."

Mrs. Tupper grinned in triumph. "Sarah, I finished two paperbacks this month. Do you want one? Or, both books?"

"Yeah, maybe ... both." I tried to sound dignified.

Anna elbowed my ribs. "You could learn some new and wicked things reading those books. Men love naughty surprises in bed."

I punched Anna's arm and Mrs. Tupper turned three shades of magenta; light, medium and dark.

"I'd like to try new sex stuff," chuckled Marie. "I mean, why not?"

"Really?" I bristled staring at the ceiling fans so I wouldn't blush.

"Girls," Anna's face lit up. "I have an idea."

"I hope it's a good one," salivated Marie.

"For Sarah's birthday, we should get the lady friend of Alexi's who gives the sex toy parties. She demonstrates the products in your living room and sells them at the discount party price."

"No, you don't. Anna, that's too much." I crossed my arms and shuddered.

Marie pushed her chair back. "Time to go. Lunch is over. Rehearsals start in half an hour." She picked up her hot pink dance bag. "I rehearse with Freddy. Don't know what it is."

"I rehearse with Borgen, too," nodded Anna. "My name was on the bulletin board. So we're together like old times."

Anna turned around and hugged me. "Don't be upset new girl in town. I'm teasing you. Learn to laugh at yourself and others. That's the only way you'll survive the CCBT and life. Take my word."

"Yeah," I sighed. "I hear you," and hugged her back.

"Still best friends?"

"Yes, best friends," I exhaled. "For a moment, I thought you were serious."

"I am serious. We girls will call the sex toy lady and throw you the best birthday ever. I get a free gift if I host the party in my apartment. I need a new vibrator."

"A vibrator? What's that?"

"Ah, Jesus, Sarah. You are naïve. You and I must have a grown-up conversation at my apartment one night. We'll drink wine and eat sushi."

"Can I come, too?" giggled Marie. "I'd like to learn a few things."

"Can I join in?" begged Mrs. Tupper reaching for her suit jacket.

"Why not? You'd probably teach us a thing or two, you sly dog reading romantic doctors as lovers."

I screwed up my face and balked. "Some friends you are."

"Yep, that's us," chuckled Anna. "We've got your back."

"And David's got your front with the good parts." Marie winked at Anna.

I couldn't look at the girls after that.

DURING THE AFTERNOON, the *Monarch* rehearsal was scheduled to end at five o'clock. I didn't know why the early finish and I didn't ask. Yuri seemed distracted and if I didn't move my hand just so or whip my head around fast enough in spot turns, he'd scream.

The office secretary entered the room carrying a plate of orange and apple slices. Yuri ran for the plate, sucked on the slices and never offered to share. He probably missed lunch because when he finished slurping, he turned into a quieter man.

At the close of our rehearsal, Yuri joked and laughed, go figure. I kissed him goodbye and waved at Alexi and Mrs. Tupper and scampered to the girl's dressing room to change.

Now wearing street clothes, I descended the stairs and spotted David in Mrs. Pace's office with the door shut. *Why?*

The two spoke in a serious, animated dialogue. I could holler,

"What the hell?" but, held my tongue. I waved and Mrs. Pace opened the door.

"Sarah ... Yuri just left in an upbeat mood. Said, 'You had an ambitious rehearsal. *Monarchs In Spring* went well.'"

I kissed David and smiled at Mrs. Pace. "Yes, it did."

"My darling girl, you make me proud. Yuri is pleased with you, his pot of gold at the end of the rainbow. He admires your tenacity and talent." She turned to David. "I'll say goodnight, Mr. Katz and Sarah," she touched my shoulder. "I'll see you tomorrow afternoon. Good luck with your doctor's appointment in the morning."

"What?"

David steered my elbow to face him. "Yes, darling, your doctor's appointment." He winked.

"Oh! Goodnight, Mrs. Pace."

ONCE OUTSIDE ON the sidewalk, I scowled at David. "What was that all about?"

"Your director wanted my assurance that you'd eat protein, sleep eight hours and visit your doctor. She insisted we use contraceptives and told me I wasn't to exhaust you sexually."

"Crap, what happened to privacy? That's none of her damn business. Uncle Al gets in trouble when Aunt Ida Mae asks his waitresses about their boyfriends. She snoops, "Are you married or living in sin?""

"Good catch, Judge Sarah. You're right but try enforcing the complaint."

"She's afraid I'll get pregnant," I mumbled watching the people pass us by.

"Mrs. Pace doesn't want anything to stop your momentum.

Eyes on the prize."

"Bubbe was fifteen when she got pregnant."

David clenched his jaw. "Bubbe didn't twirl on her toes or have the New York Times and half the ballet world anticipating her debut."

"Bubbe had sex with her clothes on."

"Brooklyn, I don't care if grandma wore sixteen pairs of socks or a bag over her head."

"I'm making a point."

"The nights you and the Russian dance are already sold out. Mrs. Pace was on the phone with the box office when she called me in. You're her cash cow."

"That's gross."

"No, it's not. You're the money-maker, and together, you and the Russian are the goose that laid the golden eggs selling tickets."

"Well, tickle me pink, I had no idea. Nothing like pressure."

"You can handle it." He turned and shouted, "Taxi!"

"Where are we going?"

"Home. And, Ed's coming over for a beer and to say good-bye."

"Please, don't discuss your trip."

He reached for my chin and kissed my upper lip, "Are you okay?"

"I have to be. The cab's here."

DAVID ANSWERED THE front door and he and Ed headed for the kitchen. I greeted the good doctor and set two beers on the table. "Excuse me, gentlemen, I'm taking a shower."

"No, you can shower later." David pulled out a chair.

"Yes, stay and chat. Nice to see you away from my office. I can tell Rebecca something about your dancing day at the ballet."

I poured myself a lemonade and sat next to David. Within minutes, Ed chug-a-lugged beer number one and banged the empty bottle on the table.

"Lady, another beer, if you please."

David sat forward. "How many beers have you had?"

"Two at home plus here? This will be the fourth."

"Maybe you should slow down."

"Why? She's seven and a half months pregnant. I can't make love to my beautiful wife so I drink. And, tonight ... I'm not on call to deliver babies, I'm free as a bird."

"Okay, fine." David raised his bottle. A night off, L'Chaim." The bottles clinked.

"Do you know what it's like to sleep next to the woman you adore and not touch her? I have a never ending boner."

David's eyes caught mine. "I can only imagine."

I took a last sip of lemonade and stood up. "I need to shower."

"No," said Ed.

"Stay, baby," smiled David. "Please."

Why? I don't wanna hear your cousin's personal life. Wasn't I humiliated enough during a pelvic exam in air conditioning so cold, my goosebumps had goosebumps?

"Ed, look on the bright side," assured David uncapping another bottle of beer for himself. "It'll be over soon."

"No, you're wrong. After she gives birth, no sex for six more weeks. Better make it a whiskey chaser with that beer. How about it, bartender lady?"

"Sarah, stay seated. I'll get the whiskey from the study."

The wall phone rang and David picked it up. "Hello, Rebecca ..."

Ed grabbed the receiver, "Yes, honey ... you have a craving for Fellini's Italian on Third Avenue? Sure. We're having one bottle of beer, that's all, just one. Sarah's here." Ed turned to the two of us, "You people want to go to Fellini's for spaghetti?"

I wrinkled my nose. "Does it come with stuffed manicotti?"

David stroked my cheek. "Whatever my lady wants? It's up to her."

"Yes, we'll go."

Ed got back on the phone then put his hand over the receiver. "You guys just made her day. What time?"

David gazed into my eyes. "Can you be ready by six?"

"I think so."

"Honey, six o'clock. Love you." Ed hung up.

David shoved his chair back. "I'm getting Jack Daniels from the study ..."

"And, I'm taking a shower."

AFTER A FUN-FILLED dinner at Fellini's, we shared a cab with Ed and Rebecca and said goodnight on the sidewalk in front their house.

David clasped my hand and walked me up the steps to his adjoining townhouse. Turning the key, he pushed open the gold latch and ushered me inside. Without turning on lights, he touched and fondled my most sensitive places. I gasped, "Oh, God," at the surprise assault. In the next minutes, his mouth slammed down on mine with the suddenness of a gale force wind. The impact, a greedy passion as if, he'd been stranded on a desert island without a woman. Scarier still, my knees buckled when he shoved the door shut, snapped the Segal Dead Bolt and pushed his face into mine squeezing my arms.

He snarled holding my shaky body pressed tight against his. "No fucking way am I making you pregnant. If I had to sleep next to you and not touch you for months, I'd go out of my God damn mind."

My lips quivered, "Not ever?"

He pulled his chest back and laughed. "Till hell freezes over!"

"What! Why are you laughing?"

"Hey," his hand lifted my chin, his eyes flashed. "Of course, I want children but not now. And you can't."

"No," I shook my head.

"So, why the hell are we discussing children?" he yelled. His face contorted in fear.

"You brought it up."

"Right because Ed can't fuck his wife."

"Wow, that's sweet."

"Yes, it is sweet. He needs to fuck her hard and often."

"Is that how you men operate?"

David pulled me close. "Yes!"

I shimmied out of his arms.

His jaw tightened in surprise. "Hey, I'm honest. You're the woman I want and can't get enough of."

"You're too demanding."

"And you aren't?" He stopped cold and glared. "Don't lie, Sarah," and he whisked my trembling body into his arms.

He carried me upstairs and kicked the bedroom door shut.

I BRACED MYSELF fearing he'd pounce and I'd be mush and bruised so I took a chance and hollered. "Put me down! Don't hurt me!"

"Hurt you?" His face registered shock but he did as I asked. "What the hell?"

"You man-handled me like a rag doll. You're scaring me."

He stepped back and bumped into the closet doors. "Ah, shit, my mind was on Ed and no sex. I'm sorry. I took it out on you."

I choked back tears watching him drop to one knee bowing his head. "I never meant to ..." He ran his hands through his hair. "I apologize, Sarah." He kissed my hands. "I can't lose you."

"Don't hurt me."

"No." His eyes smarted with moisture.

I kissed him with a generous heart. He returned my forgiving kiss and pulled us both to our feet. His strong arms wrapped me in a careful, soft, cuddle.

He turned me around and unzipped my dress. It fell to the floor and I stepped out of the skirt. He hung it up along with his jacket. He touched my back, "May I?" and swooped me up like a child's doll and laid me on his king size bed. He removed my heels and stockings.

In the nightstand drawer, he took out a tiny vodka bottle and drank the contents. He avoided my eyes as he tossed the empty bottle in a wastepaper can.

He morphed into lawyer mode.

"My behavior was inexcusable. In future, I'll try not to hurt you." He cleared his throat. "I'll make it up to you."

"Good. You do that."

He placed his hands on the sides of my face and looked deep into my eyes. "I want you," he murmured. "Sometimes, a little too much. I know you get it."

"I do," and kissing him, I realized I'd have to deal with his aggression but for now, no more talk.

I laid my head on his king size pillow and stretched out lengthwise on his wonderful, fluffy bed. He leaned forward and brushed his lips down my neck then sat up.

In an unexpected move, he kneaded and massaged my feet.

Ooooooo, my heart sang a Beatle song. Yes! I could die happy. Yeah, yeah, yeah. The pressure of his hands caressed my arches and toes too wonderful to describe. I closed my eyes and relaxed under his healing hands. *You silly girl, as if I'd ever quit David.*

He stopped the foot massage. My heart did back flips saying a quiet thank you.

"Brooklyn, what would you like?" He walked to the closet and hung up his suit pants and vest.

"Are you asking what I want?"

"Yes, do you want to watch television? Read a book? I have an extensive library downstairs or ...," his eyes lit up. "We could make love?" He unbuttoned his shirt tugging at the sleeves.

But I knew he enjoyed playing cat and mouse so I asked, "What are my other choices?"

His eyes flashed. "Your dad's right. You have a smart-ass mouth and I could show you a better way to use it ... especially on me."

I glanced up at the ceiling avoiding his eyes and tried not to cringe or laugh. He continued to act cool and slipped off his shirt, shoes and socks. Not knowing what he'd do next, I waited to see how far he'd take this charade.

"David? How about watching television?"

"Downstairs in the den or in the guestroom on this floor with the small TV?"

I met his gaze. "Kiss me."

His button-down shirt landed on the armchair and he kneeled beside me. His hands touched the softness of my thighs and he licked my skin above the knee. "You have beautiful, sweet-smelling skin."

"Damn it, David, just kiss me."

His lips moved to my face.

"Not there."

"No?" His eyes twinkled.

"No." I licked my lips.

And my underwear and his underwear flew to the armchair. He buried his head in sweet, lovely kisses until I squirmed and mumbled, "Yes," at least twenty times. My toes curled and he continued titillating until I yelled, "Stop" and pushed him away. "Too much, David."

"Never enough," he chuckled and teased me by brushing his tongue along the insides of my thigh.

His taut, muscular body rubbed hot against my soft frame sending high alerts to five senses. The heat from his breath tickled my skin. His hands clasped my shoulders and he stared deep in my eyes. A chill rippled up my spine.

"I want you," he murmured and waited for a response.

My throat closed.

He stared.

I wanted to answer a reply but my mouth went dry. I couldn't find suitable words he'd find appropriate. *Yes, appropriate, one of his favorite words in the last few days, damn it.*

His lips skimmed the top of my belly and reached my breasts. My heart pounded anticipating his next move which I knew would be kissing the soft mounds. He coaxed my shy nipples to appear. Then, moving his lips to my face, his eyes dilated. His darkened focus penetrated my pupils and witches and goblins, if you believe in such things, my soul.

I gasped feeling an electrifying energy burn through my lower body. The steam from his loins clenched my stomach and I whispered, "David, I'm ... ah ..."

He held my face and savored my lips with his trembling, burning mouth. "You're mine," he whispered, "and don't forget it." He parted my lips in a slow, wet, lingering kiss. His tongue explored my mouth and I relished the tingles and tastes. But, I didn't relish "and don't forget it" but I let it ride in the heat of passion.

The musk, citrus scent of his skin and the wetness between my legs made me dizzy. The combination, too delicious. And when he nipped the length of my neck with his teeth, I tugged on his dark, curly hair.

His hands traveled my backsides caressing with a light, teasing touch. The more he lingered, the more crazy good it got. Bless his heart, the man took his sweet time making certain I'd welcome him.

"David," I moaned trying not to leave nail marks on his back, "Why are you taking so long?"

He groaned a smug response and pushed inside me, pumping blood through my veins running berserk. I gasped, "I need ... I ... yes ..."

The man pushed gentle at first then thrust more aggressive. The slow decent heightened my nerve endings. I took in vibrating sensations to the tips of my toes and whispered his name.

Yes, I lusted after him no-holds-barred. The chemical attraction, too magnetic to stop. And, like moving trains, full throttle, we both roared into each other's bodies with no thought of the consequences.

He raised his head and exhaled a guttural roar. His eyes fixated on mine. He lowered his head and moved his chest forward to rest his weight on his hands, my heartbeat moved up the charts. His staying power lasted forever or so it seemed.

In an abrupt move, he pushed too deep and I flinched.

"You okay?" His eyes narrowed.

"Uh-huh."

Sensing I lied, he stopped moving and locked eyes. He waited for a sign and studied my face. I must have looked okay because he kissed my mouth, grabbed my upper arms and started moving again, in a deliberate, controlled rhythm. "Baby," he exhaled burying his face in my hair.

From the back of his throat, he made husky sounds that made no sense. His eyes rolled upwards. If visceral responses were tangible, he took possession of my body like property he owned. Hovering overhead to storm the castle and rescue the maiden, his energy on high alert. *Yes, he startled me. And, yes, he penetrated with such raw intensity and enthusiasm. I mumbled a quick pray for leniency and no pain.*

His mouth lingered above my lips. "Be mine."

"Yes," my eyelids fluttered. At six foot one, his brute force impacted my five foot four inch frame. I feared what he could do but couldn't do without like a moth to light.

He kissed my throat. "Trust me!"

"Yes," I answered too fascinated to say no watching a glimmer in his eyes.

He stopped moving, rose to his feet and stood at the end of the bed. His eyes widened. "Ready?"

I nodded and trembled.

Flipping me over on my belly, he grabbed my waist. His hands yanked me backwards and forced me to my knees. He slid my rear against his thighs faster than I could ask, "What are you?" Again inside me, he thrust slow and easy.

He picked up the tempo rubbing tight.

"Oh, no," I whimpered feeling the thrusting stimulate a sensitive spot. The sensations hitting the top of my belly sent my mind into orbit and my body writhing. I panted and dug my nails into the bedsheets. And then a pleasant awakening ... "Oh,

God," I shrieked, "Daaaaavid."

His hands clutched the sides of my hips and tightened when his body jerked and his breathing choked.

I started to cry, wild and uninhibited, hysterical sobs. My fists balled up, my chest heaved and I lost it. "You're leaving me," I yelled, "You're going ..."

"Shuuuush," David exhaled and turned me over on my back. His physical strength now spent, he fell against my side and partly on top of my chest. "It's a business trip."

I shivered in his arms.

He said softly to my cheek. "I'm coming back."

"I hate it."

"I know. Separation anxiety."

"What?"

"Not important."

The strength in his arms held me quiet for a couple minutes. But as the mind works in predictable ways, it leaped to hysterics.

David nuzzled his face in my hair. "It's okay, babe. Cry it out. Maybe we'll both feel better."

LATER, WE ATE Pistachio ice cream and made love again. This go round, David charged a little less frantic on a milder stampede which suited me just fine. *The man could be exhausting.*

And it would be some time before we'd see each other again. And not as intimate, until maybe ... my eighteenth birthday which seemed a million years away. *How would I manage the days ahead?* I hadn't a clue.

The heaviness of sleep overtook the two of us and we settled into a cozy spoon. David reached for my hand and whispered, "And flights of angels sing thee to thy rest. Goodnight, Brooklyn."

"Good niiii ... Grace."

CHAPTER 41

Wednesday, October 6th. Happy hands are busy hands but don't count on it.

WAKING MID-MORNING AND making love tested our give and take. David held his gymnastic prowess to a minimum and I didn't perform Ophelia's mad scene from Hamlet. At the finish, I murmured, "David, I, um ..." so full of awesome thoughts and feelings ... "wanted to tell you how much ..."

But, David's finger touched my lips indicating silence. He held me close to his chest as our heartbeats gradually returned to normal. Kissing my throat, he tumbled out of bed and headed for the shower.

I joined him for a soapy rinse-off and quickly dressed in a navy blue leotard and pink tights while he shaved. When he returned to the bedroom, wrapped in a bath towel slung low on his hips, I turned into silly putty. The halo of dark, wet ringlets surrounding his head crowned a delicious grin. I melted in his arms.

"Don't cry, babe." He kissed my forehead.

"Sorry."

"Don't apologize. Don't cry."

I sniffled.

For the record, David lied to Mrs. Pace. I didn't have a doctor's appointment. It was his answer to spending more time together and making certain, I slept eight hours. I needed the sleep because at two o'clock, I'd face the wrath of Madame Madyaslavic who'd been in a foul mood for days.

The Madame, insisted I learn the Sugar Plum Fairy variation from *The Nutcracker*. If Mr. Borgen held open auditions for this role, she wanted me prepared. Madame only told Mrs. Pace why she needed her tape recorder and the Peter Ilyich Tchaikovsky music. Having revealed her clandestine plan to teach me, pissed Madame off especially when Mrs. Pace blabbed the news to Yuri.

And I heard from Anna who was told by Yuri, "Bor-gen has sec-ret. Bor-gen teeches Ma-rie ... Sug-gar Plom Fay-reey." And Anna, told me she got really mad and asked Yuri to teach her the same Sugar Plum Fairy variation. So much for everybody having secrets and ballet company drama.

As David and I entered the kitchen, a stoic Mrs. Yee greeted us with brunch. My sweetheart ate in silence probably planning his day. Me? I gobbled scrambled eggs, lox and cream cheese on a toasted half a bagel and sliced, fresh peaches. I also popped multi-vitamins, B-complex, A & E vitamins and choked on Brewer's Yeast mixed in orange juice. Yes, I carried packets of these pills in my dance bag in case I got stranded on a subway train and needed strength to climb three flights of stairs to clear the station.

And, as I was hungry as a wolf, I ate everything knowing I'd burn calories facing the witch in Cuban heels. However, Mrs. Yee chuckled when she saw me set an empty plate in the sink. And when I helped myself to more peach slices in a clean bowl, she chuckled again.

David checked his watch, finished his second cup of coffee and looked across at me. "Ready?"

"Yes," I sipped the last drop of Tetley Tea and put my cup in the sink. "Goodbye, Mrs. Yee, thanks for a great breakfast."

"Goodbye, Miss Sarah."

I turned to leave when she stopped me with her phone number on a piece of paper. "If you need anything."

"Oh? Thanks." I reached for a hug and she tensed up not expecting the affection.

I followed David to the front door where he playfully leaned me over backwards. He reenacted Fred Astaire kissing Ginger Rogers in an RKO movie musical. His lips trembled even though he meant a whimsical goodbye. He'd miss me. I forced a giggle to join in.

"I'll call you tomorrow night around ten at Sutton Place ... if I can from Hong Kong. Only if, the long distance operator can get through to New York."

My heart raced and I clung to him. "Calling from China?" I kissed him *thinking it might as well be Mars.*

"But, if I can't get through, I'll try again Friday night." His fingers caressed my face. "I'll send telegrams. Don't let Dragon Lady take your mail."

"Dragon Lady?" My voice cracked.

"Yes, the bitch stole your flowers. Watch your back, baby."

"Anna already warned me."

"Good. Only talk ballet. Don't discuss you or me or family. Do you understand?"

"Yes, counselor." I gazed into his dreamy, ocean blue eyes.

"Tell Cook and Mrs. Williams you'll get telegrams and letters. It's against the law to give mail to anyone other than the person it's addressed to. Threaten them with jail."

I wiped my tears on my leotard sleeve. "I'll sleep home in Brooklyn on Saturday and Sunday nights."

"Maybe, I might call you there. But, calling from another country is difficult. Sometimes, impossible. Don't be upset if you don't hear from me."

He hesitated then placed his hands on my face. On an inhale, he kissed me deep, hard and urgent. *Oh, yikes*, he took possession of me with such an avalanche of emotion, *I swear* my heart stopped for two full minutes. And *geez Louise*, when he pulled away, I tasted blood on my lip.

"Sorry." He wiped my mouth with a monogramed handkerchief and shoved it in my hand.

Two knocks at the door.

"I have to go." I dabbed my eyes and grabbed my jacket from the chair.

"Next time I kiss you," he murmured. "I'll be saying, 'Hello.'" He reached over and opened the door.

"Good morning, Mr. Katz, Miss Sarah."

"Fernando," greeted David. "Right on time."

"Yes, sir, Mr. Katz. And the boss lady doesn't know." He carried my suitcase and dance bag to the car. Without a word, he sat in the driver's seat and waited, eyes straight ahead.

One more kiss later, David opened the limo door and helped me in. Fernando started the engine, drove away and I slobbered a waterfall of tears into a DEK monogramed hankie.

WHEN I WALKED in the ballet school, the lobby clock read 1:45 p.m. The company dancers sat on couches or stood talking in hushed voices. A "No Admittance" sign hung over the door to Studio A. Two rainbow girls greeted me.

Marta, the color yellow squealed, "Sarah, guess what?"

"Do I have to?"

"I think they want you and Yuri to dance on the Ed Sullivan Show."

I dropped my dance bag and covered my mouth with my

hands. "No! Really?"

"Yes," giggled Lily the color indigo. "I heard Alexi whisper in Yuri's ear just before Yuri went inside with Mrs. Pace." She pointed to the No Admittance sign.

"Where's Alexi?"

"In there with them."

I picked up my dance bag and let out a sigh. Joy crept into my heart after bawling like a baby in the limo.

Anna spotted us and hurried over. "Sarah, what's with your eyes? Have you been crying?"

"No, no, I have allergies."

"Since when? No, you don't. What's up?"

I couldn't answer because Madame Madyaslavic exited Studio A and slammed the door making us jump. The ballet mistress loved to attract attention whenever she could. Seeing me, she stomped her Cuban heels over and threw out the pre-planned red herring.

"Sa-rah, I teach you. Ve vork on jumps. Ve vork on arms, port de bras, n'est pas?"

"Bien sur, Madame."

"Maintenant! Upstairs, Studio C."

"You mean now?" I did a pretend Academy Award look of shock worthy of a Bette Davis film.

"Mais qui ... pourquoi pas?" she laughed. "Yuri in big meeting. Yuri and Sa-rah rehearse four o'clock."

I looked at the lobby clock. "Not until four?"

"Da," she smiled. "Madame teach Sa-rah, two o'clock."

I followed her up the stairs and stopped halfway. Looking back, I gave a special wave to my jaw-dropping, jealous friends.

WHILE DANCING IN Studio C, I kept checking the clock over the door. During breakfast, I heard David tell Mrs. Yee he'd be picked up at three thirty by the law firm's limo and have his suitcases ready at the front door. So, beginning at three-twenty, I eyeballed the minute hand. Five minutes later, I stopped dancing all together and froze. My mouth went dry and my pulse rate jumped.

"Sa-rah," yelled Madame. "Danse ... nyet danse!"

I exhaled an anxious sigh.

"Clock ... nyet, clock!"

"Sorry, Madame. My friend is flying out of the country." I hid my face under my arm feeling my eyes sting with tears.

"Birds fly. Planes fly. Nyet, vorry. Ver-ry safe."

"Safe? Really?" I peeked out from under my arm.

"Better get killed by taxi cab driver on New York street." She shook her head. "New York, nyet safe. Muggers in the park."

I wiped my eyes on my sleeve. "You're right, it's safer in the sky. Less traffic."

"Sa-rah danse?"

"Yes ... sorry." I blew my nose and gave the clock a last look.

Madame reached in her pants pockets and pulled out candies wrapped in red foil. "Moz-zart dark choc-co-lot from Vien-na ... ver-ry goot. Take."

I ate several chocolates and wiped my face with a hand towel. *He's gone, nothing I can do about it.* So, I smiled at Madame. "I love dark chocolates. Thank you ... okay, I'm ready to dance my best."

"Goot girl. I give Sa-rah chocolates every day." She laughed for the first time in a long time.

"Madame, I'd like to start at my first entrance and do the whole variation."

"Goot. Sa-rah danse two times ... then, fini."

IN THE GIRL'S dressing room, I stripped naked and put on pink tights and my favorite turquoise scoop-neck leotard, a recital gift from Miss Candy. I raced downstairs to find Yuri and Alexi in Mrs. Pace's office with the door shut.

I knocked and entered.

Mrs. Pace smiled. "Just in time, Sarah. I have some news since it effects your rehearsal schedule this week and next."

"Yes," I grinned with a pounding, excited heart.

"Yuri and Irina will dance the pas de deux from Le Corsaire on the Ed Sullivan Television Show of Shows."

"Oh? When?"

"A week from Sunday."

"Really!" Stomach acid swirled in my intestines. I could vomit with little effort. I crossed my arms.

Mrs. Pace reached out and embraced me. The hug so staged and condescending, I yanked myself free so I wouldn't puke on her Lord & Taylor suit. She however, kept her usual indifferent expression being born with a silver spoon up her ass and private boarding school etiquette.

I'd never experienced her kind of cold, calculated behavior growing up in Brooklyn. I saw regular people who had real, expressive feelings. No phony baloney emotions put on for show.

"Your turn will come, Sarah." She glanced at Yuri and Alexi. "We're saving you for the world première of *Colors of The Rainbow*, right, gentlemen?" She patted my head like a dog. "You understand, of course." *See Spot run. Sit, rollover, bark.*

"I see," I mumbled like a brave soldier and hated her with a passion. *From Exodus, the Torah says an eye for an eye, a tooth for a tooth ... gee whiz, why did I think of this?*

The Dragon Lady smiled. "Be patient, dear girl." *Inside my head, I swore something else but kept it to myself.*

Yuri knowing me all too well, picked up on my distress. His arm slid around the back of my waist. "Sa-rah, Yuri fav-vor-rite part-ner, rehearse *Mon-nark?* Da?" He kissed my nose and grinned pulling me into his side.

Without making a further fool of myself, I got it together fast. I smiled at my mentor and hero. "Yes, I'm anxious to rehearse *Monarch* with you." I kissed his cheek and motioned to Alexi to follow us out the door.

We entered Studio B and waved to Mrs. Tupper already seated at the piano. Just shy of four o'clock we started the pas de deux entrance.

A half hour later, Justin Sainte Claire interrupted our rehearsal. Looking sheepish and tip-toeing slower than a snail on thin ice, he announced, "Hello, beautiful people. I've brought the new butterfly drawings. They are less dangerous than my previous sketches and won't bite."

"Da?" said Yuri thumbing through the black portfolio. "Vings? Nyet vood ... nyet black mask ... goot. Vhere cost-tume? Show Yuri cost-tume."

Justin exhaled a sigh of relief, "Yes, Prince Siegfried," and ran for the door. He opened it and called his staff waiting in the lobby. "Ladies? We're ready."

Two women pushed a rolling, metal clothes rack through the open door. The rack held two, gold, orange and black patterned butterfly costumes with silk wings. The costumes were tied to hangers.

I marveled at the sight. "What lovely, flowing wings."

"Da, put cost-tume, Sa-rah. Yuri vear butt-ter-fly."

Fifteen minutes later, we danced our opening variation in the newest version of the *Monarch* costumes and the wings moved gently in the air. However, my sweetheart bodice was cut too low and my wings proved tricky. In the wrap-around Yuri body moves, I got caught in the folds and stopped the lift.

"Justin, could you cut a slit or maybe two slits along the center of each wing? I could poke my hand through it … and,"

"And, what?"

I blushed. "You have to raise the neckline up a bit. My grandmother and mother are coming to see me dance and I can't embarrass them."

"Oh, dear. Am I a bad boy? Too low for a ballet dancer?"

"Yes, way too low."

Yuri gawked at my over-exposed chest.

"Stop it, Yuri. I don't sell cigarettes in Carmen."

"Yuri like Car-men op-per-a."

"Sarah," said Justin. "I wasn't trying to embarrass you. I thought a lower cut sweetheart would elongate your neck."

"Sa-rah, beau-ti-ful breast, beau-ti-ful nip-ple."

"Wow, Yuri. You can pronounce female anatomy pretty good." *Ha! And he thought he could humiliate me but he didn't.*

Alexi chuckled, "He had a teacher in bed."

"Sarah," said Justin stepping in front of Yuri and Alexi. "Listen … your figure is far more perfect than Irina Ivanova's that's why I try things."

I made a face.

"Please, don't be upset. I'm telling you as a model, you are easy to sketch for. Your long legs and short torso are a textbook figure. You're my muse … the way you move, you're a runway mannequin whereas Irina's dumpy body." Justin stuck his finger in his mouth pretending to throw up then hesitated … "Ah, never mind, do I dare say it?"

Mrs. Pace stood in the doorway and yelled, "No, dear boy, you dare not say it! We already know what the bitch looks like."

"Oooooooo, Mrs. Pace." Justin shook his finger. "You said a naughty word."

"No, I didn't. For the record, I was never here."

I frowned at the two cynics. "Hey, Justin, can we get back to discussing my costume?"

"Yes, sweetheart, I was slumming, call me silly."

"Okay, Mr. Silly. After you make the alterations, can I keep my costume to practice in?"

"Keep the costume? Well, I guess, I could have your sample *Monarch* ready tomorrow after six o'clock and we could label it Sarah's rehearsal wardrobe. Would that make her ladyship happy?"

I looked over at Yuri, "Okay?"

"Da, re-hear-sal ward-drobe. Goot."

"I'll bring two versions of the wings. One slit versus two slits and a higher neckline, two versions ... maybe with a piece of nude cloth?"

"No, cloth. Looks too fake."

Mrs. Pace came in the room and handed Justin a check. "Mr. Sainte Claire, when Yuri approves of the final male and female *Monarch* costumes, I'll pay you the balance on two sets of finished costumes delivered to my office."

Justin took the check and kissed the back of the envelope.

"The date?" continued Mrs. Pace. "No later than seven days prior to the world premiere of *Monarchs In Spring* on Friday, October 29th. You have it in writing, dear boy, including the black and orange sequins and yellow beading on both sets of costumes."

"Yes, Mrs. Pace, the butterflies will be ready and beautiful under the theatrical lights. Sarah will sparkle and Yuri will shimmer. It will be, dare I say it, magic time!"

"Wait," said Alexi who'd been quiet this whole time. "Yuri, since the black mask is kaput, what about? A little face paint in black and yellow giving a hint of what a butterfly's facial markings are. Maybe a butterfly tattoo on Sarah's right cheek."

Yuri hesitated, "Da, Alexi, may-be. Justin, bring fo-toe … but-ter-fly face make-up … da?"

As if it were Justin's idea, he clapped his hands. "Well, ain't that the cat's meow. I had same idea and you'll love it. I'll talk to my make-up people and come up with something." He waved to his two ladies and they followed him out of the room pushing the costume rack.

When the door slammed shut, Mrs. Pace looked relieved. "Thank God in heaven, he didn't bring along that idiot fairy photographer with the Kodak Instamatic Camera. Otherwise, we'd have flash cubes popping all over my floor." And she turned and slammed the door on her way out.

YURI AND I finished rehearsing at five-thirty and I ran upstairs and changed into street clothes. When I returned to the lobby, I chatted with Anna and Marie who had just finished rehearsing with Mr. Borgen. We girls huddled in a corner when suddenly, someone took hold of my hand.

I turned around. "Eleanor!"

"Yes, my darling girl," she chirped and kissed me on my cheek. "How about coming to dinner with Harry and me at my house."

"I, um …"

"I've already cleared it with Barbara.

"Who?"

"Barbara Pace, your boss?"

"Oh, that Barbara."

Eleanor chuckled, "Yes, and Fernando can pick you up at nine so you get a good night's sleep."

"You think of everything," I giggled. "Oh, Eleanor? Meet my friends, Anna and Marie. They're dancing in *Colors* with me."

"How lovely ... a pleasure to meet you both." She sighed, "Let's hurry Sarah and grab a cab."

"No, Eleanor, not necessary," said Mrs. Pace joining our circle. "Fernando will drive you ladies wherever you want to go. Enjoy your evening."

JUST AS HARRY, Eleanor and I sat down at their dining room table, the telephone rang. Harry answered and handed me the Princess Phone. "It's for you, Sarah."

"Me?" I cleared my throat and reached for the receiver getting up from my chair. I moved away for privacy. "Hello?" *Bless their hearts, Eleanor and Harry had planned a surprise.*

"Daaaaavid!" I screamed. "Where are you? Where? TWA? What? ... Okay, okay, I'm calm ... You're leaving now? ... A seven o'clock flight?" Harry raised his arm pointing to his wristwatch ... "Oh, dear, soon. Are you scared of flying? ... No? Me? I've never been on a plane. What? ... I saw the envelope. Your itinerary? No, I didn't open it but should I? Okay, I will ... What? ... Say that again." I raised my voice and spoke loud. "You just said ... sorry, I'll talk softer, what was that again? ... Oh, God ... yes ... that's ... what I wanted to tell you this morning after we ..." I looked over at the dining room table and saw Eleanor and Harry staring at me and hanging on my every word ... "Aaaahh ... yes, David, we're all in the dining room ... yep, together ... right on ... bon voyage ..." I giggled and bit my lip ... "Goodnight, Gracie ..." Click.

I sucked in a gigantic breath of air and exhaled a grin. Harry walked over and took the Princess Phone out of my hands. "Was it a good call?"

"Yeah, I meant, yes," I giggled returning to the table. "That was a lovely surprise. Thank you both, you rascals" and sat down.

Harry winked at Eleanor and she beamed.

I sprung up from my seat, "Excuse me" and hurried to the entrance foyer. Yes, there was a 9" x 12" manila envelope in my dance bag. On law firm letterhead, a fifteen day itinerary filled ten pages. Planes, hotels, cars, maps, addresses, phone numbers and meeting dates. *Holy cow, I'd need a travel agent to interpret the abbreviations and symbols.*

WHEN I WALKED in the door at Sutton Place later that night, Mrs. Pace met me in the hall. "Sarah, you look flushed. Are you alright? I hope you're not coming down with a cold or the flu."

"No, I'm fine," I giggled *thinking more than fine I'm fabulous.*

"Odd, your face is glowing and pink."

"Really, I'm good."

I could scream since David told me he loved me three times on the phone. If that wasn't the best news ever! If I was anymore thrilled, I'd burst at the seams if I had seams. Tra la, oh, happy day. My lucky stars were shining bright.

Mrs. Pace felt my forehead with the back of her hand. "You are a little warm but there's no fever."

"See, I told you, I'm okay," and with that remark, I stubbed my toe on the corner of the rug. "Oops, a daisy." I grabbed a chair to stop from falling. "Almost landed on my butt," I giggled.

The Dragon Lady eyed me with suspicion then changed her expression and grinned showing all her teeth like Lewis Carroll's Cheshire Cat. "Yes, thank the good Lord, you didn't fall and break something."

"Whew, right." I exhaled a loud sigh watching her eyelids flutter. Could she be thinking how to spy on me and control my activities?

Better not try, Barbara Pace. The fighting gloves are on. My privacy is off limits since David taught me how boxer's bob and weave and you're gonna get my new moves.

"Sarah, did you have a nice dinner at Eleanor's?"

"Yes, they are lovely people."

"What did you talk about?"

"Why, ballet, of course. What else is there?" I furrowed my brow. "Why would you ask such a silly question?"

"That's not silly. That's polite conversation."

I moved past Mrs. Pace and stood at the bottom of the stairs. "See you in the morning."

"Wait, would you like a cup of tea?"

"No. I had peppermint tea and scones already tonight but thank you. Good night, Mrs. Pace. Sleep tight, don't let the bedbugs bite."

"I'll do that. No bedbugs. Goodnight, Sarah."

Upstairs in the guest bedroom, I showered, brushed my teeth and climbed into bed. Too excited to sleep, I replayed David's words on my lips and in my head, over and over. My joy on a scale of one to ten, hit ten sending my pulse to the moon.

Imagine that! David casually said on the phone, "I love you, Sarah," not once, not twice but three times. *Good golly, Miss Molly, can anything top that?"* I fluffed up my pillow and laid my head down. "No way, can anything top that, not evv-vverrr!"

Giggling like a five year old loon and way too loud, I felt a warmth rise up from my chest. So what if I made noise. *If anyone listened at the door, their problem, not mine.*

I prayed for my family, David's family, the CCBT and all the taxi drivers in New York City. And added, "Thank you, God, for all the blessings. I'm the luckiest girl in the world. Life is grand." I covered my legs with the blankets and turned on my stomach.

Exhausted and ready for sleep, "Goodnight, Gracie ... I love you and can't wait to say it to your face."

CHAPTER 42

Thursday, October 7ᵗʰ· Don't step on my toes.

FOLLOWING THE MORNING professional class, we girls hurried to the automat. Chattering like sixth graders on a field trip to the Metropolitan Museum of Art, we were wired. For the first time, every dancer in *Colors* would meet today at two o'clock. My heart raced, I needed to dance my best. *Would I be good enough? Would I please Yuri in front of the others?*

"And guess what?" said a delighted Marie jumpy as a fly on watermelon. "I'm one of the three Eclipse Of The Sun girls. Carol Voss tore a ligament so I took her place."

"No, shit?" said Anna. "Sorry, Carol wrecked her leg but amazing luck for you."

I did a double-take. "You're dancing the Eclipse? I love it. We're all together."

"The four Musketeers," cheered Marie.

"Who's D'Artagnan?" smiled Anna.

"Who cares? One for all and all for one."

"I knew she was in *Colors*," said Mrs. Tupper hugging Marie. "I played her first rehearsal last night."

"Why, Mrs. Tupper?" I cocked my head. "Wow! This is the first time you actually hugged somebody."

Anna shook her head. "Seeing is believing. I guess people do change. By the way, I should put on my orange rainbow leotard. Let's hurry back."

I lifted my blouse. "I'm already dressed in red, ta da and you, Marie? What color are you?"

"Nobody gave me a color."

"No color? Why not?" I picked up my dance bag and took Marie's hand. "We're asking Mrs. Pace for your colored leotard right now."

"God only knows what shade that could be," groaned Anna.

"Justin Sainte Claire," I giggled, "would never pick halucious-yellow or chartreuse-green."

"Wanna bet? Got a nickel?"

BACK AT THE ballet school, Mrs. Pace had to call and order Marie's Eclipse colored leotard.

"It'll be delivered tomorrow afternoon," she assured a very upset Marie and me. "In the meantime, just wear what you're wearing."

"She can't," I said. "Her leotard is fire engine red."

"Okay, Sarah," said Dragon Lady taking a key from her desk drawer. "Unlock the wardrobe room and find something for Marie to wear."

We searched through the shelves and found Marie a white leotard that fit. She changed and we returned the key. Seeing Anna and Mrs. Tupper in the lobby, we hung out with them.

Anna, now wearing the orange leotard started fidgeting. "I have to pee" and she hurried to the bathroom.

Seeing her run away, Alexi swooped in to join us. He whispered, "Yuri spent last night at Anna's apartment and he's done it before." He flipped his eyebrows up and down imitating Groucho Marx holding a cigar.

I narrowed my eyes. "What are you saying?"

"Why?"

"Because I have a sudden urge to slap you." *Like my dad does to Jeff and Max on the sides of their heads.* "It's none of your business, that's why. Don't talk about her behind her back. Got it? Alexi?"

Oh man, I still have her letters hidden in my basement. Should I tell her or burn them?

Marie punched his arm. "Why do you talk about her behind her back? That's chicken shit. She doesn't tell your secrets. God only knows what or who you sleep with and we don't want to know and don't care."

Mrs. Tupper agreed by helping Marie and me, stare him down until he walked away.

"Good riddance to bad rubbish," said Marie.

Of course, I'd never repeat what he said and neither would Marie. But, Mrs. Tupper? At age thirty-three? She couldn't stop the girlie giggles. When she saw Anna walking back to join us and during the next day at the automat, she twittered like the "three little maids in school are we from The Mikado."

Holy shit! Mrs. Tupper must never know I spent nights at David's. She'd have a cow and probably chirp the aria from "Aida" at Horn & Hardart's. And her reading fifty cent romance paperbacks? Definitely, not good. Too many active verbs and descriptions for her to digest.

At two o'clock, Yuri appeared in Studio A emotionally charged. He announced with misty eyes, "Tank you, eve-ry-buddy, Yuri dream ... hap-pen-ning to-day ... I luv-va you. Danse goot!"

The dancers hooped and hollered.

I whispered to Anna, "I know the ending. Nobody else does. Tra la."

"Okay, hotshot, what is it?"

"Nope. It's Yuri's ballet. He tells the story, morning glory."

"Jesus, Sarah, you're such a baby."

The studio door swung open and Mrs. Pace entered with the scenic designer Tule Jethro, carrying his two, 3D models of the set. And behind her, strutted Justin Sainte Claire, carrying his costume designs in a black portfolio. This would be everybody's first look.

"Good afternoon, welcome to The *Colors of The Rainbow*," said Mrs. Pace standing at the piano. She indicated Tule Jethro should set his two, set-to-scale 3D models down on the closed baby grand top.

We dancers circled the piano viewing the Act I opening set which contained a painted scrim at the proscenium. Next to it was the Act II, Scene One set. This showed a heavy rainstorm with lightning streaks. Yuri waved his hands, "Nyet, touch."

Justin placed his costume drawings on the long black benches in front of the mirrors. The 10" x 13" watercolor drawings encased in plastic were carefully considered and judged by the group. On a separate 3x5 card and added to every sketch, Justin noted the character and dancer's name or names.

When Yuri had enough of the floor show, he announced, "Yuri tell stor-ry. Sit, sit, sit." He observed eight male dancers sitting on the floor at his feet. "Vhat? Nyet vo-man?" He looked dejected.

The men snickered and the women booed.

In half Russian and broken English, Yuri began the story. Alexi translated. "Certain percussive instruments in the orchestra play the roles the dancers represent. A flute alternating with a French horn played the Red Rainbow theme while drums, cymbals, tympani and gongs played the dramatics of the Rain Men and the Thunder and Lightning Bolts."

"What part are you, Yuri?" asked Luke Pendragon rising to

his feet.

"Yuri ... hot, burning Sun ... a trum-pet."

"I figured. A wise decision," chuckled Luke Pendragon sitting back down on the floor.

"Alexi," said Yuri. "Tell ball-let."

"Okay. The curtain opens on a fading rainbow scrim. The Sun pops out and begins to shine but it starts to rain again. A violent storm occurs. After thunder and lightning, a rainbow forms in the sky. The Sun refuses to shine and waits for the four or five rainbow colors. But this time when the Sun peeks out from behind a cloud, there are seven brilliant colors in the rainbow. He falls madly in love with the color red. The beguiling Red Rainbow's dancing is sensuous and enticing for a purpose. Red Rainbow tempts the glorious, golden Sun for her gain which is to keep all the rainbow shades in the sky as long as possible."

"Right on, sister," whooped Anna while Marie shot a triumphant hand in the air and whooped in solidarity.

Alexi made a face. "Can I continue?"

"Yes, go for it." Anna waved her hands in the V victory sign.

"The Red Rainbow teases and temps the Sun into submission. Towards the end of the ballet, the six colors fade away leaving only the color red."

Yuri suddenly interrupts Alexi by flexing his arm muscles like a wrestler. "Da!" he yells with a grin. "Sun make love ... Red Rainbow. Da!"

"Okay, now it's my turn," snickered Alexi.

"Yes, Alexi, please, go on," said Mrs. Pace.

"The highlight of Act II ... is a love duet of continuous contact lifts. The Sun's adoring brilliance melts The Red Rainbow."

Marie and Lily both moaned dramatically.

"Girls, stop it!" ordered Mrs. Pace.

"Her death," continued Alexi. "Causes him to go berserk. An

eclipse of the sun at high noon, saves his sanity."

Some dancers applauded and others moaned. Natasha started to cry and Mrs. Pace dabbed her tears with a hankie.

"That's why you rehearsed us in small groups," said a sarcastic Marta. "So, we wouldn't guess the story.

"Marta, nyet, tell story ... nyet talk. Yuri kill Marta."

"Really, Mr. Konstantinov?"

Alexi said sharply, "Marta, he means, no one in this room is to tell the story of *Colors of The Rainbow* to their family or friends. It's a huge secret. We want the story to come alive on opening night to the press and critics."

"Absolutely not. No one is to reveal the plot ... that goes for all of you," said Mrs. Pace. "Now Yuri, what's next?"

"Da. Tell who dance vhat in ball-let." He pointed to the men on the floor.

Luke Pendragon jumped up and introduced himself and the two other Thunder and Lightning Bolts. They applauded themselves and some girls yelped. Next, Yuri introduced the five Rain men and they applauded themselves.

"Sit, sit," he said pointing across the room. "Three Eclipse Of The Sun girls. Ver-ry pret-ty." And he continued to raise his voice over the applause, "Seven rainbow girls. "Anna ... orange, Marta ... yellow, Natasha ... green, Suzanne ... blue, Lily ... indigo, Marisa Albanese ... violet and Sa-rah danse Red Rainbow."

I smiled until Yuri held his hand up to halt the clapping. Standing at a distance of ten feet, Yuri changed his grin to a serious frown. He rung his hands in front of his chest, "Sarah... try to be sexy ven Sa-rah danse Red Rainbow. Da?"

My heartbeat sputtered, my knees weakened and I thought I'd die on the spot. To hear him say this in front of my peers. *How humiliating!* Emitting no sound, I moved my lips, "What?

I'm not sexy enough to dance Red Rainbow? You tell me now?"
I wanted to hide. But where?

"Da, da, got you!" he broke up laughing and ran to me and
picked me up by my waist. He spun me around laughing even
louder. "Da! Sa-rah sex-y," he yelled. "Yuri make joke. Da,
beaut-ti-ful dans-ser. Every-body love sex-y girl. Big joke!"

"Not funny!" I slapped his face.

The dancers in the room reacted in shock. Some of them
groaned. Alexi ran over and yanked Yuri's arm.

Yuri set me down and kissed my mouth, hard and deliberate.

Mrs. Pace hollered through clenched teeth, "That's enough!
Play nice in the sandbox."

Yuri glared at me and panted.

I glared right back. My face flushed and my chest heaved up
and down breaking out in hives.

Mrs. Pace turned to her company of dancers. "Everybody,
please. Take a fifteen minute break. Then, we'll start the rehearsal. Thank you." She walked over to where Yuri and I
moved to a corner with Alexi.

Glaring at her two money-makers, she spoke in a very quiet
voice. "Both of you come with me. Alexi, stay out of this. I can
handle naughty children, especially the young man."

Yuri whispered in Mrs. Pace's right ear. "Yuri nyet think-
king. Yuri sor-ry."

"Right," she whispered back in his left ear. "You'll be sorrier
when I take away your Bloomingdale's credit card which I just
might do."

AT TEN MINUTES to three, the rehearsal began on a somber note.
Mrs. Tupper played the Overture and indicated the percussion
parts.

The Sun performed his short solo to express a warm and

sunny day. The weather changed and one by one, the five Rain Men danced a variation. Light rain turned into a heavy, threatening rainstorm of jumps and leaps.

During the three hours, there were plenty of rough moments. Some dancers forgot the choreography and others, remembered it too well to the point of debate. The last Rain Man bumped into Marta and Suzanne, the yellow and blue rainbows while exiting the chalk-marked stage floor. All three dancers landed on their rear ends laughing.

"Nyet funny," screamed Yuri pulling his ponytail.

And during a series of rainbow pique turns in a serpentine circle, Yuri waved his hands. "Tuppervare, stop mu-sak. Wrong rain-bow ... Alexi, rainbow fo-toe ... run, get fo-toe."

Alexi returned with the pictures from National Geographic. The order was always the same arc in the sky. Red, orange, yellow, green, blue, indigo and violet.

We girls giggled because we had the green reversed with the indigo and the yellow was on the end instead of the violet.

Anna punched Marta. "Mellow yellow? You're number three behind me, you ding-a-ling. Not on the end, silly."

"Go figure," Marta giggled. "And not only me. The blue and the green were reversed. Stop laughing, violet. You're mean."

Mrs. Pace got up from her bench and walked over. "You know girls, there's an easy way to remember the list. It's called a mnemonic."

"What? Is that even English?" Natasha rolled her eyes.

"Yes, it is ... just remember to recite: 'Richard Of York Gave Battle In Vain' then you'll always have the correct line-up of colors."

Anna smirked, "You expect us to relate to that. We're not British."

"You're trying my patience, as always, Anna," hissed Mrs.

Pace and she left the rehearsal.

Yuri scratched his head. "Nyet, understand."

Alexi chuckled, "I'll explain later over vodka shots."

"Da, girls, regardez fo-toe … get the place."

The rainbows scrambled into their rightful places and repeated the serpentine of pique turns.

"Goot!"

The next screw-up occurred when the Rain Men anticipated their entrance too early and collided with the Thunder and Lightning Bolts. A few punches were thrown when Luke Pendragon accused the Rain Men of doing it on purpose, four musical bars ahead of their leaps and somersaults onto the stage. *Holy smokes, this fighting was scary. Luke bellowed like a big brown bear standing on his hind legs.*

Alexi and Yuri soothed Luke's ego and promised him drinks and dinner after the rehearsal. That invitation appeased Luke's hurt feelings.

Although we didn't progress far enough into the first act, Yuri insisted he and I dance the "Sun meets Red Rainbow duet" at the end of Act I. When we finished our duet, the cast of *Colors* applauded and yelled, "Bravo," in awe of the special lifts and choreography never seen before in a New York ballet.

"That was moving and unique," exclaimed Mrs. Pace to Yuri and me. She blinked and wiped her eyes with a lace hankie.

To say, we danced at our very best and emotionally-charged was an understatement. After the verbal thrashing and threats we got from Mrs. Pace in her office during the fifteen minute break was enough to damage our egos for days.

As a result, we could strangle each other if given the chance or make love uninhibited and undying if alone. The energy of pent-up anger burned brighter than the lights in Manhattan on a dark and cloudy night. However, since the duet moved the hearts of our audience ... *Too bad it wasn't filmed so Yuri and I could watch it and duplicate the performance at a later date.*

The rehearsal ended at six o'clock and the cast of *Colors* exited the room exhausted. The enthusiasm and chatter that entered the room at two o'clock disappeared into silence.

I changed into street clothes in the girl's dressing room and ran downstairs looking for my partner. I needed to apologize and make things right again.

Anna yelled over her shoulder heading out the front door. "You're SOL Sarah, Yuri left with Alexi and Luke. They took a cab to Elaine's."

"What's SOL?"

"It's slang for shit out of luck," chuckled a male dancer walking alongside.

"No! I meant Elaine's. Where's Elaine's?"

"Second Avenue at eighty-eighth," yelled somebody else.

I threw my dance bag at the wall. "SOL!"

COOK HAD VEAL chops waiting when I walked in the Sutton Place kitchen. And, tapioca pudding with fresh slices of nectarines. "Cook, you're a mensch."

"Don't know what it means?"

"It's a compliment."

"My pleasure, sweet girl. Are you okay?"

"No. I had a rotten day."

"I'll leave you be. I'm watching television."

Eating alone, I nearly choked crying over Yuri. Why did he tease me? *Gosh darn.* Why did I slap him? *How stupid!* First thing, tomorrow morning, I'm going to apologize on bended knee. I'll ask Fernando to drive me to a flower shop and buy

Yuri flowers as a peace offering. As Bubbe would say, "Make nice." *Okay, stop crying stupid. I have the apology plan.*

I called Dad and heard the news from Grossinger's. Aunt Ida Mae won the five hundred dollar jackpot at bingo. She spent the winnings on Lucy, Sophie, Bubbe, Mama and herself. They all had the hair bleaching and perms at the beauty salon and massages at the spa. Daddy laughed saying, "The girls left as brunettes and they're coming home as blondes."

I assured him blondes had more fun in the TV commercials and he replied, "Not your mother."

I took a quick shower and waited for David's phone call thinking about more of what Dad said. How, "Uncle Al nearly had a heart attack when Ida Mae told him she spent all the money."

I sneezed on the truth and muttered, "You can't take it with you, Uncle Al." The clock now read five minutes past eleven time for bed. David did say don't be upset if you don't hear from me. Okay, I wasn't upset. Reading his itinerary, when would he have time to call? *Duh!*

"Please, God," I prayed. "Help Yuri and me be friends again and not fight. I'd really appreciate it. Thanks, I have to be nicer."

Will David try calling tomorrow night? Will Yuri love the flowers? "I hope so ... Goodnight, Gracie."

CHAPTER 43

Friday, October 8th. Why is this day unlike any other day?

FERNANDO TOOK ME to the florist and I bought a small bouquet of orange lilies and yellow daisies. When I returned to the car, Fernando continued driving me to the ballet school when suddenly, a taxi driver rear-ended the limo.

"Ma'am. Step out of the car."

"Huh? Yes. Please, officer." I stepped out clutching my dance bag and the flowers. "Can I catch a cab?"

"Wait on the curb."

"I have to be in a ballet class by eleven. I'm a soloist with the City Center Ballet."

The officer peered over his sunglasses. "Ma'am, I need you as a witness to answer questions. I need to write a report."

I hyper-ventilated and grabbed a paper bag from my dance bag. Breathing in and out, I tried to act desperate. The officer raised an eyebrow and probably thought I was bluffing. He moved to the front of the limo.

A second NYPD officer walked past me.

"Oh, ah, officer? I really need to get to my job. It's only a silly fender bender. Why all the fuss?"

"Ma'am, step back on the curb. It won't be long. Thank you."

But, the taxi driver worked for the Staten Island Cab Company and he complained Fernando stopped short without signaling. The cabbie felt a sharp pain in his back and claimed whiplash.

"Oh, save me from phonies," I mumbled to a third officer moving alongside.

"We don't know that, ma'am. That's why Officer Michaels is writing up a detailed report."

"But my Uncle Al said, 'If somebody rear-ends you, it's their fault.'"

"Ma'am. Just be patient and let him do his job. We'll get through this faster."

After fifteen minutes, the cop finished writing and the ambulance took the taxi driver away.

Fernando drove to the school and dropped me off. I dreaded facing Madame and Mrs. Pace. Hiccup.

I OPENED THE front door ... hiccup. And, hurried down the hall and saw my class in the lobby. I knew why I was thirty-three minutes late ... hiccup. But what was their excuse?

My peers stood talking in small groups in excited voices. The tension in the room could be cut with a knife and Madame was nowhere in sight.

Lily ran up to me and sniffled. "You should have seen his face."

"Who's face?" Hiccup.

"Yuri's, when the two NYPD detectives escorted him out the front door to the police car."

"What?" I dropped my dance bag as my hands flew to my mouth.

Lily caught the small bouquet of lilies and daisies. "How pretty. Who are they for?"

"Yuri. I wanted to apologize. Lily, what's going on?" My hiccups stopped.

"They took Yuri to the 17th precinct on East 51st Street and 3rd Avenue. They wanted to question him in connection with a fight he had with Karl Kreisler."

"A fight?" A lump formed in my throat and my brain scrambled.

"Sarah, what is it?"

"Um, I don't get it. The detectives already asked him about a fight two and a half weeks ago."

"Maybe they found something new. A witness might have come forward."

"Right, who knows?" *My senses signaled fear.*

"The older detective told Mrs. Pace, it's a preliminary inquiry and he questions persons of interest at the precinct."

"He's a person of interest?" My voice choked as I backed away. "That's scary."

"You're right," said Marie now joining Lily and me. "Mrs. Pace freaked when she heard the detective's explanation. I stood next to her and listened."

"When was that?" asked Lily.

"About twenty minutes ago."

Natasha, the green rainbow jumped up from the couch. "Hey Marie, I saw Alexi whisper in your ear."

"Uh-huh, he did. Alexi was in the office and heard Mrs. Pace speak to her attorney's partner who said, 'her attorney was in court and she should relax. Most of the time this means nothing. Only routine questioning.'"

"I pray he's right," I mumbled.

"However, Alexi got mad," added Marie, "the detectives refused to let him go with Yuri to the station. They had a Russian translator. They didn't need his help."

"Where is he now?" I said scanning the lobby.

"I don't know."

Anna entered the room and rushed over. "Sarah, this looks bad for Yuri. I hope the newspapers and TV reporters don't show up. They'll want to interview Mrs. Pace or anybody who'll talk."

Lily smiled. "That's a good thing. Free publicity always sells tickets. We should give interviews and tell the press he's innocent."

Mrs. Pace waved at me to come to her office.

"You'd better go," said Anna picking up my dance bag and shoving it against my chest. "It's the boss."

I stood stunned.

"Sarah, you okay?" Marie touched my shoulder.

"No, I'm not. I wanted to apologize to Yuri and now I can't."

Anna touched my arm, "You'll apologize later today. Mrs. Pace is waiting. You'd better go."

"Wait, Sarah, your flowers," said Lily handing me the small bouquet.

"Who's the flowers for?" asked Anna.

"Yuri." Lily and Marie answered in sing-song.

MRS. PACE, RED-EYED and looking terrified, paced back and forth in high heels. The carpet's worn spot looked worse than last week.

"My poor Yuri," she lamented twisting a blue handkerchief. "He must think the cops are the KGB. He's probably scared the police will send him back to Russia and to a workhouse in Siberia."

I set my dance bag and small bouquet on a bookcase and stared at Mrs. Pace. In a quiet panic, I bit my thumbnail. I knew some of the truth but I didn't know if Yuri left his apartment that night. Goosebumps covered my arms under my long-sleeved black leotard. *Oh, crap!* I looked down at my chest and a rash started to form. *Hives!*

What if the detectives returned to the school and took me to the precinct? How would I explain myself? Or, explain to my family and David? My knees started to buckle and I sat in the desk chair.

Mrs. Pace stopped pacing and regarded my presence. "Well, at least you're not part of this awful mess. I don't have to worry about you."

"Ah, ah, oh," I stuttered.

"Huh? What is it? Spit it out."

"I saw the fight in the Osborne lobby. Mr. Kreisler and Yuri hit each other pretty hard."

"Jesus, Mary and Joseph." She made the sign of the cross.

I shrugged and started to cry.

"My dear, don't cry. I'm sure Yuri won't tell the police you were there ... unless?"

"Unless what!" My spine stiffened.

"He needs you to prove Karl started the fight and he never saw him again that night. Didn't you eat Chinese take-out with Yuri, Alexi and the neighbor with the cat? I tried to get you to leave his apartment. You even refused Fernando's offer to drive you later, to Sutton Place in the heavy rain."

Two men, dressed in dark blue suits and carrying brief cases knocked on the office window.

Mrs. Pace said softly, "For right now, Sarah. Say nothing to anyone. Please open the door for the attorneys and leave."

I scooted past the two men and into the lobby where I noticed the door was open to Studio B. Peeking inside, six dancers including the principals, Irina and Sonia were warming up for

Mr. Borgen's rehearsal. I glanced back at the lobby and decided to join my friends.

Anna sounded positive. "No news is good news."

"Since when," snapped Lily. "No news means they're still questioning him, you twit."

"Hey, cool it," said Marta. "Yuri could return any minute. Let's hope for the best."

The male dancers in *Colors* were scheduled to rehearse at two o'clock. The Rain Men and Thunder and Lightning Bolts stomped around the lobby as panicky temperamental race horses at the starting gate. They'd eaten their brown bag lunches and changed into clean dance clothes. And like rabbits, they hopped to the telephone if it rang or bounced to the front door if someone entered.

Mrs. Pace escorted the attorneys out of the building and returned to the lobby.

"Gentlemen," she scrutinized the male dancers. "If Yuri doesn't return by two o'clock, will one of you take the lead and start the rehearsal?"

"But, but, Mrs. Pace ..."

She held up her hand. "No buts, gentlemen." She waved at Mrs. Tupper. "Can't you eat a peanut butter and jelly sandwich faster than a snail? And do, join the men in Studio A."

The pianist nodded and took the last several bites.

"And, Mrs. Tupper?" added Mrs. Pace. "Begin with the entrance music for the Rain Men in Act I."

The male dancers huddled like football players on a practice field. Minutes later, the tallest Thunder and Lightning Bolt, Luke Pendragon said, "I'll do it." He stepped out of the huddle and put his fists on his hips imitating Superman. He tossed his blonde hair out of his eyes and declared, "I'm familiar with the choreography. I can lead the men."

"Yes," snickered Mrs. Pace twirling her pearls. "You can lead the men in many directions at the same time, Mr. Pendragon. I've seen you in action."

He beamed. "You know girlfriend," and he snapped his fingers at Mrs. Pace. "I'd do anything for you and the CCBT." He swaggered over to Studio A, opened the door and raised his voice. "Come girls, single file, we're rehearsing Act I. Bright-eyed and bushy tailed." He patted the last Rain Man's ass as he entered Studio A.

"Don't touch me, Luke, I'm warning you," said the Rain Man.

Luke smiled, "Such a tease you silly, silly tail."

"I'm not teasing."

"Okay, so I'm quivering in my ballet slippers."

Mrs. Pace yelled from the lobby. "Mr. Pendragon? Are we rehearsing the men?"

"Yes, Mrs. Pace, we are. Ready, girls … warm up those heavenly, divine, bodies." Then he vocalized a high "A" trill making Mrs. Pace cringe and run to her office and shut the door.

Alexi sashayed over to where we girls were standing and spoke only to Anna. "Mrs. Pace sent the two lawyers to the precinct to get Yuri released from custody. So, for now, it's wait and see."

"Any idea of time? How long?" Anna looked ready to cry.

Alexi shrugged. "Don't know."

"Where's Madame?"

"She left to get money and legal advice from the Russian community on the lower Eastside. She knows a Ukraine attorney who helps immigrants."

"Okay, that's it," said Anna. "Let's go to the automat. I'm so stressed, I need sugar and a thousand calories. Maybe some Lemon Meringue Pie and Peach Cobblers out of those little glass windows in the wall."

Marie perked up. "Lemon Meringue is my favorite and I've got plenty of nickels for the both of us."

"Let's all go," I said. "Marta, Lily, Natasha?"

Anna added, "Alexi?"

"No," replied Alexi. "I'll wait with Mrs. Pace and if I hear of anything, I'll run to the automat and tell you."

Anna kissed his cheek. "Thanks."

Marie and I recoiled watching Anna being nice to the man who gossiped about her, behind her back. Marie nudged my ribs. "If she only knew what a snake in the grass he is."

"You tell her," I whispered.

"Not now, later when she's not worried about Yuri."

AFTER WOLFING DOWN enough desserts to feed a class of first grader's at a birthday party, we girls returned to the ballet school.

My stomach hurt. Eating apple pie, cherry pie and drinking cider at the automat was a dumb idea. No happy, sugar high for me now. Unlike five weeks ago when David and I giggled eating Peach Melba and Charlotte Russe at the Russian Tea Room. *Meeting David was the best day of my life. Oh, noooo ...*

David, please don't call tonight. I know that sounds looney but there's too much to tell and too little time. And you know when I lie. I hope the Hong Kong operator screws up your call and dials Brazil.

I bummed two Bayer aspirins off Mrs. Tupper and an Alka Seltzer from Anna. Two pills "down the hatch" and "plop, plop, fizz, fizz," yep, I felt better. But where the physical pain disappeared, the emotional upset remained. *Please God, free Yuri fast.*

Like a cyclone, into the lobby stomped Madame. She pounced on us girls and spoke fast. "Mrs. Pace, Alexi go jail ... I leave-ed them. Talk to a lawy-yer man. Talk to a Yuri. Every-buddy talk-king."

She further explained, she couldn't meet with the Ukraine attorney because he'd taken the train to Peekskill on business. She agonized, "I need ... do some-ting ... busy bee."

"No shit," mumbled Anna. "You're a tornado circling the Bahamas and I say that in the nicest way."

Like the wise old owl, Madame ignored Anna's apology and kiss on the cheek. She waved at dancers across the room. "Who vants? I teach morn-ning class? Maintenant? Studio B?"

Her question got answered fast. "I do, I do, I do."

Other company members in the kitchen, bathrooms and dressing rooms rushed out when they'd heard the news. Madame's suggestion was an unexpected relief to worry.

"Da, goot! I vake up Ser-gei!" She smoothed the loose strands to her bun and hurried to the tiny private office in the back. According to Anna, "Sergei loved the brown couch."

At three forty-five, Mr. Borgen's rehearsal finished in Studio B and Madame's class entered and began warming up. By four o'clock, twenty-two dancers stood at the barre, in second position ready to grande plie. Happy faces ready to stretch backs and arms in port de bra.

In a corner, I set the small flower bouquet on top of my dance bag. The flowers looked better than me. The pies at the Automat didn't agree with my stomach acid. I gagged and thought ... *Don't call, David. I can't pretend life is peachy-keen when it isn't.*

I bummed two Bayer aspirins from Mrs. Tupper and an Alka Seltzer from Anna. Two pills "down the hatch" and "plop, plop, fizz, fizz," yep, I felt better. But where the physical pain disappeared the emotional upset stayed. There's no magic pill to cure being terrified.

Please God, free Yuri. Put him in a cab back to the school.

I held onto the barre with both hands, closed my eyes and shuddered. *I had secrets.* I clutched my throat in fear.

Madame barked, "Allons-y! A la seconde. Grande plie, releve ... port de bra ... tendue, quatrieme position ...grand plie."

The old man played a Chopin Polonaise. My blood pulsated through heated veins. Hiccup. Sweat covered my brow and I wiped my face with David's monogrammed handkerchief. I tucked the hankie between my breasts. *Close to my heart brought tears to my eyes.*

I muttered, "Focus Sarah." Hiccup. "Nothing matters but the class." I fixated to keep from going bonkers. Hiccup.

When the class ended, I changed into street clothes and ran downstairs for news of Yuri. The office secretary made an announcement.

"Mrs. Pace is at the precinct with Yuri and her attorney. The two homicide detectives are out of the station on another assignment. They have to wait for the detectives to return and decide if Yuri can be released."

Madame waved her handkerchief and screeched. "Vait and see ... vhat vait? I can't vait. I must see Yuri face."

And poor Anna. She stopped taking Madame's class early on because she kept crying and upsetting the other dancers. She finally stopped the hysterics and waited in the lobby in case, Mrs. Pace telephoned again.

After class, she said, "Sarah, if I hear of something, I'll call you later. Okay? Love you. And, if Mrs. Pace tells you something." Anna couldn't finish the sentence and sobbed.

I hugged her. "Yes. Whatever Mrs. Pace says, I'll call you right away. Love you, Anna. Take care."

Fernando entered the lobby and reached for my dance bag. "Miss Sarah, let's go."

"Huh? Oh, wait."

"No, I can't wait. Mrs. Pace told me to pick you up now! We're leaving."

"But I never said goodbye to my friends upstairs."

I ATE DINNER, showered and watched television. I waited for Mrs. Pace to come home and *no, no, no* ... I waited for David to call. Neither of them did. I threw out Yuri's bouquet of wilted lilies and daisies. The orange lilies stunk.

At several minutes past the hour of eleven, I crawled into bed feeling numb. I prayed extra hard hoping God would listen. When I closed my eyes, I didn't have the heart to say, "Goodnight Gracie." I couldn't be frivolous. Life was too sad, not with my hero and mentor at the precinct.

I hoped David would understand.

CHAPTER 44

Saturday, October 9ᵗʰ. An Indian summer Manhattan day.

I WOKE UP before the alarm with a headache and antsy as a cat sensing fear. A black cloud hung in the air. I dressed in pink tights and a turquoise leotard with crisscross straps in the back. I slithered into blue jeans, put on sneakers and repacked my dance bag. Feeling like shit, I grabbed my car coat and dance things and went downstairs.

Cook, wearing hair curlers and plaid pajamas turned at the stove and jumped a foot. "Heavens to Betsy, Miss Sarah, you caught me off guard. What are you doing up with the chickens?"

"I couldn't sleep … did Mrs. Pace come in last night?" I dropped my stuff on a kitchen chair and yawned.

Cook hesitated, struck a match and lit the gas stove. "Had to be after I went to bed if she did. Never heard the woman and she didn't leave written instructions."

"What instructions?" My heart skipped a beat. "Would it be news of Yuri?"

Cook hesitated. "I was referring to …" She set the kettle on the back burner. "The to-do list for the day. Shopping at Gristede's and the A&P and taking clothes to the cleaners."

"Does she talk about us dancers and the ballet school?"

"Good Lord, no," said Cook, picking up the New York Times. "Only if I prepare a special dinner for her patrons."

Cook tossed the paper on the kitchen table. "Here, do something useful. Read while I'll make you scrambled eggs and slice cantaloupe."

I grit my teeth and opened the paper looking for ... "Oh, God!"

Cook turned, "You okay?"

"Yeah." I blew a slow stream of air fearing the worst. At the bottom of the page in tiny, black print ...

The Russian Premier Dancer, Yuri Konstantinov, who defected from the Leningrad-Kirov Ballet in February of this year while performing in Paris, was questioned yesterday by the NYPD regarding a homicide. The body of Karl Kreisler was discovered on September 19th in his mid-town penthouse apartment. A neighbor found the choreographer's body shortly before noon when she noticed his open front door. Mr. Konstantinov and another person of interest were allegedly detained by homicide detectives for several hours. The detectives, after extensive questioning had no reason to hold the men. They were reported to be clear of suspicion and released.

I sprung to my feet and hugged Cook.

"Miss Sarah, stop. I'm cracking eggs."

"Thank you, God, he's okay," and poured two glasses of orange juice. I raised the glasses and gulped to celebrate.

"Slow down," chuckled Cook. "You'll get a tummy ache, silly girl."

I slammed the glasses on the table. "Yuri must have gone home when we left the school. That's why we didn't know."

"Know what?"

"He's not a suspect."

Cook stuck out her chin. "What?"

"I'm talking about a ballet premiere. My hero is back." I twirled and bumped into the table.

Cook tapped my shoulder. "Sit down."

I sat and sprung back up. "When I'm happy, happy, I get very, very hungry. Make me a toasted bagel with lots of cream cheese and three eggs and oodles of cantaloupe and, um, where's Fernando?"

"Won't be here for another hour and please, sit down. You're wound up like a ten-day clock. I'll make breakfast and get dressed."

I made a leap towards Cook and fumbled with her curlers.

"Stop, Miss Sarah."

"Yep, put on a dress and comb your hair." I ran around the table and out the door with the curlers in my hand.

Cook muttered, "Impossible girl."

"Catch me if you can."

"Saaarah."

In the living room, I dropped the curlers in Cook's apron pocket. "There! Just come get me when Fernando's here."

"You have to eat your breakfast. Boss's orders."

"I changed my mind. I'm not hungry."

Cook grabbed my wrist. "But happy, happy is hungry and where are you going?"

"Upstairs to pack a bag. I decided to go to Brooklyn after all. I'm leaving at the end of the day."

"Does Mrs. Pace know?"

"Well, not exactly."

Cook yanked my wrist and pulled me back to the kitchen. "Someone has to tell her Ladyship and it won't be me."

"So what? It's my dad. I'm going home." I plopped down on the end chair.

"You do that and I'll throw out the Snicker Candy Bars you hid in the closet."

"Huh?" *My heart pounded the Beatle's Let It Be. The cleaning lady snitched.*

Cook dumped the bag of bagels on the counter. "Kindly observe, Miss Sarah. I'm toasting you a bagel and scrambling eggs." Her right hand whisked three eggs to hell and back in a ceramic bowl and her left hand, popped a bagel in the toaster.

I had no defense. "Yes, ma'am."

I'm thankful Cook meant well but a royal British pain in the arse.

Okay, so I stayed seated and held my head. The throbbing I felt earlier, gone. A sudden warmth rose from my chest to my face.

Cook stopped folding the eggs in the copper pan and rescued me with a hug. "Don't cry, Miss Sarah. Stiff upper lip."

"No, no, it's happy tears," I blubbered. "I can't wait to see my dance partner."

Cook kissed my forehead. "Good! Stay happy. You're my ray of sunshine in this gloomy house." She handed me a tissue. "Blow your nose."

Honk, honk.

WHEN I RUSHED through the front door to the ballet school, several colleagues were hanging a sign, "Welcome home Yuri."

"Wow! The best sign ev-vver!" I shouted getting goosebumps.

"Yes, it is!" beamed Thomas, one of the Rain Men. "We painted it in the kitchen. Hope Mrs. Pace doesn't see the mess."

"Oops-a-daisy," I muttered.

More dancers walked through the front door and upon seeing the sign, they squealed with joy. Their enthusiasm resembled the happy faces when the Christmas tree at Rockefeller Center lit up the night. Excitement and noisy voices soon filled the room.

Minutes later, Madame and Mrs. Pace entered the lobby arm in arm in silence. Both women looked pale. They didn't greet anyone as they approached the office. A few stranglers followed and quickly found a spot in a corner. Madame entered the office and shut the door. Mrs. Pace stayed in the lobby and looked around.

The noise and happy faces disappeared.

"Last night," said Mrs. Pace. "The detectives released Yuri at six-thirty and sent him home to his apartment then ..." Her chin dropped to her chest.

"Then what?" bellowed Luke Pendragon pushing his way through the crowd. "What is it, Mrs. Pace?"

"Lord in heaven," she screeched. "The police arrested Yuri an hour ago for the murder of Karl Kreisler. He's no longer a person of interest, he's a suspect!"

My heart stopped and I began to shake. I heard Lily cry out, "What will we do?" Hers, was the only voice I recognized but there were other similar comments and sobs of disbelief.

In a quick move, Luke Pendragon rushed at Mrs. Pace who started to collapse. I ran to her, screaming, "Nooooo."

I caught her left side and dangling arm and hung on tight. "We got you," I whispered. "You won't fall." I held her clammy hand and she opened her eyes staring into mine.

"My attorney, is with him. They're booking him on suspicion of first degree murder. God help him, Sarah."

My head spun in circles. *First degree murder? The NYPD thinks he killed Bozo Karl the Clown?*

Hot tears filled my eyes. "Mrs. Pace, what can I do to help?"

"Pray, sweet girl."

She let go of my hand and sort of smiled at Luke as he carried her to the couch and sat her up. She waited but not long. "My strength is back. Thank you, Luke ... Sarah."

She took small, deep breaths and stood tall on three inch patent-leather heels. Sweeping a hand across her short, blunt-cut bob, she grimaced.

The room hushed.

"My dear company," she said barely audible. "Yuri didn't kill Karl Kreisler and he kept saying this over and over to the detectives. He said it in English and he yelled it in Russian. I want you to know, our man is innocent and I'll get the best attorneys to defend him."

Several listeners nodded and whispered their support. Mrs. Pace acknowledged their hope and sat back on the couch between Luke and me.

Suddenly, Anna entered the lobby looking surprised at the meeting. *Where had she been?*

"Anna!" yelled Marie from across the room.

"What?" Anna smiled and shrugged in innocence.

"Come here," answered Marie.

Anna moved towards her as if performing Peter Pan on stage flying in and out of windows. Not a care in the world and gorgeously dressed.

Why was she spared the agony of hearing of Yuri's arrest? Would a friend later sugar-coat the truth?

I gasped, "Holy cow!"

Marie, Lily and Marta made a bee-line straight for me, seated on the couch. *Please, no confrontations.*

I patted my boss's hand. "I'll be right back" and turned to Luke. "Watch her, I have to do something."

"What do you think I've been doing, bitch!!!!!"

"Oh, dear, sorry."

"Barbie Doll is sorry?"

Did he just call me Barbie Doll like Mr. Kreisler? My blood boiled and I shot myself out of a canon, four feet in the air off the couch ... a very pissed Jack-in-the-Box.

"I hate you, Luke Pendragon."

"If that floats your boat?"

"It does." *Damn! That felt good.*

I started making my get-a-way when two, hard-bodied males, seated on the floor blocked my path. In an attempt to jump the guys, I bumped into Marie, Lily and Marta. *Oh, crap!* Next, came Anna.

"Whew!" *What else could go wrong? I didn't choose the meeting place.*

Anna hugged me until my crying forced her to stop. A smokescreen never fooled street smarts.

"Okay, what's up?" Her dark eyes zeroed in on my green eyes.

Geez, how do I answer?

Before I could, Anna saw past me and got a close-up of Mrs. Pace. She clutched my elbow. "What's the matter with the Trojan Horse? Drunk or tripping on acid?"

"Don't be cruel."

Mrs. Pace, now a propped up scarecrow in Luke's arms, said nothing. She stared at us five girls looking glassy-eyed. Luke stared looking stupid.

At that moment, Madame Madyaslavic, who'd been hiding in the office all this time, opened the door and stepped out. When she saw Anna, she rushed over.

"Anna, I call you. No ans-sir. Yuri arrest-teed! First de-greed murr-derrr!!!!"

"No!" shrieked Anna and passed out.

We girls caught her before she hit the floor.

DURING THE NEXT hour, no one left the school. We comforted each other feeling scared and uncertain of what to do next. The five of us sat huddled on the floor. A way-too-quiet Anna worried me.

My pulse rate spiked if I thought of her going off the deep end. She loved Yuri and being headstrong and impulsive, I feared for her life.

But so much for concern, she fell asleep.

Should I tell her or give her the letters I took from under the desk? I read hers but I never read Sonia's or Marie's. Why didn't I read theirs? I could have discovered why Bozo Karl hid them. Blackmail? Money?

"Was the killer after the letters to cover something up?" I bit my lip tasting blood.

In Studio A, a few company members, limbered up and stretched their legs. Luke organized a group of friends and led them in barre exercises. He whispered the commands which seemed weird. No one woke up Sergei, on the couch in the back office. One small favor meaning Anna wouldn't have to endure Chopin and Yuri behind bars at the same time.

Madame Madyaslavic flitted about like a moth at a lightbulb. She was too distraught to teach a class, do anything constructive or tie shoes. She roamed from room to room and muttered in Russian. Her untied Cuban heels sounded as if icy hail fell on tin roofs during a storm. Some of us tried to tie the laces but she'd slap our hands and laugh.

Mrs. Pace canceled all rehearsals and if a pianist showed up for work, she sent them away. Even Mr. Borgen, after speaking with some of his dancers, changed his mind about holding his rehearsals and left.

Those dancers who turned to food for comfort, munched and chewed on peanuts, popcorn, potato chips and apples. A chorus of Edgar and his zoo friends sounded more polite than my teeth-mashing friends. Brown bag lunches were devoured in minutes along with endless sodas from the dime Coke machine in the kitchen. The male dancers took swigs from a bottle of bourbon being passed from hand to hand. (Of course, hidden from Mrs. Pace who probably had her own stash of gin, vodka & whiskey in her desk.)

I didn't quite get all the reactions but after I watched Madame getting nuttier than a fruit cake, I got it. Shades of Mama when I joined the CCBT. And shades of Aunt Ida and Aunt Sophie stuffing their faces when sad.

Does misery love company? "Don't ask," said Uncle Al, but, if you ask my sister? It makes more sense observing this crowd.

In an about face, several dancers packed up their things and waved goodbye. One married couple promised to return after finishing their errands. *Return to what? More misery loves company?*

I wasn't sure if any of us who hung around had nowhere to go or were lonely. Fearing the worst for Yuri, I bit my nails. A habit I'd stopped years ago when I discovered Aunt Lucy's fabulous nail polish collection. But, my love and concern for my mentor deserved a headache, nail biting and a queasy stomach. And, my body heat rose to a fever. Why? The mind never stops.

What if the NYPD drove me to the precinct for questioning? What if my family found out I slept in Yuri's bed? What if I told the detectives I stole the hidden letters? Perry Mason called it tampering with evidence. And David? Oh, my God. There'd be no more David. He'd run to the hills.

I made it to the tiny bathroom off the kitchen to vomit in the toilet and cry crocodile tears. Thanks to my fairy Godmother, nobody had to pee.

When I recovered, I washed my face and hands and returned to the lobby. Anna regained her sanity and talked a blue streak, Madame stayed meshugeneh and Mrs. Pace locked herself in the office and shut the blinds.

I asked Marie, "Who's in the office with the boss?"

She shrugged. "Not my day to watch her."

"Oh, fuck off," said Anna. "Tell Sarah who's in there."

"Yes, please, be a mensch."

"I don't know … didn't see anybody go in."

"Okay, Marie," said Lily. "Tell Sarah about the second door in Mrs. Pace's office. The door hidden by the Chinese folding eight foot screen."

I looked at Marie then Lily. "You mean someone went in a back door? What back door?"

"That's the story, morning glory. Could be a spy. Could be a lover," snickered Marie.

"Knock it off," snapped Anna. "She's got tall, file cabinets in front of the Chinese panels. How can anyone crawl through the back door unless they're a midget?"

"Still," said Marie. "It only takes a thin person and who around here is fat? Huh?"

"Nobody," laughed Lily.

I sidled up to the glass door and whispered, "Who's in there? Friend or foe?"

"Watch it. Mrs. Pace is creepy," murmured Anna.

Marta regarded Anna. "Creepy or not. I hope she's discussing a plan B to save the CCBT. I need a job."

"Without Yuri," Anna cleared her throat. "This company won't survive. He sold tickets."

Marta blew her nose and wiped her eyes. "Who can replace him now? Or, his two new ballets at this late date?"

Lily elbowed me. "Hey, look who's back!"

Mr. Borgen tip-toed in, bypassing those who wanted to chat and climbed the stairs. Apparently, Irina and Sonia met him in Studio C. The trio remained behind closed doors for the next hour then all three emerged. They descended the stairs and waved goodbye like Queen Elizabeth in her royal coach.

"The rats are leaving the sinking ship," said a bitter Anna. She gave them the finger after they passed her by.

"They're not better than us," I whispered. "I lose my job, they lose theirs, right?"

Marta agreed and Lily nodded.

Into the lobby hurried a man, wearing a red, West 55th City Center box office shirt. He knocked on the office door.

"Mrs. Pace? It's Saul. Are you in there?" He waited for a response.

The man shook his head and made eye contact with Marie. "Is she in there?"

"Yep."

The man knocked louder. "Mrs. Pace? It's Saul. The box office is getting cancelations for opening night. What do we tell the ticket holders?"

The office door swung open and there stood, Mrs. Pace, red-faced and in stocking feet.

The man stepped back. "Ah, ma'am ... do we return the money or exchange the tickets?"

Mrs. Pace twisted her pearls in pink nail-polished fingers. "That's quick." She sounded harsh. "The jungle drums beat faster than newspaper print. How does the public know Yuri's been arrested?"

"TV and radio news, Mrs. Pace."

"Get in here." She slammed the door.

I ASKED MARIE, "What will Mrs. Pace do?"

"Who knows? Return the money or offer other concerts or musicals in place of people wanting their money back."

"Weren't we sold out opening night?"

"You got me but I suspect forty-five people on the CCBT payroll will soon lose their jobs."

"I'm scared," gulped Marta. "I have to pay rent." She tilted her head towards the office door. "Guess I'll take a subway downtown to Gimbel's and Macy's and apply for a Christmas job. They'll be hiring soon." She stood up and stretched her arms.

"I need to go, too," said Lily. "I can scream in my studio apartment and drink Dubonnet Blanc."

"Me, too," said Anna rising to her feet. "I have a real urge to get shit-faced. Sarah, you coming?"

"Wait! We need to do something for Yuri."

Marie sarcastically suggested. "Take him a chocolate cake with a file in the middle."

"That's dumb," snickered Anna. "You think he can saw iron bars with your plastic nail file?"

"I feel useless."

"Damn straight," said Anna. "Like tits on a bull."

"Really, girlfriend?" I jumped to my feet. "Never heard that expression not even from Uncle Al. And you talk shit."

"Sorry, Sarah, I shouldn't open my mouth. I don't know what to do."

Hot tears rolled down my cheeks. "I hate it. He's alone and scared and it's probably my fault."

Anna grabbed my arm. "Your fault? How could you even think that?"

Because you don't know what I know.

I reached for the handkerchief in my coat pocket. When I saw

DEK, David's embroidered initials, my breathing hitched.

"What is it?" asked Anna watching my hands shake.

"Ah, um ..."

She grabbed my hankie and dried my eyes.

"I need to go home to Brooklyn."

"Yes, you do." She stuffed the hankie in my pocket. "We all need to leave."

Five friends group hugged.

SCHLEPPING MY SUITCASE and dance bag along West 57th Street, I hailed a cab to the BMT. On the subway, I tried to count my blessings but it didn't work. My mind replayed the negatives.

I dreaded the looks on Dad and Aunt Lucy's faces when I'd tell them the news. Disappointing them would be a knife in my heart. And my family? The looks, comments and recriminations.

I pictured Uncle Al seated at his dining room table. "Sarah, dancing on your toes is unnatural. Animals don't do it. Why should you? Good, it's finished. Go to college and by the way, where's your young man, David? Is he finished, too?"

Yikes!

And Mama? No, I can't go there. She'll rip my liver, spleen and guts out with guilt. A truck load of guilt I could take to the grave. She'll push marriage and a dozen grandchildren. Her family tree should have branches. Why should I be the oak and make acorns? She's got three other kids. Harass them, why don't you?

"Nu?" would say Bubbe. She'll hug me and give me a thousand kisses. "Child, we'll talk in the morning. Such a nice evening, why spoil it? Come, eat something. A little nosh-a-la."

The subway raced the tracks and squealed. I covered my ears

and thought; how strange are the things we can't control? One day, I'm dancing the lead in a new ballet and the next day, my almost career vanished into thin air. The train slowed to the next stop and the doors opened.

Poor Yuri, petrified and locked up and Mrs. Pace, panicked because her dancers would soon be out of work. Loss is powerful. *What do I do now?*

The train started and picked up speed. It lurched and my head flew back and hit the window. Covering my ears, I shut my eyes. Screeching metal against metal sounded worse than chalk on a blackboard. When the shrieking stopped, my eyes popped open. And there above me, was a Technicolor photograph advertising an island of swaying palm trees and shimmering white sand.

Spend the holidays in Nassau on sunny beaches and swim crystal-clear water. Fly the friendly skies of United Airlines to the Bahamas.

The Bahamas. Wow! *What if I ran away?*

THE END

ABOUT THE AUTHOR

Patricia Bowman-Stein, a former professional dancer in NYC until arthritis in her spine forced her to stop, loved her former life. She acted in theatre, TV commercials and became an Equity Union Stage Manager for Julie Harris in "The Belle of Amherst" and other Broadway shows.

After moving to Los Angeles, her husband died. Three children kept her in L.A. where she worked as a reporter on *Lundberg's Inweek*, an oil industry weekly, for several years and was a Writer and Stage Manager for "Women in News" for cable TV LA, hosted by attorney Gloria Allred.

Patricia studied film and became a television and film script supervisor, and married Miklos Gyulai, a film and TV editor. Her first short story, *The Long Goodbye*, was published in 2005 in the book, *A Flash of Red* (Spider Thief Publishing, Canada). The book sold in the U.S., Canada and the U.K. Her most fun writing was winning the Alaska Airlines Jingle Contest presented by the *L.A. Times*. She enjoyed driving Sunset Boulevard, seeing her ads on billboards, and magazines at newsstands carrying her print copy.

In 2014, her mystery book, *Oops A Dead Body* was published by Outskirts Press, Denver, Colorado.

Patricia's working on Book Two of *The Girl on Pointe The Ballerina* and a follow up mystery, *Oops The Mermaid Turned Deadly* based on a seafaring tail/tale.

Patricia is a member of LARA and Romance Writers of America.

www.patriciabowman-steinwriter.com

YIDDISH / HEBREW GLOSSARY

Bubbe – grandmother.

Bubeleh – endearing term for anyone you like regardless of age.

Bupkis – nothing. Something totally worthless.

Halucious – ugly

Huppah – canopy for a wedding.

Kvetch – whine, complain.

L'chaim – to life

L'chaim v'L'vrache – to life and to the blessing

Maven – accumulator of knowledge; expert

Mensch – a person of integrity and honor. One who can be respected.

Meshugeneh – mad, crazy, insane female.

Mezuzah – tiny box affixed to the right side of the doorway of Jewish homes containing a small portion of Deuteronomy, handwritten on parchment. Can be worn around the neck.

Mitzvah – good deed.

Naches – joy: Gratification, especially from children.

Nu? – So? Well?

Shaineh maidel – pretty girl.

Shikse – a non-Jewish girl.

Shiva – mourning period of seven days observed by family and friends of deceased.

Shaineh punim – beautiful face.

Smuck/Schmuck – obscene word for penis; means stupid or foolish.

Tsatskela – plaything.

FRENCH GLOSSARY

Allez – let's go

Allons-y maintenant! – let's get started now!

Alors – then

Arrete! – stop!

Advancer doucement – move slowly, gently

A tout a l'heure – in a little while

Bien sur – of course

C'est ca – that's right

C'est formidable – that's terrific

C'est magnifique – It's magnificent, gorgeous

commencons – start, begin

De quoi avez-vous faim? – What are you hungry for?

De rien – nothing

Dos bien droit – straight back

Et toi? – and you? (familiar)

ici – here

il se fait tard, allons – y. – It's getting late, let's go.

Je m'en fous dit Pierre – I don't care said Pierre

lentement – slowly

La Marseillaise – the French national anthem

maintenant – now

mais qui – but, yes

Ma petite chou – my little cabbage

Moi, aussi – me, too

Monsieurs et Madames – gentlemen & ladies

n'est-ce pas? – isn't it?

Pourquoi pas? – Why not?

Qu est quil ne va pas? – what happened?

Qui, c'est ca, formidable – yes, that's right, tremendous

Qui, j'ai faim – yes, I'm hungry

Regardez! – look!

Salope – slut

Salope, il est a moi, il 'appartient – Slut, he is mine. He belongs to me.

Tout le monde est pret? – Everybody's ready?

Tu as faim? – are you hungry? (familiar)

Tres jolie – very pretty

… une fois, s'il te plait, pour moi – one time, please, for me

Une, deux, trois, quatre, cinq – one, two, three, four, five

Vite – hurry

Vous etes prets? – Are you ready?

Vraiment? – Really?

BALLET TERMINOLOGY

arabesque – a classical pose; body is supported on one leg, on pointe, while the other leg is fully extended to the back of the dancer.

arabesque penche – a further extension of the back leg in a complete split in the air. Support leg, on pointe, in the arabesque pose. A dancer's nose can touch her standing leg knee in port de bras if choreography requires this move.

attitude pose – devised from the statue of Mercury by Giovanni da Bologna (1524-1608). The pose can be attitude devant or attitude derriere; in which the pose is supported on one leg (bent or straight) while the other leg's knee is bent in the front of the body or at a 90 degree angle to the rear. The standing leg's arm is extended a la seconde while the bent knee's arm is in 5th position en haut (overhead).

bourree – tiny steps on pointe (sur la pointe) moving front, side or backwards.

brise voile – a flying broken step, body bends forward & backwards, left leg beats right leg in rapid front & back.

developee a la seconde – in which the turned-out thigh of the working leg is raised to the knee-cap (retire) then fully extended high in the air "developee to straight leg" (to 2nd position, foot is higher than dancer's head); developee can extend a la quatrieme devant (front), a la seconde (2nd) & a la quatrieme derriere (to the rear).

en l'air – in the air.

en pointe – on the toe (standing on pointe of toe shoe – (sur la pointe).

echappes – demi plie 5th position, push off from heels, jump into 2nd position on the pointes of toe shoes, then return to demi plie 2nd position; repeat action; escaping or releasing step.

fouette – a turn usually performed 32 times or can be performed singly; a whipped movement. A step executed by the dancer on the point, in which the right working leg is whipped out to the side (seconde position en l'air) and into the knee while turning with a slight circular movement. The right leg begins devant at a 90 degree angle then whips a la seconde during the turn.

frappe – a quick beat of the foot against the ankle (usually a barre exercise).

glissades – a sliding step executed in any direction; begin 5th position extend right leg to degage positon to 2nd along the ground, weight is transferred from right foot to left foot, the right foot closes to 5th position.

grande battement – means beating; straight leg lifts high in air; performed devant, a la second, derriere or on an angle.

grande jetes – means big throw. Dancer throws one leg in air, jumps forward and lands on leg thrown into the air.

grande plie – full knee bend to floor in 1st, 2nd, 3rd, 4th or 5th positions.

pas de bourree – steps to move from one spot to another; literally three transfers of weight.

pas de chats – a cat's step; a springing movement in which one foot jumps over the other, executed on the diagonal.

pas de deux – a dance for two persons; man and a woman; premiere danseur & ballerina; entrée, adage, solo variations & concludes with a Coda.

pas de quatre – 4 girl Swans dancing in Swan Lake.

pique turns – a direct stepping onto the pointe without bending the knee into a full spin turn one pointe; the turn can be continuous in a double or in a triple.

port de bras – carriage of the arms in graceful movements.

plie – half knee bend.

releve – rise to balls of feet or to pointes of toe shoes.

ronde de jambe – circle of the leg (a terre; floor) or (en air; in the air) a rotary movement on the ground of the working leg executed from the hip, en dedors, or outwards; leg is extremely in front fully pointed foot, then swept around to the side and back and through first position again to the front (en dedors).

tendue a la seconde – extend pointed foot to second position.

tour jetes – means a thrown step; a high turning leap starting with a battement and ending in an arabesque; called also jete en tournant.

* 9 7 8 0 6 9 2 0 6 9 6 1 5 *